Published by Kensington Publishing Corporation

LISA JACKSON

NANCY BUSH
ROSALIND NOONAN

OMINOUS

ZEBRA BOOKS
KENSINGTON PUBLISHING CORP.
http://www.kensingtonbooks.com

ZEBRA BOOKS are published by

Kensington Publishing Corp.
119 West 40th Street
New York, NY 10018

All Kensington titles, imprints, and distributed lines are available
at special quantity discounts for bulk purchases for sales promo-
tion, premiums, fund-raising, educational, or institutional use.

Special book excerpts or customized printings can also be cre-
ated to fit specific needs. For details, write or phone the office of
the Kensington Sales Manager: Attn. Sales Department. Kensington Publishing Corp., 119 West 40th Street, New York, NY 10018.
Phone: 1-800-221-2647.

Zebra and the Z logo Reg. U.S. Pat. & TM Off.

First Kensington Books Hardcover Printing: May 2017
First Zebra Books Mass-Market Paperback Printing: August 2017
ISBN-13: 978-1-4201-3788-0
ISBN-10: 1-4201-3788-3

eISBN-13: 978-1-4201-3789-7
eISBN-10: 1-4201-3789-1

10 9 8 7 6 5 4 3 2 1

Printed in the United States of America

In memory of Bonzi, Ruby and the Binkster
Best writing companions ever

Part One

Three Girls

Fifteen years ago . . .

Chapter 1

They came.

As expected.

But this time there were three, not just two.

All young, on the brink of womanhood.

All with nubile, firm bodies.

All unaware that he was hidden, deep in the umbra of the woods surrounding the lake.

The back of his throat went dry, and he licked his lips in anticipation. As the tallest one began to strip in the moonlight, he felt his dick start to come alive, thickening beneath his jeans and hardening in anticipation, as if it had a life of its own. He skimmed his fingers down his zipper, feeling his boner, smiling before reaching for his belt and silently drawing his Bowie knife from its sheath. He traced the smooth steel of the slightly concave clip point with the tip of his finger and imagined the weapon plunging deep between the breasts of the girls who had gathered on the shoreline. Underage, they were here despite their parents' warnings, because they were brazen and rebellious and . . . not good girls. This, he knew. Sensed. No, they were bad.

He felt his juices flowing, that little zing that sizzled through his blood at the thought of what he would do. Ahh, yessss . . .

But first things first.

He had to wait until the precise moment.

Parting the branches, he watched, his heartbeat accelerating, his breath coming in shorter gasps.

Moonlight was a ribbon on the smooth, unbroken surface of the lake, and the wind rustled through summer-dry branches, the hoot of an owl breaking the stillness.

Come on, he thought, his blood tingling. *Take it off.* He'd been to his share of strip clubs, first sneaking in when he was underage, then later, when there was no fear of being kicked out, sitting as near the stage as possible, watching the dancers carefully peel off their clothes in the most titillating manner. Over the years he became less interested in what was obviously staged, a practiced tease to turn on the audience and draw money from the viewers' wallets. But this, three girls on a dock at a deserted Wyoming lake, this was different. More real. More raw. And the fact that these near-women had no idea that he was observing them was the ultimate turn-on.

He squinted, then lifted his night-vision goggles to get a better view. The tall one striding out to the end of the dock was a blonde with an athletic build, and he knew why. *Shiloh.* She was the cowgirl, a tomboy, though built like a woman, her pale hair braided into a rope that hung halfway down her long back.

The middle girl was shorter, but trim, a petite

brunette, her father a cop. He smiled at that. *Katrina.* Patrick Starr's kid. She resembled her mother and was a feisty thing. He knew. He'd watched. The fact that she was a detective's daughter only made her all the more interesting. A taboo.

But the third girl baffled him, and he didn't think he'd seen her before. Certainly she'd never come to swim nude with the others. He wouldn't have missed her. She was the smallest. Petite. Her hair was probably some shade of red, he guessed, pinned into a topknot on her head. Despite her small frame, she had big tits. He couldn't wait until she yanked off that sleeveless blouse she was wearing and showed 'em off.

Again his dick twitched.

He wondered at the color of her nipples. Pale and blushing? The kind that nearly blended into the surrounding soft tissue? Or big, dark discs with pointed little nubs that he'd love to suckle and nip?

Now his damned hard-on was pulsing.

But she was sitting on the edge of the dock now, hugging herself, hesitating. Come on now, girl, don't hold back now. Who the hell was she? He zeroed in on the features of her face and didn't recognize her, but he could imagine what it would feel like to have her slim legs wrap around his waist, the tightness of her moist pussy.

He had to look away for a second.

Couldn't let sex distract him.

At least not yet.

Come on, come on. His whole body tensed as the disrobing began. Of course, it was Shiloh, the cowgirl, who started the strip show. Her friends were following suit. The cop's daughter, supposedly whip smart, wasn't shy either, but the third one was still hesitating.

So, now, which one?

Who would be the lucky girl?

He adjusted his ski mask and, raising one finger, pointed at the unwitting three as they innocently removed their clothes.

Eenie, meenie, miney, moe . . .

They should never have brought Ruthie.

That was the mistake.

And a *huge* one, Shiloh thought with more than a little rancor. She shouldn't have agreed to the change in plans, should never have sat waiting in the truck she'd "borrowed" from her jackass of a stepdad while Katrina had sneaked up the well-manicured street to Ruthie McFerron's house, tapped on the girl's bedroom window, and helped her sneak out. Crap! What had Katrina been thinking when she'd suggested that Ruthie join them?

Shiloh should've argued the point. After all, she was the one taking all the chances. If Larimer Tate figured out she'd rolled his truck away from the ranch, not turning on the headlights until she was around the corner, taken his crap of a pickup without his permission, there would be hell to pay. Sometimes, she thought, shaking her hair loose from its long braid, she let other people rule her life. Always a problem. Tonight, letting Kat talk her into bringing the third girl was an example.

Obviously, Ruthie was having second thoughts

about sneaking out of her parents' house to join them, and now, of course, the little wimp was nervous, seeing ghosts in the shadows of the large aspens guarding this private lake, feeling as if unseen eyes were watching them.

The fact that the girl still went by Ruthie said it all. What sixteen-year-old would still be called Ruthie? And yet it fit, Shiloh thought, as she stripped off her dusty T-shirt and sweaty bra.

The cold breeze kissed her skin as she dropped both items into a pile on the dock. Ruthie McFerron *was* a baby. That's all there was to it. And she'd been coddled by a neat, little holy-roller family, unlike the patchwork of weirdos Shiloh called family. Her mother had married a string of losers—the last, Larimer Tate, to whom Faye was still married, being the worst of the lot.

"But I think I saw something," Ruthie whispered again.

"Like what? It's dark as hell out here," Shiloh grumbled as she worked at the top button of her jeans. She was having none of it. "You're imagining things."

"No, I think—"

"Shhh!" Katrina, a few steps behind the other two, hissed a warning. "No one's out here. Just us."

"Then why do we have to be quiet?" Ruthie's round eyes were visible in the moonlight, the whites shimmering.

She was *such* a wuss.

"I think someone or some*thing's* out here. There. Over there!" She pointed to a thicket of trees where the undergrowth was the darkest.

"Oh, for the love of God," Shiloh muttered, kicking off her cutoff jeans and panties. They landed close enough to her T-shirt that if she had to grab them quickly, she could scoop up all of her clothes at once. Good enough if, on the off chance that Ruthie was right, there *was* someone hiding in the copse of saplings surrounding this lake. "It's probably just a deer or a cougar, maybe a bear."

Ruthie gasped. "A cougar? No, it couldn't be a—"

Shiloh shrugged. "Then a wolf."

Planks creaked underfoot as Ruthie backed toward the center of the dock. "Can wolves swim?"

"Stop it!" Katrina warned angrily. "Why do you do that? Huh? What's wrong with you?" she asked, and Shiloh knew the question was aimed at her.

She didn't answer. Girls like Katrina and Ruthie didn't have a clue about the hot mess that was Shiloh's life; they didn't understand how living at home was far scarier than anything these woods could hide.

With a little less anger, Kat said, "Don't mess with her. It's her first time. She's not used to disobeying her parents."

Shiloh snorted to herself. Like Ruthie was some fragile china doll. But there was no talking Katrina down when she found a cause to get behind, and right now, Ruthie-damned-McFerron was her cause du jour.

Rebuked, Shiloh decided not to wait. Sucking in her breath, she made a shallow dive into the icy water. She barely made a splash in the still, humid night. Grateful for the frigid grip of the lake and the silence it brought with it, she swam deep under the water as if she could get away from the sting of Katrina's words. But the question *What's wrong with you?* chased after her, echoing through her brain.

Not for the first time.

Maybe it was her needy mother and the slew of broke-ass stepfathers who always eyed Shiloh with more than a little lust. Larimer Tate was the worst of the slimy lot, a sick bastard if there ever was one.

Or maybe she'd just been born with a bad attitude. Who knew? And really, who gave a crap? She tried to ignore Kat's question, attempted to shrug it off, as she did with anyone's criticism, be it constructive or not, but the words burrowed deep in her brain: *What's wrong with you?*

Nothing! She let a few bubbles escape from the sides of her mouth, and they rose around her, catching the moon's reflection in the inky depths. Really, it was all Ruthie's fault. Not hers.

Skimming along the bottom, she wondered why she'd ever allowed Ruthie to come anyway. The girl was the daughter of a minister, one of those fire-and-brimstone types who were always condemning sinners to hell. Shiloh had known sneaking Ruthie out and heading here to go skinny dipping was asking, no, make that *begging*, for trouble, but Katrina seemed hell-bent on making friends with wimpy Ruthie.

For the life of her, Shiloh didn't understand why, but she sure wasn't surprised that the girl was jumping at shadows. Well, fine. Katrina had wanted Ruthie to come along, so now she could deal with the girl and her case of nerves. Served them both right.

Her lungs started to ache, and she shot upward to

the surface, tossing her hair from her face. Treading water, she observed the moonlight shining through the trees to show in stippled lines upon the lake's dark surface. Ripples moved around her as she turned onto her back, her bare breasts exposed. At least her muscles were finally relaxing after a day filled with dust and chaff from bucking hay and training a particularly stubborn colt. She enjoyed the horses, hated hauling the scratchy bales into the barn, detested working with her useless stepfather, though. What a douche.

Ruthie and Katrina were still on the dock, where they were finally removing their clothes. About damned time. Katrina was probably having to convince the younger girl that being naked was okay. What a head case!

She turned again, and from the corner of her eye, she thought she saw movement, just the barest alteration of the shadows in the foliage flanking the lake. Her muscles tensed as she blinked away the drops of water clinging to her lashes. Telling herself that they'd distorted her vision, she focused hard but saw nothing she shouldn't. She gave herself a quick mental shake. Ruthie's overactive imagination was infecting her. That was all.

Damn. Shiloh had come here all summer long and never once seen or heard anyone. Nothing had changed when Katrina, thinking a swim sounded good after a greasy, smoky shift washing dishes at Big Bart's Buffalo Lounge, had started tagging along. So why would that all change. Because of Ruthie?

It's nothing. With a kick, she turned over and dove deep again, but the eerie sensation chased after her into the murky depths.

* * *

"Shiloh?" Ruthie McFerron called nervously.

"She's fine." Katrina couldn't keep the irritation from her voice as she peeled off her tank top. Shiloh could be such a bitch, a hothead who was always barreling through life and damning the consequences.

Well, fine. Let her swim off alone. Cool her jets. Katrina could deal with Ruthie. "Don't worry about her. She talks before she thinks." Standing near the edge of the water, Katrina tightened the band pulling her hair away from her face and noticed that the greasy smells from the fryer at Big Bart's still clung to her.

She glanced at her friend. Ruthie was having one helluva time taking off her clothes. Katrina unhooked her bra and tossed it onto the small heap where she'd kicked off her flip-flops. Then she dropped her shorts and panties in one fell swoop. "Come on," she said to her newfound friend.

Anxiously eyeing the surroundings, Ruthie was carefully undressing, even bothering to fold her skirt and sleeveless blouse over her sandals. "I don't know about this," she whispered but managed to take off her bra and tuck it under her blouse.

"You wanted to come," Katrina reminded her. The truth was that Ruthie had practically begged Katrina earlier in the day when the preacher's daughter had come into the diner for an iced mocha and had overheard that Kat was meeting Shiloh for a midnight swim.

"I know, but . . ." Ruthie held her hands over her breasts. "But it's all kind of weird, and I swear I saw something. I mean, Shiloh, she was just joking about cougars and wolves and all that. Right?"

"Of course she was," Katrina said tautly. But she slid another look into the fringe of trees surrounding the lake. There was something off tonight, a little bit of electricity in the air she couldn't explain. Or maybe Ruthie's case of nerves was just making her edgy.

"Well, it's not funny. I know I'm a little jumpy, but I'm still not used to the country. When we lived in Denver, everything was total suburbia. Malls and neighborhoods and Blockbusters and stuff. Dad said the area was losing its frontier charm. I've only been here a year, and the wilderness takes some getting used to. I really did see something. It's . . . it's probably nothing," Ruthie said. "My mother accuses me of jumping at my own shadow."

"Yeah, well, don't worry about it." Katrina tried to soothe her friend, tried to ignore the skin-crawling doubt, that little bit of subconscious anxiety suggesting that things weren't as they appeared. A warning. She narrowed her eyes on the darkest spot in the surrounding trees, where the tree limbs nearly canopied over the narrowest point of the lake. A frog was croaking and mosquitos were buzzing, a fish jumping in the water and sending out ripples. But she saw no one lurking in the shadows.

The thought was ridiculous, wasn't it? No one would be out here.

For a fleeting second, she thought of the two girls who had disappeared two years before on a summer night just like this. Not here at the lake, but at a brook where they had gone wading. Rachel and Erin, two teens from good families. Katrina's father was still working on their missing persons cases. And then, just last month, Courtney Pearson had also gone missing one night after fighting with her boyfriend, Rafe. No one had been surprised about Courtney. She had been suspended from Prairie Creek High School numerous times because of her piercings and tube tops with jeans cut so low you could just about see her girl parts. Katrina and Courtney had been lab partners in earth science class, with Courtney repeating the class after failing it twice. Courtney Pearson had gained a reputation as the bad girl of Prairie Creek High School. Her image wasn't helped by the fact that her boyfriend was Rafe Dillinger, a spoiled rich kid who'd gotten caught stealing a few times.

Three girls gone. Some people, like Shiloh, discounted them all as runaways, but Katrina wasn't sure that was correct. Since the girls had vanished on Patrick Starr's watch, she had overheard a lot of the details, and it sounded like none of the girls seemed eager to get out of town. Kat worried they'd been kidnapped, and her father seemed to agree. Dogged as he was, Detective Starr wasn't giving up the investigation, not until he found them.

Katrina shook off her dark thoughts and lifted her arms to the humid velvet air. She was safe with her friends. "It's a good night for this." She glanced back at Ruthie. "Are you coming or not?"

"Sure." Ruthie didn't seem sure at all with her arms folded to cover her breasts.

"Then come on. We'll ease in from the beach."

Ruthie let out her breath. Stepped out of her panties. Hid them in her tidy stack of clothes. "Okay," she said, tentatively following Katrina off the dock to the sandy shore. They waded into the lake, the water so cold it could steal your breath.

Katrina hissed, sucking in air through her teeth, her abdomen concaving.

"Wow," Ruthie whispered as she checked to make sure the pins holding the knot atop her head were secure. "It's freezing!"

"You just need to get used to it." Katrina scanned the lake. Shiloh had submerged again. Insects buzzed over the surface, and she felt rather than saw a bat fly by, but she wasn't going to say a word about it and spook Ruthie even further as they picked their way carefully over slick stones and sand.

Katrina loved coming here. To get away. Not only from her summer job as a waitress at the diner, but from other troubles—troubles related to her family. Her father was wrapped up in his work, a detective who worked overtime. Sometimes Katrina thought work was just a handy excuse for Patrick Starr to avoid facing what was happening at home. With Mom.

"She hasn't come up." Ruthie was eyeing the water, searching the depths.

"She will. It's a game Shiloh plays, holding her breath for as long as she can. Ignore her." She was done pandering to the anxious girl. In one quick movement, Kat dived in and knifed through the water.

Shiloh was untamed and tough, sixteen going on forty, or so Kat had overheard her father grumble once. As a lawman, Patrick Starr didn't really approve of his daughter's association with Shiloh and the troublesome Silva clan, but he tried to keep himself from nagging too much, she could tell. No doubt he would prefer to find out that Kat was hanging out with Reverend McFerron's daughter, since Ruthie walked the straight and narrow as a rule, while Shiloh didn't give a hot damn for convention of any kind.

"Hey, wait up!" Ruthie called, and Katrina saw that the timid girl had actually started dog-paddling after her.

Katrina began swimming again.

Suddenly, a hand grabbed her leg.

Her heart leapt to her throat, and she yelped in shock.

The hand slid away, and Shiloh shot out of the water not a foot from her.

"Gotcha," Shiloh said, grinning as she tossed her wet hair from her face.

"I knew you were there," Kat lied, more than a little pissed. She was nervous enough as it was with all of Ruthie's fears coming to the fore. She didn't need Shiloh playing her stupid games.

"Nah. Ya didn't. Race ya."

"You'll lose."

"No way." Shiloh grabbed Kat's shoulder and pulled her back.

"Hey!" Kat sputtered, spitting water.

"That's cheating," Ruthie called from across the lake, but even she was laughing as Shiloh started swimming again and Katrina, still burned, her heart racing, took off after her, only to be beaten.

Shiloh heaved herself onto the shore, moonlight dappling her sleek skin. "You should have seen your face," she said to Kat, who glowered at her from the water. "Looked like you saw a ghost."

"More like the bogeyman," Kat snapped back.

"Shhh. Don't say that," Ruthie said, slowly making her way across the lake, all the while careful to keep every strand of her red hair piled high and dry on her head. "You shouldn't talk about the bogeyman," Ruthie warned in a worried whisper as she reached the opposite bank. "That's tempting fate."

"Oh, it is not." Kat kicked and splashed water at her. Ruthie pulled away fast. "Don't tell me you're superstitious."

"I'm not. Not really." But the tremulous tone of her voice said differently.

Another splash.

"Stop it! You'll get my hair wet! My dad will notice."

"He already thinks you're in bed, so he won't see you when you sneak back in," Kat assured her for the thousandth time. Maybe Shiloh was right; maybe she shouldn't have let Ruthie come along. Even now, as if tired of Ruthie's complaining, Shiloh had slipped back into the water and vanished without making a ripple.

"She's a damn fish," Kat said, half admiringly.

"A cold fish," Ruthie agreed. "She doesn't like me."

"She doesn't like many people." Why try to argue when it didn't matter anyway? It wasn't like Shiloh and Ruthie were going to start hanging out.

Especially when Ruthie, standing chest-deep in the water, was once again staring anxiously at the darkest spot in the thicket of trees, trying, it seemed, desperately to pierce through blackness to discern what might be hiding behind the thick boles. "We should go back." Nodding to herself and worrying her lower

lip, Ruthie added, "Yeah, I think it's time. You know . . .
it might not be so safe here. Let's go."

Shiloh broke the surface of the water again to
stand next to her. "What are you talking about?"

"Ruthie's thinking about the missing girls," Kat
said.

"I didn't say that!" Ruthie protested.

Kat said, "But you were."

"No, I—"

"But nothing happened to them, okay?" Shiloh
cut in. "Some people don't know this, but Rachel
and Erin took off after going to a rodeo—happens
all the time. Sometimes teenagers just don't come
home." Shiloh barrel raced in the local circuit, so she
considered herself an expert on all things rodeo.

"Rachel Byrd wouldn't just not come home!" Ruthie
argued.

"You know her?" Shiloh was skeptical.

"No, but her family attends a church where my
dad sometimes preaches."

"Oh God." Shiloh rolled her eyes. "So what? Here's
a news flash, Ruthie: Even churchgoers cross moral
lines, just like the rest of us. Trust me, I know. Some of
them are the biggest hypocrites around!"

"No—" Ruthie started to argue, but Shiloh ran
over her with, "Even the police think those girls ran
away. End of story. No big deal, really. Maybe they
needed to leave. Maybe things weren't all that great
at home. Maybe they were really bad." Her expression, already shadowed in the moonlight, turned
even darker. "When I turn eighteen, believe me, I'm
taking off."

"You mean to college."

Shiloh shot her a searing look and didn't bother keeping the sarcasm from her voice. "Sure. College. That's the plan."

Stung, Ruthie winced, but asked, "Where would you go?"

"Somewhere else. Anywhere else." Shiloh was emphatic. "Like those girls who got the hell out of here."

"They didn't just run away," Ruthie said, spinning in the water. "Isn't that right, Kat?"

"Why are you asking me?"

"Your dad doesn't think they're runaways. That's what you said about Rachel and Erin, right? And Courtney Pearson . . ."

"Give it a rest," Shiloh muttered, her voice hissing across the lake's surface.

But Ruthie went on, "Courtney's been all over the news, and I told you, Rachel used to attend our church. But everyone talks about them. Right, Kat? And . . . and, Shiloh, you really shouldn't use the Lord's name in vain."

Shiloh snorted. "Kat's dad is a detective. He's paid to be suspicious, but no one's saying anything bad happened, like—foul play." She looked to Kat for corroboration.

"Not officially," Kat agreed, "but Dad doesn't tell me everything. He can't." Especially when he wasn't around all that much, when he was avoiding coming home.

"I'm telling you all that's going on is that a couple of girls took off to get away from some kind of bad situations. They probably had dads or stepdads who knocked them around and had weak mothers who didn't believe them, or even want to believe them. Or maybe their mom was a drunk, or on pills, or a sicko cousin or some creeper of an uncle tried to get into their pants."

Ruthie actually gasped, treading water with some difficulty.

"Oh, get real!" Shiloh rolled her eyes at the younger girl's naïveté. "For God's sake, Ruthie, it happens, okay? Not everyone has a perfect mom and dad who go to church picnics and hold hands and dote on their children and wear halos over their damned sanctimonious heads!"

"Shiloh, enough," Kat warned.

In the moonlight, Ruthie's face started to crumple, but she kept her head above the waterline and managed to lift her chin a fraction. "Why are you so mean?"

"I've had lots of practice," Shiloh said tautly. Not backing down an inch, she added, "Remind me again, would you, why you were so hell-bent on coming here?"

Ruthie's lips tightened. "I don't know anymore." She spun in the water and took off for the dock where they'd left their clothes.

Kat glared at Shiloh. "Do you always have to be such a bitch?"

Shiloh was hot. "Yeah. I think I do."

"You went too far this time. Look what you did."

"What *I* did? What *you* did," Shiloh shot back furiously. "Bringing her was *your* idea." Before Kat could say a word, Shiloh dove deep and disappeared again.

"Damn it." Pissed as hell, Kat saw Ruthie's head bobbing over the water's surface. What a colossal mistake this whole skinny-dipping thing was. Well, it was the last time. Shiloh was right: Ruthie was a wimp, but with three girls missing, it was kind of stupid to be out here like this. And Ruthie wasn't wrong about Shiloh, either. At times Shiloh was an angry, heartless bitch.

Who needed either of them? Kat thought, as she cut across the water after the shyer girl. She had her own problems. Big ones. Unbidden, her mind drifted back to her mother, never far from her thoughts. *I'll . . . dying . . .* And no one in her family knew what to do.

Nope. She didn't need Shiloh or Ruth. She vowed with each stroke that, starting tomorrow, she was going to find new friends. *Normal* friends.

Chapter 2

Ruthie shivered and tried not to think about someone hiding in the woods, about the eyes she felt watching her, about sensing an evil presence. The other girls would just laugh at her, but as she worked her way across the lake, she scanned the perimeter, searching the gloom and feeling a gnawing fear.

Beneath the surface, something slimy slid across her leg, and she let out a startled cry, but whatever lurked in the water moved on. Or maybe it was just in her mind.

It was all probably because of Shiloh. The truth was, Ruthie was starting to think she wouldn't really care that much if Shiloh left town. *Good riddance to bad news.* Isn't that what her mother always said? For once, maybe Beverly McFerron had a point.

Katrina had said Shiloh was fun to be with, sort of, but she also had a blazing mean streak and the tongue of a viper. It was almost as if she reveled in being a bad girl or a rebel or whatever. The bottom line was that it was dangerous just hanging out with her.

Ruthie had been a fool.

What had she been thinking, sneaking out here in the middle of the night? Just to fit in? Just to make friends? Well, no, there was more to it than that, of course. It was because she needed to get close to Kat to gain access to her brother. Ethan Starr was like a real-life cowboy, having won junior rodeo competitions in barrel racing for the past few years running. So adorable, and humble too, as he said hello to Ruthie every morning when they passed in the hall at school. Some days she lived just for that hello from Ethan. She knew he didn't have a girlfriend, so why the heck couldn't it be her?

Because everyone knew Ruthie was a minister's daughter, doomed to be chaste and boring until she got married.

She bit her lip and mentally chided herself. Coming out tonight had been a stupid idea. If Ruthie happened to get caught by her mother or father as she tried to sneak back into the house, she'd be in deep, deep trouble. Punishment at the McFerron house was meted out by measure, determined by the magnitude of the crime, and usually accompanied by a stern reprimand from her father while her mother's eyes welled with tears. Ruthie shuddered to think what her father would consider appropriate for lying and leaving the house without permission, allowing her parents to think she was safely asleep in her bed when she was out wandering the countryside and swimming nude while dreaming of Ethan and what it would be like to kiss him. Or more. She blushed at the thought.

Sin after sin after sin.

Quickly she climbed the slimy ladder onto the dock and, feeling goose bumps rise on her flesh, bee-lined for her tidy stack of clothes. She was reaching for her underwear when she heard a noise.

The rustle of dry leaves?

Big deal. A breath of wind, that was it. Nothing sinister or menacing.

The crack of a twig snapping?

Footsteps drawing nearer?

Her heart froze.

But the other girls were still in the lake. She could see their dark forms as they swam closer to the shore.

She was alone.

Right?

Don't do this, Ruthie. It's just your imagination gone wild.

But there it was again: the steady footsteps of something or someone drawing nearer. Thoughts of a wolf prowling, hidden in the night, its head low, its eyes focused on her made her heart thump. Slowly she lowered herself to the pile of clothes, then gasped at the sudden flash of light in the trees.

Heat lightning?

Dear God, please *let this be my imagination.*

Shivering, she folded her arms across her chest as she heard splashing, the other girls arriving. Good. Then they could leave!

Shiloh dragged herself from the water one step behind Katrina and gave her body a little shake as she made her way down the dock. Katrina stood in front of her, smoothing her dark hair back from her face, a sheen of water shining on her skin.

"Finally," Ruthie said. "I keep seeing something in the bushes."

"Take it easy." Shiloh was stretching toward the sky, eyes closed, trying to rub the whole naked thing in Ruthie's face, when she saw the flash of light. "What the hell was that?"

"Lightning?" Katrina asked, wincing.

Trying to peer deep into the darkness, Shiloh saw a movement, the dark shadow looming, stepping away from the undergrowth.

What the hell?

No way!

But even as she was denying it, telling herself she was letting Ruthie's stranger-danger fear get the better of her, the hairs on the back of her neck sprang to attention.

A huge bear of a man rose from the scrub. A dark, moving shadow, he charged toward them. *Shit!*

Fear sizzled down her spine.

Panic gripped her soul.

Who the hell was it?

Why was he here?

For no good reason.

"Run!" she screamed as a flash of light burst before her eyes, blinding her. "*Run!*" She took off, stumbled, her heart racing as she scrambled over the shoreline and dived into the foliage. "Oof!" She hit the ground hard but pushed herself upright. She heard the other girls running, feet pounding, breathing hard. She blinked and scrambled for footing. The bastard must've had a flash camera. But she couldn't worry about that.

Run, run, run!

Blood thundering in her ears, she raced barefoot through the foliage. Thorny branches scratched her legs. Leaves and limbs slapped her face. Still, she kept moving, plowing forward, adrenaline firing her blood. Faster and faster, her hands outstretched so that she didn't run headlong into a tree.

Who the hell was the voyeur in the woods?

Her *stepfather*?

She wouldn't put it past Larimer Tate, that raving perv, to follow her out here. Inside she withered. Would he? Was he that much of a sicko? Had she stupidly lured her friends out here just so that he could . . . what? Take nudie pics? For what purpose? To leer at her image as he jacked off? Her stomach revolted at the thought.

Faster! Faster! It didn't matter who the creeper was or what his intentions were. She had to get away, put distance—miles, if possible—between him and herself. And her friends, she reminded herself. Katrina and Ruthie.

Veering around a thicket of spruce, Shiloh picked up the pace, her eyes readjusting to the dim night, her long legs stretching with each stride as she found the wide path they'd used to get to the lake. Now, with moonlight giving her some visibility, she flew along the dirt trail, dry weeds brushing her ankles.

Where were the other girls? Had they gotten away? *Oh please . . .*

She nearly screamed when some lumbering creature, a skunk or porcupine or whatever, waddled across the path in front of her, but she kept going, all the while feeling its beady eyes watching her. Well, fine, she'd take her chances with the beast rather than whoever it was who had followed them out here.

Her heart was pounding, her lungs beginning to ache. She stubbed her toe on a hidden root, but managed to keep her balance and keep running. *Go! Go! Go!* She heard footsteps pounding behind her, the rustle of branches being parted. Her heart leapt to her throat as she ran frantically. Whoever was chasing her was breathing hard, audibly.

She didn't even bother glancing over her shoulder, just shot forward.

Was her pursuer the perv with the camera?

Or his accomplice? Oh God, what if there were more than one of them?

More than *two*?

No, no, no! It could be Kat on her heels. Or even Ruthie.

Please let it be one of the girls! she silently prayed and wondered fleetingly when was the last time she'd tried to talk to God. Ages. Months. Maybe even years.

Who cared? Whoever was behind her was breathing hard, gasping. Gaining? Oh God!

She spurred herself to run even faster, kicking up dust, feeling a warmth sliding along the bottom of her foot, her toe bleeding and aching. Still she ran, terror urging her forward, a slow-burning anger edging into her consciousness. What did that jerk-wad think he was doing, spying and taking pictures? What kind of creep does that? How did he even know they'd be there? Geez-God, was it Larimer? The guy was built like her hated stepfather, and she wouldn't put it past the bastard. Oh great. Wouldn't that just be perfect?

"Jerk," she muttered and spat as she ran, sprinting through the trees. She heard the creek tumbling over rocks before she saw it, a silver slash in the dappled movement. Without breaking stride, she splashed through the icy water and slipped a little on the muddy bank, her already stubbed toe hitting an exposed root.

"Ouch!" Pain ricocheted up her foot. "Son of a bitch!" *Just keep moving!*

Gritting her teeth, she pushed on, upward over the slippery edge and onto the dry earth again. Her strides lengthened, but she heard the sound of footsteps pounding the ground behind her.

Was he gaining?

Oh. Dear. God.

Suddenly the aspens gave way to a clearing, a wide patch of grass and weeds, broken only by a few large boulders, huge huddling masses scattered in the dry field.

Shiloh propelled herself to the back of the largest rock and gasped for breath. Only then did she remember that she was nude, sweating and breathing hard. Her clothes were where she'd left them on the bank of the damned lake.

Idiot! Now what?

She flopped back against the rough boulder and tried to regain her wits as she heard the footsteps again. Fast. Wild. Oh Jesus. Squinting, pulse pounding in her ears, she dared to peer around the sharp edge of the stone to spy another person flying from the woods.

But not a man. A smaller woman, running as if Lucifer himself were on her tail.

Katrina!

"Kat!" Shiloh stage-whispered, and her friend, also still naked, looked sharply in her direction "Over here!"

Kat veered toward the boulder, sliding to a stop behind it, nearly crashing into Shiloh. "What the hell was that?" she rasped, gulping for air. "Was that sick freak out here with a *camera?*"

"At least it wasn't a gun."

Katrina bent over, hands on her knees, trying to catch her breath. "Not that we saw. I don't know about you, but I couldn't see much. That damned flash!" Still drawing in air, she peered into the darkness. "Where's Ruthie?"

"I don't know. Haven't seen her." Or heard her either. Once Katrina appeared from the woods, the sounds of footsteps and something crashing through the undergrowth had stopped. "Maybe she ran the other way."

"The other way was the lake," Katrina reminded, an edge to her voice.

"Then she could've stopped to grab her clothes—"

"I don't think so. Damn it!"

"Shhh. Listen." Shiloh was straining to hear something, *anything* to indicate that the other girl was bearing down on them, ready to burst from the forest flanking this field. She found herself rooting for the girl she'd so recently thought of as a wimp or a baby. *Come on, Ruthie. Come on. Just show up. Please!*

"He's got her," Kat said, voicing Shiloh's worst fears.

"You don't know that."

"But it's a pretty good guess." She shook her head. "She could've angled off . . ."

"You don't believe that any more than I do." Kat straightened and swore. "I should've brought my cell phone."

Kat was the only girl of the three who had a mobile flip phone.

"Why didn't you?"

"I don't know. I just didn't. Look, we have to go back."

"Are you crazy."

"We can't just leave her out here. With that maniac."

Shiloh wanted to argue. "I know, but you don't know that she's not safe."

"You want to take a chance?"

Shiloh shook her head. "No."

"Then we have to go back," Katrina repeated.

Before Shiloh could argue, a raw, terrified scream tore from the quaking aspens and pine trees.

"Oh Jesus. Ruthie!" Katrina started sprinting back the way she'd come, heading for the opening in the dark forest from which they'd both just emerged.

"Damn it," Shiloh growled out and was right on the shorter girl's heels. No way could Katrina handle the guy alone. No doubt Ruthie would be of little help.

Her toe throbbing, she chased Katrina along the path and through the creek back toward the lake. While she ran after Kat, she played out the scene they were sure to find: Ruthie being mauled or raped or tortured or killed by the psycho with the camera. *Shit!*

Unless the guy had been scared off by Ruthie's scream. Maybe he'd taken the picture and left before anyone showed up.

Oh, please.

As they neared the lake, Katrina slowed and motioned for Shiloh to move off to the side, to split up so that they could approach from different angles. Shiloh eased away from Kat, taking a small spur in the trail, one that opened up to the lake twenty yards beyond the dock area. Her heart was a jackhammer in her chest as she reached down and scraped up a rock she found on the trail. About the size of a baseball, it was rough against her palm—heavy, and the only weapon she could find.

After the one bloodcurdling scream, she'd heard nothing. No, that wasn't quite right; there was another noise, deep-throated grunts, the kind of rutting noises she'd heard through the paper-thin walls of the house where she lived. Oh God. Without another thought about her safety, she stepped from the foliage. "Stop!" she bellowed, spying the huge bear of a man, his pants at his ankles, lying atop a wan, unmoving Ruthie. "You son of a bitch, stop right there!"

"Wha–?" He looked up, his eyes zeroing in on Shiloh as she hoisted the rock high. God, who the hell was he? With the dark ski mask on his head, the only features she could make out were his body type and his beady, cold eyes.

He rolled off her and onto his feet in one motion. Ruthie whimpered. Only then did Shiloh see the knife, a curved blade winking evilly in the darkness.

"Oh Jesus," she said under her breath, and this time it was a prayer.

"Whatcha got there, girlie?" he asked with a sneer. "A pebble?" Waggling the knife, he laughed, a cruel guttural sound that was eerily familiar, as if Shiloh had heard it before. But where? When? Who the hell was he? "You think yer gonna hit me with that itty-bitty rock? Go ahead and try."

Amen to that! Without waiting a second, Shiloh hurled the stone with all the force she could muster. The rock hissed through the air, straight as an arrow, and hit the bastard square on the forehead.

Thwack.

The blow knocked him to his knees. He sputtered, tried to scramble to his feet, but his pants were like shackles around his ankles, and Katrina flew from her hiding place, a stick in her hand. "You sick bastard," she cried and whacked him hard on the back of the head.

Craaaack!

The dry branch splintered in her hands.

Groaning, he fell forward.

His face landed on the dry ground.

Thud!

"Let's go!" Shiloh yelled and raced for Ruthie.

"Oh Jesus. Are you okay?" Throwing herself onto her knees beside the stricken girl, she felt renewed panic. Ruthie lay staring upward at the sky, her eyes wide open, her expression blank. "Ruthie!" The girl was nearly catatonic. "Ruthie! Come on. We gotta get out of here!" She pulled on her arm.

Nothing. It was as if Ruthie's bones had melted, her arm going slack.

"For the love of God, move it!" Shiloh ordered.

"Let me." Katrina was at her side. "Ruth. Come on, honey. It's all right."

A low moan from the lump nearby indicated that no, they hadn't killed the bastard. At least not yet.

"Get his knife," Katrina ordered Shiloh. "And our clothes." She was forcing Ruthie to her feet. "Come on, honey, we have to leave. Now!"

Ruthie wasn't arguing, but she wasn't actively helping.

Shiloh tried to pick up the knife, but the guy moved, his fingers finding the hilt. With a roar, he lunged upward, the blade whispering against her calf, and Shiloh reacted, kicking his face, smashing his nose, and hoping to hell that she'd killed the bastard. Who the hell was he? Not Tate, she knew that much, but the features of his face, deep in shadow and covered with the ski mask and shaggy hair, were undefined.

"Come on!" Katrina ordered. She had Ruthie on her feet but was half dragging her to the trail.

Shiloh ran to the dock to snag their bundles of clothes and silently cursed the fact that she hadn't been able to grab the bastard's weapon or his camera. Her leg throbbed from the gash he'd made with the knife. She could feel blood running from the wound, but she ignored the pain.

"Where's your cell phone?" she asked, catching up with the other two, something, a bra or panties, flying from the pile of clothes she'd tucked under her arm.

"At home, remember?"

"Great."

"We'll find a house," Kat said.

"Out here?"

"There's got to be one. A farm. A ranch. Something."

"We just have to get to the truck." Which, of course, was parked half a mile away on the nearest stretch of road to the lake. "Come on. Run!"

Ruthie's legs began to move of their own accord, thankfully, but Shiloh was forever looking over her shoulder, certain the assailant would reappear. Terror drove her forward. She didn't want to ever see that bastard again.

"I can't," Ruthie finally said, and Shiloh took it as a good sign. At least she was talking; at least she was turning back into the naysayer she was.

"Sure you can," Kat encouraged as they hurried along the path.

"I—I need my clothes." It was as if Ruthie had just realized they were naked.

"Shiloh's got them."

Only some of them, Shiloh thought. She'd dropped some things in the race to leave the bastard behind. But she kept her thoughts to herself and prayed that she at least had her cutoffs and the keys to the truck in the pocket. If they didn't have the keys, what then? She kind of knew how to hot-wire a car, had seen it done a couple of times, but out here in the middle of the night? Oh no, she couldn't think of that now. "Just move it!" Dear God, did she hear someone lumbering in the woods behind them? She grabbed Ruthie's arm and propelled her forward, dropping another article of clothing in the process.

Into the clearing they ran, past the boulders, toward the far end of the small canyon where the truck was parked. Shiloh's lungs were beginning to burn, her heart thudding, and beside her, Ruthie was gasping for breath.

"I can't . . . I just can't," Ruthie rasped.

If the poor girl hadn't just been through a horrid trauma, Shiloh would have stopped in her tracks and shaken some sense into her. Instead, she said, "Sure you can, Ruthie, we're almost there." That was a lie. The old Dodge was more than a quarter of a mile away, but Shiloh wasn't going to admit it. Not now.

"That's right. Come on," Katrina encouraged as yet another piece of clothing—a blouse?—slid out of Shiloh's arms. Damn it, she was leaving a trail for the psycho if he was chasing them, the scraps of apparel just like the breadcrumbs for Hansel and Gretel.

"I—I can't go home," Ruthie said.

"What?" Shiloh kept running, pulling her. "We sure as hell can't stay here."

"My dad will *kill* me."

"He's not the one I'm worried about." Shiloh hazarded a glance over her shoulder, and her blood turned to ice. She thought she saw something, big and dark, running after them, cutting between the boulders. "Hurry!" Spurred on, she pulled Ruthie with her. "He's coming."

"Noooo!" Ruthie wailed, but suddenly she began to run in earnest, her speed surprising Shiloh. She let go, as did Katrina. Separately, they flew across the dry Wyoming grass and weeds, the palest of moon-light guiding them.

Faster, faster, faster! Shiloh was in the lead, the other girls close behind. She saw the truck at the end of the trail, and her heart soared. They could make it. They could! "Come on!" she cried and another piece of clothing fell. Damn! Holding their precious garments to her chest, she was gasping, her lungs burning, her leg throbbing and bleeding, her feet bloodied by the time she reached the old Dodge parked in an open field. All of the clothes tumbled from her arms and onto the ground as she grappled with the door handle. "Crap!" With a groan of old metal that rubbed in all the wrong spots, the door lurched open. Then she dropped to the hardpan and, scrabbling frantically, searched through the bras, undies, and blouses, throwing them onto the front seat until she found her cutoffs.

"Yes," she whispered under her breath and yanked on the pair of frayed shorts, then reached into her pocket.

Nothing.

What? No!

Katrina and Ruthie appeared.

"Get in," Shiloh ordered.

"But our clothes . . ." Ruthie began.

"Are inside. Just get in!" she yelled, freaking out. The keys! Where were the damned keys? She searched her pockets again.

Empty. *No!*

And then she saw him. Emerging from the dark-ness. Running at them.

Christ! Now what.

Ruthie screamed as she scrambled into the truck. Oh God, oh God!

"Shiloh! Hurry!" Katrina, usually calm, sounded panicked.

"Get the flashlight. In the glove box!" Shiloh said. "Now!"

"But—"

"I dropped the flippin' keys!"

"No!" Ruthie's voice was high and screeching. "Shiloh, no! He's coming! Oh no, no, no!"

"Shhh!" Katrina hissed.

Shiloh scoured the ground frantically on her hands and knees, thinking the damned keys fell out when she'd dropped the rest of the clothes. She raked her fingers through the dry grass and dirt. A fingernail broke and something sharp poked her palm, but she didn't give up. *Come on, come on, they have to be here! They have to!*

She could hear him now, breathing and running, his feet pounding the ground awkwardly. Fear turned her insides to jelly.

"Lock the door!" she ordered over her shoulder as she still desperately tried to locate the keys. What if they had fallen out on the path? What if they'd slid from her pocket as she'd scooped them up? Jesus, dear God, no! Her heart was thudding, her skin damp, her terror increasing. Again and again, she swept her hands over the uneven ground, feeling only rocks, weeds, and dust. "Oh come on, come on, come on," she muttered as sweat ran down her face. Never had she felt so vulnerable in her life.

Ruthie whispered, "But—"

Damn it all to—

"Move over," Katrina ordered Ruthie, then leaned out the open driver's-side window. She was holding a flashlight and switched it on so that a frail beam of light appeared, a fragile yellow glow casting thin illumination on the dry stubble. "Lock the doors," Shiloh repeated as Katrina swung the flashlight, casting a wide arc around the battered Dodge. "Roll up the windows and lock the damned doors!"

Katrina kept shining the light, leaning farther out the window.

"Did you hear me? Roll up the windows and lock yourselves—"

Then she saw it: a fragile wink against the flashlight's thin beam. Could it be? She hardly dared believe it. Her heart soared. She stretched forward, her fingers curling around the keys.

Finally!

Now all she had to do was—

Too late!

Wheezing and huffing, the monster reached the truck. "You little bitch!" he roared, towering above her.

And then she noticed the knife in his meaty hand.

Jesus!

He lunged.

No!

Scuttling backward, she hit the side of the truck, then scrambled quickly beneath the bed.

He dropped to all fours.

Oh crap!

Heart thudding, pulse pounding, she scooted to the far side of the pickup. She could barely breathe, the air was so full of dust and oil. She scraped her butt against the ground but didn't care. She still clutched the damned keys in a death grip. From inside the cab came frightened screams. Ruthie freaking out. If only Kat had brought her damned phone. If only Shiloh hadn't dropped the keys. If only–

A long arm extended beneath the truck, swinging in a broad arc, the knife slicing low to the ground. Shiloh pressed against the tires and sucked in her gut. Then, seeing how near the tip of the blade came, she rolled through the open space between the wheels, her shoulder jarring against the undercarriage.

Another fast swipe of the knife, the blade hissing as it cut through the air.

Shiloh threw herself to her feet. Yanking on the passenger door, she wrenched her shoulder.

Locked.

"Open up!" she screamed and beat on the window with her fist. "Ruthie, dammit, open the damned door!"

Ruthie's white face appeared.

Click!

The door flew open, and Shiloh jumped in, nearly flattening the smaller girl. "Lock it!" she ordered as she climbed over the others to fall into the driver's seat. In the side-view mirror, she caught the ghastly shape of the assailant as he struggled to his feet. "No way, fucker!" She jammed the key into the ignition and pumped the gas as Ruthie, for once, did as she was told and locked the passenger door. "Hold on!"

Thud!

The entire truck shook. As if he had kicked the back panel or—

Threw himself into the bed?

No, no, nooooo!

The damned truck didn't start.

"God damn it!" Katrina cried.

Shiloh twisted the key so hard she thought she might break it.

Again she pressed down the accelerator, remembering Larimer Tate's warning *"Now, don't flood the damned thing. This here's a classic. 1964."*

Shit, shit, shit!

"Don't do this," she said as the engine coughed and died.

"What's wrong?" Ruthie wailed, then looked through the small window cut into the back wall of the cab. Her face drained of all color, and she started to hyperventilate. "Oh no! Oh no! He's . . . He's in the back!"

Shiloh gave it another go. "I know." *Come on, you miserable bucket of bolts*—The engine sputtered to life just as a meaty fist bashed against the small window in the back of the cab, a window that was already cracked, and stupid-ass Larimer Tate had never bothered to fix it.

Ruthie squealed and jumped.

"Get us the hell out of here!" Katrina ordered.

Shiloh hit the gas.

The pickup lurched forward, bouncing over the dry grass and rocks. The fist kept pounding.

Craaaack!

The window split, then began to splinter, glass falling out of the frame.

"Nooo!" Ruthie leaned hard into Katrina.

Shiloh gunned it. "Son of a bitch!" Driving like a maniac, she cranked hard on the steering wheel while stomping on the accelerator, driving in tight circles, only to slam on the brakes and jam the truck into REVERSE.

The pickup shuddered and shook, its rear end fish-tailing, its wheels spinning wildly, kicking up great plumes of dust.

It didn't matter.

No matter what she did, the creep held on to the opening with one hand and rammed the knife through with the other, swiping crazily in the air, the blade slashing through the interior.

Son of a bitch!

Ruthie was on the floor in front of the passenger side, Katrina huddled near the door. Shiloh tried to avoid being cut as she steered back and forth in wild arcs, hoping like hell to throw him out of the truck's bed.

Still the bastard clung on.

Still the knife swung furiously through the cab, hissing with each cut.

"Open the glove box! For God's sake, grab something! Hit him! There's . . ."

Bam!

"Oh crap!" The front wheel hit the side of a boulder, bouncing off. The truck went airborne for a few seconds and even Katrina shrieked.

Landing hard, the Dodge shuddered, its tires spinning. With a jolt, the truck sprang forward.

The psycho screamed as if his arm were being torn off, but somehow he hung on and kept slashing.

Who was this maniac? No time to think about it. "Get the hammer! In the box!" she yelled over Ruthie's terrified screams. "Get it!" She cranked on the wheel hard. The back end of the truck spun. Katrina's head bounced off the passenger window. *Crack!*

Ruthie howled. "She's hurt!"

"She's fine!" Shiloh snapped. "Get *something!*"

Katrina opened the glove box.

The arm swung again, this time connecting, slicing into Shiloh's shoulder. She yelled and swore as hot pain radiated and blood began to run down her back. "You son of a bitch."

At that moment, Katrina pulled a screwdriver from the glove box, and when the hand appeared, she jabbed the head of the tool deep into the flesh of the back of his hand. As she did, Shiloh hit the gas again and aimed for a huge mound just in range of her headlights.

Yowling, the man yanked back his arm.

"What do you think you're doing?" Katrina whispered as the hillock loomed into view and the truck sped forward.

"Getting rid of bad news."

Katrina sucked in a breath and whispered, "You're going to kill us all."

Ruthie started screaming.

"Hang on!" Shiloh set her jaw, tromped hard on the accelerator. The truck hit the rise full throttle. Speeding up the incline, Shiloh sent up a prayer that she wasn't about to kill her friends. The truck went airborne.

"Holy shit!" Kat yelled.

They soared over a shallow creek bed, the truck landing hard, tossing them about, jarring their spines and rattling their bones. Ruthie squealed. Katrina's head hit the roof. Shiloh clung to the steering wheel with all her might.

The freak in the bed flew out, his body thudding against the ground.

Praying they hadn't broken an axle, Shiloh floored it.

"He's gone?" Ruthie stammered against the jarring ride as she crawled upward onto the seat and peered through the shattered back window to the night beyond.

"Finally," Kat whispered, rubbing her head. "Jesus."

"Don't take the Lord's name in . . ." Ruthie started, then shook her head as she stared into the darkness. "Where is he?" She shuddered, and rubbed her arms, then more panicked, repeated, "*Where is he?*"

Shiloh glanced into the side-view mirror. In the half-light she caught a look at the man, a crumpled heap on the ground. A dark, unmoving blot on the landscape.

At the moment, Ruthie saw him too, her eyes rounding. "Oh dear Lord." She swallowed hard. "You—you killed him."

Shiloh hit the gas again and tore through the dry hardpan toward the road. As they passed through the broken-down gate and onto the gravel road, she said through her teeth, "We can only hope."

Part Two

Shiloh

Now . . .

Chapter 3

"God help me," the woman whispered, pleading, heartsick, knowing that after all this time there was no escape, no rescue. She was trapped in this hell-hole of a room with its rough-hewn walls and smells of dirt and must. The only light came in through a small window high overhead, a slit in the wood not more than six inches high and about double that in length. Tucked beneath the rafters, it provided no air but allowed her to tell the passing of time, day to night.

Not that it mattered.

She'd been held prisoner for years, too many to count, at least half her life, and though she had never lost the desire to escape, she now felt that no one would take her back now—this scrawny, tired shell of a woman. Gone was the girl who had taken a stupid risk in trusting him. Like a moth to the flame, she had been drawn in and singed.

At first, when she'd been young, she'd thought she would escape or that she would be rescued. Her parents. The police. There would be a massive man-hunt, and she would be rescued under the whoosh of helicopter blades, the chopper's bright lights almost blinding. Police with dogs that would snarl, officers outfitted in black, assault weapons poised, would break down the dead-bolted door to save her and take her to the loving arms of her distraught family.

Were they even still alive? Had the loss of their daughter ultimately destroyed them as well? She felt the burn of tears, but no drops wetted her eyes nor drizzled down her cheeks. All her tears had been shed years ago at the hands of the monster who had abducted her.

The four walls closed in on her. Aside from a cot and small table, there was no furniture in the room, no electricity, no lamplight. He'd left her hand-me-down clothes and books that she'd read over and over again. Once in a while, he'd replenish the meager stack, but never allowed her magazines or newspapers. She really wasn't sure what year it was. Every day, he'd let her out, but he'd never allow her to get more than five feet from the rickety porch where he stood, knife in hand, gun visible in a holster. She'd tried to run several times, and each time, he'd caught her and placed her back in her room. That was her punishment—a month or so of confinement to the shack without fresh air and sunlight. A dreary absence of life in a life of absence.

She'd learned to be obedient because she lived for those few short moments outside—usually at twilight, when she'd spy a hawk soaring overhead or glimpse a squirrel or rabbit darting out of sight or a timid deer nearly hidden in the surrounding umbra of the forest. Based on those precious moments, she knew her shack was surrounded by mountains, canopied by firs and pines. In the winter, she nearly froze to death because all he gave her were layers of clothing and a down sleeping bag, her only insulation from the bitter winter's cold.

How many times had she tried to escape?

A hundred?

A thousand?

More?

And still she was here, held captive and used as a whore. She closed her eyes and took in a deep breath, her mind returning to that fall evening when fate had turned on her and she'd allowed herself to be vulnerable to this horror.

If only she hadn't been walking alone. If only she hadn't been bold and sassy, thinking she could handle herself. If only she'd never gotten into that car with the friendly man who flashed her that sexy grin from behind the wheel.

"Need a lift?" he said, pulling over.

She'd known him. Trusted him. Well, kind of. There had been an edge to him that she'd found fascinating, and when he'd reached across the console and passenger seat to unlock the door of his pickup, she'd ignored all the warning signals in her mind and cast aside her parents' admonitions about taking rides or being alone with strangers. She'd rationalized that he wasn't a stranger. Her parents knew him, did business with him, so with only the slightest trepidation, she'd climbed inside.

Big mistake.

He hadn't been kind or sexy or decent.

He'd kidnapped her then and there, locking her inside, threatening her with his knife and binding her wrists and ankles, then blindfolding and gagging her before driving for what seemed like hours to this remote spot in the middle of no-damned-where.

And she'd been trapped with him forever.

She knew it would never end.

Not until one of them died.

She also realized it wouldn't be the bastard. She'd plotted his demise a thousand times in murderous fantasies that included a deep, hellish pain and an ugly, drawn-out death, but none had come to fruition. So she couldn't inflict her revenge against him for all the pain and horror he'd put her through.

At first she'd fought him, but he'd prevailed in his twisted sexual fantasies. Then, when she realized that her physical battles, the screaming and flailing and biting, excited him even more, she'd tried the psychology of just letting him use her. Not saying a word, not begging, not even whimpering, just lying there like a limp doll while he did what he pleased. At first he'd been frustrated and angry. Punishing. But nothing had changed.

Nothing, she realized, would ever change.

Her feeble attempts at escape had proved useless.

Her hopes for rescue had long ago faded.

She looked down at the barbed wire binding her wrists. Though she knew that she'd lost weight since her capture, the sharp barbs still cut deep when she moved. The skin around her hands was scraped and raw from her efforts, with angry, wormlike scars visible.

Soon, she thought, there would be more.

She walked to her cot, where, tucked into the sheathing that surrounded the metal frame, she'd found a tiny hiding place in the space between the rail and the stretched cotton. It was here that she'd tucked away a piece of the barbed wire that had broken off her manacles.

She'd thought she might wound him with the small shard, but she never got the chance. And unless she slammed it into his eye socket, it would do little damage.

To him.

But with the right amount of effort and courage, she could break the nearly translucent skin over the underside of her wrists and puncture a vein and slowly bleed out. There would be pain, of course, but nothing as savage as what she'd borne at his calloused hands. No.

Judging by the daylight seeping in through the window, she figured she still had several hours until dusk, maybe more. He wouldn't be back until evening, so there was plenty of time. She found the barb in its hiding place and fingered it.

She eyed the piece of wire.

Her death.

Her salvation.

Just do it! Now!

Holding the precious piece of metal between her lips, she twisted her hands, ignoring the pain in the bite of the barbs. She'd practiced the move over and over again, perfecting it after trying for weeks to rid herself of the sharp manacles. Removing the barbed wire had proved impossible, but this twisting of her hands, slightly stretching the wire and allowing the cruel handcuffs to bite into flesh, worked. Sweating with the effort, she clenched her teeth, and with the heels of her palms pressed together, she slowly inched her way around until the fingers of one hand could touch the inside of the opposite wrist.

Then she lowered her head and opened her mouth, releasing the barb to her thumb and forefinger. She nearly dropped it as her fingertips were oily, but she managed to hang on. Clutching the thin wire with renewed determination, she found that vulnerable spot. Slowly, she drew the barb along the fragile skin and watched the first scrape, and then another, and still another. Finally, she pierced the skin and a small drop of blood formed.

Closing her eyes, she whispered, "Please forgive me." And then, using all her strength, pressed deeper and harder until the blood began to flow slowly but steadily. She felt a strange, sad sense of peace and relief. She knew, given enough time, she would finally be free.

Shiloh had sworn she'd never return.

Promised herself she wouldn't ever set foot in this part of Wyoming again.

And she'd kept that vow. For fifteen damned years, but now it was over, Shiloh thought, glancing at the WELCOME TO PRAIRIE CREEK sign as she passed it on the way into town. Flanked by pine trees, the wooden greeting had been brightened with a fresh coat of paint, but Shiloh wasn't fooled by the spit and polish. As she maneuvered her ten-year-old Ford Explorer through the town's streets, she saw past the western

store fronts and façades to the heart of Prairie Creek.
And it was dark as the devil.

*But you're here, aren't you? You can denigrate this
little Wyoming hamlet all you want, but you, Shiloh
Silva, came back.*

She bristled a little. That stupid little nag of a
voice in her head was usually what kept her in line,
ensured that she walked the straight and narrow, but
now, mocking her, it was a pain in the butt.

"Hypocrite," she muttered, slowing for a stop sign
and catching her expression in the rearview mirror.
The same green eyes that had hitchhiked their way
out of this town glared back at her, her eyebrows
drawn together, her jaw set as rigidly as it had been
when she'd left fifteen years earlier.

To avoid the silent accusations as much as the
harsh rays of a late June sun, she slid a pair of sunglasses over the bridge of her nose and couldn't help
wondering about Katrina and Ruthie. What had happened to them? Had they stayed in this hellhole or
escaped, as she had? It was strange that they'd never
seen each other since that fateful night, never once
spoken. Well, she couldn't speak for Ruthie and Katrina; for all she knew, they could be best buddies
now. Maybe they were young mothers who planned
PTA events, went to soccer games, or saw each other
once a month at bunco parties or something. All
Shiloh knew was that she'd never seen or heard from
either of them since, and the few times when she'd
talked to her mother on the phone, she'd avoided
asking about the other two.

That had been the plan.

Ruthie's choice.

And Shiloh had honored it. No matter how many nights she'd woken up in a cold sweat, reliving the terror, seeing the blade of a knife slashing in the night, sensing the monster's presence, haunted by the fact that she felt as if she should have known him, that, if given the chance, she could even have ID'd the son of a bitch, that even now he'd still be behind bars—

Beep! A sharp honk woke her out of her reverie. In the rearview mirror, she saw the driver of the pickup behind her lift his hands in a "What're-ya-thinking?" gesture. "Cram it," she muttered as she drove through the intersection.

She hadn't even realized she'd been daydreaming.

Not a good sign.

Hitting the gas, she refused to dwell on the concussion she'd suffered less than a month ago when she'd taken a spill. It still galled her to think that she, a horsewoman by trade, a woman who some had actually referred to as a "horse whisperer" because of her seeming intellectual link to all beasts equine, had actually been scraped off by a low-lying limb when Ike, the most stubborn sorrel she'd ever met, took a notion to empty the saddle. Of her.

She was still burned when she considered it.

Another glance in the mirror, and she saw that the old pickup was following her. No big deal, right? Small town, not a lot of streets, but as she passed the police station and the largest grocery store in town, the truck was still right behind her.

Get over it. You're jumping at shadows because

you're anxious about being back. He just honked be-
cause you idled at the light.

But she couldn't shake her case of nerves. Being
back here would take some explaining. Some major
explaining. To the cops. To her friends. To . . . everyone she'd allowed to think she was missing. She hadn't
even called her mother for a month, had let the woman
worry and suffer, thinking her daughter, like the three
girls who'd gone missing before her, might be kidnapped or wounded or dead.

Shiloh still felt guilty about that.

But really, hadn't Mom been the one who had let
Larimer Tate beat the crap out of her when he'd discovered Shiloh had rolled his pickup out of the driveway? At the time, Shiloh had figured it served Faye
right to be worried about her because her mother
hadn't stepped in and stopped Tate from using the
belt on her.

"Bastard," she muttered and would spit on the old
man's grave if she got the chance. Not that she'd
take a step near the cemetery.

Past the post office and veterinary clinic she drove,
and the damned truck was right on her ass. Really?
Was the guy pissed enough to chase her down? Road
rage in Prairie Creek? On the far side of town, she
picked up the pace, driving five miles over the speed
limit, then ten. The damned truck didn't let up, and
her heart froze a little.

What if the driver was the maniac from that night
fifteen years before? What if he'd gleaned that she
was returning? What if he'd been lying in wait? She'd
had the eerie feeling that night that she'd known
him. What if he was still here? Oh. Dear. *God!*

No. He was dead. He had to be. Right? Just because a body had never been found didn't mean he'd survived. All these years she'd believed the unnamed psycho was dead, and she wasn't going to let some testosterone-driving, macho pickup driver freak her out now. At the far edge of town, she hit the gas, glanced in the rearview and saw that the driver was now backing off, a cell phone to his ear. Well, good. She put some distance between her and the dented rig, then squinted through the Explorer's bug-spattered windshield as she closed in on the ramshackle ranch where she'd grown up. Her insides tensed, and the hunger she'd felt for the past two hours dissipated as her hands sweated over the wheel.

Her mother's last phone call had been the impetus that had forced her to pack an overnight bag and hit the road.

Shiloh had been working with a particularly ornery gelding, and afterward, dusty and parched, she had walked into the house and noticed that Mom had called three times in an hour. Seized with trepidation, Shiloh had taken a deep breath and phoned back.

Faye hadn't even greeted her. "You need to come back. Come home," she'd rasped in a barely recognizable whisper.

"I don't think so."

"Now." There was a new urgency in Faye's weak voice.

"What? Why?" Geez, it had been a decade and a half, and though Faye had often asked to see Shiloh, it had never happened. She just hadn't wanted to return to the scene of the crime. Even when Faye had

wheedled and begged—tossing out the guilt trip that
Faye wanted to see her and that it was way past time
she met her sister—Shiloh had resisted. Sure, she'd
been tempted, but of course, Larimer Tate had always been around. Shiloh had declined, even when
her mother had used her favorite ploy: "The police
still don't believe me that you're okay."

"After all these years?" Shiloh had snorted her disbelief. Faye had been known to use any angle available to get her prodigal daughter to return home.
Okay, so it was true that Shiloh had never officially
checked in with the authorities, but she just didn't
want to open that particularly distasteful can of worms.

"Yes. They think you might be . . . well, like those
other girls who went missing." Shiloh had heard it
then, that little telltale lisp that indicated Faye had
drunk more than a couple of glasses of wine.

"Maybe I am like them. They probably all just ran
away."

"They've never turned up, and, God, what those
poor parents have gone through, worrying and not
knowing."

"Well, at least you don't have that. You know."

"Oh, for the love of God. Please, Shiloh, come back. I,
we, could use the help around here. You're so good with
the livest . . . livest . . . the oh, you know, the horses and
cows."

"No, Mom. Not happening. Not now."

"Your sister needs you."

That whispered phrase had caused something inside her to break, her conviction to erode. It happened whenever she thought of the girl who was so
much younger than her, her half sibling.

The sister you've never met . . . never wanted to meet.

Shiloh swallowed hard and remembered another phone call, the fateful one that had once, years before, nearly caused her to return.

Faye had been pleading with Shiloh to return when she'd dropped the bomb.

"Your sister needs you."

"My *sister?*" she'd repeated in shock.

"Her name is Morgan," her mother had said twelve years ago, and there had been a swell of pride in her voice as she'd told her eldest of the pregnancy and birth, while Shiloh, for once, had been silent, dumbfounded, and more than a little horrified that at thirty-eight, Faye had been pregnant with Larimer Tate's child. The thought had sickened her. And if she did the math, that meant that the girl was twenty years her junior. Hell, Shiloh was old enough that Morgan, age-wise, could have been her own kid.

"Are you still with Tate?" she'd asked when she'd finally found her tongue.

"He's my husband." Again that ring of false pride.

"Then you've made your choice," Shiloh had declared and clicked off, refusing to answer when her mother had called back not once, but six more times that evening.

Now Shiloh felt heartless. She'd made a mistake. She should've returned to Prairie Creek before it was too late. She was an adult. Strong. Knew her rights. Tate couldn't hurt her.

But what about Morgan? His own kid? Would he have used that skinny little leather belt on her?

She'd asked, of course, several times over the years,

and after each inquiry her mother had sounded horrified at the thought, that no way would the little girl's
father do anything the least bit harsh to the girl.
They were, after all, a loving family.

"Yeah, right," she muttered now as she spied the
end of the lane with the mailbox, bashed in on one
side, the letters reading L. TA E, as it had for years.
She suspected no one had bothered to find another
"t" to make it read TATE. Clearly no one cared enough
to pound out the dent.

Dry grass and weeds grew tall around the fence
post supporting the mailbox, and the curving lane
leading to the ranch house was in serious need of
fresh gravel to fill the potholes and combat the pig-
weed and thistle that grew in abundance.

Shiloh's insides tightened at the sight of the house:
a long, low structure built on a rise and surrounded by
outbuildings, most of which were going to seed. The
house itself was in sad shape, as it had always been,
though a few fresh shingles appeared in the roof and
the sagging porch had been shored up, propped by
fresh 2x4s, and a few new floorboards were visible
against the weathered original planks.

That surprised her.

She cut the engine and sat behind the wheel for a
second, needing to brace herself. She'd never met
her half sister, so there would be that emotional ride,
and then there was Mom, her time running out, no
longer a vital woman, now a sorry case. Guilt consumed her, and she silently berated herself for her
own stupid pride, her stubborn self-righteous streak
when it came to returning to these weedy acres. Her
hatred of Larimer Tate had overridden her love for

her mother or even her curiosity about her half sister.

She yanked the keys from the ignition. So she'd made mistakes. So what? She couldn't fix what had happened now, could she? She'd just have to live with the errors, move forward, and count them among the flotsam of faults that was forever flowing under the bridge that was her life.

She'd expected the place to be run-down; Larimer Tate had never been one for maintaining it, and now that her mother was ill, no way could Faye be repairing roof shingles or setting posts or putting in new floorboards.

She cut the engine.

Then she took in several deep breaths. The last time she'd actually seen her mother, Faye had been cowering in a corner, hands over her mouth, appearing horrified as Larimer had slipped his belt from his pant loops with a hissing *sssst*.

A cruel grin pinned on his unshaven jaw, he'd jerked on the worn leather.

The belt had snapped like a bullwhip.

Crack!

"Who d'ya think you are?" he'd roared, advancing. "Sneakin' in here like a damned thief after takin' my truck?"

Shiloh had backed up, glanced past him to her mother, still cowering in the doorway to the bedroom she'd shared with this beast.

"And look at 'cha. Half naked." His eyes raked over her body. He was right. She was in her cutoffs and a shirt, no bra, no underwear, both items having been lost in her race through the woods. She doubted he could tell she was missing her panties, but her breasts were visible through her T-shirt. "You been out whorin'."

"No, we . . . we just went skinny-dipping."

"You and who else? Some horny fuckin' teenage boy?"

"Larimer," her mother whispered, but he paid no attention.

"No!" Shiloh wasn't about to give him the names of her friends. Who knew what he'd do?

"I won't have it. Not in my house." Again he cracked the whip, and she witnessed pure evil in his eyes. Her blood pounded through her veins. Given the chance, he would seriously hurt her in as many ways as possible.

"Larimer, she's just a girl," her mother pleaded.

He turned his head to glare at his wife. "Shut up, bitch," he growled.

Shiloh hadn't waited. As Tate's focus had shifted, she made a lightning-quick decision. She had to leave. Right then. No turning back. She bolted through the open door and took off, first on foot, racing across the summer-dry fields. Then when she reached the county road, she stuck out her thumb and hitch-hiked the rest of the way out of Prairie Creek.

She might never have come back at all except for the urgency in her mother's voice last night, and the sound of her cough, a wet rattle that was far worse than the usual dry hack caused by Faye's cigarettes. "If you won't come back for me, do it for Morgan."

Still, Shiloh had resisted. "I don't know Morgan."

"She's your blood, Shiloh. Your sister. The only one you'll ever have. I didn't tell you, but your father died last year."

"What?" Not that it really mattered; she couldn't remember the bastard who'd sired her, married Faye in a shotgun wedding, and then took off. Still, it was a shock.

"And I might not be long for this world."

"Mom—"

"Come home, Shiloh. Morgan and I need you." Another chest-shuddering cough, and Faye, out of character, hung up. When Shiloh had dialed her back, the phone hadn't connected, a busy signal bleeping in Shiloh's ear. All night. So she'd packed up the next morning, made arrangements with Carlos to take care of the horses, then hit the road.

Now she stared at the screen door, and all the old memories washed over her. Of swimming in the pond in the nude, of the old tire swing on the long-downed tree in the backyard, of crushing super hard on Tommy Monroe before he'd moved away, of the first stubborn colt she'd ridden after being scraped or bucked off what had to have been fifty times or more. And then the darker memories of Larimer Tate and the night that had propelled her out of Wyoming, when Ruthie had been assaulted and the three girls had nearly died at the hands of the madman.

Damn it all, they should never have remained silent, never have agreed to Ruthie's desperate pleas. They'd been young and foolish and scared.

Tires crunched against the sparse gravel, jolting her back to the present.

She looked over her shoulder to see the same
beat-up pickup that had been following her driving
up the lane. He'd been following her *all this time*?
What kind of small-town road rage was this? Or . . .

She was starting to connect the dots when the
truck stopped. A tall, rangy man in faded jeans and a
ripped T-shirt climbed from the cab. With wide
shoulders, slim hips, a hard jaw, and hair that hadn't
met a comb recently, he glared at her as if she were
the interloper. A dog that looked part German shepherd hopped to the ground and trotted toward her.

She braced herself.

The dog gave her a once-over, then beelined for
the front porch.

He asked, "Can I help you?"

"Help me? You followed me here."

A thin smile stretched over a beard-stubbled jaw.
"I think you led me."

"Why are you here, and who are you?"

His eyes narrowed, and that damned good-ol'-boy
grin tightened a bit further. "Funny. That's just what
I was gonna ask you."

"I live . . . I used to . . ." She snorted in annoyance.
"My mother lives here," she finally got out. Something flickered in his eyes. Recognition? But she'd
never seen him before. Or? Was she wrong? Had her
mother moved? No way. Shiloh had spoken to Faye
just yesterday, and there had been no mention of a
move.

Before he could say another word, the screen door
banged open, and a girl flew out. Gangly and tanned,
with wild, strawberry-blond curls and freckles dusting
a tiny nose, the girl, around twelve, stared at Shiloh

with wide, suspicious eyes. "You're Shiloh," she declared.

"Uh huh." Shiloh recognized the kid from a few
pictures Faye had sent over the years. "Hi, Morgan,"
she said, but the girl didn't smile, just turned her attention to the man standing next to her.

"We have to go!" she said tightly. "I called nine-
one-one. The ambulance came. They took her to the
hospital." Her eyes dampened as she ran toward the
stranger and vaulted into his waiting arms.

"It's all right," he murmured into her hair, his
voice rough. He gazed over her shoulder, his intense
hazel eyes finding Shiloh's. "We'll go there." Morgan
was sobbing now, her shoulders lifting and falling as
she buried her face in his neck.

"Now?" the girl whispered.

"Yes." He gently turned her toward his truck,
throwing over his shoulder to Shiloh, "You coming?"

"Who are you?" she asked again, but she knew,
deep in her gut, before he could say a word.

As he helped Morgan into the cab and she scrambled over the driver's seat and console to the passenger side, he sent Shiloh another hard look. "I'm
Beau."

As in Beau Tate, Larimer's son, whom she'd never
met and had only heard mutterings of "that damned
no-good kid" from her stepfather before she'd hightailed it out of Prairie Creek. She saw now that Beau
resembled his old man, from his sun-streaked brown
hair to his deep-set eyes and strong jaw. Yes, he had
Larimer Tate stamped all over him.

He hauled himself behind the wheel and yanked
the door shut. The dog whined. Through the open

window, Beau said, "Don't know how long I'll be, so you'd best stay."

Was he talking to her or the dog?

"Hold on, Tate. What happened? It's Mom, right? Something happened."

His silent stare through the window said it all: Faye was in really bad shape.

"But she'll be okay."

When he didn't respond, the breath rushed out of her lungs in a whoosh. It was this serious? As in life and death? "What . . . what hospital?" As far as she knew, the nearest hospital was hours away.

"Let's go!" Morgan cried. "Come on!"

"It's in town. North End," he said to Shiloh. "Where the old video store and the Snow Bird Café used to be. You can't miss it." With that, he twisted the key in the ignition. The engine fired, and he backed up, swung his truck around, and hit the gas.

Her heart was a stone, her legs wooden as she strode to her SUV and slid into the warm interior. By rote she began driving, but she didn't see the fence posts shooting by, nor the geese flying in formation in a blue Wyoming sky, nor even the back end of Beau Tate's battered old truck as it kicked up dust before turning onto the county road.

No, in her mind's eye she saw Faye as she had been the night she'd left: fearful, weak, and trembling.

You should never have gone. Never left her alone with that maniac. You were the stronger one. Always. You left her to get pregnant and bring another girl into that hell of a marriage.

Rationally, she knew she was being too hard on

herself; that she'd been the child whom her mother was supposed to protect. Still, of the two of them, Shiloh was the one made of tougher stuff.

She flashed onto the day that her mother had married Larimer Tate, how happy and full of hope Faye had been, her blond hair twisted into a chignon, her dress a gossamer frothy ivory, her face filled with expectation. At sixteen, Shiloh had known the man was bad news, but Faye, forever a romantic dreamer, had thought Tate would turn their luck around, help save the ranch, help her deal with her headstrong, wayward daughter.

What a joke.

Shiloh set her jaw and felt the sting of tears.

She'd always thought there would be time to repair their broken emotional fences, to reconnect with her mother. Now, it seemed, it was too late.

Chapter 4

The hospital was built on a hillside where once a strip mall from the fifties had been perched. Constructed of stone and glass and flanked by a wide parking lot, Prairie Creek Hospital was small by big city standards but a major upgrade from the clinic that had serviced the area for previous generations. EMERGENCY ENTRANCE was clearly marked in red letters, and as Shiloh grabbed her purse and swung out of her vehicle, she noticed a helicopter landing pad close by.

Beau Tate's truck was parked haphazardly, taking up two spaces, but he and Morgan were nowhere in sight.

Already inside.

Shiloh made her way to the entrance.

A double set of automatic doors whispered open, and she had to dodge an elderly man in a wheelchair. In a bathrobe and slippers, clutching a plastic bag of belongings, the patient barely glanced at Shiloh as he was pushed to a waiting vehicle. Inside, she spied Tate talking to a woman seated behind a large circular desk. Next to him, bouncing nervously from one foot to the other, Morgan was fighting tears.

As Shiloh strode to the desk she heard. ". . . sorry. Nothing I can do." The receptionist, whose ID tag read NINA CORTEZ, was petite and sharp-featured, her black hair shot with strands of silver and tucked into a neat bun at the base of her skull. She was also wearing a practiced smile that didn't quite touch her eyes.

"I want to see my mom!" Morgan insisted, alternately glaring at the woman and glancing beseechingly up at Beau.

"I think it's important," he said.

"I understand, but the doctors are with her now." Nina didn't waver.

"I'm Faye Tate's daughter," Shiloh said, walking up to them. As the next of kin and an adult, maybe she could make an inroad past the roadblock of Ms. Cortez. "Shiloh Silva."

Nina's intractable expression cracked a little, and her gaze shifted, her dark eyes narrowing. "Shiloh Silva?" she repeated. "Wait a minute. I think I read about you . . ." Disbelief clouded her features. "I thought—"

"I'm her daughter too!" Morgan interjected, shooting an angry look at Shiloh.

"I understand," Nina said to the girl, but her eyes were on Shiloh. "Right now no one can see her. Not yet. If you'll all just take a seat, someone will be out to update you shortly."

Morgan was having none of it. "But—"

"It's no use, Morgan. We'll have to be patient," Beau said, and with a big hand placed over her shoulder, he effectively guided his distraught sister from the desk.

Nina said, "You're one of those girls who went missing, what, about ten years ago?"

"Fifteen," Shiloh corrected.

"I thought . . . the whole town thought you were dead." Nina was sizing her up, mentally trying to connect the image of the woman standing in front of her to pictures that had been all over the newspapers years before.

"Not everyone." Shiloh didn't elaborate. Her mother had known she was alive, and possibly a handful of other people.

Nina obviously didn't approve.

Shiloh didn't care. "Look, I just want to see my mom and make sure my sister sees her, too."

The receptionist's face returned to its original bland expression. "You'll have to wait with the others. But if you're the legally responsible party, you need to go to the next desk and fill out some paperwork, insurance information, medical history."

"I don't know if I have any information that will—"

"Right there," Nina said, pointing emphatically to the next desk. "Rebecca will help you. Now, next in line, please." Nina rained her smile on the woman behind Shiloh, a twenty-ish mother holding a whimpering baby.

Fine, Shiloh thought and, with a last glance at Beau and Morgan, now seated on the bland chairs flanking the windows, made her way to the next desk where blond, cheery Rebecca Aldridge was ready with forms and questions that Shiloh had no way to fill out or answer.

The wait was excruciating. Sitting in the uncomfortable chairs, staring at the clock, holding Morgan and trying not to show his irritation at Shiloh, Beau tried to hang onto his patience. Both he and Shiloh had been to the desk several times, asking for information, and had been put off each time.

"I want Mom," Morgan whispered as she sat next to him. "Why won't they let me see her?"

"Rules," he said.

Her face crumpled. "But—"

"I know." His heart tore a little bit. Why the hell wasn't someone giving them an update? He was about to storm to the information desk again when a doctor approached. Tall and reed-thin, in green scrubs, he paused only to confirm with the desk before heading in their direction. His face was somber, his eyes, behind rimless glasses, dark and serene.

"Ms. Tate?" he asked Shiloh as they all stood.

She didn't correct him. "I'm Faye Tate's daughter. Shiloh."

"Me too," Morgan said, fear showing in her eyes. "I'm her daughter too."

The doctor's sober gaze shifted to Morgan for just a second, and he paused a moment before addressing Shiloh directly. "I'm Dr. Sellers. I was your mother's ER physician."

Was. Past tense. The word rang through Beau's brain. He braced himself and felt, rather than saw, Shiloh do the same.

"I'm sorry. We did everything we could, but your mother was too compromised when she came into the hospital. We tried to revive her, but it couldn't be done."

Beside him, Shiloh took in a sharp breath.

"But she's okay?" Morgan demanded, hearing the unspoken message but refusing to believe. "She'll be okay, right?" Tears began drizzling down her cheeks as she turned to him. "Mom's sick, but she's going to be okay."

He put his arm around her. "I'm afraid not, honey."

Morgan protested, "But she has to come home, she has to—"

"She was just too sick."

"No!" Morgan fell into broken sobs.

Beau turned away from Shiloh and guided Morgan toward the door. She clung to him and wept against his neck. Hot, pained tears. His heart ached for his sister, but he couldn't stay in the hospital a second more. There was just no reason. Let Shiloh work things out with the hospital accounting department, let her decide what would happen to her mother's remains, let her deal with the mortuary. For now, he needed to get his broken twelve-year-old sister home.

Not a whole lot else mattered.

By the time Shiloh drove back to her mother's home, it was dusk, the sun no more than a brilliant glow beyond the western ridge, the first stars winking high in a lavender sky. She'd rolled down the driver's-side window, allowing the warm Wyoming air to tangle her hair and kiss her cheek. It had been a long, emotionally wrought day, with hours in the ER, then more time spent making funeral arrangements before meeting with Faye's lawyer, all the while dealing with the brutal fact that her mother was dead. As in forever.

Heavy bands seemed to tighten over her chest, and she found it hard to believe that she hadn't made it in time to say "good-bye" or "I love you."

Fingers clutching the wheel, eyes squinted into the gathering night, Shiloh felt a growing numbness deep inside. She'd not been close to her mother, not for years, but the finality of Faye's passing, her death, hit her harder than she'd imagined it would. A small part of her had irrationally believed that Faye Renee Wilson Silva Tate would always be there for her. Oh, maybe not just around the corner, but always just a phone call away. The fact that this wasn't the case, that Faye had died, was a shock. Already there was a hole in her life, an empty space she'd never thought she'd feel. Apparently just knowing that Faye was living here had been emotionally settling for Shiloh.

"Don't be such a basket case," she muttered under her breath as she eased into the corner of the lane leading to the ranch house.

What now? She couldn't help but wonder. The future stretched out before her, in many ways no different than it had been twenty-four hours earlier, but in other ways it was vastly changed.

She was now responsible for her sister, a girl she barely knew. Morgan. She'd heard Morgan was headstrong and smart, and, right now, she was shattered, her life imploded. It was up to Shiloh to provide some stability.

Not exactly her strong suit.

Then again, neither had it been Faye's.

But that was just the beginning of the life changes. Shiloh would also have to deal with her stepbrother, the son of a man she detested, a cowboy who was outwardly sexy, she'd give him that, but inwardly, she suspected he was as distant and cold as a Canadian blizzard. Then again, he seemed to care for Morgan and the little girl for him. So there might be a chance that Beau Tate's chest wasn't empty, that somewhere deep inside he actually had a beating heart. Not that it mattered. She'd deal with him, heart or no. She had to. She had already stopped by Faye's attorney's office, paid a past-due bill to the taciturn receptionist, and gotten a copy of the will from C. Lewis Cranston. Faye's meager belongings were in trust for her underage daughter, and the kicker was that Faye had appointed both Shiloh and Beau to be Morgan's guardians. Together, as each was related equally to their sister.

"Swell," she said under her breath, the beginning of a headache starting to throb at the base of her skull. "Just damned peachy." Her SUV bounced along the rutted drive, weeds scratching the undercarriage. Shiloh had only planned to be in Prairie Creek a week, maybe less, though she'd made arrangements to have her job in Montana covered for longer. She was a horse trainer and worked out of a ranch near Grizzly Falls in the Bitterroots and had found someone to help her out. However, she doubted Carlos would appreciate her being gone indefinitely as her absence doubled his workload at the Rocking M.

And then she'd have to deal with the police and the people who thought she'd vanished along with Rachel Byrd and Erin Higgins. Another girl, Courtney Pearson, had disappeared soon after the others, just before the monster had attacked Ruthie. Shiloh winced at the thought. They should have known better than to sneak out at that time. By going to the pond, had they inadvertently set up Ruthie's rape? Had Ruth's rapist been involved in those other girls' disappearances, or were they runaways, as she'd always believed? These same torturous thoughts had dogged her for fifteen years.

She sighed and brought herself back to the present and the gathering gloaming. The lights in the house had been turned on, warm patches of yellow glowing over the darkening landscape. The dog, Rambo, was lying on the porch and lifted his head, perking his ears and giving a soft "woof," announcing her arrival as she parked near Beau's beat-up truck.

Cutting the engine, the headlights of her Explorer dimming, she sat in the dark for a few minutes, content to stare through the bug-spattered windshield at the coming night. She thought of Kat and Ruthie, girls she'd steadfastly pushed from her mind, but who had haunted her dreams, the nightmares that punctuated her sleep.

She yanked her keys from the ignition.

She was out of the cab and walking up the path to the house before she noticed Beau seated on the darkened porch, his hips resting on the railing. "'Bout time you showed up," he drawled.

"I've been busy." She couldn't keep the snap from

her voice. "You left me to deal with all the paper-work."

"Had my hands full."

She couldn't argue the point and instead asked, more calmly, "How is she?"

"Not great, as you can imagine." He turned his head, stared across the shadowy fields. "She's resting." He frowned, dark eyebrows drawing together. "Exhausted. Can't say as I blame her."

"Yeah."

"It's gonna be rough for a while."

Maybe longer. "Do you know anything about Faye's will?" she asked and saw him scowl.

"Nope."

"Then you probably don't realize that you've been named as Morgan's guardian."

"Is that so?" He didn't seem surprised.

"You and me."

His head whipped around so fast it startled her, and even in the darkness she felt the intensity of his gaze drilling into her. "You and me," he repeated. "Both of us together?" He sounded about as thrilled as she was.

"That's the way it's laid out in the will. Morgan will inherit everything when she turns eighteen. Until then, you and I are supposed to take care of her."

"Well, now, how's that supposed to work, seein' as you don't live anywhere around here and Morgan and I do?"

"I guess I'll have to move," she said, though she didn't mean it. She just said it.

"Well, I guess you will." He didn't bother hiding the disdain in his voice. "Or more likely, I could petition the court to be her single guardian, and you can go off and hide again, pretend you don't exist or whatever it is you've been doing for the past decade or so."

Shiloh gritted her teeth. "I'm not abandoning her."

"You don't even know her, Shiloh."

"But I will."

"Don't you have a life somewhere, maybe a husband or a kid or a job?"

"A job, yes." Why was she even having this conversation? "Look, for now, I'm staying, that's all."

"For now," he repeated knowingly. He pushed himself off the railing and stood over her, a good head taller than she was. One long arm stretched toward the entrance to the house, where the screen was shut but the heavy wooden door was ajar. "That girl in there has been through a lot. She's lost a father and now a mother, and she's only twelve, so what's not gonna happen on my watch is that she gets attached to someone who has no intention of sticking around. No more abandonment. Not from you. Not from anyone."

Her back teeth ground together, and though he was intimidating, Shiloh wasn't about to back down from Larimer Tate's son, not the way she'd run from the old man. "That goes double for you. Morgan seems to have some attachment to you, so I expect you to stick by her and help out."

"That's exactly what I intend to do."

"Good."

"Good."

They paused a moment, staring at each other like boxers in their corners. Then he extended his hand and gripped hers for a quick shake, surprising her. In the awkward aftermath, she headed inside to check on Morgan and tried to shake off the nagging feeling that she'd just made a deal with the devil.

Chapter 5

Morgan had claimed the bedroom that had belonged to Shiloh when she'd lived here, so after Shiloh quietly checked on her sleeping sister, assured that Morgan was curled up atop the covers of the very same twin bed that had been Shiloh's, she found a quilt in the closet and tucked it around the girl. Morgan, exhausted, barely moved. The girl's face looked pale against the pillow case, her hair a riot of untamed curls falling across her cheeks.

Sleep tight, Shiloh thought but didn't utter the words. Her throat was suddenly thick as she realized the girl was an orphan, as was Shiloh. Morgan was alone aside from Shiloh and Beau Tate.

All in all, it was going to be a difficult situation.

For all of them.

She turned to find Beau standing in the doorway. He was silently observing her, as if he couldn't quite trust her. She couldn't help but bristle and didn't say a word as she passed by him and walked the few short steps from the hallway to the main living area, a space that hadn't grown cozier, or cleaner, or more tended over the years. If anything, the living room, dining area, and kitchen seemed drearier than ever, the walls dingy, the furniture sagging, the lingering scents of bacon grease and Faye's last cigarette still faintly noticeable.

Shiloh was reminded of her own childhood in this dreary, unhappy home, and her guts tightened. But Larimer, the brutal tyrant, was long gone, along with Faye, his dutiful if long-suffering wife, and now the house was empty—devoid of life, rough as it had been for Shiloh.

She heard Beau close Morgan's bedroom door, the latch clicking before he walked into the living room.

"You're staying here?" He pointed a finger at the floor to indicate the house.

"Of course."

"Okay."

"You thought maybe I was going to book a room at Prairie Creek's answer to the Ritz?"

He snorted, as close to a laugh as he was going to come. "Maybe stay with a friend."

"I don't have any friends here," she said, and in her mind's eye she saw Katrina Starr as she had been: short, athletic, tough. A cop's kid. And then there was Ruthie, with her pale, terrified China-doll face. They'd undoubtedly changed since then, were probably married and had kids, maybe moved away. Ruthie most likely went by Ruth now that she was all grown up. Who knew? Certainly not Shiloh. She hadn't kept up with them. Or anyone. By design. That had been the plan, the oath she'd sworn, and she'd stuck to it, never once asking her mother about the other two girls, cutting them out of her life completely, never expecting to see either of them again.

Until now.

Because everything had changed.

"What about you?" she asked him.

"I've got a bunk over the garage."

Shiloh remembered the old attic as a musty collection area for unwanted, broken-down furniture, picture frames, suitcases, and bags of clothes that had never made it to the thrift store. She'd had friends over, and they'd hung out there when she was a teen; she'd even stolen one of Tate's whiskey bottles and, with Tommy Monroe, sampled her first searing swallow of Jim Beam when she'd been in the tenth grade. The place was uninhabitable, or had been the last she'd been up there. "*You* live here?" Oh no, that wouldn't work. She couldn't imagine waking up to Beau Tate or trying to sleep when he was nearby.

"No. I don't live here. Or I didn't." His lips compressed. "I have my own place, but since Faye took ill a few months back, I've stayed here off and on."

"Well, you can go home now," she said emphatically.

"I'll stay tonight."

Man oh man, this wasn't going how she'd planned. "So where do you really live?"

"Outside of town, not far from the Kincaid ranch. You know where that is?"

Of course she did. Anyone who grew up in the area knew about the two major spreads in the area. The Rocking D was owned by the Dillinger family, the other was the Kincaid place. "Yeah."

"I work for the Kincaids. Blair and Hunter."

"Not the Colonel . . . no, wait, I mean the Major?" she asked, referring to the Kincaid patriarch.

Beau gave a quick shake of his head. "Nope. He passed on a couple of years ago."

"What about his wife?"

He grimaced. "I keep forgetting that you weren't around. Georgina's still alive, I think, but she's not in Prairie Creek." Shiloh waited for more, but he walked to the window, looked outside, as if thinking about how much he should share about the family that had hired him. "None of the Kincaids talk about it much, but rumor has it she's in a private care facility somewhere in Colorado, I think. Denver, maybe."

"Because . . . ," she prodded, sensing there was more to the story.

He seemed reticent to gossip and shrugged. "I guess she lost it after her husband died, got herself into some kind of trouble, and ended up there." He met her gaze. "I don't pry."

"So, then, who's in charge of the ranch?"

"Blair's the overseer. All the Kincaids own a share of the ranch, as I understand it, but Hunter and Blair actually work on the day-to-day dealings. Hunter's married, a fireman, and he needed help with a spread that big, so he practically begged Blair to come back and help out."

"And he came? Just like that?"

Beau lifted a dismissive shoulder. "Just what I heard. I work with a few of the hands, Scott Massey, Roland Gonzalez, and Belle Zeffer."

She'd heard of Massey and Gonzalez but didn't recall Belle Zeffer.

"You'd have to ask Blair what really brought him back to Prairie Creek. Again—"

"I know, I know." She held up her hands as if in surrender. "You 'don't pry.'" Still, she was curious as she remembered Blair from her youth as being kind of a rebel.

Beau slid a glance her way before walking to the short hallway, where he peeked inside Morgan's bedroom.

"She okay?" Shiloh asked.

"Still asleep."

"Good."

He added, "So the long and the short of it is that I live near the Kincaid ranch and work for them too. Blair's my immediate boss. I don't deal much with Hunter or his wife."

"Who'd Hunter marry?"

"Delilah Dillinger."

"*Dillinger?* Really? But I thought . . . huh . . ." A person couldn't have grown up in Prairie Creek and not known that the Dillingers and the Kincaids were sworn enemies, two ranching families whose animosity had gone on for decades.

He seemed to read her mind. "Heard they've got a baby, too, but yeah . . . a lotta bad blood there. Big ranches, big families, and even bigger egos. At least back in the days when Major Kincaid and Ira Dillinger were in charge. Guess Hunter got over it, now that the Major's gone. Ira's lost some of his fire too. He's letting his kids run the Rocking D." He walked into the kitchen and, as if he owned the place, opened the refrigerator and pulled out a beer. "Time has a way of making people forget the bad times."

"Does it?" She didn't believe it. Not after what she'd been through. If so, she would have forgotten about the night of Ruthie's rape, the horror of nearly being killed, and, of course, of the cruelty of Larimer Tate. Without thinking about it, she rubbed the scar on her shoulder where the would-be killer's blade had sliced through her skin.

"Usually." He studied her for a second so intently that she felt a wave of heat rise up the back of her neck. "Maybe not always."

It was as if he knew about that night, which, of course, he couldn't.

"Want one?" He held up a long-necked bottle, and she shook her head.

"Not now."

"Suit yourself." He twisted off the top and took a long swallow. Again, as if he'd done it a hundred times and was comfortable in her mother's home.

"So the feud is over?"

"I wouldn't say over. Seems unlikely, y'know. For now, though, it's at least buried." His brow furrowed. "Things seemed to have calmed down a lot since Hunter and Delilah's wedding."

"Sometimes marriage only makes things worse."

"Tell that to Sabrina Delaney. She's marrying Colton Dillinger. In September."

"Sabrina Delaney." Shiloh wasn't certain she remembered her, but, of course, she'd run into all of Ira Dillinger's kids growing up. Colton had been way ahead of her in high school, but that boy had caused more than one teenage girl's heart to pound. "Well, good luck to them on making it work," she said dryly.

"Speaking from experience?"

"Thought you didn't pry."

"You seem to have a tainted view on marriage."

"Well, yeah. I've seen enough bad ones." *And one of the worst happened here, within these four walls.* "Everyone thinks marriage will make things better, improve their life."

"Not everyone."

Fine. Your turn. "So now *you're* speaking from experience."

He smiled faintly. "If you're asking if I've ever been married, the answer is 'no.'"

"I wasn't asking," she said, lying a little. "So how'd you get involved with the Kincaids?"

"I'd just come back to town and ran into Blair down at The Dog. The ranch is massive, and they needed a foreman."

She nodded, remembering the Prairie Dog, a local watering hole.

"Blair and I were in school together, and I knew most of his brothers and sisters. We got to talking, and I said I'd run several other spreads out of state. He was looking for someone, so it was kind of a perfect deal. They needed a foreman. I needed a job. The rest, as they say, is history."

"Recent history."

He took a long pull from his bottle. "Right."

She looked around the kitchen, wishing his big body was not in it. "Look, I've got this. At least for tonight. You really don't need to hang out here."

He shook his head. "I'm good. If she"—he hooked his thumb toward the hallway and the closed door beyond—"wakes up, she'll want me to be around."

"You don't trust me."

"Course not. I don't know you, and neither does Morgan. You're a stranger to her, someone she's heard about but never met."

He waited for her to argue. She couldn't.

"So for the next few days at the very least, I'll be around. Until the dust settles and I see that she's good." Another drink and the beer was gone. He set the empty on the window ledge.

"And your job?"

"Don't worry about that. I've got it handled."

That's more than she could say. "All right. Fine."

"Glad you agree," he said sardonically, then he checked on Morgan once more, whistled to the dog, and walked out the back door.

Through the windows, she watched as he crossed the dry patch of lawn to the garage. With Rambo at his heels, Beau mounted the steep exterior stairs that led to the attic tucked under the ancient building's rafters.

Why, she wondered, did it seem so obvious that he belonged here while she felt like a damned intruder?

Shiloh Silva.

Beau should have expected her to show, but she'd stayed away for so many years, who would have thought that Faye's last dying plea would get to her? He unrolled the sleeping bag he'd brought with him and spread it on a folding camping cot that had seen better days. A dusty rug covered the ancient floorboards, and haphazard junk, the detritus of a hardscrabble life, surrounded the small open area. He'd opened the two dormer windows earlier so the heat of the day was slowly dispersing, and he could hear the sounds of the night: a faraway train rattling on distant tracks, a night owl hooting softly, the flutter of insect wings drawn to the attic light. He eyed his surroundings and smiled to himself. He'd slept in worse. More times than he could count, once in a while with a woman, often alone.

He glanced through the open window to the house, where lights glowed in the living area, though the bedrooms remained dark. Again, his thoughts turned to Shiloh. Tall, athletic, with wide, green eyes that narrowed on him with distrust. As if he were cut from the same cloth as his old man.

So now, she was back? In worn jeans, a loose blouse, curly blond hair clipped at her nape, and carrying a don't-mess-with-me attitude as if she had every right to be here.

He opened the backpack he'd left propped against an old bureau capped with a cracked mirror, opened the flap, and pulled out a bottle of Jack that was about half full. With a flick of his wrist he uncapped the bottle, then took a long pull. The whiskey warmed a familiar path down his throat and hit his empty belly hard. He didn't need the distraction of Shiloh or any other woman now. The kid needed him, and he had a ranch to run, a mortgage to pay, the damned Dillingers breathing down his neck. Hell, no. Shiloh Silva was a distraction of the worst order, but luckily she despised him.

"Thank God for small favors," he muttered to himself and took another swig.

So why the hell was she so damned intent on staying? Through the window, he watched her move through the living room to the kitchen and back again. She had a natural grace to her, a fluidity of movement. Long legs, rounded butt, high breasts, not too big, not too small, and straight shoulders. She claimed she'd never married. He decided she was probably telling the truth, though he hadn't heard much about his step-sister. Faye had mostly kept mum about her, though there were a few pictures of Shiloh as a girl or teen in which she'd always been standing rigidly or riding a horse of some kind.

Those pictures were on the mantel, and he knew them by heart. In the first photo, Shiloh had been standing next to a docile pinto pony, reins gripped loosely in one hand. She must've been around seven or eight, her freckled face tipped up beneath the brim of a pink cowgirl hat that was buckets too big, her smile wide but missing one front tooth.

Next to the first was a slightly larger framed shot. Shiloh had been older, around fifteen, and the picture had been taken after a barrel-racing competition, Faye had explained when Beau had picked up the dusty picture. The spotted pony in the first photo had been replaced by a black horse that looked part Arabian. Astride the gelding, Shiloh was definitely on the edge of womanhood. Her cheekbones were high and pronounced, and her lips, without the slightest hint of lipstick, were full and lush, but now the earlier wonder in her eyes replaced with a mixture of innocence and suspicion, at least in Beau's estimation.

"She's beautiful," Faye had murmured once, when she'd caught him looking at the photos.

"If you say so."

Shiloh's mother had smiled knowingly. "I do. But she's a handful. A real pistol. Never could get along with Larimer, rest his soul."

Beau had doubted that the old man's soul was resting at all. If there was a hell, Larimer Tate was surely a deep-seated resident.

He took another sip, then recapped his bottle.

Never before, to his knowledge, had his stepsister shown an iota of interest in her mother or sister. So now she was back? Intent on staying? Going to, what, "mother" Morgan? Like that would fly. If nothing else, his half sister was stubborn and knew her own mind. Morgan would peg Shiloh fast.

So what was the deal?

Did Shiloh think she had to come here to stake her claim?

Was she angling for ownership of this scrap of land?

Or feeling some latent sense of remorse for taking off and barely communicating with her mother?

Shiloh had left years before under a cloud of suspicion, around the same time other girls had gone missing. Some people thought she'd been abducted, others considered her a runaway, but Faye had always maintained she was fine, had even talked to the police and insisted her wild child was just "growing up" and "finding herself." No one had said differently, but Beau had suspected her abrupt leaving had to do with his old man. Larimer Tate's quick temper and liberal use of "corporal punishment," which of course was abuse, was a widely known secret around these parts.

Beau grimaced. It made him ill to think Shiloh

might have been on the receiving end of Larimer's cruel sense of justice. Hadn't Beau been the object of his father's rages more often than not while growing up? He'd certainly felt the bite of his belt more times than he wanted to remember. Beau doubted that Larimer's warped sense of values had stopped at "disciplining" a child just because she was a girl.

Was that why she left? The thought made him go cold inside. Sure, it had crossed his mind, but he'd preferred to believe Shiloh was spared, that she'd escaped what Beau had endured—abuse that hadn't abated until Beau turned sixteen and grabbed that sharp leather snake that kept a drunken Larimer at bay. They'd been in the barn in the sweltering heat of summer, Beau raking out the stalls, getting rid of the urine-soaked straw while flies buzzed near his head. Larimer, who'd been visiting Beau's mother, had wandered out to the barn and had seen it as his opportunity to offer up his special brand of parenting, starting by badgering Beau and commenting upon how slowly he had been working.

"You're a lazy son of a bitch," his father told him, and Beau could smell last night's alcohol seeping through the older man's skin as he sauntered into the building. Larimer paused at the stall where Beau was working and looked over his son's shoulder.

Beau hadn't responded, knowing his dear old dad was baiting him. Trying to tamp down his rage, he'd kept raking, dropping the filthy straw into a rapidly filling wheelbarrow.

"A do-nothin," Larimer goaded.

Beau's jaw had tightened, and his hands gripped the smooth handle of the rake until his knuckles showed white. He'd been tired and dirty and had better things to do than clean the stalls, but he'd acquiesced, figuring it was a way to avoid his old man. Obviously, he'd figured wrong, so he kept on working, sweat pouring down his neck and shoulders, his T-shirt clinging to him.

"Won't amount to nothing." Larimer scowled into the stall.

"If you don't like the way I'm doing this, then why don't you do it yourself? Or better yet, just leave."

"You need to listen to me."

"And you need to screw off."

"What's that, boy? What'd you say?"

Beau had turned then, standing as tall as the man who had sired him, his shoulders flexed, his fists balled, his gaze staring straight into Larimer's. With more calm than he felt, he clarified himself. "I said, screw off, but I meant fuck off. If you don't like what I'm doing, then either you grab a damned rake and do it yourself or get the hell away from me."

"That's no way to talk to your father, boy."

"You're right. But then you're not much of a father, are you? So go on. Go back to your other family. Mom and I don't need you." He'd turned back to the job at hand, but every one of his muscles was stretched tight, and if he didn't control himself, he'd swing the damned rake right in the old man's face.

"You want to fight me?" Larimer challenged.

You bet! "Not worth the trouble." But, yeah, what Beau wouldn't give to square off with Larimer, punch his lights out.

"You need a lesson in respect."

Then he'd heard the familiar hiss of a belt being

stripped from Larimer's jeans. The same sound he'd heard as a boy of not more than five. His heart stilled. *Bastard,* he thought. Beau then turned, dropping the rake in the same motion, and his father had drawn back and started to crack the slim leather over his head. As it whipped toward him, Beau had deftly caught the belt in one hand. Sharp leather cut into his fist, but he barely felt it.

"You ever try this again, I swear I'll kill you," he warned in a low voice. Larimer tried to yank his weapon away, but Beau had wound the snake-like strap around his fist, drawing his father closer until they were glaring eye to eye. His father's nostrils flared, and Beau smelled the stink of whiskey and tobacco on his breath. A drop of sweat drizzled along the old man's hairline.

"You don't have the guts."

"Oh, sure I do."

"You'd spend the rest of your life in prison."

"No court in the county would convict me." With his free hand he lifted his shirt to show the scars that were visible on his skin. "You wanna take your chances?"

"You're just like me," Larimer insisted. "You look like me, and now you're acting like me."

"I'll never be like you, you sick piece of shit."

Surprisingly, the old man had backed down. For the first time in Beau's memory, he dropped his belt and backed out of the doorway of the barn, his looming silhouette visible against the backdrop of the setting sun. Beau had gone about finishing his chores, then later swung his leg over the saddle of his miserable excuse of a motorcycle and roared off.

He'd never seen Larimer Tate again.

And he hadn't regretted it.

Still didn't.

Except for the terrible thought that Larimer might have hurt Shiloh while Beau had turned a cold shoulder to his father's other family.

Shiloh took one step into Faye's bedroom, then backed out and closed the door. No way could she stay in the room where her mother had slept, at least not yet. The ghosts were too nearby. A single glimpse of the bedroom, with its faded floral wallpaper, yellowed curtains, patchwork quilt, and a bureau of Faye's things, including her wedding picture to Tate, was enough to convince Shiloh that she wouldn't be comfortable occupying a space that was so intimately Faye's. Maybe she'd change her mind. Someday. Then again, more likely not.

So she turned and nearly jumped out of her skin when she spied Morgan standing in the doorway of the other bedroom.

"That's Mom's room," the girl said.

"I know."

"You're not gonna sleep in there, are you?"

"No."

"Good."

There was a heavy silence before Shiloh said, "Are you okay?"

"No."

Shiloh's heart twisted.

"Are you?" Morgan asked.

"Not . . . really."

"Are you staying here?"

"For now."

"Why?"

"Well . . . because of you."

Another long pause, then Morgan said, "You don't have to. Beau's here . . ." Her eyebrows knotted. "Isn't he?"

"In the attic over the garage."

"He should be in here."

"His choice." Shiloh took a step closer. "Can I get you something?"

Her eyes narrowed. "No."

"Maybe a glass of water? Or . . . hot cocoa?"

"I'm not a two-year-old!"

"I know . . . I'm just trying to help."

"Then leave."

"What?"

"You don't belong here," she charged. "You really want to know what would help? If you left."

Shiloh wanted to fight back, to mention the fact that Faye had been her mother as well, but she knew she would only be wading into deeper, darker emotional waters, and Morgan was only twelve and hurting.

"You should have come back when she was alive. She wanted that."

Guilt jabbed at Shiloh, but she didn't explain.

"But . . . you . . . didn't, did you?"

"It was complicated."

Morgan crossed her arms over her chest, her chin tilted at an imperious angle. "What? You can't explain? You don't think I'll understand?"

"I don't—"

"Never mind. I can tell you're going to lie."

"I'm not going to lie," Shiloh shot back. "Okay, the truth. I left because I didn't get along with my step-dad, your father." That was sugarcoating it, but the little girl didn't need to know what a perverted creep her father was, and Morgan was still very, very raw from Faye's death only hours before.

"Dad's been dead a long time." She pressed her lips together.

"I know, but by that time I had my own life."

"That's what Mom said, but you know, I think it's all just a big excuse." Her last words quavered, and she cleared her throat. She wasn't nearly as tough as she wanted Shiloh to believe.

"Okay, look. You're right. I should have been closer to Mom while I had the chance. I get that. And I get that you're mad at me because you think I didn't treat her right, but, we have to go forward. So maybe you and I can start over."

The glare she received could have melted granite. Without a word, Morgan stalked past her and into Faye's room. She shut the door so fiercely the timbers creaked. A second later, the lock clicked.

Shiloh closed her eyes and slowly counted to ten. She'd tried. She'd failed.

Frustration boiled inside, and she nearly started beating on the door, to try and engage her sister, but that wouldn't work. Instead Shiloh reminded herself she just needed to give the kid some space. Everyone grieved differently. Morgan was hurting and transferring the source of that pain onto Shiloh.

Made sense, but just the same it didn't feel good.

"Wonderful," Shiloh hissed beneath her breath. "Just . . . fabulous."

Chapter 6

"Shiloh Silva's back in town?" Kat repeated, staring at her father in surprise. She was standing in his tiny office, a storefront, its only nod to décor a few fishing poles and nets tacked neatly onto the gray walls.

Patrick Starr was seated behind his desk, a newspaper spread on the scarred top, coffee warming in a glass carafe on a hot plate situated on the credenza stretched behind him. Since retiring from the force, Patrick Starr had worked as a private detective, renting this hole-in-the-wall office space in a strip mall. His private detective business was wedged between a taxidermist, who doubled as an accountant when tax time rolled around, and a bakery that specialized in a wide array of cupcakes. The freshly made pastries were so special that most mornings a line of patrons snaked from the counter inside Betty Ann's Bakery and out the front door, even in the middle of winter with the temperatures freezing. So far, Kat had resisted temptation and hadn't sampled Betty Ann's fare.

"I saw Shiloh myself." He folded the paper as she dropped into one of the side chairs. His hair, once as dark as hers, was now shot with silver, and his sharp eyes had dimmed a bit, forcing him to wear glasses that he vociferously hated.

"I didn't think she'd ever return."

"Her mother passed away a few days ago."

"I heard. But—" There hadn't been a lot of love between Faye and her firstborn daughter. And once Shiloh took off, she'd never returned. Nearly vanished. Kat hadn't heard from her. Not a word.

"I know, I know. I didn't expect her to ever set foot in this town again. She was vehement when I talked to her." While on the force, Detective Patrick Starr had been working on the investigation of the teenagers who had gone missing fifteen years earlier. Erin Higgins and Rachel Byrd had never been located, and their missing persons cases had crushed Kat's father. Sometime after their disappearances, a third girl, Courtney Pearson, never returned home. That was about a month before Ruthie's rape, and she'd never been seen again, either.

That was the one that really gnawed at Kat. Her worst fear was that Courtney had fallen victim to the same man who'd raped Ruthie—and that she and her friends could have prevented it if they'd only stepped forward.

Kat had wanted to come clean about the night at the lake. It was hell keeping mum, but she'd made that promise to Ruthie. But what if the three girls' silence had put Courtney Pearson at risk? Could they have prevented her disappearance? If they had just gone to the police, told what they knew, maybe talked to a police sketch artist and come up with some kind of composite picture of the attacker, would things have turned out differently? Would the son of a bitch be serving time?

Worse yet, Kat had been forced to face her father every day, the very man who was leading the investigation, a man who had poured his heart and soul into his job rather than deal with the pain of a sickly wife. Those had been horrible years, when only Kat, it seemed, faced the fact that Marilyn Starr had been dying bit by bit, that the chemo hadn't been working.

Even now, seeing the lines on her father's once-ruddy face, she felt a renewed sense of guilt. And still, to this day, when she was a detective with the department herself, she'd held her tongue. Though she'd never actually lied to her father, she knew now that there were lies of commission and lies of omission, and she was certainly guilty of the latter.

"I think I'll look Shiloh up," she said. It was time to rectify her mistakes.

"I always liked that kid, but I thought she got a raw deal with that stepfather of hers. A mean cuss. No one ever filed any charges, you know, but I had a gut feeling about him." Patrick's face tightened. "I should've asked some questions, y'know."

"It's long over."

"I know, but there's the right thing to do, and then there's the wrong. Not a lot of gray area in between. I didn't do the right thing."

"We've all made mistakes," Katrina said, meaning

every syllable. She desperately wanted to get the story on record, but first she had to talk to Ruthie, and with Shiloh back, maybe the two of them could convince her to come forward. Ruthie, or Ruth, as she apparently went by now, had recently returned to Prairie Creek after years away, though Katrina had yet to run into her.

Ruth hadn't made any concentrated effort to connect with her onetime friend, either. Since in a town the size of Prairie Creek that was nearly impossible, Kat guessed it was by design rather than happenstance.

But with Shiloh back in town, there was no more waiting, as far as Kat was concerned. The three of them needed to come clean about the night of Ruth's rape.

"I was just too involved with my job at the time to take on much more," Patrick was saying. "And then there was your mom, may she rest in peace."

Kat watched as a particular sadness settled over him the way it always did when he spoke of his wife. Though Marilyn had been gone nearly fifteen years, he'd rarely dated, though he'd had many opportunities. He'd struggled to be around Marilyn while she was dying. He'd loved her fiercely, but he couldn't watch her suffer. Kat understood that now, though at the time she'd been deeply angry with both her father and her brother for leaving her with the bulk of her mom's care. She'd forgiven both of them over the years and had forged new, happier relationships, but it had been a long struggle.

"You look like her, you know," her father said wistfully.

"Yes." She'd heard the same thing all her life. While Ethan was tall and rangy like their father, she'd inherited her mother's shorter height, if not her sunny disposition.

"You may have gotten my temperament, but thank God, you got her looks. She was a beautiful woman, Kat. You're lucky."

"I know, Dad."

"I should have paid more attention those last years. Been there with her," he said.

"I know that too." She sought to head him off from the maudlin track he was about to embark on.

He nodded, just managed to stop himself from going there. A big, strapping man who thought nothing about staring down the barrel of a shotgun pointed in his direction, Patrick Starr had been leveled by the insidious disease silently killing his wife. Rather than sitting for hours at her bedside, he'd found excuses to be away. He'd turned his attention to finding the missing girls most people thought were runaways. That was his way of coping.

Still, despite his efforts, every lead in the investigation had turned into a dead end.

Patrick smiled sadly at the picture of his deceased wife, and Kat's restless mind wandered back to the investigation that had become her father's Waterloo. Rachel's parents, Paul and Ann Byrd, had never given up hope that their daughter would someday be found. With their remaining daughters at their side and the news cameras rolling, they had let it be known they blamed the police as a whole for not finding Rachel—and Patrick Starr, in particular. Anytime there was an issue in the family that required involvement with the Sheriff's Department—and there was a small one developing now—Paul Byrd used the opportunity to complain anew about the department's failings.

Erin Higgins's parents, Alan and Dora, though divorced, were united in their belief that Erin was alive. They were less angry with the authorities than the Byrds, but they were steadfast in their belief that their daughter would come home someday. Their son, Bryce, had been one of the most loyal searchers for Erin and had never given up trying to find her.

And Courtney Pearson's mother, Jan, believed that the Lord would bring her daughter back to her. Courtney's father wasn't in the picture and was in fact, long gone; broken, he'd walked out soon after his only daughter disappeared.

When Shiloh had first disappeared, Faye Silva-Tate had shrieked at the police to find her baby, too. Kat had been miserable and had been on the verge of telling her father about the attack at the lake, but again Ruthie had shut her down.

"What good would it do?" she'd demanded. "Did you recognize him? No. None of us did."

"He'll have wounds on his body that we inflicted. Scars now, maybe."

"It won't help. It's not enough. And my father will kill me, if it comes out. He'll kill me!"

They had been walking down a park path after school; Ruthie had chosen the venue because she didn't even want to be seen talking to Kat. Their burgeoning friendship had been cut off by the events of the night at the pond, and they'd all stayed away

from each other by unspoken rule, but now Shiloh
was missing.

"You really think Shiloh's been taken?" Ruthie had
queried, her face screwed up in misery.

Kat shook her head. No. Shiloh had taken off a
few times before for periods of time; Kat knew that
from overhearing her father discussing Larimer Tate
on the phone with someone else at the department.
She really hadn't believed Shiloh had been caught by
the man who'd taken Ruthie, but what she said was,
"All I know is we need to go to the police about your
rape. Or at least my father. It wasn't your fault. For
God's sake, you were attacked, Ruthie. *Violated.*
You're the victim here. Your father will understand
that."

Ruthie shook her head so hard her hair started to
fall from its knot at the top of her head. "He'll . . .
he'll . . ." She swallowed. "He'll make an example of
me at church. I . . . will be like Hester Prynne in *The
Scarlet Letter.* You know that one?"

"Yeah, I know that one."

Ruthie had then swiped at her eyes and stopped,
leaning on the trunk of a massive tree for support.
"He'll show no mercy. He'll be mortified. He sets his
family up as this . . . this godly example."

"But you didn't do anything wrong."

"He won't see it that way."

"Other girls are missing—"

"I know that! Don't you think I know that? What
would you do if it were you? Would *you* tell *your* father? And the police. Could you confide in some officer who looks at you as part of the job? And what

about the people at the hospital or, worse yet, the local clinic? Sandi Thompson's mom is a nurse there, and she goes to our church and . . . oh, can't you see?"

The truth was Kat did see. Much of what Ruthie feared was true. Gossip spread like wildfire through the streets and shops of Prairie Creek.

"But—"

"Just think about it, okay?" Ruthie said, clearing her throat, seeming to pull herself together a bit. "What possible good would it do? You can't ID him, and neither can I. It would be a great big, horrible circus, and I'd be the main attraction. All of my family would be dragged into it." She squeezed her eyes closed and balled her fists. "I don't know what to do, Kat. I want to tell the police, but it won't help. All that will happen is that I'll be humiliated. My father will never forgive me, and my whole family will have to move. *Again!*" She shook her head. "I should have gone in right after it happened," she whispered. "You know, when they could do those tests."

A rape kit, Kat had thought, but hadn't said it.

"But it's too late now. I mean." She blinked again, fought for control. "I must've showered a thousand times, trying to get him off me. And I've prayed. I've prayed and prayed and prayed and still . . . still . . ." Letting out her breath slowly, she grabbed Kat's hand, letting the tears she'd been battling run down her cheeks. "I . . . I . . . just . . . I just can't."

Kat had felt her own eyes burn, and she had never brought up the subject again.

Some of Kat's anxiety lessened when, shortly thereafter, Shiloh called her mother to tell her she was fine, that she just wasn't coming back. Faye Silva hadn't been convinced that she was, so she'd forced her daughter to speak on the phone to the lead detective on the case, Patrick Starr. Faye was afraid that a kidnapper was forcing Shiloh to make the call, even though Shiloh had assured her she was perfectly fine. Shiloh had then gone to a police station in Helena, Montana, where an officer had confirmed that she was well, and, having just turned eighteen, was not a runaway.

Faye had been relieved. Yet over the years Shiloh's name had become lumped in with those of the three missing girls. Her "miraculous" reappearance had given the parents of Rachel Byrd, Courtney Pearson, and Erin Higgins hope that their daughters were safe, a hope that had yet to come to fruition.

Detective Patrick Starr hadn't been sidetracked by Shiloh. He'd doggedly kept on working on finding Erin, Rachel, and Courtney, though the department had never officially listed them as missing persons. Even after his retirement, Patrick kept a list of names with pictures of his suspects, a list that Kat had caught glimpses of over the years and now knew by heart. Those suspects had been interviewed several times when the case was hot, but nothing had ever come of it, and now the missing girls were assumed to be runaways. No crime had been committed, as far as anyone could prove, and since Ruthie hadn't come forward about her rape, the three missing teens— now women—were a cold case . . . actually, hardly a case at all.

Skip Chandler.

Calvin Haney.

Rafe Dillinger.

Those three were at the top of Patrick Starr's list because they'd all left town about the time girls had stopped disappearing, though none of them had ever been charged with the crime. Coincidentally, they were all three now back in Prairie Creek. Back when the girls disappeared, Calvin Haney, a loudmouthed womanizing wildcatter, and Skip Chandler, a known thief and con man, had taken off without telling anyone, including their relatives, where they were headed. The third man was one of the Dillinger cousins, Rafe Dillinger, a dropout who had dated Courtney Pearson. When Kat was a teenager, Rafe had been a notorious bad boy, stealing cigarettes and beer from Menlo's Market, driving girls around in his truck, giving alcohol to minors, even, supposedly, getting Darla Kingsley pregnant, though that was never confirmed. Unlike other petty criminals, Rafe had the Dillinger fortune as a safety net when he screwed up. He'd left town around the same time that Shiloh had done her own disappearing act; some said Ira Dillinger had had enough of the boy.

There were others on Patrick's list, but the three that had hightailed it out of town for a while were the ones he'd focused on. Kat wondered if one of them had been Ruth's rapist. The problem was, even if Kat thought she could ID the man, there would be no proof of a rape, nor any conclusive evidence, such as DNA collected in a rape kit.

Kat looked at her father, seeing his florid face. With

lack of evidence, no bodies, and no found kidnapping victims, no arrests had been made—and that, coupled with his lifestyle, had nearly killed Patrick Starr.

After the heart attack, he'd given up the cigarettes and booze, but he'd never let go of the case.

Now Patrick rubbed the back of his neck and said, "You and Shiloh were thick as thieves for a while in high school."

"Eons ago. I'm surprised she came back."

"Well, there's her kid sister, you know. Morgan's around eleven or twelve, I think, and now she's lost both parents. I expect Shiloh had to return to settle things." He waved a hand. "Not just her sister, but all the red tape that comes when a person leaves this earth. Funeral arrangements. Wills. Whatever." He reached for the half-drunk cup of coffee situated between a few scattered piles on his desk. "You want a cup?"

She was slinging the strap of her purse over her shoulder when she glanced out the window to spy a familiar pickup fly into the lot. Her heart jolted as she watched Blair Kincaid park next to her car, hop out of the cab, adjust his aviator sunglasses, and stride into Betty Ann's. Tall and rangy, with thick hair and a body hard from work around the ranch, Blair was too handsome for his own good. He now ran the family's ranch, and Kat had run into him far more than she wanted. She'd never really liked him, she reminded herself.

"Kat?" her father said.

She turned back to him. "Sorry. I need to be at the office, like ten minutes ago."

One eyebrow rose over the rim of his glasses. He could always spot her when she told a lie. Well, almost always. He'd never guessed what had happened the night of the attack. "Tomorrow, then? A rain check?"

"Sounds good." In an effort to divert his attention, she asked, "Maybe you could sneak over and grab a couple of those red velvet cupcakes at Betty Ann's before I get here. They're supposed to be spectacular."

"You heard that from me."

From the corner of her eye, she spied Blair return to his truck carrying a cup of coffee and white sack. He climbed into his truck and roared out of the parking space as quickly as he'd flown in.

"You okay?" her father asked.

"Yeah, fine. Just thinking about my calendar. Okay, tomorrow. Cupcakes for breakfast. I'll be here at seven-thirty."

He slid her a smile, and his eyes twinkled a bit. For a second, there was a glimpse of the strapping man he'd once been, the no-holds-barred detective with a quick wit and dogged take-no-prisoners attitude— the man he was before the heart attack and his early retirement from the force. Once he recovered, he'd thought he'd spend his hours fishing and golfing, but boredom had set in early, so he'd started this private detective agency.

"They also have a killer German chocolate," he said, walking her to the door.

"Whatever you want. For today, we'll indulge."

"You got it, kiddo."

As Kat left, she walked by the plate-glass window with his name inscribed in gold leaf, and she caught a glimpse of her father returning to his desk. In her heart of hearts, she knew that he'd started this one-man agency not just to fill his time chasing down perpetrators of insurance fraud or proving that a husband had cheated on his wife or vice versa. No. He still was chasing his white whale: a case involving three missing girls.

Chapter 7

"I'm not sure when I'll be back," Shiloh said, cradling her cell phone between her ear and her shoulder as she dried her hands on a towel in the kitchen of her mother's house, then tossed the damp rag onto the counter.

Carlos Hernandez was on the other end of the wireless connection. "I don't know how long I can cover for you," he said, and she imagined fine lines drawing his dark eyebrows together. "The wife, she's not all that crazy about me not seeing the kids."

"Look, I'll have a definitive answer in a few days." Would she? She wasn't certain. Not of anything right now. Faye's funeral was scheduled for later today, and after that? Who knew? The thought of actually laying her mother to rest in a plot next to Larimer Tate's was depressing.

Nearly a week had passed since she'd first returned, and she still felt uneasy, as if she didn't belong. She'd kept herself busy by cleaning the house and yard and working with the horses, something that had actually interested Morgan. Shiloh had caught her sister watching her from the window and then the porch, but when she'd asked the girl to join her, Morgan had scurried back into the solitude and safety of the house. Not good. Not good at all. Now Shiloh cast a glance out the window to the garage, where Beau was just coming down the exterior stairs. She and he were getting along, though, she knew, their affability was all a show for Morgan.

Crossing the fingers of her free hand, she said, "I'll figure out what I'm doing in the next couple of days, I promise."

"Okay . . ." Carlos still sounded unconvinced, but he finally acquiesced, and she hung up wondering what in the world she was going to do.

Could she really make Prairie Creek her permanent residence? A place she'd sworn she'd never set foot in again? But that was before Larimer Tate had kicked off, and now Faye had died, and the responsibility of her half sister had been laid at her feet.

Against her nature, Shiloh had played it cool, avoiding confrontation as she'd slowly tried to get to know Morgan and figure out what she was going to do. She would never be able to sleep in Faye's room, though, no matter how much she tried to rationalize that it didn't matter—her mother was gone, so what if she'd spent her last days there? Or, years before, made love in that bed with Larimer Tate? No amount of talking to herself worked.

Instead, Shiloh had taken to sleeping on the back porch on an old lounge chair. From her position, she was able to watch the stars appear and the moon rise before drifting off to the sound of a soothing breeze rustling the leaves of the aspens and cottonwoods rimming the property. Once in a while, she'd hear the howl of a coyote or the flap of an owl's wings or be awakened by a chorus of frogs, but these were comfortable, familiar sounds of the night.

More often than not, she'd catch a glimpse of Beau Tate, backlit by a single lamp as he leaned against the window before shutting off the lights of the attic over the garage, and those images were unsettling.

She'd thought him to be like his father, cut from the same cruel cloth, but she was slowly learning she'd been wrong. Or so it seemed on the surface. She wouldn't go so far as to say he was pleasant—quite the opposite—but he'd been rock steady and was incredibly kind and tolerant of Morgan. So far he'd kept his promise, and though he was often gone during the day, at work on the Kincaid ranch or tending to his own place, he and Rambo returned in the old battered pickup each evening. Once he'd come back with a pizza, another time with sandwiches from a local deli, each at the request of Morgan. The girl flat-out adored her older half brother, while with Shiloh she'd continued to be petulant and distrustful, never missing a chance to sling some guilt her older sister's way.

"Mom was always worried about you, you know," she told her at breakfast on the first morning, after Shiloh had suffered a fitful night's sleep. Nightmares had peppered Shiloh's slumber, vicious dreams of Larimer Tate and Ruthie's rape and her mother falling off a cliff and into a bottomless chasm as Shiloh desperately reached for her. She'd awoken with a headache.

Morgan's remarks had cut deep, but Shiloh had sworn to herself she wouldn't react, so she kept quiet.

Not so Morgan, who picked at the pancakes Shiloh had made her and added, "It *killed* her that you never called."

"I did call."

"When was the last time?" Morgan demanded, swirling a piece of pancake in a lake of maple syrup on her plate. She'd been perched upon a stool at the small table pushed against a window to the backyard.

How long had it been? Shiloh hadn't remembered. As if realizing she couldn't answer, Morgan had just stared at her.

Shiloh had reached for a nearly empty bottle of ibuprofen that had been left on the windowsill and plopped two in her mouth, swallowing them dry. That had ended the conversation.

There had been other attempts at communication between Shiloh and her half sister in the days that had passed since, but none had turned out any better.

Now, the screen door to the back porch creaked open, and Beau stepped into the kitchen. Shiloh's muscles tensed a little, just as they always did when he was around. It was as if the air between them changed, a sudden electricity building, whenever he came near her.

"Hey," he said, peering down the hall. "Where's Morgan?"

"On her phone. In her room. Wasn't interested in breakfast."

"Maybe I'll take her out for lunch," he said. "Wanna come? We could all go to the funeral together."

"Okay," she said reluctantly, her stomach in knots. "This isn't going to be a walk in the park for Morgan."

"For anyone," he agreed, and his gaze touched hers for a moment, a bit of sadness and empathy in his eyes. For the first time, he seemed to acknowledge, if silently, that she too was hurting.

A lump formed in her throat, but she fought it back. No need to get maudlin now. Today was going to be tough enough as it was.

Morgan had barely touched her burger and ate only a handful of fries, and Shiloh also had no appetite and hadn't been able to finish her salad. Beau, however, mowed through a French dip at the Lazy L Café. Afterward, they drove to the funeral home and sat through the short service in the front row of the stuffy central room. Morgan was pale but dry-eyed, while Shiloh was the one fighting tears. The windows were open, a warm breeze attempting to make up for the fact that the air-conditioning was on the fritz. The preacher, who'd never met Faye, stumbled through the biographical part of the service, which was based on her obituary and a few questions Shiloh had answered. Prayers were said, and a singer had tried her best but had trouble keeping with the pianist as she'd warbled her way through "Amazing Grace."

Later, at the grave site, Morgan dropped a single white rose onto the lowered coffin, and at that point Shiloh stared at the trees across the way, tears running freely. It wasn't so much a personal pain she felt, but empathy for the grief evidenced in her stoic little sister's eyes. Dear God, what was she going to do? No way would she abandon this child, but obviously Morgan didn't want anything to do with her.

Beau grabbed her hand and gave it a quick squeeze for half a second before he turned to Morgan. His tender gesture brought on a fresh spate of tears, which Shiloh desperately fought back. Head bowed, she stood as the preacher mumbled his way through another prayer, and bees buzzed through the cemetery, where dandelions and small daisies poked their heads through the fading grass growing between the headstones. The graveyard was positioned on a small rise and flanked by a copse of trees, the graves in rows marked by tombstones, the view toward the valley where, three miles away, the town of Prairie Creek was sprawled.

Shiloh thought of her mother, of the fact she'd never see her again and that there were so many things she hadn't said. It was too late for recriminations. She would just have to live with the fact that she'd never resolved some issues.

She closed her eyes for a second, and in that moment she felt as if she were being watched, that someone was observing her. She glanced up, but saw no one staring, no one even glancing at her from the corner of their eye.

Why, then, did the hairs on the back of her nape lift? Why did she feel a darker presence?

Then her gaze dropped to the ground, and she understood.

Faye's fresh grave was cut into the dry earth near that of her late husband, Larimer Tate. As best as she could, Shiloh kept her eyes averted from the final resting place of Beau's father, where a single flat marker was etched with his name and the date of his entering and leaving the planet.

Rest in peace, you bastard, she thought; then, before she actually spit on his grave, she returned her attention to the last part of her mother's burial service. Tate was dead. But being near his grave was what was causing her to feel nervous, that she was being watched by some sinister presence, just as she had when he was alive. She slid a glance in Beau's direction and saw that he too avoided a glance at his old man's final resting place.

She'd been wrong about Beau, it seemed. Dead wrong. He was nothing like his father. Since she'd been in town, she'd witnessed firsthand that he was hardworking and seemed to sincerely care about his half sister, *their* half sister.

No, Shiloh couldn't fault him about his relationship with Morgan. It appeared solid. Genuine. Something she couldn't say about hers.

On the way to her SUV, she caught sight of Kat, one of a handful of mourners who had shown up at the burial site.

Not now, she thought as Kat approached, but managed to pin what she hoped was a welcoming smile on her face.

"I'm sorry about your mom," Kat said.

"I guess we both know how it feels. I'm sorry you lost yours too." Shiloh hadn't been around when Marilyn Starr had passed away.

"It was tough, but you move forward," she admitted. A pause, then, "Any chance you can find time to get together?" The seriousness in her eyes said that

the conversation wouldn't be girl talk or just catching up.

"Sure."

"When?"

"Tomorrow? Today's . . . well, you know."

"How about at the Prairie Dog? Five-thirty, after
work?"

"Sure," she said. She didn't ask about Kat's job.
Shiloh had already heard that Katrina Starr had followed in her father's footsteps and now was a cop with
the Prairie Creek Sheriff's Department.

In Kat's case, the apple hadn't fallen far from the
tree.

The next afternoon, Beau arrived at the house earlier than usual. He'd run into town to check on an
order of lumber for a new barn under construction at
the Kincaid ranch and had decided to make a detour
to check on Morgan. Since the funeral, the kid had
seemed even more withdrawn and quiet, as if the rit-
ual of burying her mother had made her situation
more final, as if deep-down she'd been harboring
some hope that the doctors had made a mistake.

Or maybe he was reading too much into the situation.

He pulled up and cut the truck's engine. Things
would have to change. Currently, the three of them—
Shiloh, Morgan, and he—were living in limbo, existing
together in a surreal state, one that couldn't continue.

When Shiloh'd first landed in Prairie Creek, she'd
told him he shouldn't stay here, that he had a home
and should go there. Now that the funeral was over,

her words rang even truer. He'd been camping out over the garage for Morgan, or so he'd told himself, but Shiloh being here had played into things, messed with his head.

He'd stood at his window and watched her sleep, not twenty yards away. As the bullfrogs croaked and crickets chirped he'd witnessed the rise and fall of her breasts and the way her hair, caught in the moonlight, fell over her cheek. He'd felt like a voyeur and had snapped the dusty blinds shut in disgust . . . then had splayed out on his back on the old cot and fantasized about her.

Telling himself that he was losing it, that he'd been too long without a woman, that Shiloh Silva was *not* the right woman to let into his brain or his dreams hadn't helped. Every morning since she'd arrived, he'd woken up with an aching hard-on that wouldn't quit. He knew the source: erotic dreams where the both of them were stripped naked, their skin covered in perspiration, their bodies clinging together. While in slumber, he'd run his tongue over the shell of her ear, heard her moan with desire, and felt her guide his fingers inside her as he nipped at her breasts. Each night, if only in his mind, she'd rocked his world. Only a shower as cold as an arctic storm had been able to cool his blood and ensure that his cock would relax.

Something had to break.

With Rambo trotting behind, he walked through the front door, left open, the screen in place. It squeaked as he opened it, and he called for Morgan as he walked through the house. "Hey! Morgs?" he yelled down the hallway, though he sensed no one was inside. A quick scan of the bedrooms confirmed his suspicions.

The shepherd was already heading to the back door, which, like the front, was only secured by a screen. Rambo didn't wait but nudged the screen door open and took off across the dry patch of lawn and through the nonexistent gate, and loped down the worn dirt path to the pasture nearest the barn. In the enclosure, Shiloh was brushing a sorrel mare, while Morgan, balanced on the top rail of the fence, looked on.

As the dog gave out an excited bark, Morgan looked up, shielded her eyes, and spying Beau, hopped to the ground. His heart did a stupid little flip when he saw the hint of a smile on her freckled face.

"Hey, Morgs," he said as he reached her and she flung herself into his arms. "Learning something?"

"What?"

"From Shiloh?"

The girl glanced over her shoulder. "Nah. I'm just bored."

"What can we do about that?"

"Ayla called and asked me to come over, maybe stay the night."

"And?"

"*She* said 'no.'" Morgan hitched a defiant chin in Shiloh's direction. "*She* said she didn't know Ayla or her parents, and so unless you said it was okay, I couldn't go there, but Ayla could come here."

"Sounds fair enough to me."

Morgan's smile faltered, and he saw hurt in her eyes. He reminded himself that she was still raw inside.

"Hey, I didn't say I'd say 'no,' did I?"

"But you didn't say 'yes' either," she countered. From the corner of his eye, he saw Shiloh approach. She'd released the mare, who was tossing her head and galloping to join the rest of the small herd, her coat glistening a fiery red in the late-afternoon sunlight.

"She's been workin' me," he said, motioning to Morgan with one hand.

For that he received a glare silently calling him a traitor.

"I said she could go if you okayed it," Shiloh said.

"You're not my mother!" Morgan spat.

"Whoa, whoa." Beau held up his hands as in surrender.

"No one said I was," Shiloh retorted.

"And I'm not your dad," Beau put in quickly, "but right now, this is what we've got. The three of us have to figure this whole family thing out."

Morgan's face crumpled into a scowl, and she crossed her arms belligerently over her chest.

"The way I see it, you can go to Ayla's. You're talking about Ayla Dunbar, right?"

Morgan muttered, "The only Ayla I know."

He ignored her jab and said to Shiloh, whose face was set in stone, "The Dunbars are good people. Frank, Ayla's father, is an insurance salesman and does horseshoeing on the side. I've known him for years. His wife, Betty Ann, owns the bakery in town."

Morgan rolled her eyes.

Shiloh nodded. "Then let's set it up. I'll call Ayla's mom and introduce myself."

"How embarrassing!" Morgan cried. "It's like you don't trust me."

"I just don't know the Dunbars," Shiloh said, echoing Beau's words of a week before. "I'll talk to Betty Ann, and if it's on, we'll make it happen." Shiloh paused.

"Just let me shower first." She brushed her hands together and whipped her phone from the back pocket of her jeans. Morgan seemed to want to fight, but she reluctantly checked her own phone and gave Shiloh the number to call Betty Ann. The whole exchange took less than five minutes. "Okay, we're good to go," Shiloh said and hurried up the back steps.

"Can't you take me?" Morgan asked Beau once the screen door banged shut.

"What's the problem?" In his opinion, Shiloh was handling the situation perfectly, and that surprised him.

"I don't know," Morgan mumbled.

"Give 'er a chance, Morgs."

"Easy for you to say." With that she stomped off.

Beau watched her leave, but his mind was still on Shiloh. He'd thought a lot about her over the years, but never had he thought she had any bit of maternal instinct.

Beau Tate didn't like to be wrong.

Worse yet, he didn't like admitting it.

This time it looked like he'd have to.

Chapter 8

Shiloh parked her truck at the end of a long line of similar vehicles outside the Prairie Dog Saloon. Most of the pickups were dusty, with gun racks visible in the back windows and tool boxes spanning their beds. There were only two that were washed: a gray Dodge Ram that looked like it had been used hard, and a bright-red Ford F50 that gleamed beneath the sun, damn near enough to burn her retinas. No tool box on that one, but, oh yeah, the gun rack was there.

The Dog, as the bar was called by the regulars, was a long-necked Budweiser kind of place with a dark interior, booths and tables scattered in the open area, and a bar that stretched across the back wall. Pool tables and neon beer signs vied with televisions turned on to muted sports channels. Country music filled the area. A bartender poured drinks and swabbed down the bar, while a thin woman in tight jeans and a black T-shirt with the logo of THE DOG stamped across the back worked the tables.

Shiloh searched the dim interior but didn't see Kat among the patrons, who sat on stools near the bar or crowded into booths and around tables, deep into conversation over pints and peanuts. A couple of guys were arguing over a baseball play, and she thought she recognized them as two ranch hands who had been around town years before. It took a moment, but she came up with their names. One was Scott Massey, who Beau had said worked with him at the Kincaid ranch. He'd done something with the rodeo too, back in the day. Like Kat's brother, Ethan Starr, who'd been a bronc rider until he'd broken one too many bones. Massey wore a Dodgers baseball cap as he huddled over his beer. The second man was harder to recognize, but she felt she'd seen him somewhere before. He slid a glance her way, and when their eyes met she felt a little shiver run down her spine. Hank Eames was peering at her from beneath the brim of a black Stetson. He had always nailed people with a cold, fish-eye stare, ever since he got injured in a tractor accident. He had worked for the Kincaids, the last she knew, and he was also a friend of Larimer Tate's.

As if he read her thoughts, he smiled coldly at her with a hated recognition.

She turned away first and almost made her way back out the door, but she held her ground, scolding herself for her cowardice. She had nothing to worry about. As far as she knew, Hank wasn't dangerous. But anyone associated with Tate gave her pause. She'd even questioned her own mother's sanity for staying with such a slime.

As Hank turned back to the game, she noticed two

men playing pool, their long-necked bottles resting on a nearby table, billiard balls clicking with each shot.

She'd never been in The Dog; she'd been too young to patronize the bar before she left, but this was the place Larimer Tate had called home more often than not. Her stomach turned at the thought, but she told herself to bury the past. If she could. Living on the same plot of land as his son made it difficult at times.

"Shiloh?" A deep male voice caught her attention.

She jerked involuntarily as she spied one of the men who had been playing pool approaching. "Shiloh Silva?" He was still carrying his cue in one hand, while his opponent sent a withering glance his way, returning his stick to the rack mounted on a plank wall.

He was vaguely familiar, slightly older than she was, but she couldn't place him. His jaw was covered in a three-day growth of dark beard, and his skin was dark, from hours in the sun.

"We went to school together," he said. "A long time ago." He waved to the passing waitress. "Mellie, can you get me another?" He jiggled his empty at the waitress. "And one here, for my friend."

"I'm meeting someone," Shiloh interjected, just so he didn't get the wrong impression.

With a lift of his shoulder, he said, "It doesn't hurt anything to have a beer before he shows up."

"She," Shiloh interjected.

"All the better. We can sit here, and you can watch the door for your friend."

She hesitated.

His smile was dark, his eyes a bit dangerous. Dressed

in a western-cut shirt and faded jeans, he stuck out his hand and introduced himself. "I'm Rafe."

Now it clicked. "Rafe Dillinger."

"That's right."

Rafe was some kind of distant Dillinger cousin, a black sheep of the family. He'd been ahead of her in high school, at least when he attended, but everyone knew Rafe as the bad boy of Prairie Creek. He and Courtney Pearson had been an item for a while: two delinquents in love. She shook his hand carefully.

"You've been big news around here," he said. "Or at least you were a while back. I've seen pictures."

Her skepticism must've shown on her face as he went on, "And I heard about your mom. It's still a small town." He slid into one side of a booth, she opposite him, just as the waitress delivered two frosty glasses and a couple of beers to the table. "Put it on my tab, darlin'," Rafe said, and Mellie cast him a saccharine smile. To Shiloh, he said, "Sorry for your loss." Ignoring his glass, he took a long swallow from his bottle.

She pulled her bottle closer. "Doesn't she get offended when you call her something like 'darlin''?"

"Probably." His lips twisted into a smile that said, "Who the hell cares?" Another swallow. "I can't spend my time worrying about what does or doesn't offend others. All that PC bullshit. Not into it."

"So . . . I hear there's a wedding coming up."

He didn't respond.

"Colton and Sabrina?"

He looked away, and Shiloh realized he might be persona non grata or the fallen son of the family.

"There's a good chance I'm not invited." And this time there was no humor in his eyes.

"Yeah, well, I'm not invited either," she said, wondering why she bothered being nice to Rafe Dillinger, who'd barely acknowledged her back in high school. "I have to admit, I'm surprised to see you here. I heard you skipped town too." She didn't add that she'd heard he'd left to escape charges in the abduction of Courtney Pearson.

"I left, I came back, I left again." He shrugged. "I guess this town's like a bad addiction. Hard to shake it."

At that moment, the guy he'd been playing pool with stopped by the table and slammed a couple of twenties onto the hard surface. "There ya go," he said a little bitterly. "I'll get ya next time."

"If there is one."

The opponent, shorter than Rafe by a couple of inches, was muscular, tightly compact, with a horseshoe mustache and deep-set eyes. Shiloh thought she recognized him too, but she couldn't place this one.

"Oh, there'll be one," he blustered. "And next time, I'll be collecting."

"Wouldn't count on it."

The guy finally looked at Shiloh, and his eyes narrowed at her.

A warning bell went off in Shiloh's brain.

"Shiloh Silva," Rafe introduced. "You remember Jimmy Woodcock?"

The muscles tightened in Shiloh's body. "Oh yeah," she said without enthusiasm. A little older than she, he was the son of the owner of the local paper. Back in school, Jimmy had earned a reputation as a bully. "The mustache threw me off, but I remember you," she said, thinking of a girl who had been crying in the lavatory at a basketball game because Jimmy had smacked her around in the parking lot.

"Wondered when I'd run into you," Jimmy said, his face becoming more animated. He looked like a young Yosemite Sam. "I run the paper now, *Prairie Winds*, you remember?" She made a noise of acknowledgment. "It's been fifteen years since some of the local girls went missing, and I was thinking of doing a story about them. Your take on it and what happened to you would be an interesting angle."

"No, thanks." The only thing Shiloh would gain from the publicity would be trouble.

Ignoring her reticence, he plowed on. "Oh come on, maybe we could generate some interest in what happened to them—you know, get the police interested again? Get some computer-enhanced pictures made of what the girls would look like now."

"But nothing happened to me," she reminded him. So this was going to be how it was, everyone in town wanting to hear her tale? "I just left, and my mother knew that. I was never a missing person."

"It would still be a great perspective." He reached into his pocket and slid a business card across the polished wood. It landed against her sweating empty glass. "Think about it," he suggested, and it sounded almost like an order.

"The lady doesn't want to," Rafe said.

"The lady can handle herself," she said evenly.

Jimmy sent Rafe a satisfied look, as if he'd won that round, before he walked out the door.

"I don't need anyone fighting my battles," Shiloh told Rafe. Part of her wished she'd never sat down with him, though, in truth, she would have drawn more attention to herself if she'd taken a seat alone.

"Okay, okay. Just so you know, Woodcock's a dick. Been with the paper for years, inherited it from his old man. And he can't play pool worth shit." He folded the twenties and dropped them into his breast pocket.

At that moment, Kat walked in, and Shiloh breathed a little easier since she now had an excuse to get away from Rafe. Though she didn't love the way Rafe eyed her petite friend with interest, Shiloh could see why. Still trim, with shoulder-length hair, Kat had an energy about her that drew attention. She'd always been quick, her humor and temper at the ready. Spying Shiloh, she headed to the table, but stopped short when she saw Rafe.

"Must be your date," Rafe said casually. "The lady cop."

"You know each other?" Shiloh asked.

"Of each other," Kat replied.

"We could be closer . . . ," he said with a smile. Kat regarded him with cool tolerance as she slid onto the bench he'd so recently occupied. He tipped his hat to her as he made his way out of the bar.

"Making new friends already," Kat observed dryly.

Shiloh grinned. "Geez, it's good to see you," she said and felt a small lump form in her throat. For all her talk of hating Prairie Creek, all her determination to brush the dust of this little town from her boots, there were good things about it too, things she'd missed. Katrina Starr was definitely on the list, though they'd steered clear of each other after that fateful night.

"How are you, Kat?" she asked as they sat on opposite sides of a booth on the wall opposite the bar.

"All right." She set her purse on the bench beside her. "So you know Rafe Dillinger."

"Not really. But he recognized me . . . acted like I was some kind of celebrity or oddity."

Kat glanced at the doorway where Rafe had disappeared. "He left town about the time you did, and that's when the disappearances stopped."

Shiloh too swung her gaze to the door, but Rafe was gone. "Those disappearances have been on my mind ever since I got back. You think Rafe was involved?"

"Hard to say. My father has an unofficial list of suspects, and Rafe's near the top. Doesn't mean anything to anyone but him . . . and me . . . because the girls are still considered runaways."

"Rafe recognized me."

Kat said, "He could've just recognized you from seeing your picture in the paper. You were big news back then, for a while. Until your mom said she'd been in contact with you."

"I took off a few times, but it was bad when I returned, so that time I left for good." Shiloh didn't want to think about how she'd had to up and leave and let her mother worry for days before calling.

"Your stepfather?" Kat guessed.

"Yeah, well, he was a bastard." She drew a breath and exhaled. "So, you're a cop now, right? A detective. Like your dad." Shiloh finally took her first sip of the beer Rafe had bought for her.

Kat smiled faintly. "Who woulda thunk?"

"Me," Shiloh said. "I'm not surprised."

"Maybe me, neither," she said truthfully. "I'm sorry about your mom."

Shiloh nodded. "Me too." She cleared her throat and looked away. "We, um, weren't that close."

"Still . . ."

"Yeah." Then she added, "And yours too. That was bad."

"It was a long time ago." Kat made a face. "Hard on all of us, at the time, but we got through it. Ethan left for a while. Came back a few years ago. You still into horses as much as he is?"

"He's a bronc rider. But, yeah, I'm still into horses. I work on a ranch in Montana."

"Ah. Ethan *was* a bronc rider," she corrected. "Now he's a horse trainer, and a coach, and a whole lot of other things."

"How is he?" Shiloh asked.

"Fine. We see each other some. He lives his life, and I live mine."

"Doesn't exactly sound like brotherly and sisterly love."

"Well, you know, you work through things. He's happy, I think."

And what about you, Kat?

Mellie floated over, a tray of drinks balanced in one hand. "Ready for another?" she asked, and Shiloh shook her head. "Still working on this one."

The waitress turned her attention to Kat. "How about you?"

Kat eyed the beer, then said, "Club soda."

"You got it." She turned her attention to another group.

Shiloh guessed, "You're on duty."

"Wouldn't look good for me to be knocking back a beer in the middle of the day."

"This is kind of a special occasion," Shiloh said. Kat regarded her thoughtfully and Shiloh asked, "What?"

"I was just thinking . . . about everything."

"Yeah."

Kat had come into The Dog tense and somewhat stern, and now she took a deep breath and seemed to force herself to relax as Mellie brought her her soft drink. Maybe that's what being a cop was all about, Shiloh thought.

They brought each other up to date on their lives. Kat explained that she'd lived in Prairie Creek until her mother's death, then went off to college and came back after graduation. Shiloh, in turn, told how she'd hitchhiked out of town to get away from her stepfather and eventually landed at a farm in the Dakotas, where she'd earned her keep mucking out stalls and caring for the horses. When it was apparent she had a connection to the animals, the elderly couple who'd taken her in and let her sleep in what had been their son's room helped her start training horses. When they had to sell the place, she moved on, working from one ranch to the next, gaining a solid reputation, until she settled in Grizzly Falls, Montana, in the Bitterroot Valley, not far from the Idaho border, which was where she still was.

"And so now I'm back," Shiloh said as she finished her beer.

"Fifteen years . . ." Kat made a face. "Half the town still thinks you and the other girls that went missing met with the same fate."

"Maybe we all did. Maybe you and your father are wrong about them being missing."

"So far, you're the only one who came back. Rachel, Erin, and Courtney didn't. No one knows what happened to them."

"Maybe they'll turn up. Like me." Shiloh heard the lack of conviction in her voice just as Mellie drifted over. "You still good?" she asked them.

They both nodded.

"Okay, then." Mellie turned her attention to a table of four women sipping wine.

Kat said, "You seriously think the missing girls— well, *women* now—will return after fifteen years of silence?"

"It could happen." But Shiloh was playing devil's advocate because Kat's conviction made her feel itchy and uncomfortable and guilty. "It's a long shot, I know."

"It is a long shot," Kat agreed, taking a shallow sip from her soda. "I'm not trying to make it all sound like it was your fault."

"Good, 'cause it's not my fault."

Kat lifted her hands in surrender at Shiloh's irritated tone. "It's high time we came forward—you, me, and Ruth—and told what we know about the guy who attacked Ruthie that night."

"After all this time?"

"Yeah, after all this time."

"Have you talked to Ruthie about it? I mean, if we say something and she denies it . . . well, it won't work. Do you even know where she is?"

"She's here."

"In Prairie Creek?" Shiloh was dumbfounded. "She never left? Like you?"

"Ruthie did leave and ended up in California somewhere. Santa Barbara, I think, or somewhere around there. She went to college, got married, had a kid, a girl, then divorced and ended up back here. I really don't know all the details."

"You haven't talked to her?"

"Not yet. I heard she's a psychologist."

"Wow."

"And she goes by Ruth now."

"As in Dr. Ruth?"

"As in Ruth Baker, LPCC. I understand she goes by Dr. Baker, but I'm sure clients love calling her Dr. Ruth."

Shiloh absorbed that, then said, "Sounds like she's been busy."

"Yeah." Kat circled the bottom of her glass against the table, smearing the condensation. "We have to get Ruth on board, which might be a trick. Or maybe she'll agree to it now. It's not like she's a teenager who'll get punished for sneaking out of the house."

"She was sure scared of her dad at the time."

"She was a kid."

"We all were."

"And we made some dumb choices. Even if we can't fix the mistakes we made, we can try to make them better. So . . . ?" She raised her eyebrows.

Shiloh finished her now room-temperature beer. "If Ruthie—Ruth's—in, I'm in. Only then. Otherwise we'll have to let sleeping dogs lie."

"Wish I could do that, but I can't." Kat grabbed

her purse and dug out some bills, which she dropped on the table. "Whether Ruth agrees or not, I'm working up to put the truth out there. I'm a cop now, and I can't go on with a secret that might be obstructing an investigation. We need to tell what we know, and maybe it'll help break something open."

So she was back. Shiloh Silva had returned to Prairie Creek. She was the wildest of the three—the crazy blonde—and he did like them with a wild streak. It had taken her mother's death to drag her back here, but now, he thought, as he sat on his porch and honed the blade of his Bowie knife, the time was right. He'd waited a long time for the revenge that was due him.

The scar on his forehead, where she'd hurled the rock at him fifteen years earlier, seemed to throb. It wasn't even noticeable any longer, but he reached up and traced the thin line with his thumb. The scar was a reminder that his work wasn't finished. He had another small scar on the back of his hand from the screwdriver one of them had jabbed him with. Payback was coming . . . oh yeah.

Licking his lips, he examined his newly sharpened blade. It winked in the light of the fading sun, reflecting gold on its nearly mirrorlike surface. Perfect for slicing. Perfect for carving. Perfect for getting a little of his own back.

His cock twitched at the thought.

So now all of them were back. All three of the bitches who had tried to kill him.

Good. His jaw tightened. He'd managed to contain his urges, keeping with one girlfriend for a long time now. Longer than the fifteen years since those three had turned on him. Now the thought of taking them all made him go hard.

Revenge and lust in one fell swoop. The time had come, at long last. Anticipation warmed his blood. Recent losses became memories.

Stretching, he picked up the package lying on the porch, scowled at his dried lawn, then circled the house to the flight of stairs that led to the basement. He used the knife to slice open the package. There were several items inside, but it was the four pairs of handcuffs, their cuffs covered in fuzzy pink padding to shield the skin on the wrists, that he drew out. Pink. He smiled grimly. Good quality. No more barbed wire, except for what was out of reach in the shack. A woman couldn't be trusted with it.

At his workbench, he opened a drawer filled with nuts, nails, and screws, all arranged perfectly in little glass jars the size of baby-food containers. Reaching to the back of the drawer, he pushed a button. The spring latch released, and he was able to pull on the inner lining of the drawer, removing it from its resting space in the drawer casing. Carefully he set the lining onto the workbench's surface, just behind the old vise that had been clamped in position for as long as he could remember.

Still within the drawer were several plastic bags, carefully sealed, the pictures within preserved. He flipped through them until he came to the handful of photos he sought, photos he'd processed himself in the small darkroom he used to use.

"Payback time," he said, eyeing the girls by the

lake. In the photos, he had caught them splashing in the water or stretching their arms to dive off the dock. Their young, nubile bodies with high breasts and dark triangles at the joining of their legs brought back memories. His mouth turned dust dry with desire.

Katrina, the detective.

Ruth, a mother and psychologist.

And now, Shiloh, the runaway cowgirl.

All home to roost. At least for a while. He didn't know, hadn't heard how long Shiloh intended to stay.

He'd have to work fast.

He stared at the images.

He couldn't wait.

Chapter 9

Seeing Kat again brought back all the old memories, painful thoughts that Shiloh had tried like hell to tamp down. But as she drove back to her mother's house, she couldn't shake them. It was as if the ghosts of the past, her mother, Larimer Tate, and that damned bastard who'd attacked them swirled over her vehicle as it rolled home over the hot asphalt.

Once parked in her usual spot, she noticed that Beau's truck was missing. Unbidden, a drip of disappointment ran through her blood. "You're an idiot," she told herself as she shielded her eyes and headed inside, where despite the windows being open, the house was hot. Stuffy. Empty.

For the first time since landing in Prairie Creek over a week earlier, she was alone on the property. Inside the little house, she felt suffocated. According to her mother's lawyer, the place had been left to Morgan for use as a home while she was raised by Beau and Shiloh. *A bad arrangement,* she thought, and again felt her mother's spirit hovering nearby, which was flat-out ridiculous.

She opened the refrigerator, poured herself a glass of water, and took a long swallow.

Setting down her glass, she eyed the Formica table where she'd sat for so many meals. She could envision her mother seated in her favorite chair. Over the years, Faye had given her advice from that very seat: "Eat your asparagus; it's good for you." Then, "I wouldn't worry too much about what Mary Jordan thinks, or anyone else, for that matter." Or, "Be careful, Shiloh. I know you don't get along with Larimer, but all this wild acting out is not going to help." Over the years, her mother's face had grown thinner, the lines more visible, the bits of silver showing through her naturally blond hair, while Larimer Tate had become more and more of a presence to the point that Mom had seemed to shrink as he'd loomed larger. She'd withered beneath his shadow.

But was it fair to blame Beau for all his father's faults? Probably no more than it would be to point a finger at Shiloh for Faye's failings or for the genes of Frank Silva, her dead father.

Things had changed so much since she'd first come here. Her whole attitude about the town, her family, and especially Beau Tate, had altered, which was probably a mistake. "You're getting soft, Shiloh," she chided herself, and thought about calling Morgan's phone to see if she was okay, or Beau's to make certain the girl had been dropped off at Ayla's place.

Again.

She wasn't used to this mothering thing, or the big sister thing. She didn't recall ever having an emotional tie to a younger, dependent human being. Now, being another person's guardian and provider felt right, before it felt wrong, before it felt awkward.

Give it time, she thought she heard her mother say and took another swift glance at the table to see if Faye's ghost was there, smoking a cigarette while flipping through the coupon section of the weekly freebie advertising paper.

With all the memories, ghosts of the past, and recriminations crowded in her head, she drained her glass, then slammed it onto the counter, nearly cracking it.

Enough!

She had to clear her head, get rid of the images of the past, and look to the future, whatever that might be.

Walking onto the back porch, she couldn't help a glance at the windows to the attic over the garage. If a light burned within, she wouldn't be able to see it as the glass panes had become opaque with the reflection from the evening sky. The vibrant colors of a Wyoming sunset were the only thing visible.

What did she care if Beau was inside, which he wasn't? He was an irritation. Nothing more. Larimer Tate's son.

But her thinking about him had changed. He wasn't the same kind of man as his father. If anything, he seemed nearly diametrically opposite to the man who had sired him, at least from what she'd observed in the past week or so. He was kind to the animals, had a sense of humor, and was straight and caring with Morgan. Shiloh had assumed that his connection to their mutual half sister might be tenuous at best, or even all for show, but from the moment she'd first spied him with Morgan, Shiloh had been aware of the incredibly strong bond between Beau and his only sibling.

Not faked.

Not temporary.

The real thing.

Shiloh was the outsider.

She was the one who didn't belong, the sibling Morgan didn't trust—and with good reason. Morgan hadn't known her. She was a stranger.

She crossed the porch that had become her bedroom and jogged along the path leading to the barn. The horses were grazing in the closest pasture, so she grabbed a bridle from the tack area and called to Dot, a dappled mare with more than a little fire in her eye. "Come on, girl, let's go," she said.

With the bridle in place, she flung herself onto the gray's back and headed toward the back end of her mother's property. Along the western border, a creek snaked beneath the fence line, and a pool collected in the surrounding pines. Leaning forward, she urged the mare faster, and the horse responded, stretching out, galloping across the dry earth and the sun-bleached grass. Squinting against the brilliance of the western horizon, Shiloh felt the gray's muscles bunch and stretch beneath her. The wind tore at her hair as Dot's hoofs threw up clouds of dust, thundering over the song of crickets greeting the coming night.

Riding had always been an exhilarating experience for Shiloh—her escape—and often she found being around horses easier than dealing with people. She pulled on the reins, and Dot, breathing hard, slowed to a walk to pick her way through the scrub brush and pines where the creek flowed. The sound of water rushing over stones and roots filled the air. It was cooler here, and Shiloh relaxed as she guided Dot to an area where the water eddied and swirled, the stream colliding with another brook and creating a pool deep enough to submerge in when the winter snow melted and the icy spring runoff filled the banks.

She dismounted, kicked off her boots, and hesitated for a moment, while Dot bent her head to the dry grasses. Then she thought what the hell and stripped out of her clothes. One step into the cold stream nearly changed her mind, but then she walked on into the water, which was still cold enough to cause her breath to catch in her lungs. "Geez," she whispered, and Dot nickered softly, as if in agreement.

She waded deeper, sucking in her stomach, then finally taking the plunge and letting her entire body be enveloped in the frigid creek. Beneath the surface, she blew out her breath, watching the air bubbles rise, and couldn't help thinking back to another time, another place, another body of water.

Don't go there, she warned herself, but images of the horror of that night, pictures in her mind of a bloody knife, of poor Ruth being raped, of a monster of a masked man intent on murder, all slipped through her mind in a kaleidoscope of brutality.

She flung herself to the surface and tossed the wet hair from her eyes.

For a second, while water drops clung to her eyelashes, she thought she spied the silhouette of a man in the shadows.

Her heart began to pound, and she glanced at her mare, still plucking at a few blades of grass poking up from the ground. Dot was as calm as ever, her bridle jangling softly as she moved toward another riderless horse, Thor, the largest gelding in their small herd.

What the devil—

"Hey!" a male voice said, and she gasped just as she recognized that it belonged to Beau. He stepped away from a low branch, and she saw him, all six feet of him, on the bank.

"What're you doing here?" she demanded, heart still racing. She eyed her messy pile of discarded clothes.

"Spying on you, I guess."

She hoped the water was moving quickly enough and the evening shadows were long enough that her body was at least distorted. What were the chances of that in this clear mountain water? "Wanna hand me my clothes?" She raised an arm out of the pool.

"Want the truth?" He smiled lazily.

"Come on, come on," she said, wiggling her fingers.

"Maybe you should come get them."

"And maybe you shouldn't be such an ass about it."

He didn't move, and that damned smile stretched a little wider. He was enjoying this.

Narrowing her eyes, trying to figure him out, she wondered at the game he was playing, flirting with her when she was pretty certain he resented her being on her mother's plot and taking up residence in Faye's house. She laid her hand out flat, and eventually he reached for the pile of clothes—bra, panties, T-shirt, and shorts—that she'd dropped on the bank.

"A shame," he said, reaching over the water and handing her the clothes.

"Is it? I don't think so." She snatched her belongings and, before she could think twice, grabbed his empty fingers with her free hand and yanked. Hard. Momentum pulled him forward, and he tumbled into the pool, splashing and gasping in surprise. "Damn!"

"Serves you right," she mumbled under her breath as she tried to climb to the shore while keeping her clothes dry.

No such luck. She was halfway out of the pool when she felt strong fingers wrap around her ankle and give a sharp tug.

"Beau!" Falling forward, she lost her footing. Her four pieces of apparel flew upward to flutter down into the water just as she too slid under the surface again. What a colossal mistake!

Why had she baited him? Sputtering to the surface, she found him next to her, his wet face inches from her own.

"To think I was worried about you," he said.

"Worried? Why?"

"You weren't at the house, but your Explorer was there."

"And that concerned you?"

"Yeah, a little. 'Til I saw Dot wasn't in the herd and figured you might've gone for a ride. I rounded up Thor and thought I'd check it out. See that you were okay."

"I'm perfectly fine."

"I can see that."

Inching her chin up a fraction, she said, "Trust me, I can take care of myself."

Again the amused grin, but he was so much closer now, his eyes as clear as the water, his gaze finding hers and causing her heart to beat faster once more.

"I can," she insisted, though the fact that he'd just toppled her into the pool argued the point.

"Let's see." There was a bit of mischief in his expression, a touch of the rebel boy she'd imagined he once was. She wondered fleetingly if, had they met as teenagers, sparks would have flared, if a wild, almost taboo, romance would have ensued? He was, after all, not just Larimer Tate's son, but her stepbrother as well. Not that it really mattered. Except in her mind.

"What are you thinking?" Geez, did she sound breathless? What was wrong with her?

His gaze took in every dripping inch of her face.

Her blood began to pound in her ears.

Get out of the water, Shiloh. Whatever you're contemplating, forget it. Any involvement with Beau Tate is a mistake of cataclysmic proportions.

"How about this?" he asked, and before she could back up, he licked a drop of water from her chin. When she gasped, he kissed her on the mouth. Hard. Warm wet lips met hers, and strong arms surrounded her, wrapping around her naked torso and crushing her to him. Though she wasn't able to stand, he was, and he held her floating above the bottom of the pool.

Her eyes closed, and her mind spun. Despite the cold water, a flush spread up her body, radiating from her core outward, causing her skin to tingle and her brain to fill with the same incredible, erotic visions of her dreams.

This is dangerous, Shiloh. Get out now. While you still can.

Calloused fingers splayed over her back, and she ignored the warnings sliding through her mind, chased them away as she let herself go . . . let herself get caught up in the wonder of him.

Why not throw caution to the wind?

What would it hurt?

Everything. Every damned thing. Think, Shiloh, think!

But she didn't, and when she felt him start to slide out of his jeans and shirt, she helped him shed the clingy wet clothes until she felt skin on skin, body on body, desire on desire.

He never stopped kissing her. Not when he removed his shirt or kicked off his Levis and boots. Not even when she lifted her face for air. Instead he trailed his lips down her neck to her collarbone, to kiss her chilled skin, causing it to heat, creating a fire within at odds with the icy water.

"I don't . . ."

"Sure, you do," he said, and before she could utter another protest, he lifted her upward and settled her onto him, the apex of her legs opening as he thrust hard, upward, and pulled her down against him.

She gasped, her organs clenching around him, her whole body jerking. Shuddering, she closed her eyes and gave in to the rhythmic and sensual rubbing, the fire he stoked brighter and brighter within. Her breathing became rapid and ragged, echoed by his own hoarse breaths. Her fingernails dug into the slick, hard muscles of his shoulders, while the water swirled around them.

Raw emotion captured her soul, while her skin was on fire, and every nerve ending was alive with his touch.

God help me, she thought as control fell away.

All doubts fled as the very center of her universe seemed to be the physical connection between them, the upward thrust, the downward pulls, the pure ecstasy of becoming one.

Faster and faster.

Her soul soared until it seemed to splinter somewhere high above the rugged mountains. She let go. A cry of satiation sprang from her lungs and joined with his own orgasmic roar.

He pulled her tight, her breathing rapid against his wet, heaving shoulder. The arms surrounding her seemed a safe haven, a place she could close her eyes and let the worries of the world pass her by.

It was a false security, she knew that, but for a few minutes, as the stars appeared in the darkening heavens, she let herself believe in the gossamer fantasy with Beau Tate. . . .

Astride her bay gelding, Addie Donovan glanced at the lowering sun. The sky over the western hills was flaming a bright orange to brilliant pink, the forested peaks becoming silhouettes, and yet it was still warm, heat rising from the ground near this spring that cut through the pines.

Sweat beaded on her brow, and she felt it trickle

between her breasts and cause her T-shirt to cling to her back.

The creek was too small, barely a trickle, so she couldn't take a quick swim, but she climbed off Falconer and kicked off her cowboy boots to wiggle her toes in the clear water. Bridle rattling, Falconer snorted, shaking his head, his forelock falling over his blaze as he drank from the stream.

Was it her imagination, or did she hear voices over the sound of the water? Distant voices from somewhere upstream? She glanced longingly to the Crofts' property, the adjoining acres that butted up to her parents' place, and hoped she'd spy Dean, but of course that was impossible. He was away tonight, spending time at his cousin's place.

A jab of loneliness cut through her.

Addie knew she should get back. If she didn't return by nightfall, her parents would freak. But then they always freaked. Last year, when she'd just turned seventeen, her mother had caught her adding water to the vodka bottle to replace what she'd taken to a slumber party, and then they'd found cigarettes in her purse. Luckily, so far, they hadn't discovered the weed she kept in a tiny plastic bag hidden in the barn. She was saving the marijuana, tucked in a bale of old straw that she used as a bench when she was caring for the horses, for this weekend when Elle, her best friend, would be staying the night. If they could sneak out without Mom catching them. Fortunately, Addie's father snored so loudly Mom wouldn't be able to hear them slip from the room.

She hoped. She crossed her fingers.

Her parents were just so out of it.

Didn't they know she was almost a woman?

It was getting pretty obvious with the changes in her figure. She'd gone from a flat-chested tomboy to a teenager wearing a 36D bra. She already knew her shape was a blessing and a curse. A lot of the girls were jealous, and she got more than her share of attention from the boys, but sometimes she felt that her boobs had betrayed her. She'd wanted a killer figure, but . . . she really didn't want to stand out this much.

Fortunately, Dean saw beyond her boobs. Oh, he liked them. A lot. But Dean Croft was better than the other boys. More mature. He loved her. For her. She was sure of it, and she dreamed about him day and night. They would be married. For sure. But first college, and getting engaged, and then a wedding that would rival the Dillingers' nuptials that all the town was talking about.

It would be spectacular. Addie knew. She'd been clipping pictures out of bridal magazines for months and had paid attention to the dresses, especially the dresses. She couldn't wait to walk down the aisle of the Pioneer Church and hear all the guests gasp at how beautiful she'd be. And Dean, he would cry when he first saw her. Either that or she'd turn around and come back in again on her father's arm, just to insure Dean gave her the proper reaction.

Oh, how she loved him. More than any girl or woman had loved a man. She was sure of it. And Dean, he'd told her he loved her too, especially when he was feeling her up and caressing her breasts. Yeah, he liked them, and she never felt more in love than when he'd take one into his mouth and suckle it. Even now she thrilled at the thought of it and couldn't wait until they could marry.

In four years.

Four long years.

The shadows were growing longer, and all of a sudden, she felt as if someone was watching her.

Had Mom followed her out here? Or Dad? Maybe even her little nerdy brother, Gil? It would be just like him and his friends, all of thirteen and major geeks who ogled her when they thought she wasn't aware, then pretended they didn't see her boobs. Pains in the butt, all of them.

Or maybe Dean was looking for her?

Her heart soared. When he found her, they would kiss and touch, and she'd let him explore all the feminine places in her body that she'd decided were just for him and him alone. Forever. Infinity. Eternity.

And yet, there was something not right about this. Something was off.

Casting a glance over her shoulder, she saw no one, but the goose pimples running along the back of her arms warned her that she wasn't alone.

From an upper branch of one of the pines, a crow let out a screech, and she actually jumped. Then again, she'd been a little nervous ever since she'd spied a few vultures up on the ridge and figured a wild animal was dying or dead.

Time to get going.

She wasn't even supposed to be on this stretch of government land that ran along the back of her family's property, but she knew of a place where the fence was down, and she liked riding through the trees, away from the feeling of being penned in. Away from Mom and Dad, and especially Gil.

She wished she was going away to a four-year university rather than living at home and commuting to the nearest community college, but there just wasn't enough money to send her, and she didn't want to take out loans. Most of all, she didn't want to be away from Dean, and he was attending the same two-year school, so Addie was okay with putting up with Mom and Dad . . . but not Gil. He just bugged her so much.

But in four years when she was through school and she and Dean were married—

Snap!

The crack of a breaking twig startled her, and she jumped.

With a snort, Falconer lifted her head and turned, her large eyes focused on a thicket of saplings.

Her gaze glued to the shadows, Addie grabbed her boots.

The looming shape of a man appeared from the gathering shadows.

Oh, shit! Her heart nearly stopped.

Not caring that her feet were muddy, she yanked on one boot and considered leaving the other.

"Hey. Didn't mean to scare you," the guy said, and she stared up at him, a handsome guy, but old. Maybe close to forty. He had the whole cowboy thing going, like everyone else in town, in jeans and a cowboy shirt, snakeskin boots, and a scraggly growth of stubble over a tanned jaw. He held his hands palms out as if he really didn't mean to startle her.

"Well, you did."

"Just out here looking for a couple of strays."

"Strays?"

"Calves." His gaze moved to the underbrush. "You haven't seen 'em, have you?"

"No." She tugged on her second boot and told herself the guy was okay. "But . . . I did see vultures up over the ridge."

"Damn."

Still nervous, she glanced behind him. No horse. No ATV, which of course she would have heard approach. All-terrain vehicles were usually pretty loud. "How'd you get here?"

"Horseback, like you." He was moving closer to her and making her more nervous.

She wished she'd left five minutes earlier.

He hitched a thumb to the ridge. "I left Diablo to check the stream myself." He frowned. "No calves here? You're sure."

"Yeah. I mean, no. No calves," she said, unable to contain her case of nerves. Did she know him? He was kinda familiar. A dad of someone, or uncle maybe? Or maybe not. "Uh. I've been here a few minutes . . . maybe fifteen. I haven't seen any cows."

He was still approaching, his gaze wandering over the surrounding terrain as if he were searching the umbra for the missing livestock, but still, it was weird. Unsettling.

She stood quickly.

"Look, I gotta go." Why was she explaining anything to him? And why did she feel she knew him? That she'd seen him before?

"Well, if you see a couple of Herefords on your way out, give a whistle, would you?"

"Yeah, sure." She had the reins in her hands and one boot in a stirrup. She started to hoist herself into the saddle.

He pounced. Leapt on her like on prey, strong arms binding her, her back pressed hard against him.

She screamed.

Falconer spooked, rearing and neighing.

The man's muscles clenched around her.

No! No! No!

With a snort, her horse jumped forward, yanking her with him.

The attacker held fast, digging in, but the heel of her boot caught in the stirrup, dragging her forward.

Pain ripped up her leg.

Squealing, she thought she was going to be ripped in two as her hip was yanked from its socket.

The man holding her sat back on his heels, and the horse reared again.

Terrified, Addie clawed wildly, trying to free herself, agony tearing through her muscles and tendons. She nearly passed out.

"Son of a bitch," the man swore.

Suddenly her foot slid from her boot, and the horse bolted. Leaving her. No, no, no! Her leg was on fire, but she fought and clawed. "Let me go, you bastard! Let me—aaarrrggh!"

A new searing pain shot through her.

Her entire body jolted.

Her muscles spasmed uncontrollably.

Oh. God.

She couldn't focus, her eyes seeming to jiggle in their sockets.

What had happened, she wondered wildly above the pain, but she caught a flash of something in his hand. A weapon. Like a stun gun or a compact cattle prod or something horrible.

She tried to fight and failed, her body jerking spasmodically of its own accord.

How had this happened?

Why?

All of her parents' warnings rattled through her brain in quick bursts that didn't connect. She felt herself being hauled, twitching, onto his back. Every effort she made was useless.

Though she didn't know she was crying, tears filled her eyes.

The only thing she knew for certain was that she was doomed.

Chapter 10

Shiloh rolled over, opened a bleary eye, and realized she'd fallen asleep in the attic space over the garage. In a sleeping bag. Naked. With Beau Tate.

Oh. God.

She hadn't been drunk. She'd just been out of her mind. After the wild lovemaking in the creek, she and he had thrown on their clothes, hers relatively dry, his wet, and ridden back to the house where, after opening a bottle of wine, they had ended up here and made love until after midnight.

Now, as morning sunlight streamed through the open windows, she noticed an empty wine bottle and stained glasses that sat on a scarred side table that had once been her grandmother's. Her clothes were strewn over the old braided rug that had been rolled up on the attic floor when she was just a child. The oversized sleeping bag had been centered in the room, but over the course of the night of lovemaking, it had shifted and now was wedged against a bookcase of forgotten paperbacks.

Lying on the floor, they were surrounded by left-over furniture, books, records, and boxes filled with the detritus that had been part of Faye Tate's life.

Shiloh closed her eyes for a second and let out her breath.

What had she been thinking?

That was the trouble, she hadn't been.

She looked down at Beau, still sleeping, eyes closed, breathing slowly and evenly. His hair was rumpled, his jaw even darker with beard shadow, his naked chest exposed as a corner of the sleeping bag had flipped back.

Images of the night before played inside her mind. His lips on her neck. His hands sliding down her spine to cup her buttocks, his tongue running along her skin, the taste of wine in her throat, and the earthy smell of him in her nostrils. He'd brought her to a climax more than once, and just thinking of him propped on his elbows, thrusting inside her made her tingle in places she'd nearly forgotten.

He'd seen the scar on her shoulder, the remnant of the wound from Ruthie's rapist's blade all those years ago.

"What's this?" he'd asked, touching the scar.

"Nothing." No reason to confide in him. "Happened long ago."

His lips had flattened. "Who did this to you?"

"It was an accident."

"You're sure?" he'd asked.

"I should remember."

"But Larimer. He didn't . . ."

"Oh, hell no." She'd wrapped her arms around him and kissed him to stop the interrogation. He hadn't been able to resist as she rubbed against him, and she still remembered how her nipples had tightened and the juncture between her legs had pulsed with desire as he'd begun stroking her.

"Oh God," she whispered, wondering what would happen now.

He opened an eye and gazed at her. "Mornin', sunshine," he said, and part of her melted. There was a tenderness in his voice she didn't expect, a familiarity that touched her.

She started scooting from the bag, working her way out. "This . . . this was a mistake."

"Umm. Can't argue with you there."

"We have to forget it happened."

He cocked an amused eyebrow.

"Okay, that is not going to happen. We can't forget. But . . . but this . . . whatever this is, is never going to work. I mean, I'm only here because of Morgan and you too . . . Oh God." She flung herself back onto the floor. "Morgan." If their half sister ever got wind that they were . . . what? That they had . . .

"What about her?"

"She can't find out that you and I were . . . together."

"She's not going to find out anything," he said and chuckled.

"I'm serious, Beau."

"Me too." Quick as lightning, he grabbed her again. One arm circled her naked waist, his other hand tangled in her already mussed hair. Holding his face a hair's breadth from her own, he stared at her, and his eyes darkened with desire. He whispered, "This is our little secret."

Before she could object, he kissed her, and once again she was lost. *Just one more time*, she thought as her blood heated and her body responded. *Just one more time.* But even as she made the promise to herself, she knew, deep in her heart, that this was just the beginning of what could only become a disaster.

Kat was running late and wasn't surprised to find her father had already set his desk up as a table on which half a dozen cupcakes were displayed.

"Beginning to think you were gonna stand me up," he said with a smile.

"Nope. But I gotta make this quick. You know the Crutchens burglary, where beer and cigarettes were taken, some petty cash?"

"Teenagers again?" he asked, reaching for a German chocolate cupcake.

"Yeah, but the bad news is, this time the Byrds' grandson, Noel, could be involved."

Her father grunted. "Uh oh."

The Byrds didn't much like the Prairie Creek Sheriff's Department as a whole, and Patrick Starr in particular. Paul and Ann Byrd felt there'd never been enough done to find their daughter, Rachel, and they specifically blamed Patrick, which was entirely unfair, but there it was.

Kat had mainly told her father about the theft as a means to provide herself a quick exit. Her father always liked to visit a little longer than Kat did. However, the burglary and theft at Hal Crutchens's farm were the crimes she was currently working on. She'd already interviewed several teens who had been involved, and they, and their parents, wanted this latest round with Mr. Crutchens to just go away. They'd offered the older man remuneration, but Crutchens, whose garage had been broken into and whose property was stolen, had demanded that they be prosecuted to the full extent of the law. Crutchens had a history of making complaints about all his neighbors and the community at large, and naturally wasn't well-liked. His attitude had made him a target for teen pranks and vandalism over the years, and this latest one was no exception.

"You see Shiloh?" her father mumbled around a last bite of chocolate cupcake.

Kat had just bitten into a red velvet one. "Mmm."

"How is she? The same?"

She swallowed. "Yeah, maybe a little toned down."

"Not a wild child any longer?" He threw the wrapper from the German chocolate cupcake in the trash can beside his desk and reached for a lemon chiffon one, peeling back the paper. "Good. I was afraid a kid like that might go off the rails."

Kat bit back an automatic warning about his diet. *You told him to get the cupcakes. You said it'd be okay for today.* "She seems solid." She took another bite of her own cupcake, and conversation stopped for a while as they made their way through their "breakfasts."

Before her father could ask more about her conversation with Shiloh, she threw a glance at the clock and said, "Gotta run."

"So soon? We've barely had a chance to catch up."

"Next time," Kat promised.

"Maybe you should take a couple of these for the

road." He motioned to the two lone cupcakes, but he looked longingly at them.

"They're all yours. Just don't eat 'em all at once."

"I'm perfectly healthy."

"Uh huh."

Hurrying outside, she placed her sunglasses over her nose and climbed into her Jeep.

She parked in the lot at the back of the building. On her way inside, she waved at a couple of officers, dropped her purse into her locker, and grabbed a cup of coffee from the carafe in the lunchroom.

She nodded to Ricki Dillinger, then punched in Ruth's number on her cell as she threaded her way to her desk. The door to the sheriff's office was ajar, and as she passed, she caught a glimpse of Sheriff Sam Featherstone, ear pressed to his phone, his eyes steady on a computer monitor on the corner of his desk.

Ruth's voice mail answered.

With an inward sigh, Kat left her name and number, clicking on her cell phone as she pulled out her desk chair. Ruth hadn't replied to her text from the night before, sent after the meeting with Shiloh. Was Ruth actively avoiding her? Her old friend hadn't made any attempt to connect with her since she'd returned, but then Kat hadn't exactly been the Welcome Wagon, either. The fact was, all three of them were reminders to each other of that terrible night, and Ruth was the one who'd been attacked and hurt the most.

And now she was a single woman with a private practice and bound to be extremely busy.

Since seeing Shiloh last evening, Kat wanted action. She was over wrestling with her conscience. Maybe she should have confided in her father about the rape. Maybe waiting for Ruth meant waiting forever. Maybe she should run back over to his office and just lay it all out.

Kat picked up her cell phone in a rush of momentum, then set it back down again. No. She needed to talk to Ruth. She couldn't blindside her. There was a way to bring this all forward, and it wasn't helter-skelter.

Her desk phone rang. Naomi, from the front office. "Paul Byrd called again and asked for you," she reported.

Kat grimaced. She knew for a fact that Byrd hadn't called because he wanted her help with his grandson's case. Nope, her last name was Starr, like her father's, and though Paul Byrd was upset about Noel's problems with Crutchens, it was his anger toward Patrick Starr that drove him to ask for Kat. Since Byrd believed the Prairie Creek Sheriff's Department had failed on all accounts to find Rachel, who was better fit to listen to his vituperative complaints than retired-cop Patrick Starr's cop daughter? "Okay, I'll call him back," she said, trying hard to keep the dread from her voice.

Beau finished fixing a broken pipe that led to the watering trough near the barn. With a final turn of the wrench, he straightened, then twisted on the handle and watched water pour into the trough without leaking all over the side of the barn. Satisfied, he filled the trough, walked into the barn, and slipped the wrench back into its spot on the workbench.

He ran his hand over the stained wooden top and wondered how many hours his old man had spent here. Probably not that many. And it didn't matter now. He headed out of the barn again and, stepping into the bright sunlight, spied Shiloh with Morgan and one of the mares.

Morgan was astride the roan, Shiloh patting the horse's neck. The sun was high in the afternoon sky, a slight breeze moving the branches.

Beau was surprised that the sisters seemed to be getting along, though he'd sensed a bit of a shift in Morgan's attitude when he'd picked her up from Ayla's and brought her back here.

"You like her, don't you?" Morgan had accused as he'd nosed his truck up the lane and the tires had spun a little on the gravel as Faye's house had come into view.

"Like who?"

"Shiloh." Morgan gave him the look that said she wasn't going to let him wriggle out of this conversation. Rambo sat on her lap, his head out the window and his tongue lolling out, and Morgan had been absently petting him. But her eyes were laser-focused on Beau's face.

"She's all right." He'd tried to shove off any further conversation on the subject. Ever since waking up this morning, he'd replayed the events over and over in his mind. How they'd made love in the stream and back in the attic and how, this morning, after she'd left, all he'd wanted to do was call her back.

"Just all right?"

"Okay, yeah, I like her." He'd shrugged, eased off the gas as they hit the pothole he had yet to fill in the drive. "And you should too. She's your sister."

"I think it's weird if you like her."

"And I think it's weird if you don't."

He'd pulled up to the house, and she and Rambo had tumbled out, leaving the dust the old truck's tires had churned up to settle and Morgan's pointed questions to hover in his brain.

Beau prided himself on knowing his own mind. He usually figured out what he wanted, went after it, and either ended up with the prize or didn't beat himself up for losing out. He just moved on.

But he'd never met Shiloh Silva before, and now it felt like there'd been a tectonic shift; she'd somehow changed everything, put a damned wrench in his whole outlook on life.

He'd woken up after a night of lovemaking and found himself considering new options in life, options that included not only Morgan, but now Shiloh as well.

It was crazy, really.

Yeah, he'd been attracted to her from the get-go.

Yeah, he'd known she was trouble.

And yeah, he'd told himself not to get involved.

That hadn't happened, and now he was stuck with the knowledge that rather than want her out of his life, as he'd once thought, he couldn't imagine life without her.

* * *

Kat had been at the station for nearly two hours and had managed to stay calm during Paul Byrd's latest tirade—one hell of a phone call, to say the least—when she heard footsteps approaching her desk. As she turned away from her computer screen, a tall woman with spiky red hair appeared. In slacks, a print shirt, and a vest despite the heat of summer, she forced a smile over lips that trembled and showed a hint of lipstick that had worn off. She was pale beneath a tan, her eyes haunted. She looked as if she hadn't slept in days. "Are you Detective Starr?" she asked before her gaze landed on the name plate on Kat's desk. "Oh. I see. The woman at the front, Naomi, sent me this way."

"Yes, I'm Katrina Starr." Kat stood. "How can I help you?"

The woman lifted one hand in a helpless gesture. "I know it's only been a little while. Well, I mean it seems like forever since last night, and I don't know if there's some rule about waiting twenty-four hours, but I'm just so worried." She ran anxious fingers in her hair, making the spikes stand even straighter.

"What happened?"

"My daughter . . . she didn't come home last night, and oh, it's not like you think!" she interjected. "I mean she wasn't on a date or anything. She was just out riding."

"Why don't you have a seat," Kat invited, motioning to one of the two side chairs on the other side of her desk. "And start from the beginning. Maybe you'd like some water or coffee or—"

"I just want my daughter back!" the woman declared, then dropped into the offered chair and held her forehead in her fingers. "Sorry. It's just that this is so unlike Addie. She's very responsible and never gives Jeremy and me any trouble, not like Gil, our son."

"Let's start with your name," Kat said as the woman seemed well on her way to falling completely apart.

She took in a long breath. "I'm Deb, Debra Donovan, and my husband is Jeremy. We own the feed store, you know, the Seed and Feed, just outside of town." She went on to tell Kat that her daughter, Addison, had gone riding alone last evening, but before sunset. She didn't show up, but her horse did. One of Addie's boots was there, caught in a stirrup. The family, thinking an accident had befallen Addie, had searched the property, to no avail. They'd talked to the closest neighbors, then checked with Addie's friends and boyfriend, Dean Croft, none of whom had spoken to her.

"You're sure about her boyfriend?" In Kat's experience, teenage boyfriends and girlfriends tended to protect each other and always tried to sneak away from their parents' prying eyes.

"Dean's a good kid. The Crofts, a fine family." She licked her dry lips and tried to dispel the doubt in her eyes. She seemed to be trying to convince herself. "He's out of town. I checked with his parents and talked to him. I thought . . . well, maybe she staged the whole horse returning and had actually taken off with him, but he'd left too early, and now he's so upset that he's coming back. I really don't think Dean's involved . . . oh dear, I said 'involved' as if something nefarious and horrible has happened."

She appeared about to collapse and struggled to find some kind of inner strength. "I know there can't be any connection. I mean, it's been so long, but I just can't keep thinking about those families who lost their daughters years ago. I mean, Addie was only three at the time, and Gil wasn't even born yet." She swallowed hard. "The Byrds, Ann and Paul? They're members of our church. Ann was Addie's Sunday school teacher, and even though they have the other girls, Rinda and Ramona, who are grown with children of their own now, and the younger one, Rhianna, it's not like Rachel can ever be replaced, y'know? You never stop loving a child." Deb was worrying her hands now. "Even with the grandchildren, there's the void, the not knowing."

Paul Byrd again. The man's stinging words were still in her ears. If he'd only known how much Patrick had worried about those missing girls, how much he still did.

". . . what happened all those years ago can't have anything to do with Addie, but I keep thinking about it," Deb was finishing.

"What about Addie's cell phone?" Kat asked.

"She left it in a charger at the house. I brought it with me. Along with her iPad. Other than that she uses our desktop. But there's nothing there, and the fact that she didn't take her phone with her . . . it makes me think she thought she would be coming right back. She's never without it." She dug through her bag and dropped the phone and tablet onto Kat's desk. Sighing, Deb added, "The code's 4567. She just plugged it in and never changed it. She trusts us." Deb's eyes filled with tears, and she brushed them away, almost angrily. "She didn't plan to be gone long or she would have taken the phone with her. Though reception is spotty out there near the mountains. You know how that is. But Addy's never far from her phone; it's almost attached to her. But last night . . . last night . . ." Her voice cracked, and she took a moment to gather herself. "We . . . Jeremy and I, we even went to the hospital in town. We . . . we've called everywhere, searched high and low." She bit her lip and brought her gaze up to meet Kat's squarely. "We need the police to help us find our daughter."

Chapter 11

"Soooo, what's going on?" Morgan asked as she walked out of the house and found Shiloh and Beau in deep discussion. It was afternoon, the sky blindingly blue, the smell of freshly cut hay from the neighboring property heavy in the air. And Shiloh had been telling Beau that it was crazy, just plain nuts, to think they could ever repeat their lovemaking of the night before.

"What do you mean?" asked Shiloh.

"I meant, what's going on between you two." She looked at Beau, who was leaning against the railing. "You sound like you're fighting."

"Discussing," he clarified.

"Discussing what?" The girl swept her gaze to Shiloh. "Like if you're staying or leaving?"

"I'm not leaving," Shiloh said, and she meant it. She planned on calling Carlos in the morning, then the ranch owner, to tell them she was pulling up stakes. Permanently. Well, at least for the next decade. She had already decided that she was going to stick like glue to Morgan. Shiloh might not be the most exemplary mother figure, but she'd give it her best shot, and, it seemed, Beau had already stepped into the father role.

Crossing her arms over her chest, Morgan couldn't hide the defiance in her voice. Shiloh considered herself at Morgan's age and then during the following years, how her rebellion had grown until she'd finally left town. Yeah, the next few years, dealing with a teenager who had already stated she didn't like her older sister, were not going to be a damned picnic, but too bad. Shiloh wasn't known for backing down from a challenge.

Bring it on.

"I'm sure."

Morgan rolled her eyes, and Beau stepped in. "Look, Morgs, we've got to stick together."

"So now you're on *her* side?" Morgan did her best to appear crestfallen and disappointed.

"I'm on *our* side."

"Like we're all together?" the girl asked, staring at her half brother as if he'd changed his name to Benedict Arnold. "Oh come on."

He reached out to rumple her hair, but she jerked her head away.

"Don't!"

He pulled back. "I'm just asking you to do the same."

"You're not my father!"

"Nor is Shiloh your mom, but hey, we've got to find a way to make this work."

"And how are 'we' going to do that?" she asked, making air quotes.

"By taking one day at a time and eventually maybe adding onto the house, so I don't have to camp out over the garage."

"You have a place."

"Yeah, I know, but I think I'll move here. To be closer." He threw a look Shiloh's way, a glance that Morgan didn't miss.

"What is it with you and *her*?"

His smile stretched wide. "We found out we have a lot in common," he said and pulled Shiloh closer. She let him tug her to his side but wasn't comfortable with it.

Morgan's mouth dropped open.

"You know Shiloh and I are your guardians. Both of us. Together. So we've decided to work together rather than separately."

"You're getting married?" she practically shrieked.

"What? No!" Shiloh took a step away from Beau. This was getting way out of hand. "No," she repeated. Marriage? God, they weren't even a couple. Or were they? "What he means is that instead of fighting about how to help raise you, we're going to be on the same page. We will take care of you. We will put you first."

"And we won't let you get away with anything," Beau said, his eyes glinting. "Anything you can think of doing, well, we've already done it, so don't think you can buffalo us or work one of us against the other."

Morgan glared at him. "This is weird. All I asked was if something was going on. Geez!" She stalked back into the house and let the screen door slam behind her.

"That went well," Shiloh said.

"She just needs to know where we stand."

Shiloh almost laughed. "*I* don't even know where we stand."

Beau's eyebrows raised a little. "That makes three of us."

A few clouds had gathered in the afternoon sky as Kat drove out of town. Bugs were splattered across her windshield, and the heat in her vehicle was intense. She rolled down the window, letting in a stream of summer air and trying to set aside the sense of unease that had been with her ever since Debra Donovan strode into her office and fell apart in the visitor's chair.

After a last, and surprisingly fruitful, meeting with Hal Crutchens—the families of the teens had upped the remuneration, and Crutchens had finally taken the offer and dropped all charges, a fact Kat herself had reported to Paul Byrd, who'd merely grunted a response—Kat had spent most of the day making inquiries about Addie Donovan. What she had wanted to dismiss as an overly protective mother's concerns now struck her as serious. Something had happened to the girl. The horse returning without Addie hinted that there had been an accident, but when Addie couldn't be found on the fenced property and the surrounding acres, Kat had called in the troops, and the search had widened. An Amber alert had been posted, and the sheriff was currently calling in local law-enforcement agencies to assist in an organized search that would include manpower and helicopters with infrared scanners.

She rounded a corner on the country road and

found herself behind an old John Deere tractor chugging along at about twelve miles an hour. At the straight stretch, she passed the farmer, who sat huddled at the wheel, the bill of a faded trucker's cap shading his face.

She had checked on everything the girl's mother had said, and Deb was right. None of Addie's friends knew what had happened to her. None copped to her having secret plans, and the idea of the horse being sent back to the barn as a camouflage for some other plan was tossed out.

Dean Croft had returned and seemed genuinely upset.

Stunned, he'd answered Kat's questions without any apparent guile.

Yes, he'd been with friends.

Yes, he'd had a few beers the night before.

No, he hadn't seen or heard from Addie since leaving.

And yes, oh God, yes, Dean would do whatever he could to help find her!

Kat had believed him. The innocence and concern on his eighteen-year-old face had been convincing.

From all accounts, Addie was obsessed with her boyfriend, and when they'd looked at her cell phone and computer, that information was confirmed by the sheer number of texts and social media posts/tweets/pictures and so on. Kat couldn't help but wonder if the girl had decided to ride toward his house since the Croft property wasn't far from the Donovan place. The only properties between the two family ranches were an arm of government land and the place that had been owned by Faye Tate, where Shiloh was now staying with her kid sister.

Kat headed toward the Tate place, figuring to warn Shiloh about the missing teen and ask if Morgan had any association with the older girl. It would be a huge help to have an expert rider like Shiloh to search for signs of Addie in the parkland behind their ranch, which was mostly inaccessible by road. Passing the Tate mailbox, with its missing letter, Kat wished she had something to report about Ruth, but Ruth hadn't returned any of her calls or texts. Ruth was avoiding her, plain and simple, and Kat got it that she didn't want to dredge up those terrible memories. But it was time, past time, for something to be done, and since in Wyoming there was no statute of limitation on sexual assault, they needed to get the facts of the rape out there.

Kat wheeled into the long drive of the Tate property, twin ruts of sparse gravel interspersed with potholes and dry weeds. The house, located on a small rise, wasn't in great shape, though it seemed there had been some work done recently, as evidenced by the fresh rails on the porch and visible patches of new shingles on the roof.

She parked and made her way up the path to knock on an already open door, only a screen blocking her entrance. "Shiloh?" she called, and a girl of about twelve, carrying a cell phone, appeared.

"Who're you?" she said through the screen.

"I'm Katrina Starr. I work for the Sheriff's Department, and I'm a friend of Shiloh's," Kat said showing her badge. "You must be Morgan."

The girl stared through the mesh at Kat's ID. "Are you here to arrest her?"

"No, just talk to her."

"Oh." She almost looked disappointed. "She's in the barn, around back." She lifted the hook latch on the screen and motioned Kat toward a small living room and through a dining area to the kitchen, each room following after the other, shotgun style, or maybe like an older-model mobile home. At the rear of the house, Morgan pointed out another open door. "Out there," she said.

"Thanks." Kat paused. "Nice to meet you, Morgan. I'm sorry about your mom."

The girl lifted a slim shoulder. "It's okay."

No. No, it isn't. It never is.

Kat simply nodded and kept her thoughts to herself. There were no words of sympathy that would strike a chord.

"You need me to show you the way?" Morgan asked.

"If you want, but I see the barn." She smiled at the tween. "I think I can find it."

Morgan's phone jingled musically as a new text came in, and she turned her attention away from Kat and onto the small screen. Kat made her way past some outdoor furniture as she crossed the wide porch, then hurried down a few steps to the path, which led through an open gate. The yard was patchy, but sparse, mostly dry. The surrounding fields were much the same, the landscape dotted with a herd of horses trying to graze on dry grass near the barn.

Kat noticed Shiloh standing next to Beau Tate. A

dog lying in the sun next to him, Tate was working on a latch on one of the gates. The dog stood up as it heard Kat approach, and Shiloh looked around. She said something to Beau, who lifted his head from his task.

"Hey. What's up?" Shiloh asked.

"Working a case. One of your neighbor girls is missing as of yesterday," she said and saw Shiloh's expression turn wary.

"Missing?"

"Addison Donovan. She's eighteen, just graduated from high school and went out riding last evening." Kat explained what she knew about the case, including how Addie's horse had returned without her.

"I remember the Donovans," Shiloh said, hitching her thumb to the north.

"Good people," Beau said.

Kat nodded. "We've checked the Croft property and every piece of land surrounding the Donovan ranch."

"You think she might have ridden over here? On my—er, our land?" She glanced at Beau.

"Part of the western end of your property butts up to US Forest Service land, which is practically inaccessible due to the ravine. Lots of scrub brush and downed trees. There are a few tracks back there that a truck could probably make, but it's always easiest to explore on foot or horseback. I thought we might check there." She saw the skepticism in her friend's eyes. "I know. It's a long shot, but . . ."

Shiloh inclined her head. "Whatever it takes. I'll round up the horses."

"What about Morgan?" Beau asked and glanced at the back porch.

"I don't think she should come." Shiloh glanced up at him, and something, some kind of understanding, passed between them, almost as if they were parents . . . or at least a couple.

"I'll see what she wants to do," he said, squinting toward the porch and waving. "If she wants to ride, I'll stick with her and pull up if we locate anything . . . disturbing. If she doesn't want to come, she'll have her phone, and Rambo will be here."

Kat eyed the shepherd, who wagged his tail at her. "Yeah, great guard dog."

Beau snorted. "Well, I was thinking more like he would keep her company. We'll figure it out."

As it turned out, Morgan wouldn't be left behind, and they all rode through the series of paddocks and fields while grasshoppers flew out of their path and the sun rode low in the western sky. At the edge of the government land, Beau opened the final gate, and all four horses filed through before he latched the fastener behind them and climbed astride his gelding once more. Single file, they guided their horses through the brush and around pines with low-hanging branches, along a deer trail that led to the bottom of the ravine. Far overhead, sunlight filtered through the canopy of trees, dappling the ground, where pinecones, sticks, and rocks littered the dry soil.

They didn't speak, just searched the gloom, looking for anything that might lead them to the missing girl, as they worked their way in the direction of the Croft property. This was a long shot at best, Kat knew, and more likely a wild goose chase. She followed Shiloh, who rode a dappled mare. Kat was on Toby, a bay quarter horse, followed by Morgan on a mare and Beau on his gelding. The horses snorted, their hoof beats softened by the soft dirt on the trail. All the while Kat scanned the area, her eyes narrowing against the umbra.

She felt uneasy on the horse, not that she hadn't ridden often as a younger woman, but today's mission, coupled with her own worries about Addie Donovan, made the forest seem ominous. At the bottom of the ravine, the trail followed the edge of a stream winding its way down from higher elevations. Her eyes were on the ground, ever searching, when she heard Beau say, "Buzzards."

She glanced up to the sky, and, sure enough, there were two large birds high above.

"Let's go," Beau said, and Shiloh picked up the pace, urging her mount to move quickly through the underbrush.

Behind her, Beau told Morgan: "This might not be good. You should probably hang back. It's probably a calf, dead or dying."

"I can handle it," Morgan replied.

"You're sure?" He didn't sound convinced.

"I'm not a baby!"

Kat let them argue about it and kept riding, Toby keeping pace with the horse in front of him. They splashed across the stream, crossing to the other side onto the path that started up the opposite bank. They rode upward through the Ponderosa pines and firs, the horses straining, Kat's heart hammering.

Beau was probably right. Some poor dying or recently dead animal had probably lured the birds of prey that were hovering aloft. Certainly whatever they'd discovered wasn't an eighteen-year-old girl. No way. And yet the uneasy feeling that had been with her all day increased, and dread along with curiosity propelled her forward. A fly buzzed past her head. As she swatted at it, she caught the first whiff of a distinctive odor. Whatever the buzzards had found was already dead.

Not necessarily human.

She set her jaw.

Ever upward the trail wound until the trees gave way to the top of the ridge, a stony outcropping high above the valley. The sky was blue, the sun still visible over the treetops, the heat of the day still simmering.

Another powerful whiff of death and something else. Kat was about to turn in the saddle and warn Morgan when she heard Shiloh's voice ahead of her.

"Oh, dear God!"

Kat's stomach dropped.

Shiloh's mount snorted and shied. "Morgan!" Shiloh cried. "Go back!" And she was off her horse.

Kat squinted ahead to see if they had found Addie, but her gaze landed on the body of a woman about Kat's own age. Stark naked, she lay spread-eagle upon the rough stones. Her face was turned to the heavens. Her skin was rotting away, and the stench of death was heavy in the air.

Based on the level of decay, this corpse had been here for more than twenty-four hours. It was not Addie, though that was small relief.

"Go back!" Kat yelled to the horse behind her, but it was too late. As she climbed off her bay, she whipped her cell phone from her pocket and heard Morgan's horrified gasp.

Geez, the poor kid.

Shiloh was standing over the corpse, trying to shield it from Morgan's view.

Kat's stomach tightened, and she had to fight a wave of nausea roiling up her esophagus as she stared at the body. The woman's wrists were wrapped in rusted barbed wire, and she looked as if she'd been lying here for days, if not weeks. Her eyes were gone, and bits of flesh had been torn away, showing bone.

One thing Kat knew for sure: this was not Addison Donovan.

And that other scent . . . gasoline? It looked like the body had been doused in it.

With unsteady fingers, Kat snapped several pictures of the body with her cell, then put in a call to the Sheriff's Department. The woman seemed familiar, like someone Kat had known, though age and death had altered her features.

Then she saw it. Something about the hair, the line of her jaw, what remained of her lips . . .

"I know her," Kat said in shock, staring down at the decomposing body of the most notorious of the three missing girls from fifteen years earlier, her ex-earth science lab partner who'd been suspended from Prairie High more than once: Courtney Pearson.

Part Three

Ruth

Chapter 12

I see you everywhere.
  Your thick, strong hands with stubby fingers.
  Your wooly body, furred with man hair.
  And your huge stature . . . giant and grotesque.

Just like the bear of a man packing bags into the back of her car. A solid young man with broad shoulders and thick biceps. Great guns. Built like a truck, just like *him,* her rapist.

Standing back as he loaded the bags, Ruth Baker couldn't help but stare.

The clerk—PETE, his name tag read—was aware that she was watching intently. "Don't worry, ma'am," he said. "I'm being real careful. I know you got eggs and bananas in there."

"Right." She noticed the hands lifting her bags— hands that could palm a football. But they were not the hands of her attacker. Too thin, fingers too long. And his legs, visible below his khaki shorts and long apron, were hairless and tanned.

Pete was probably an athlete, maybe even in high

school. Fifteen years ago, this young man was probably still potty training. She could let him off the hook.

Although it had been fifteen years, she still had a vivid memory of the details she had observed of her attacker. Certain images had broken through to her in the first year, sharp and distinct as the jangle of a wind chime, and she'd held them tight, clutched them as ammunition against a future attack.

Wide girth, furry skin, thick hands.

His face had been covered, but that had only made her cling to the scant features she could see. Wide girth, furry skin, thick hands . . . her mantra for years.

In those first terrifying years after the attack, there had been nowhere to turn, no one to share the heavy burden with here in Prairie Creek. She had avoided curious eyes in church and lived in fear of having her shame made public. Eventually she learned that she could hide her sins from her father and the congregation, but she could not stem the panic that flowed whenever she saw a man who fit her attacker's profile.

All that changed when she went off to community college in Santa Barbara and discovered a rape crisis center just off the main drag of State Street. There she had found people who would listen without judgment, therapists who focused on healing instead of shame. Through her involvement with the center, Ruth had become inspired to study the field of social work and counseling.

She had learned not to condemn men like Pete, though her vigilance remained. As she told her clients, recovery was a process. Of course, she didn't tell them that hers was still in progress. Every now and then, she had to remind herself that she had studied self-defense techniques and learned to avoid dangerous situations. She had moved on with the knowledge that it was a little silly to keep looking for a man who had sprung on her fifteen years ago. But sometimes threads of memory still snagged in her mind, and she let herself go through the list.

Wide girth, furry skin, thick hands.

She thanked Pete and handed him a few singles, which evoked a huge smile and thanks. As he pushed the cart back toward Menlo's Grocery, she opened the car door and paused with one hand on the warm roof of the car. The cerulean sky vaulting over the mountains that framed the horizon reminded Ruth of how the weather used to energize her this time of year. Wyoming summers were full of activity from sunrise to long after dark, when starlight splattered the sky and fireflies filled the air. As a kid, she had savored the endless hours of freedom, swimming in lakes, catching fish and flying kites, caring for a friend's horses, riding bikes into town with a pack of girls to buy ice cream or penny candy from the general store. Those were sweet days, a childhood spent in a bubble of faith and hope.

Until a masked man ripped away her innocence and changed the path of her life.

Changed but not destroyed, she reminded herself, as she pressed the starter and began to back her Chevy Cruze out of the parking lot. She'd come back to Prairie Creek to give her daughter the kind of childhood she'd enjoyed—lakes and horses and family and a sense of community at the foot of the Wind River Mountains. She had also returned to prod the sleepy town forward in terms of mental health services. The next time a woman in this town was raped, Ruth wanted to be there to help her through recovery. Someone had to let these women know that they were not alone.

She thought of the teenager who was missing, Addie Donovan. The girl had gone riding, and her horse had returned without her, though there was some talk that she might have run off to join a boyfriend.

I hope so. Because disciplining a recalcitrant runaway daughter was far better than trying to mend the tattered shreds of a girl's soul, her essence and identity.

As she pulled up to the exit of the parking lot, the shriek of a siren made her hit the brakes. Two vehicles from the Sheriff's Department zipped through the streets, lights flashing, sirens popping. Two shrieking police cars were a rare sight in Prairie Creek. Ruth tried to see if Kat Starr was behind the wheel of one of the Jeeps, but the vehicles flew past so quickly it was hard to tell. Like her father, Kat had joined the Sheriff's Department. Ruth owed her a phone call— Kat had left a series of messages, but Ruth hadn't summoned the nerve to call back yet. Besides, she'd been busy settling her daughter in, laying the groundwork for her practice and now setting up the hotline. She would have just enough time to put the groceries away before her meeting with Chrissy Nesbitt, the mayor's wife, who was funding her hotline, and Doc Farley, who had been giving her client referrals. So far he'd sent her a teenaged girl named Brooklyn, who was working through anger management, a housewife named Lorelei, who'd suffered domestic violence, and Hank Eames, a fiftyish cowboy who was recovering from a traumatic brain injury caused by a tractor accident. Yes, her plate had been full since she'd moved back to Wyoming, but wasn't that the point? She'd come with a mission to help the women in her hometown, women who had nowhere else to go, and she wasn't going to rest until she'd made some inroads.

Addie lay on the dirty cot in the shack, staring blankly at the way the tall windows caught the orange sunset for the first time that day. Sunlight was supposed to be a sign of hope, but for her it marked the end of day two—at least twenty-four hours during which no one had come for her.

No one.

Where were her parents—her mom and dad, who would both cry when they learned what he had done to her? Where was the Sheriff's Department and the neighbors and all the people from church who rallied together when bad things happened to someone in Prairie Creek?

And Dean? Oh please, Dean. *Come rescue me and tell me you still love me.*

In the alone hours, between the times when he was poking and prodding at her, violating her body and expecting her to do disgusting things to him, Addie listened hard. She listened for sounds of the searchers, the distant call of her name, the whir of helicopter blades, the squawk of a police radio.

But the only sounds came from him and the wilderness. She was used to birdsong and the cry of a hawk.

The odd whine of mule deer. The scurry of raccoons, hares, or squirrels. The scuffle of coyotes, wild goats, or bobcats. The wilderness was her backyard.

But she would never get used to him. His smell. His calloused touch. His greed.

"Do you understand about sacrifice?" he'd asked her that first day in the gloomy shack, counseling her like a minister. "The sacrifice of one can save the lives of many. That's what we got here. You're helping me, and you're saving others because of it."

She didn't understand what he was talking about, but that was no surprise. The man was a psycho with a capital P. "Leave me alone," she'd cried, jerking away as he grabbed her by the shoulder. "Keep your hands off me."

"I can't keep my hands off you, darlin'," he'd growled in a low voice. "From now on, you're here for me."

"Who are you?"

"Call me Lover . . ."

She bit back a cry when he took her by the shoulders and pinned her down on the dirt floor. When he climbed onto her, she closed her eyes. That way, she could keep him out of her soul. All the force and pain and savagery hurt her body, but she refused to let him inside.

He would never have her soul.

When Ruth returned home, she was dismayed to find the screen door of her parents' house unlocked. "Hello?" she called, stepping inside the tidy house.

"In here," Bev McFerron called from the kitchen.

Ruth locked the door behind her. "Mom, you left the door unlocked again."

"That's what folk here do," Bev said as she peeled and pitted a peach with lightning speed and added it to a large pot to prepare for canning. "Living in Santa Barbara really put you in fear of your fellow man, Ruthie."

With her short, over-dyed red hair and wide smile, Bev McFerron had an air of confidence and concern that served her well as a minister's wife, though it wasn't entirely genuine. Sometimes Ruth wanted to call her on it.

If you'd been paying attention, you would know that this has little to do with Santa Barbara. You would have noticed that I was nearly catatonic with fear my last two years of high school.

Shaking off her resentment, Ruth asked. "Is Penny upstairs?"

"She's out in the potting shed with Jessica." In the past few weeks, her eight-year-old daughter had begun to stick like glue to one of the neighborhood girls, and Ruth had been grateful for her mother's pleasure at having the two girls over while she attended to business. "Penny wanted to put together some flower bowls for your front porch, and I let her have at the marigolds and petunias."

Ruth pushed the starched white kitchen curtains aside to peer out back. She couldn't see Penny from here, which tightened her stomach. She couldn't help thinking about Addie Donovan, who would most likely turn up quickly, but what if she didn't? Bev didn't understand why Ruth rarely let her daughter out of her sight, but Ruth knew there were bad people out in the world.

"How'd your meeting go?" asked Bev.

"Great. Chrissy Nesbitt is a real go-getter. She got some funding for the hotline and has offered to volunteer her time. And Doc Farley was more receptive than I expected. He's agreed to open his office, day or night, to treat any emergencies that come in through the hotline. Honestly, I didn't think an old-school doctor would be that attentive, but he told me he's had some very sad cases with women who won't admit to being beaten. Doc suspects rape, but he thinks the women are too frightened to speak honestly."

"It just breaks your heart, doesn't it?" Bev shook her head sadly. "I would just love to reach out and help women like that."

Her mother seemed sincere, but Ruth wondered how deep that compassion ran. Would it apply to her own daughter if Ruth told her about the events of that horrible night fifteen years earlier? Maybe. Or perhaps the shame of an ugly attack would overshadow Bev's desire to be a do-gooder. "You know, Mom, you could volunteer on the hotline. Ultimately, I'll return all the calls, but we need people to answer when I'm unavailable. We have a recording, but it's so much better to get a real person on the line. We could use someone like you, a calm, soothing voice in the face of panic."

"Oh, I could never do that." Bev gave an exaggerated shudder. "You know your father wouldn't approve. He's not at all comfortable with the idea of you bringing attention to that sort of thing."

"Right." Ruth's heart sank as she prepared to have one of her father's platitudes parroted. "He doesn't believe that rape exists."

"It's just that he thinks that talking about it only encourages the bad behavior."

"But, Mom, women who've survived a sexual assault need to talk about it."

"I know." Bev patted her heart with a sad smile. "But it's not my place to argue with your father. Are you and the girls staying for dinner? I can put burgers on the grill."

"I promised the girls we'd go to Molly's Diner. It's taco night."

"I can make tacos," Bev insisted. "It's no trouble at all."

"But dining out is an event for them. How long have they been out there?" Ruth asked, stealing another glance through the kitchen window.

Bev shrugged. "An hour or so? I love the way they occupy each other."

"I'm going to see if they're about ready to go."

"Ask them if they want to stay for dinner," Bev called after her as she headed into the backyard.

Crossing the sun-dappled lawn, Ruth felt a tug of the old love she'd once known for this place, this yard, this town. Her parents' yard backed up to three land-locked acres that the neighbors had shared for gardening and recreation, and she'd spent many an afternoon back here, barefoot and blissful, picking wild berries from the fence or playing kickball. This was the sort of joyful childhood she wanted for Penny.

Although the sun was low in the sky, the air was

still baking hot, and gnats jumped from the grass as she rounded the garage. She saw the potting shed, a small hut covered in the same gray siding as the house. Its door hung open. Two plastic pots on the bench contained tender-looking yellow, purple, and red flowers that leaned gingerly against each other, as if ready to faint from the heat. Not the best day for moving plants.

The flower bowls were complete, but Penny and Jessica were nowhere in sight.

"Penny?" There was a catch in Ruth's voice, and she braced herself to keep the panic out of her voice. Penny and Jessica were safe here, in their mother's backyard, in the cradle of this slow-moving prairie town. Of course they were.

Then why was her heart pounding? Adrenaline electrified her nerves as she shouted for her daughter. Where could she be? Penny knew that she was never to leave without asking permission.

She was running now, tearing around the garden, tall blades of grass whipping at her legs as she tore through the community field and plunged into the garden between rows of cabbages and tomatoes.

"Penny, where are you?" she demanded, pausing to take in the lazy summer landscape of grass and plants, sweating shrubs and trees. "Where are you?" The words stuck in her dry throat.

She paused, listening, but there was no answer in the birdsong, the buzz of a distant lawn mower, and the pounding of her heartbeat. Should she return to the house and alert her mother? Call the police? Search the potting shed? Maybe they were hiding, playing a trick on her. Or maybe they'd gone to Jessica's house without asking permission.

Ruth was headed back to the shed when the sound of voices and a child's scream sent her wheeling around. Oh God, where had it come from?

There were two screaming voices now, shrill and young, and they seemed to be coming from one of the nearby yards to the west, where the setting sun was ablaze in the sky. These properties were fenced off, but she followed the fence lines, some of them post and rail, others six-foot wooden fences.

"No! Stop!" came a young voice, followed by another shriek.

It was Penny.

Oh God, something terrible was happening.

Memory jarred her, the darkest moments of her life replaying in her mind. It couldn't be . . . not Penny.

Galvanizing herself against the memory, Ruth ran into the blinding sunlight to save her daughter.

Chapter 13

"Penny!" Ruth shouted, racing to the source of the sound. "Penny, where are you?"

She couldn't see over the fence, but the gate sat ajar and unlatched. Rusted hinges screeched as she yanked it open and combed the yard for her girl. Her view was blocked by a fat oak trunk and an overgrown lilac bush that lent a sweet scent to the sourness in her throat. "Penny?" she shouted, skirting the bush.

"Mom?" The hesitant whimper squeezed her heart as she caught sight of her daughter, who stared at her, as if paralyzed. Penny clung gingerly to a small linden tree just beyond Jessica, who was flitting through the yard like a moth fighting a breeze. Her shirt was removed and her orange shorts clung to her, sopping wet as she dodged the spray of a hose held by a big bear of a cowboy type who acknowledged Ruth with a sultry nod.

"What do you think you're doing?" Ruth demanded.

"Well, that's a fine howdy." The cowboy pushed off

the porch steps and went to turn the hose off. The hands that turned the spigot were thick and strong.

Wide girth, thick hands . . . His legs were covered by jeans, but the green T-shirt that stretched over his broad chest revealed arms furred with blond hair, and a tightly trimmed beard covered his jaw. He wasn't overtly menacing, but somehow that made him all the more of a threat.

Ruth braced herself to control the trembling fury that threatened to overtake her. "Who the hell are you, and what are you doing to these girls?"

"Calm down, now. This is my yard, Ruthie."

He *knew* her. He knew her, and he was trying to intimidate her. His smug grin chilled her, despite the humid air.

"I'm Cal Haney. I know your father from church. And these carpet munchers came to me, looking for water for some plants or something."

"You told us we could have water. And then you sprayed us," Jessica said, dancing in a puddle that had formed in a patch of dirt. It looked as if someone had turned the earth to plant sod and never completed the task. "That's not fair, Uncle Cal."

Uncle? Ruth looked from the man to the girl. "You're related?" Or was it one of those sick relationships in which he'd asked her to call him uncle?

Jessica nodded, brown water splashing up her legs with each step. "He's my uncle now."

"That's right," Cal said. "I got hitched to Jessie's aunt last month." He pushed back his hat to reveal tobacco-stained teeth under amused blue eyes. The band of bare forehead suggested a bald head, and he was handsome in a high-energy salesman kind of way. "Then again, if I'd known you were coming back to town, I might have held out a bit longer."

"Excuse me?"

His smile was begrudging, but a little flirtatious. "I been watching you over the years. Times you came home after college. I just never thought you were back to stay."

Stalking her? She searched her mind for a memory of this man, Cal Haney, but she couldn't place him. Had he lived here fifteen years ago? She had plenty of questions, but she didn't want to spend one more minute than necessary with this man.

"Come on, girls." She put an arm around Penny's shoulders and extended a hand toward Jessica. "Where's your shirt, Jess?"

The girl lifted her chin toward the back railing. "It's wet."

"Put it on for now. We'll get you dry clothes."

"Yeah, I got to get going anyways," Cal said. "Meeting some guys at The Dog. Business contacts."

Ruth couldn't imagine a legitimate deal transpiring over a pool table at the saloon, but she didn't pick up on his bait. Besides, she made it a habit not to converse with men who stared intently at her breasts, as Haney was now doing.

The bastard.

He'd ruined a beautiful summer afternoon, and she had to wonder if he was the man who had ruined most of her high school years here in Prairie Creek.

"I'll see you around," he called after them.

She sure hoped not.

As she guided the girls back through the common field, the truth emerged. The girls had wanted water for the plants—a liberty Bev McFerron had apparently denied them.

"Grandma said we would get all muddy," Penny admitted, her orange hair brilliant as a penny in the bright sun.

"So we went over to my aunt and uncle's to get water for the plants. But Aunt Val wasn't home. And Uncle Cal tricked us with the hose." Jessica pulled her sopping shirt away from her belly. "Still soaking wet. I'm going to catch my death of cold."

"Not in this weather," Ruth said, "but we're going to have to get a change of clothes for both of you before we head out for dinner."

"Can we still go to the diner?" Penny begged, on the verge of tears.

"After you get changed. And before we eat, we're going to have a talk about where you can and can't go on your own."

"Am I in trouble?" Penny asked. She prided herself on following the rules and doing the right thing.

"No, but we need to keep you out of trouble in the future," Ruth said, patting her daughter's shoulder. *And out of danger.*

"I won't get in trouble because Cal is my uncle," Jessica said. "I can go there any time I want."

"I wouldn't if I were you." Ruth knew she would have to talk with Jessica's parents about the new uncle. Just because someone was family did not mean they could be trusted.

"He was very mean," Penny said. "I'm never going back there."

"But it felt good to get sprayed, right?" Jessica prodded.

"At first. But then he wouldn't stop."

They loaded the flower bowls into the car, then Ruth marched the girls two blocks to Jessica's house, knowing there'd be hell to pay if she brought two wet, muddy ones into her mother's house. Jessica's mother, Fiona, offered to supervise the cleanup and find something for Penny to wear while Ruth went back to her parents' place. She could have said good-bye in a text, but the matter of Calvin Haney was too big to cover by cell phone.

She frowned at her father's Oldsmobile, parked in the driveway. She had hoped to scoot out before he got home.

Her mother was in the kitchen, chopping onions. Dad, she suspected, was off in the den they used as an office.

"Where are the girls?" asked Bev.

"They were a little too messy to traipse through here. I found them playing with the hose."

"Those little stinkers! I hope you sent Jessica straight home."

"I took them to Jessica's to get cleaned up."

"You are too lenient with Penny."

"It wasn't entirely her fault." She told her mother about the alarming exchange with Cal Haney. "It's a little scary to think of him living down the street. There's something off about him."

"Oh, I don't know. Years ago, he was in a bit of trouble. The sheriff kept questioning him about those missing girls. What were their names?"

"Rachel Byrd. Erin Higgins. Courtney Pearson."

The names were an indelible part of Ruth's memory. "Was he involved in their disappearance?" she asked, trying to hide the fear she could feel rising in her throat.

"He was under suspicion for a while, but then it eventually blew over. When the girls stopped disappearing, they said the kidnapper moved on."

"Who said that?"

"You know. People at church. That was such a sad thing. It just destroyed the Byrds, losing their daughter that way."

Ruth shivered despite the heat of the kitchen.

"But Calvin Haney has turned over a new leaf. He's a married man now, and that wildcat business is tough, but he did get one well that earned him enough to buy a house."

A wildcatter. That explained the cowboy costume. Cal Haney seemed far too soft to be a ranch hand, but Ruthie knew that a Stetson hat, jeans, and boots did not a cowboy make.

"A house and a wife might make him seem respectable, but that man is morally off center. I'm going to tell Penny to stay away from him, even if he is Jessica's uncle."

Her father came into the kitchen and, after a short nod of acknowledgment, asked his wife about his calendar in early September. The Reverend Robert McFerron had never deigned to accept his youngest daughter as a peer, and at the age of thirty-one, Ruth was beginning to accept that he never would. Still, she stood her ground in conversation with him, which he frequently perceived as a challenge.

"Your father has been approached to preside over

the Dillinger wedding," Bev said in a futile attempt to bring them together in conversation.

"You mean Sabrina and Colton's?" Ruth had heard talk of the gala wedding.

"Oh, did you know them, dear?" her mother asked.

Ruth shook her head. "I knew of him. His brother Tyler was in my class, but everyone in Prairie Creek is talking about it." Sabrina Delaney, a local veterinarian, was engaged to marry Colton Dillinger, one of the heirs to a huge local cattle ranch. It was the sort of event that sucked up the resources of local bakers and florists and sent women driving to Jackson in search of a decent dress. She knew her father would be pleased to be rubbing elbows with the wealthy Dillingers. Many of the local churches would be happy to have Rob McFerron as a resident preacher if he could draw wealthy patrons to the collection plate. "That's great, Dad. You must feel honored."

"Actually, I'm not even sure I'm doing it. There's a moral dilemma here. I'm not sure I want to have someone with the scant morals of Colton Dillinger in my congregation."

"What?" Ruth paused, miffed by the fact that her father would accept a creep like Cal Haney but reject Colt Dillinger. "You've always liked the Dillingers." Translation: sucked up to them. Dad liked the Kincaids too, though it was never an easy task to straddle the breach between those two rival clans. Still, for the promise of generous tithings, the Reverend Robert McFerron made the effort.

"It's about Colton's son, Rourke." Bev swiped at her brow with the back of one hand. "You know. Born out of wedlock," she whispered.

"Oh, really?" Ruth tried to keep her annoyance with her father's rigid views out of her voice. "It's a life, Dad. Isn't that what you're always campaigning for?"

"Not out of the sanctity of marriage." Rob McFerron pursed his lips. "This puts me in a compromising position."

"Because two people want to get married?"

"I can't condone the sins of the past."

"But, Dad, who are you to judge?"

"I am a minister of the Lord Jesus Christ, and don't take that tone with me."

"But—" Ruth had to stop herself from lashing out against her father, who had always enjoyed goading her into these infuriating conversations. "I'm just saying—I don't know how old this Rourke kid is, but if he lives in this town, I hope you're nice to him. None of this is his fault."

"As if I'm ever anything but nice." He took a long swallow of lemonade. "Now that we've heard from liberal California, what's the plan for dinner, Bev? I'm leading the men's Bible study at seven."

"And I've got to get the girls to dinner," Ruth said, grateful for a reason to duck out. "Thanks for watching them, Mom."

Forty minutes later, Ruth was relieved to step into the cool air of the diner, where Cordelia, the no-nonsense waitress, let the girls take the last available booth. Before leaving with the girls, Ruth had spent a few minutes explaining her confrontation with Cal Haney to Fiona, and Jessica's mother had shared her sense that there was something off about the man.

"I'll lay down the law," Fiona said. "Jessie is never to go there again."

Ruth had also gone over the need to stay close to the house and use caution around strangers. This time, both girls had listened quietly and promised to follow the rules. Now, as she sank onto the cool vinyl upholstery and sipped her ice water, Ruth looked over at her daughter with pride. The incident this afternoon could have been worse if Penny hadn't been cautious. She was a good kid, and she deserved the simple, wholesome childhood that Prairie Creek had to offer.

"How are you doing tonight, Cordelia?" Ruth asked the waitress when she came to take their order. Cordelia greeted most guests with a deadpan look, though she seemed to have a soft spot for Penny.

She shrugged. "I've had better nights. Everyone here's feeling the strain right now."

"Too hot for you?" Ruth asked, noticing that the usually animated restaurant did seem a bit subdued tonight, with diners murmuring in low, doleful voices. An elderly woman across from Ruth frowned down at her plate as her husband stared off sadly, hands tucked under his chin.

"It's not the weather as much as the bad news. We got one girl missing and another one . . ." Cordelia nodded toward the girls. "I don't want to ruin anyone's meal." She poured water into three glasses on the table. "It's a real heartbreak."

"I heard about Addie Donovan," Ruth said, trying to stay calm. "Do you know her?"

"She's been in here with her family. A good kid."

"I hope they find her." Ruth tried to sound positive.

Cordelia nodded, pressing the bridge of her nose

as if to stave off tears. "She was just out riding, and her horse came back without her." She looked away. "Her parents, Deb and Jeremy, were freaking out last night, and now, with this other girl . . ." She took a calming breath. "It doesn't look good." The waitress walked off, replacing the water pitcher at the service stand.

Something was wrong . . . very wrong. Now Ruth noticed the subdued voices at the tables around her. Bad news had obviously hit the diner, one of the centers of town gossip. What was the story with the "other girl"?

She checked Penny and Jessica to see if they were curious, but they were pointing out items on the dessert menu, making big plans. Scooting out of the booth, Ruth stepped away from the table and followed the waitress toward the kitchen.

"Cordelia," Ruth called, pulse pounding. "Who's the other girl you mentioned?"

"Oh, they found a kid who went missing years ago. You just moved here, so you wouldn't know her." Cordelia didn't realize that Ruth had attended high school in Prairie Creek.

"My parents have lived here for years. Did they find one of the girls who disappeared fifteen years ago? Is she all right?" The look on Cordelia's face said it all, and suddenly Ruth knew. They hadn't found a girl. They'd found a corpse.

"One of the deputies found the remains of a young woman up on the ridge near the Tate land this afternoon. They said she might be Courtney Pearson."

Chapter 14

Ruth didn't know how she made it through dinner that night. The tacos seemed leathery and tasteless, and the hot sauce started a burn in her throat that lasted throughout the meal and beyond.

One girl dead and another girl missing . . .

Actually, Courtney Pearson wouldn't be a girl anymore. Older than Ruth by a couple years, she would have been in her early thirties had she lived. Memories of that summer long past consumed Ruth. Thank goodness Penny had Jessica to keep her occupied, because her mother was about as responsive as a zombie.

She couldn't stop thinking of Courtney Pearson. Although Ruth's family had been living in Prairie Creek for only a year or so when Courtney went missing, the girl's disappearance had made an impression on Ruth because of the way so many people had written her off. Granted, the girl was no angel, but she caught everyone's attention in the hall at school or when she walked in town. With her trampy clothes, big hair, multiple piercings, and loud laughter and shrieks, Courtney filled a room.

When she first disappeared, most of the kids at school thought that a larger-than-life person like Courtney couldn't have been hurt, that she had simply left town and hitchhiked her way to excitement in a city like Denver or Vegas. People like Ruth's father passed judgment in a different way, claiming that Courtney deserved whatever happened to her because of her bad behavior. That condemnation had seemed wrong back then. Now, Ruth knew it was deplorable. Today, a kid like Courtney was exactly the kind of girl Ruth wanted to reach.

"Chocolate tacos?" Jessica rolled her eyes, drawing Ruth's attention back to the here and now. "That's just crazy."

"Can we get dessert, Mom? Please, please, please? I know it's not a weekend, but I've never had a chocolate taco." Penny's brown eyes were so earnest that Ruth couldn't help but suspend the family rule.

"We'll make an exception tonight." Anything to prolong a feeling of normalcy. Ruth knew that the moment she stopped gathering memories from her high school years, she would have to face the tough reality that held an imminent threat.

An eighteen-year-old girl was missing. Some monster was out there.

Again.

Could it be the same man who had struck fifteen years ago, taking Rachel, Erin, and Courtney? She wondered if the same kidnapper had been the masked attacker from that summer night.

Wide girth, furry skin, thick hands . . .

No! There was no proof that the same man had taken those other girls, and Ruth wasn't going to make this about herself. She had gone through steps toward her own recovery, acknowledging her trauma, accepting support, moving on, and now giving back. She was here in Prairie Creek to give back to the community, not to impose her personal fears on it. While there was a slim chance that her attacker had gone after Addie Donovan all these years later, Ruth had to remember that she hadn't returned to Prairie Creek to start a police investigation; she was here to help. Maybe the best way to start was to offer support to Addie's parents, though she needed to find an entrée to the couple.

When Cordelia came by with the check, Ruth asked her what she knew about the circumstances of Addie's disappearance.

"I don't know about the details." Cordelia nodded to a table by the window, where a couple Ruth's age sat with two children, one in a high chair. "Ask Jimmy."

Jimmy Woodcock, the most recent owner and editor of *Prairie Winds*, sat texting on his phone while a sullen-faced woman talked at him. He and Ruth had talked on the phone when he was gathering information for two short blurbs about her local practice and the hotline, but she doubted he'd remember that. Ruth hadn't recognized him at first, as he'd grown a mustache that gave him a cowboy look, but he was still a big man, a T-shirt stretching over his chest and biceps. From the look of those soft hands, she doubted that he'd ever even been on a horse, though his hands did seem strong, with short, thick fingers.

Strong hands, wide girth . . .

She was about to turn away from the broad-shouldered man when he caught her looking.

He lifted his chin, arrogant as ever, and smiled, his eyes shining dark over his mustache. The woman looked up in annoyance, chewing in silence as he motioned Ruth over.

"Well now, if it isn't the minister's daughter. Ruthie McFerron."

"It's Ruth Baker now," she said, a bit surprised that he knew who she was. After the rape, she had kept a low profile in high school. "I went to California, got married, and had a kid." He studied Ruth intently as he introduced his wife, Desiree, and kids. Desiree nodded but suddenly seemed more interested in wiping the baby's hands.

"That's right. I did a piece on you, right?" he asked. "About you moving back."

"We talked on the phone." Ruth turned to the bland wife. "I've moved back for good, with my daughter." She nodded toward the girls. "I'm working as a thera-pist, setting up a small practice. I've got an office next door to Emma's shop."

"Yeah? It's gonna be a real small practice here," Woodcock said. "Plenty of crazies, but none of them know it. Trust me, I've seen it all, covering the local news." He held up his phone. "See that? Something breaking right now. Just when you think Prairie Creek might be a nice, peaceful town, some shit breaks."

"And ruins your dinner," Desiree said with a scowl.

"Is that about Addie Donovan?" Ruth asked. "I was wondering if you knew the details of her disappear-ance."

"He knows everything," Desiree bragged. "Gets updates straight from the Sheriff's Department."

"That one's a simple story. Girl, eighteen, went riding alone, and her horse came back without her. The boyfriend was out of town, so the parents thought it might be a ruse to get with him. He says no, but off the record? These things are always about sex. Looking for love in all the wrong places." He grinned— not a wholesome "dad" smile, but the sort of inviting look you might get in a singles bar.

"I see." Ruth folded her arms across her chest. Apparently Jimmy didn't have a lot of respect for his wife and kids. "So the police think she's safe with her boyfriend?"

"I'm working on confirming that right now. In fact, I'm going over to the office to get some confirmations and post the story. Got to keep the website updated. It's the only way for a newspaper to survive these days. Subscriptions are down, but there's money to be made through advertisers on the web." Jimmy pushed his plate away and tossed down his napkin. "You want to come see, Ruthie? Check out the operation and get the latest on the story?"

She didn't. The last thing she wanted was to spend time alone in a hot office with a guy who had all the charm of a lizard. Ruth suspected that a look under the table would prove that Woodcock was living up to his name.

"I need to get the girls home," Ruth said, gesturing toward the door with her thumb. "But thanks for the information. And sorry to interrupt your dinner." This was directed more toward Desiree, but the woman was chastising the baby about something. Ruth backed away, glad to escape the dour couple.

He watched her leave the diner, her head held high and those voluptuous breasts leading the way.

Well, aren't you looking pretty, Ms. Ruthie McFerron Baker, the minister's voluptuous daughter. Ripe as Eve just kicked out of Eden. He had busted the cherry on that one when she was just a filly. His only regret was letting her get away. He should have kept her when he had the chance, dragged her to his place and added her to his collection.

But too many things had gone wrong that night. Wrongs that still had to be righted.

He watched from the shadows of Main Street as she guided the two young girls. Now that she had a daughter and a full, ripe woman's body, she would have so much more to offer. She would know how to use those hands and that mouth to tease him to a frenzy.

His cock was a rocket in his pants, aching for release. That girl in the shed was just not enough. He needed more, and here was the minister's daughter, ripe for the picking. But she was older now, smarter. This time he would have to plan carefully if he wanted to hold on to her.

For now, he would watch, wait, and find another way to relieve himself. He pressed a hand to the hard rod between his legs and smiled. *You had to love Prairie Creek. Come into town for dinner, and you got so much more.*

* * *

When Addie Donovan was not found by Saturday, the police announced that they were working with nearby law enforcement agencies to broaden the search, but that was little consolation to the people of Prairie Creek. The newspaper website reported that some folks were beginning to lock their doors, kids were having nightmares, and the sheriff's office was advising young people and women to travel in groups, especially at night.

Ruth was feeling the crunch at home, with Penny worrying that a bad man was lurking in the cluster of bushes across the street from their house. "What if he's living there, watching me from the bushes?" Penny asked one night as Ruth sat in bed beside her, reading yet another chapter of Junie B. Jones aloud to soothe her daughter. "What if he catches me and takes me away, the way he kidnapped Addie?"

Those damned bushes! Ruth had been attracted to the rental home because it faced a tall wall of trees that allowed privacy from the small park beyond it, but now both she and Penny were beginning to see potential danger in each dark space.

"You're safe in our home," Ruth assured her, not wanting to reveal any more facts than Penny needed to know. It wasn't easy to mask her own fear and insecurity, but she didn't want her daughter to be traumatized by this. "Addie went riding alone, something you will never do."

"But I still want to learn to ride."

"I know, pumpkin. You're all signed up for lessons. You and Jessica start this week."

"Do you think it's safe?"

From the mouths of babes . . . "You'll be with an in-structor the whole time, at the Dillinger ranch, where people will be around." She rubbed her daughter's thin shoulder and kissed her forehead. "Totally safe."

"So maybe I can be a cowgirl after all."

Ruth smiled, thinking that it was an odd goal for the daughter of a therapist and a software engineer, but Penny had always taken to the horses and animals whenever they'd visited here. Such a country girl! Sometimes it was the little surprises from her daughter that reminded Ruth of the light in the world.

That week, Ruth received the first call on the hot-line. It rang through to her cell phone late Thursday night as she was washing up for bed. Fortunately, Penny was fast asleep. Suddenly alert, Ruth blotted her face and answered the call.

"This is Ruth, and you've reached the Sexual Assault Support Line."

There was silence on the line, a heavy silence that made it clear someone was struggling, suffering.

"I know this is hard, but you need to tell me what happened to you," Ruth said. "I've been there myself. You can talk about anything you want if it helps you get started. Tell me about the weather, your pet turtle, your favorite kind of music."

"You can call me Lily."

"Lily, I'm glad you called. It takes a lot of courage to do the research to find someone like me. But it takes even more courage to make the call."

"I'm not brave. I'm a coward."

"Why do you say that, Lily?"

"Because I didn't turn him in. He raped me, he

kidnapped me and . . ." Her voice cracked with a sob. "I'm sorry, but I can't."

"No rush," Ruth said in a calm voice. "Take a breath. Take all the time you need. I'll still be here."

After a moment, Lily went on. Guided by Ruth, she told her story. One minute she was hanging out down by the creek; the next minute he was there, dragging her away to his lair, some old hunting shack in the wilderness. Once in captivity, she was raped, forced to let him use her body so that he could re-lease his sex drive and escape arrest "out there," he had told her.

"You're calling on a phone, so I'm assuming you got away from him?"

"Yes, but I feel so guilty that he's still out there. I know it's terrible, but I couldn't stick around to re-port him. I wasn't the only one."

"What do you mean?"

"I had to get away, I couldn't stay!!"

"Many of us don't have the resources or strength to go after an attacker," Ruth said. "It's not your fault, Lily."

A heavy pause. Ruth sensed the woman's high emotion and silent tears.

"I need to go, and . . . I'm sorry I bothered you," Lily said glumly. "Talking about this won't solve any-thing."

"But talking about it can help," Ruth assured her. "Talk therapy is an effective way of working through issues."

"It won't help. Nothing helps." And then the line went dead.

Ruth exhaled heavily. She noted the call and content in her log, hoping that the woman would call back. She had a bad feeling about her comment that she wasn't the only one. Did she know of more victims?

On Sunday, Ruth joined her mother to hear her father deliver the sermon at the Pioneer Church, a newly rebuilt edifice that used to be on Kincaid land before it was deeded over to the church. Truth be told, it was only the second time Ruth had heard her father speak from the pulpit since she'd returned, as she preferred to attend the Unitarian Church, where the mission was more about living together in peace than damning the errant soul to hell. But today she had come with a mission of her own. Her mother had promised to introduce Ruth to Addie Donovan's parents, regular patrons of the Pioneer's Sunday services.

At the door, they stepped out of the bright sunshine to be greeted by two men in the cool, shadowed vestibule.

"Hey, Bev." An older man with a bulbous nose and a rubbery smile, whom Ruth recognized as the pharmacist, handed them programs. "Come to see Rob today?"

"Haven't missed a Sunday with my husband yet," her mother said, chatting with the man.

When Ruth turned to the other man, she realized he was closer to her age and—and extremely familiar. Tall with broad shoulders, thick dark hair that curled off to one side, and clear eyes that seemed to see deep inside her.

She had heard he'd left town, but here he was, the object of her teenage fantasies: Ethan Starr.

Her throat tightened as he handed her a paper fan with an advertisement for the Mercer Funeral Home printed on one side, and she noticed his hands, which were calloused, with long, graceful fingers. Oh, thank God, her instincts about him had been right. She had only been in a discussion with him a handful of times, but she had sensed kindness in his low, gravelly voice.

"Would you like a fan, Ruthie?" he asked in that deep voice, which had grown sexier with age. "Once the place fills up, it's going to be hot in there."

"You remember me?" She accepted a fan, noticing the navy button-down shirt and khaki pants. Not quite the bronc rider she remembered.

"You were the ghost girl I passed every day as I was leaving the chem lab in senior year of high school. I could always count on you to say hello, but you disappeared pretty fast after that."

She was surprised and tickled that he knew her. "You were a big rodeo star back then."

He smiled. "I was out of my league."

"Oh come on. You were hot. I didn't think you'd notice a nobody like me."

"Everybody's somebody," he said as Ruth's mother touched her arm.

"We need to go," Bev reminded. "Can't be late."

Ruth nodded at Ethan, reluctant to leave.

"There's a lemonade social after the service," he said, handing a fan to Bev before they walked in. "I hope to see you both there."

Organ music filled the small, airy church as they slid into a pew in the second row.

"You know Coach Starr?" her mother asked under her breath.

Ruth leaned back against the cool wood of the pew. "From high school," she answered, trying to keep it simple. "He's a coach now?"

Bev shushed her and handed her a song book as a flourish of organ music signaled the first song.

There was comfort to be had in some church rituals, but during the first two songs and opening reading Ruth had trouble keeping her thoughts from straying. Thoughts of Ethan Starr were like mind candy, and she wondered if he was single, why he'd come back to town, what had become of his rodeo career. She longed to twist around in the pew like a five-year-old and search the congregation for his earnest blue eyes. Restraint, she reminded herself.

Ruth's interest was drawn back to the moment when her father focused his sermon on the tragedies that had befallen Prairie Creek in the past few days. He intoned gravely, "I invite you to join me in praying for the safe return of Addie Donovan, a young lady from this congregation. Her parents, Debra and Jeremy, are here with us, and I pray that they'll feel a groundswell of God's love and support."

It was more compassion than she had ever seen from Robert McFerron. He spoke of the importance of pulling together as a community to support families in crisis and maintain the safety of children and young people. "God bless Addie Donovan and her family."

Would you have talked that way if I had been snatched away in high school? Would you have supported me if you found out I was raped?

Shifting on the pew, Ruth realized her father was a fine public speaker, but a lousy human being. Handsome, engaging, narcissistic, and quick to find fault, Rob McFerron had been a charming but harsh father. For a preacher looking to ward followers off sin, that quality could be helpful, but Ruth had learned the hard way that a hypercritical bent made a man a terrible father or husband. How had her mother put up with it all these years?

Ruth knew how unbearable a man like that could be; she'd been married to one too. So classic to marry a man like your father, warts and all. She had hooked up with Sterling Baker because he seemed so sure of right and wrong. But as she grew and learned to stand on her own two feet, she felt smothered by Sterling's way of life. It was a relationship so tight, she could barely breathe.

Five years ago, when she asked for space, Sterling refused to let go. For a time, she worried that he would snap and get violent. She began making preparations to leave Santa Barbara, knowing that she was walking a tenuous line by taking their daughter out of state without having full custody. She began to take Penny to their favorite places in Santa Barbara—the palm-lined beach, the pier, the zoo. They went for pancakes at Sambos and ice cream at McConnell's on State Street. In Ruth's mind, they were saying good-bye before heading across the country to anonymity.

Thank God, Penny had proven to be the great equalizer. Sterling could be selfish and depraved, but even he would not knowingly harm their child. Besides, he'd started having an affair with Suki, so he had a woman to take Ruth's place.

She had been grateful when he found Suki and started a family; he'd even lost interest in playing father to Penny, agreeing to let her move back to Wyoming with Ruth so that he could focus on his wife, and his twin sons, designer dogs, and sports cars.

"Brothers and sisters, let us pray," her father said, spreading his hands wide. "Father God, we ask that you grant the safe return of Addie Donovan."

"Amen," the congregants agreed.

"And God bless the soul of Courtney Pearson," said the minister. "May she rest in peace."

"Amen," said Ruth softly, thinking: *There but for the grace of God go I.*

After the service, the Donovans were surrounded by congregants who lined up to offer support. Ruth went to the opposite end of the reception room, deciding to wait for now and avoid overwhelming the tense couple. She saw Jan Pearson, bent over and pressing a handkerchief to her mouth, being guided away by a man and woman, whom she believed were Rachel Byrd's parents. Ruth's heart ached. She wanted to offer them all comfort, but sensed that Jan, and maybe the Byrds as well, wanted to escape too much attention. Earlier she'd thought she'd recognized Erin Higgins's parents, but they were nowhere to be seen now.

Then she saw Cal Haney in line with a short, doe-eyed woman, his wife, and her decision to back off from the man was affirmed, especially when he spotted her and gave her a wink.

She moved toward the refreshment table in the corner, saying hello to a few people who remembered her from high school as she passed. Her return to Prairie Creek had made her realize how isolated she had become in high school after the trauma. With no friends and no emotional access to her parents, she had spent the last two years of high school in a stoic zombie mode, pushing herself to survive, get her diploma, and escape this place.

As she sipped a glass of lemonade, she overheard people talking about the Prairie Creek football team, one man encouraging the other about a son who had been dropped from the roster last year because of grades.

"Wyatt's a gifted player. He's pretty tricky out there as a running back. Let him know that this is his time for a second chance. If he can apply himself and get the grades this year, I'd be thrilled to play him." The coach's voice was low and gravelly. She shot a glance over and saw that it was Ethan.

"I'll let the boy know," the player's father said. "Coming from you, Coach, that'll mean a lot to him."

"And you tell him that we can get him with a tutor if he needs help with academics. It's up to him. If he's willing to apply himself, there's no limit to where he can go."

"Thanks, Coach. Much appreciated."

As the player's parent walked away, Ethan turned to Ruth. "And that would be the summer recruitment portion of my day."

She laughed. "So you're the football coach. You must be pretty popular." Out here, high school football was the only thing happening on a Friday night. "Still competing in rodeo?"

"Not for years. That last bronc ride earned me a spinal injury, and I had to switch professions from entertainment to education."

"Oh no."

"Nah, it's fine. I give horseback riding lessons out at the Dillinger ranch, but mostly I've moved on to teaching and coaching."

"Do you miss the rodeo?"

"I'm pretty happy where I am. Though it appears I'm a disappointment to my father."

"Really? He says that?"

"Not to me directly, but it's there."

"You two had a falling out?"

"More like the old man is disappointed that I didn't follow in his footsteps."

Ruth recalled that Patrick Starr used to be a detective. "He wanted you to have a career in law enforcement? Isn't that what Kat chose?"

"He's still a little uncomfortable having a daughter in a traditionally male profession. I think it's getting better. We all made our choices quite a while ago. But I'm definitely the outcast."

"That's a shame. It must be hard on you."

"I don't want to talk about it. Oh, wait—I just did."

He gave a casual smile. "See how you did that? You must be a kickass therapist, Dr. Ruth."

They both chuckled, and Ruth realized it was the first light moment she'd experienced since the bad news had broken this week. It felt good to laugh, even if just for a moment.

"How is Kat doing?" she asked. "She must be busy with everything that went on this week."

"I'd imagine. We have dinner together whenever we can, but she's been canceling lately, blaming it on work, which, unfortunately, is probably the truth. She's still single, like me. I don't think there's a man alive who could put up with her stubbornness."

"Underneath that shell, there's a heart of gold." Kat had been kind to her, but they were both too young and immature to help each other through the trauma of that night.

"Does she know you're in town?" he asked. "You two used to be friends, right?"

Ruth thought of the recent phone calls and texts she'd ignored. "That was fifteen years ago. A lot of things have changed."

"True, but you didn't turn into an asshole, and neither did Kat. You two could meet on common ground." He held up a finger and glanced in both directions. "Okay, I've got to stop with the potty mouth. This is a place of worship."

"Right. Save it for the sidelines, Coach."

"We should get together," he suggested. "The three of us. Kat will want to see you."

"Oh, I don't know."

"Am I being too pushy?"

"No. It's not you. It's—it's me."

"That is the oldest blow-off in the book, Ruth. You've got to come up with something more original than that."

He scared a laugh out of her. "Sorry, I just . . . can't do it now. Building a business, settling in with my daughter."

"Fair enough. So I'll give you some time. How does two weeks sound?"

She looked away in regret. She couldn't tell him that it was his sister she was avoiding. She saw that the group of people on the other side of the room was dispersing and said, "I need to go over and speak with the Donovans. It's been great talking with you, Ethan. I hope to see you around."

"Same." The glimmer in his eyes made her want to stick around, and it had been a long time since she'd felt this way about any man.

A long, long time.

The sun blazed low in the sky as the two lovers peeled their naked bodies apart and began to pull their clothes on. Through the field glasses he had watched the two of them, Shiloh Silva and Beau Tate, mating like pigs in spring at their favorite spot by the river where they thought they were hidden from view.

Wrong.

Sunday was supposed to be a day of rest, but they'd gotten their rocks off. He'd gotten off too, but barely. The new girl was too young and inexperienced. Stiff as a board and always whimpering like a puppy.

His cock hardened at the memory of Courtney.

She'd had a reputation, that girl, but it had been all talk. She hadn't known what to do with a man at all. But he'd taught her. He'd taught her good. Her body had ripened into a fine specimen of a woman, with round breasts and hands that he'd trained to service him. She'd learned where to stroke and when to let go, schooled her in all the tricks of a whore, things no decent woman should know. With Courtney, he had been able to get it all out, all the rage and roaring sexual desire that drove him stir-crazy when it was pent up inside.

And he'd loved her husky voice when he prodded her to say, "Only you can do it for me, Lover."

Damn, but he missed her. He'd actually teared up when he found her body; getting soft as an old hag, he was. He'd had to get rid of the body, and his plan had been to burn her remains, remove any trace of possible DNA he might have left on her. But the damn fire starter hadn't sparked, and he'd run out of time, and now he was fucked if they found something that would give him away. Maybe the gasoline would destroy evidence. He'd even gone so far as to put some inside her.

But it was all wrong anyway. The police were beating bushes and buzzing through the sky in their helicopters like pesky overgrown insects, but they didn't get it. They kept saying she'd been murdered, but it wasn't true. He would have never killed her. Killing wasn't his thing . . . as a rule. Sure, he'd killed once, but only because he had to. That bitch had tried to *kill him*, so he'd had to stop her. That was the one and only reason. Well, that and the fact that she planned to run home to tell the cops everything. RIP, little bitch.

But she was gone too. Long gone. And now clumsy, simpering Addie was a poor substitute.

He needed another. A ripe, experienced woman.

Shiloh Silva would fit him just fine. Or Ruth Baker . . . but with Shiloh back in town . . .

She could teach the younger one a thing or two, bring her from an awkward filly to a galloping mare. He'd had two at the same time before. Double the pleasure. And he had no trouble handling them.

Thinking of her caused his cock to go hard, despite the pounding he'd given Addie earlier.

He needed more.

He wanted Shiloh, the wild girl. She owed him for leaving a wound on his flesh, the little bitch. He would tease her and pin her and give her more of a pounding than Beau Tate would ever deliver. He would get her, and good.

Soon enough, she'd get her invitation. After that, it was just a waiting game until he could pounce on her when she was alone.

Just a matter of time.

Chapter 15

"That's the latest news, right there." Jimmy Woodcock motioned Ruth to come around his desk so that she could see the monitor he was turning her way.

Although she had been avoiding the office of the *Prairie Winds* for weeks, Ruth's encounter with Woodcock at the diner had reminded her that it was high time to buy advertising for the rape hotline in his newspaper and on his media website. This shell of a storefront with a handful of abandoned desks was emptied of full-time reporters and photographers after the last economic downturn had hit town, and she found it a little creepy that Jimmy worked in a desk set at the dark back of the cave. Reluctantly, Ruth came around behind him and squinted at the screen to avoid getting too close to him. Although Woodcock was smooth and attractive in a lost cowboy sort of way, something about him repelled her.

Her jaw dropped at the headline: COURTNEY PEARSON 15-YEAR SEX SLAVE.

It was a confirmation of the fear that had shadowed her all these years. There was a brutal predator out there, and he was a monster.

Woodcock pointed to the screen. "The police think Courtney spent the last fifteen years as a prisoner. Someone's sex slave, right here in our own backyard. Ha!" He swiveled his chair toward Ruth, causing her to take a step back. "That's a story if there ever was one."

"That's absolutely horrific." Ruth found his enjoyment despicable.

"A terrible thing," he agreed, "but tragedy sells papers. I was just polishing off this draft to get it online. I'll fill out the story for tomorrow morning's edition of the paper."

"What are the police basing their theory on?"

"Some wounds and long-term scarring around the wrists and ankles. The girl was kept shackled up. Some malnutrition, too. Some of her teeth went bad." He shook his head. "Did you know her, back in the day?"

"I knew who she was. She seemed so tough and determined. When she disappeared, I wanted to believe that she went to Vegas or Dallas and found the excitement she craved."

"Well, isn't that a sunny point of view," he said with a flirtatious grin.

Ruth frowned, kicking herself for opening up to him at all. "That's highly disturbing news, but I stopped in for something else. I tried to book some advertising on your website, but I couldn't find any way to do it."

"Yeah, well, we're not as tech savvy as those bigger

papers over in California. It's just me here at the helm. But I can do that for you. Have a seat," he said, turning his computer monitor back toward the corner as she sat down on a hard wooden chair and found the notes in her bag.

"I want to run some advertising for my hotline." She handed him a typed sheet with the details, and they discussed the logistics. When he gave her the price, she bit her lower lip.

"Any chance you could do it as a donation? We're a non-profit, and need to keep our overhead low. Doc Farley is donating his service, and I'm not compensated for my time."

He was shaking his head. "Sorry. I'm a businessman, not a philanthropist."

"Then how about a discount?"

"I'll think on it and get back to you." He found a pen amid the cluttered mound of papers, protein bar wrappers, and dirty mugs that consumed his desk. "What's your cell phone number?"

She reluctantly gave it to him. She'd rather not, but this was business.

He punched her number in on the keyboard and clicked a few items. "There we go. I'll text you the information. In the meantime, let me get you a printed form." He rose from the computer, stroking his mustache. "I think they're in the back. Hold on." He grabbed something from a shelf in the hall and continued into the darkness.

As he disappeared into the dank, narrow hallway, Ruth got out of the chair and paced toward the front of the office, eager to get out of there. She had appointments, and her instincts told her that it wasn't wise to be alone with Jimmy Woodcock. There was something feral about him, like a hungry animal ready to snap. Was it any surprise that all these desks were empty? This man did not breed employee loyalty.

"Jimmy?" she called, walking toward the back. "I need to get going."

No answer.

She moved toward the hallway and listened. There was a whirring sound. A bathroom fan?

A narrow shelf that lined the hallway was stacked with magazines. She assumed that they were some sort of reference material for the newspaper, but a provocative cover at the top of the stack caught her eye. Moving a bit closer, she was glad she hadn't touched any of them. The shelf was filled, floor to ceiling, with pornography.

Her pulse was hammering in her ears, her senses on alert. Maybe she was being overly cautious, but she had learned not to ignore these warnings. Fear was a gift, instinct a guidepost.

Time to leave.

As she turned toward the door, she caught a glimpse of Woodcock's computer monitor displaying a photo of a well-endowed brunette with her legs spread. The next photo was a blonde in an even more compromising position.

Her throat knotted as beads of sweat broke out on her brow. A porn screen saver?

What a guy.

Without another word, she escaped to the heat of the street, grateful for her instincts.

* * *

The first client of the day was a referral from Doc Farley, a sullen fortyish woman named Maureen Everly. She sat down on the couch without a smile, her hair tied back and concealed under a cowboy hat with a long scarf trailing behind her.

"Would you like to take your hat off?" Ruth offered.

Maureen declined. It turned out that the hat was covering her dirty, badly matted dark hair, which had been neglected for weeks. "It's embarrassing, but I can't get to it," Maureen admitted. "I can't get anything done. I can barely get out of bed in the morning, let alone get anyplace on time." Soon after she began talking, tears began to roll down her cheeks.

Ruth handed her a box of tissues and listened.

Maureen had lost her job and friends, and what little family she had was on the verge of disowning her. "My mother was the one who made me come here. She got together with Doc Farley and tricked me. Told me the appointment was an hour ago so I'd be on time. I hate being tricked."

"I understand that, but your mom was just trying to help." Ruth talked about the need for a few sessions to introduce Maureen to Cognitive Behavioral Therapy. "CBT is a process, but in a nutshell, it gives us a chance to change our behavior to improve our mind-set."

Through her tears, Maureen agreed to give it a try, and she would start by keeping a journal of her daily moods, diet, and sleep patterns. Before she left, Ruth gave her a worksheet on unhelpful thinking styles, such as jumping to conclusions and all-or-nothing thinking. She also made a note to check with Doc Farley about prescribing antidepressants.

Maureen was still crying as she went to the door. "Tears of relief," she said.

"Crying is a part of healing," Ruth told her, giving her a few tissues for the road.

In the reception area, Ruth closed the door behind her patient and considered Maureen's treatment plan. If Maureen stayed in therapy, she had a chance to transform her life.

Just as I transformed mine, Ruth thought, recalling Dr. Boden, the therapist who had pulled her out of the pit of fear. And one of the first things she had told Ruth was that crying was a part of healing.

Ruth went to the window and watched the woman maneuver gingerly across the street. It was people like Maureen who reminded Ruth of why she had come home. Ruth could make a difference here.

She wanted to stay.

As long as Prairie Creek was a safe place to raise her kid.

Right now, she knew that Debra and Jeremy Donovan did not believe it was safe, and she couldn't blame them. But she would do her best to help them through this difficult time. And any information she could extract from them would come in handy in her profile of Addie's kidnapper. No, Kat and the sheriff's office hadn't asked her to be involved, but she had been pulled in fifteen years ago when a monster pinned her to the ground.

*   *   *

"Hurry, Mom! Can you drive a little faster? I can't wait to meet my horse!" Penny was bobbing in the car seat as the car trundled down the long road leading to the Dillinger barn.

"Yeah," Jessica seconded, craning her neck to look out the front window.

"Patience. We're almost there." Ruth had budgeted an hour between sessions to deliver the girls to the ranch and get them started on their lessons, and she was glad to be able to be a part of the process instead of handing the task off to her mother.

As they walked up to the barn, the place seemed fairly deserted but for a black Lab resting in the shade and two horses that seemed to get taller and taller as Ruth approached them. "These don't look like ponies," Ruth said aloud.

"Wow!" Penny exclaimed. "They're ginormous!"

Enjoying her daughter's amazement, Ruth looked for their instructor. "Hello?" she called through the barn as the girls stood on the rail of the fence, admiring the horses. "Anyone here?"

"I'm here." A lean, twentyish woman with ginger hair emerged from the shadows and strode to the horses without looking at Ruth. She went to one of the horses, checked the saddle and tightened the belt under its belly.

"We're here for a lesson. That's Jessica and this"— she placed her hands on Penny's shoulders—"is my daughter Penny."

"I'm Kit."

"We're really excited to learn how to ride," Penny said.

When Kit didn't respond, Jessica asked if the horses had names.

"Kaspar and Strawberry."

"Strawberry!" Jessica rolled her eyes. "What kind of name is that?"

Again, Kit didn't answer, and Ruth realized that small talk was not her thing. Kit had a wild, edgy look about her. With a smattering of freckles across her face and fiery red hair braided behind her back, she had a youthful body that seemed honed by hard work and time outdoors. Judging by the way she avoided eye contact, Ruth wondered if she was on the spectrum for autism, which would not prohibit her from being an effective teacher, in any case.

"I assume you'll bring the girls back here when the lesson is over," Ruth said.

"You'll have to ask Rafe. He's their teacher."

Ruth glanced past the saddled horses to the paddock area. "Where is he?"

"On his way over. He just ran up to the bunkhouse for a minute."

"Okay. I guess we'll wait," Ruth said, heading over to the corral to keep the girls company.

Ten minutes later, there was still no sign of the teacher. "You know, it's getting late, and this is cutting into their session time."

"Yeah, I know." Kit stared at the horse she was grooming. "Just tell Rafe."

"I would if he were here. I'll take the girls to find him."

"Suit yourself."

"What does he look like?"

Kit shrugged. "A little older than you. A Dillinger cousin."

"Wait. Rafe Dillinger?"

"Yes. You can talk to him direct. You pay him too."

The image of a nasty, spitting cowboy seared Ruth's mind as she tried to remember the young man who had blazed a trail of trouble back in high school. He'd been a few years ahead of her, but everyone knew of Rafe. He'd been questioned by investigators when Courtney disappeared because he'd been her boyfriend at the time. With numerous arrests and a rowdy reputation, Rafe was not an appropriate choice for an instructor of two eight-year-old girls.

And now Courtney was dead, held prisoner for fifteen years!

Ruth took a deep breath to calm down. She didn't want to give Kit a hard time, but Rafe was not going near her daughter, and she didn't want to disappoint the girls. "Is there someone else who can do the lessons?"

"Rafe's gonna be their teacher."

"What about you?" Ruth asked. "I'll bet you're an excellent rider."

"I don't teach. Rafe's on his way from the bunkhouse."

The sound of approaching horses had them both turn toward the trail that led from the foothills, where three riders were coming in.

"Is that Rafe?" Ruth asked.

"No. That's another lesson."

When Ruth held up a hand against the glare of the sun to see the riders, she let out a laugh. "You're kidding me."

The other teacher was Ethan Starr.

"Okay, Kit. I'll need to talk to your boss, or whoever oversees the lessons because we need another
teacher. Rafe Dillinger is not an appropriate teacher
for eight-year-old girls—or any kids, for that matter."

"Davis went in to town. He's the boss. He'll be
back this afternoon."

"Well, maybe we'll have to reschedule this lesson
for tomorrow until we can get everything straightened out."

"Mom?" Crestfallen, Penny shook her head so
hard her ponytail whipped around. "No!"

"Pumpkin, I'm trying to work this out, but if that
doesn't happen, there's always tomorrow."

The little girls moaned at the possible disappointment and went over to watch Kit untether Kaspar
and move him out of the sun. This time, Kit answered their questions, and Ruth was glad to see her
engage, even if bluntly. The dog shook itself from
sleep, took a few licks from the watering trough, and
joined the girls.

Ruth watched as Ethan and his students rode in.
The students were teenaged boys, and they were
laughing together as they approached the stables.
She waited in the shade of the barn as he finished
with the guys, then ambushed him as he headed
away smiling.

"Okay, Starr. I'm throwing myself and two eight-
year-old girls at your mercy."

"Ruth." He paused to take her in, his blue eyes
glimmering. "I knew you couldn't be serious when
you blew me off yesterday."

"I didn't blow you off, and watch out for big ears.

I'm here with my daughter and her friend, who've been promised riding lessons. But it turns out their teacher is supposed to be Rafe Dillinger."

"I see." He tipped back his Stetson. "Is Rafe giving you a hard time about switching?"

"He's a no-show. But Kit doesn't give lessons, and Davis is in town. I'm wondering if—" Just then the pounding of horse hooves indicated that someone was coming. They both turned to see a gray gelding galloping in at breakneck speed.

With broad shoulders and head held high, Rafe cut a fine figure on his horse.

Until he slouched to the side and nearly fell out of the saddle, catching himself at the last minute. Drunk, Ruth realized.

"Aw, man. Rafe." Ethan moved toward the listing cowboy. "You're in bad shape."

"I'm fine and dandy." Rafe's words came out in a low, slow drawl.

"You're drunk. You can't come to work that way."

"It's not the first time, and it's not gonna be the last." Rafe removed a pack of cigarettes from the folded cuff of his T-shirt, struck a match on the wooden rail of the fence, and lit one. In his dusky blue shirt, jeans, hat, and boots, he could have modeled for *American Cowboy* magazine. Except that his arms were thick with hair. And his fingers . . . short, stubby fingers pinched the cigarette.

Fear clawed at Ruth, squeezing her in a tight fist of panic.

Wide girth, furry skin, thick hands.

No. It couldn't be.

She backed up into a bale of hay, the bristly fiber forcing her to stop as it poked into her white linen dress pants. Calm down. Deep breath. Feet solid on the ground. She ignored the sweat beading on her upper lip and brow, swallowed back the fear rising in her throat as she stood strong and stared into the face of the beast.

"You've got a lot of nerve coming here," she said.

Rafe didn't seem to hear, though he straightened and squinted toward the corral. "Where the hell are the students? Got to give a god-damned lesson."

"The students are kids," Ruth said, trying to tamp down her panic and fury, "and you're not going near them."

"Shit. Who's this bitch?" Rafe swung around and locked a searing gaze on Ruth. "Hey, I know you." He gave a laugh. "The minister's daughter. Sorry, darlin'. I didn't mean to fuck with an angel."

Chapter 16

Ruth gasped at the crude comment. It was just an expression, wasn't it? As he loomed closer, pinning her with his lewd grin, she shrank against the wall of the barn and wondered if he could have been her attacker.

Even if he wasn't the one, the potential for danger was there, setting every nerve in her body on edge. Adrenaline coursed through her veins, imploring her to rush over to the corral, grab her daughter, and blaze a trail out of town.

But she couldn't run from the question: *Did you rape me?*

She wanted to ask, to prod Rafe for a confession, but he was too drunk for a reliable answer, eyes rolling shut as he took a heavy drag on the cigarette and then stumbled back, groping in the air for the fence.

Ethan lunged forward and grabbed Rafe by one arm, yanking him back onto his feet. "You're going back to the bunkhouse. Get some coffee or sleep it off. Whatever you need to do. Just get the hell out of here."

"Get your hands off me," Rafe growled. "I can walk just fine."

"Then go," Ethan said, pushing him back toward his horse.

Holding her breath, Ruth watched as Rafe stumbled off. After he managed to heave himself into the saddle, he raised his head and trained his simmering gaze on Ruth. Putting two fingers up to his eyes and then pointing out to her, he pinned her with a hateful look. "I've got my eyes on you, girl."

Silence overcame Ruth and Ethan as they watched him gallop off.

"What do you think that meant?" Ruth asked, pressing the back of one hand to her sweaty upper lip.

"He doesn't know what he's saying. That's the whiskey talking."

Was it? Rafe's anger had rough edges and muscle, the kind that pummeled another man unconscious in a barroom brawl. And if he directed that fury toward a woman . . . she didn't want to think of the consequences.

Or the fact that he knew her name. How had he known? Had he been watching her? Or was he her attacker?

She wished she could share her fears with Ethan, fill him in about the trauma that had sent her running from home, but that was not going to happen, especially with her daughter yards away, wondering about her riding lessons.

"Are you okay?" Ethan was noticing her damp skin and lightning nerves.

"I'll be fine." She tried to take on a joking tone as her crazed heartbeat began to slow. "You know, being in my profession, I expect to counsel some people who are on the edge. But this town seems to have more than its share of them."

He cocked his head to one side. "Been that kind of morning?"

"Don't get me started. Let's just say that I'm going to start making a list of these characters."

"Keeping a scorecard?"

"Definitely. My roster of people who have a screw loose."

"A screw loose? Did you attend the Three Stooges School of Therapy?"

"I'm just saying, we've got a disproportionate psycho population in Prairie Creek."

"That's a topic for later discussion, which I'd love to have over coffee or a beer sometime," he said, looking over at the girls. "For now, let's see if we can salvage a riding lesson."

On Tuesday afternoon, Shiloh swallowed the last of her iced tea and pressed the cold, damp glass to the crook of her elbow. It was hotter than hell in this house.

Beau had to drive over to Jackson for tractor parts, so Shiloh decided to delay her grocery run into town. Neither she nor Beau wanted to leave their younger sister alone for too long now that Addie Donovan had gone missing in the prairie beyond their back acres.

If the sorrow of losing her mother wasn't enough for Morgan, the fear of a kidnapper out there and the discovery of a corpse in the hills bordering the ranch had been a real kick in the ass—for her and for all of them.

Morgan buried her grief and fear in discontent. "There's nothing to do here," she complained as she flopped down at the table in a bathrobe, with hair wet from the shower.

"I didn't hear you saying that this morning when Beau and I were mucking the stalls," Shiloh pointed out. "Oh, that's right. You were still in bed."

"Because I was up late, talking to Ayla."

"You going to the pool with Ayla today? It's a scorcher."

"She has to watch her brothers."

"What about Sandi?"

"I told you, she's got summer school every day."

"Well, if you get dressed, we can go for a ride."

Morgan took a sip of milk. "Maybe later."

"Now would be better. You need to get out of here. I'll get the mail while you get ready." Leaving Morgan in the kitchen, Shiloh rousted Rambo and headed down the long drive to the mailbox. Her thoughts were on Beau—and decidedly pornographic. Her brain was on a track, recalling every detail of their coupling, his body, her soaring desire, the smell and taste of him . . .

With an effort, she dragged her thoughts back to the present. She and Beau had been piecing together her mother's fiscal life, and so far the outlook had been better than Shiloh had expected, with just a two-thousand-dollar credit-card debt that would be covered by Faye's small life insurance policy. When the last of the bills came in, one of the things on her list was to get this smashed-up mailbox replaced. She reached inside and took out a stack of mail that seemed to be mostly junk mail. Hallelujah.

When Shiloh returned to the house, she was bothered to find her little sister parked on the couch in front of some reality show. In the days since they'd stumbled on that corpse out on the range, Morgan had barely budged from the house.

Leaving the mail on the kitchen counter, she stepped into the living room. "You're not dressed, and it's hotter than the bowels of hell in here. How can you stand it?"

Morgan scraped her wild red hair back into a high ponytail. She moved slow and cool like a cat, but the sheen of sweat on her face was a dead giveaway. "I'm watching my show."

Hands on her hips, Shiloh stared at the girl freaking out on the TV screen. "That one is a spoiled brat."

"She's upset because Brandy is trying to steal her boyfriend."

"Yeah? Well, any boy that can be stolen isn't yours in the first place," Shiloh said, surprised at the words of wisdom slipping from her mouth. This responsibility thing was really getting into her psyche. "Come on, let's move. Turn this thing off and take the horses out." Without waiting for a response, she snapped off the TV and put the remote on a high shelf. "Get dressed, and don't forget sunscreen and a hat. You don't want to get burned."

"I don't know why we're going out when it's even hotter out there," Morgan muttered.

"The breeze sure beats this hot box."

Half an hour later, they left the ranch atop two horses that seemed just as eager as Shiloh to get away. Morgan didn't seem relieved at all by the change in venue, but at least she hadn't fought it.

"I'm not going near those hills again," Morgan said, lifting her chin toward the direction where they'd discovered the body.

"Fine by me. There's plenty of land to roam out here. And here's the thing about riding. You never go out without either Beau or me, you hear me? Never. And don't let any strangers in the house, either."

"You know I won't."

"Good."

"Do you think the person who did that to Courtney is going to kill Addie too?"

The raw fear in Morgan's voice made Shiloh's jaw clench. Fear was a terrible thing for a kid; she knew that firsthand. "I sure hope not. Maybe Addie went off on her own."

"Everyone is saying there's a kidnapper out there."

"Who's everyone?"

"All my friends have been texting me."

"Look, it's good to be cautious in the world. We need to live smart. Watch over each other and be responsible. That's all."

They rode in silence for a while, and Shiloh felt herself lulled into the clear communication between woman and horse, a bond as solid as the tumbling prairie that stretched from here to the purple rock and black shale of the Wind River Mountains. It was her bliss, to be in step with these big animals. Horses had gotten her through terrible times; they were always there to carry her away from the pain, and she wanted a chance to show her sister just what a magical relief that could be, even if just for a short time.

Suddenly, Morgan broke the silence. "I can't get that disgusting *thing* out of my head."

Shiloh grimaced. "It's awful all around. I'm sorry you went through that. My fault. One of us should have stayed back at the house with you."

"Why do you and Beau keep saying that? I'm not a baby."

"It's our job to take care of you now."

"Yeah. That means making dinner. But it doesn't mean you can boss me around."

Shiloh felt a chuckle at the back of her throat. It was good to have the old Morgan back again. "Beau and I are gonna steer you right, and that might involve a lot of bossing around. And as for dinner?" She held a hand up against the amber sun, low in the sky. "You're going to have to help."

"That's so unfair. Who do I get to boss around?"

"I'm sure Rambo would let you teach him a few new tricks."

As they headed back to the house, Morgan's snort of annoyance was somehow reassuring. Maybe Shiloh and Beau had a shot at doing this right. She hoped so. With their little sister's future in their hands, they couldn't afford another screwup. That meant keeping her safe from whatever bastard was out there torturing women like Courtney Pearson and making young girls like Addie Donovan disappear.

Back at the barn, they tended to the horses and decided on hamburger hash for dinner. Shiloh set Morgan up at the kitchen counter, chopping onions and tomatoes as she sat down to sort through the mail. A farrier's bill for two hundred and ten dollars for shoeing two horses and a gas bill for eighty dollars. Not too bad.

A slim golden envelope caught her attention, mostly because it had no address or postmark on it, though her name was printed on it in block letters. It must have been hand-delivered.

She opened the flap and found a single sheet inside—a black-and-white photo of . . .

Three naked girls.

What the hell? Biting back a curse, she snatched up the photo and strode into the next room before Morgan noticed.

It had been taken at night, eerily lit by an old-fashioned flash camera. There she stood in all her sixteen-year-old glory, breasts perky, arms lifted as if trying to capture the balmy night air. Her eyes were narrowed in suspicion, and for a moment she tasted that same fear that had rippled up her spine that night.

The photographer had caught her alongside Ruth and Kat, standing on the dock that hot summer night fifteen years ago.

The night Ruth had been raped.

And now—fifteen years later—the monster had *hand-delivered* this photo to her mailbox? A shudder ran through her at the knowledge of nearby danger. Like the adrenaline that shot through you when you realized you'd escaped death by a mere fraction of an inch.

The bastard was out there, watching, and he wanted something from her. Fifteen years she'd been away—fifteen!—and he was still trying to get a piece of her? The man was a pure psycho.

Shoving the photo back into the envelope, Shiloh grabbed her cell phone from her back pocket to call the sheriff and then paused. Crap. Anything she told them would give up Ruth's secret.

She was stuck—a walking target. And he was out there, a predator waiting to pounce. Setting her teeth, she marched out to the porch and shoved the photo under a stack of her clothes. Nothing she could do about it right now but stay safe and keep an eye on Morgan.

Kat, she thought. She could give the photo to Kat . . . may-be . . . but later . . .

But for now she would watch out for her little sister like a mother bear. And if this psycho came anywhere near them, her claws would emerge. She would rip his head off.

The air-conditioner in the window of Ruth's office made a churning noise as it struggled to cool off the room. The bright blue Wyoming sky and hundred-degree temperatures outside did nothing to brighten the sad conversation taking place within. Debra explained that her husband, a stoic, refused to come along because he didn't go in for counseling. "He's one of those who thinks you suck it up and handle your own problems."

Ruth assured her that she understood. "People work through a crisis in different ways. But you're here, and I give you credit for taking steps to help yourself. Let's talk about what you've been going through."

"The first few days, everything was about the urgency of finding her." Addie Donovan's mother, Debra, stared at the floor as she wrung her hands, picking at her cuticles and squeezing her fingers until they turned white. "The search consumed us, day and night. I kept thinking we would find her huddled by some boulders on the ridge or at the edge of a stream. Addie's an excellent rider, but anyone can get thrown, and I couldn't stop picturing my little girl unconscious and"—her voice cracked with despair—"bleeding somewhere. All alone."

Ruth nodded sympathetically, following Debra's every word but giving her space to tell her story.

"It was as if I could see her looking at the sunset and calling for us to come rescue her." Debra pressed her eyes closed for a moment. "It was horrible. Three days of constant panic as we searched. And then, when the sheriff widened the search, Jeremy asked me to stay back at the ranch in case . . . just in case, somehow, she came home to us. That's when the panic gave way to the sickening realization that someone had kidnapped our girl. She's out there—*I know she is*—but he's got her."

"Who do you think has her?"

"Some depraved man. Addie is adorable, and she has a very mature body. God blessed her with ample bosoms that—well, you probably know how men can be."

"Is there someone you suspect of taking her? Someone with a grudge?"

Debra shook her head. "I spent a lot of time crying at the house, trying to think of anyone who'd feel wronged by her. I thought of her teachers and friends. Maybe someone she babysat for, or one of our workers at the feed store. She's worked there part-time for years, so lots of people in town know her from seeing her behind the register. But the truth is, Addie is a good kid. She's not in the popular crowd at school, but she does have friends. And none of them can think of anyone who had it out for her. So now it's just a waiting game to see if—if someone comes forward and asks for ransom or—" She pressed a fist to her mouth, but a sob escaped, and her eyes filled with tears. "I'm sorry. I thought I was all cried out."

"It takes a lot of crying. Tears are a normal part of the trauma you're going through."

"I'm trying to stay strong, but sometimes I can't hold them back," Debra said, reaching for some tissues.

"They're not a sign of weakness. They're an important part of the process."

"I just want this to be over," Debra cried. "I want Addie back. If only I hadn't worked late that night. I would have been at the house, at least. I would have been closer. Maybe . . . maybe if he saw my car at the house, he would have stayed away . . ." She talked more about the past few days, the endless rides over their property and bordering lands. The repeated interviews her husband and son had sat through with people from the Sheriff's Department and the county and state police. Deputies and detectives traipsing through the house, sipping coffee and using the phone because their cell service failed out on the range.

Ruth steeled herself to counsel Debra, but inside she wanted to cry. Losing Penny would be her worst nightmare. All things considered, Debra was holding up well.

Debra didn't understand how Ruth could help her. "No offense, but I'm not going to pop any pills," Debra said. "Those prescription medications, that's a slippery slope."

"I can't dispense drugs." Although Ruth sometimes worked in tandem with a medical doctor who prescribed, she was glad that Debra did not want to go that route. "My job is to give you the tools to cope with this crisis, and the best way to do that would be to meet two or three times a week right now. Bring Jeremy if he wants to come. I can help you develop a vocabulary to describe your feelings. We can make a short-term plan to help you endure this period."

"What would that do?"

"Maybe you would plan to avoid someone at work who asks too many questions. Or you might add more rigorous exercise to your daily schedule to help you sleep at night."

"Things like that might help." Debra nodded.

"And we need to talk about the guilt and blame," Ruth said.

"We got plenty of that going around at our house."

"It's natural to blame yourself, but self-hatred is a destructive behavior. You need to stay strong for your girl, and your family," Ruth said. "Food and rest are important. And hope."

"I'll never give up hope," Debra vowed. "I won't give up on my girl."

Ruth gave a nod of encouragement, hoping that Debra's steadfast faith would be rewarded. She prayed that the deputies would find her daughter and bring her home soon.

Addie was baking in a huge oven, about to explode in a fireball, as he stoked the flames and tossed more wood onto the fire. Addie whimpered, wanting to give up, but knowing she had to try and stay alive for the people she loved: her mother and father and Dean. Even Gil—what she wouldn't give to see him again . . .

Her head lolled to one side, and her eyes slid open. The rough cot and the bare shack showed her that it was a dream.

Except for the heat.

It was hotter than hell in here. Suffocating. She pushed up with an effort, handcuffed to a chain and tethered inside a shack like a rabid dog, waiting to die. He'd brought her two buckets, one for water and one for waste.

She went to the water bucket and splashed her face, neck, and breasts. No worries about getting her clothes wet since he had taken her clothes away.

"You girls are so modest," he'd told her, staring at her breasts. "You're not gonna run off while you're naked."

Ya think? Just watch me, dickhead.

Addie worked at the cheesy handcuffs lined with pink acetate fur, twisting and tugging, trying to imagine a way to slip out of them. He disappeared for long blocks of time. He must have some kind of job that kept him busy, which she was grateful for, because otherwise she knew he'd spend even more time with her. She shuddered and looked down at her cuffs. They were causing blisters on the skin of her wrists. He'd bragged about them, saying she was the lucky one, that the other girls hadn't had it so good. The idea that she should be grateful for having fancy new handcuffs while the other girls hadn't just showed how crazy he was.

And what other girls? As far as she could tell, she was the only person stuck here.

Which could only mean two things: either the other girls had escaped, or they were dead.

Maybe they died in these very chains, their eyes on those windows up above, clinging to the light as hope drained from their bodies.

A whimper escaped her throat. *Mom and Dad, where are you?*

She sputtered and swiped water from her face with her forearm. These cuffs weren't going to slip off anytime soon, but maybe she could wear down the chains. She would have to find something hard to file them down, and it would take years.

She sniffed, and then bit her bottom lip.

Might as well get started now.

Chapter 17

"I've done some very bad things," he said in a voice laced with regret. "I hurt some women, real bad."

Ruth shifted in her chair, frowning. This didn't sound good at all.

It had been a relief when her client, fifty-three-year-old Hank Eames, finally agreed to face away from her on the sofa and remove his black Stetson. Straight on, the man was intimidating. This was his sixth session, and even facing away, he still made her feel uncomfortable, partly because of his constant cold glare, and partly because he fit the profile of her rapist with his wide, thick-fingered hands, large build, and arms covered by dense, dark hair.

Normally, Hank would not be someone she was interested in taking on as a client. In the past, he'd been a surly man, too much of a handful for Ruth, or so she thought. But Doc Farley had appealed to her desire to help. Since the tractor accident, Hank had lost the ability to drive himself long distances, and Ruth was the only therapist in town, and he needed help to get the basic functions of his life back on track. Furthermore, despite Hank's cold scowl, his injury had affected the aggressive tendencies he once had. He was not quite a lamb, but he was no longer a lion.

They had been working on coming up with varied menus that Hank could prepare, as well as a list of places he could go to get him out of the Prairie Dog Saloon at night. So far, he hadn't had great success with the second part, but some behaviors were difficult to alter.

"What do you mean, Hank? How did you hurt women?" she asked.

"Bad things. Like, maybe I tortured them. Maybe I came on too strong."

Ruth swallowed and called on her courage. "How did you torture them?"

His stubby fingers tapped nervously on the arm of the sofa. "You know . . . like tie 'em up and have at it."

"Sexually? Do you mean you raped women?"

"Wasn't really rape."

"You're saying it was consensual?"

Silence. Hank didn't have an answer.

The air in the room was suddenly icy cold, sending a chill down her spine as the air-conditioner rattled on, a constant racket that would cover up the sound if she were to scream. Moving silently behind him, Ruth shut the unit off and forced herself to take a breath in the subsequent stillness.

She worked to keep her voice steady, not wanting him to know that her heart was pounding in her chest. "What was it, Hank? When did this happen?"

"That's the thing I'm kind of foggy about. I mean, I'm not completely sure. Maybe I just saw it in a movie, or maybe I just thought about it. You know how that is, darlin'. Like fantasies."

"Stick to the rules, Hank. You can call me Ruth or Dr. Baker."

"Oh, yeah. Sorry 'bout that, but you know what I mean, right? Sometimes there's a fuzzy line between what you've done and what you wanted to do, and when you add in the accident for me, a lot of things before that time just don't make sense. This head of mine is like a dark, abandoned well. No telling what's been shoved down there."

Was he telling the truth, or toying with her? It wasn't the first time she sensed that Hank had retained more of his long-term memory than he was letting on, though it was hard to tell what he remembered and what he was fabricating from television shows or stories he'd heard. But damn it, she wanted to know if his guilt was based on reality.

"You know," she said, "there are treatments that might help unlock the memories. If they've been suppressed because of post-traumatic stress, memories may be retrieved through hypnosis or guided imagery."

"Really?" He shifted on the couch, casting his ravening gaze on her. "Can you do that for me?"

She angled her body away from him, trying not to feel pinned down by his stare. "It's not my specialty," she said, "but I'll look for someone in Jackson."

"I can't go that far. Can't drive anymore."

"I'll find a specialist who's willing to come here," Ruth said. She would pay the fees herself if it meant coming closer to unlocking the mystery of that night long ago.

Was she crossing a line of professionalism, now that she felt she might have a personal stake? Maybe. But the fact remained that she was the only therapist in town. Hank Eames needed help, and for now she was committed to helping him discover the truth.

Late Thursday night, Ruth was reading in bed when her cell phone rang—another call from the hotline. She was pleased to hear Lily's voice again.

"I was hoping you would call back," Ruth said. "Our conversation was so short. I didn't get a chance to tell you the different ways I could help you."

"I'm not calling for help. Nobody can help me more than I've helped myself by getting away."

"Distance can help facilitate healing," Ruth agreed. "I did that myself. Left Prairie Creek and went off to college and didn't come back for a long time."

"But I'm never going back anywhere near Prairie Creek."

"I'm not trying to pressure you to return," Ruth said.

"That's good, because it would be a lost cause. Like I said, I'm only calling you to warn you. I do Internet searches on Prairie Creek news every day. Kind of sick, I know, but it's the only way I can stay in touch with my home. When I read about Courtney Pearson and Addie Donovan, I had to warn someone."

Ruth stilled. "Do you have information about the crimes? Something the police should know?"

"I'm not calling the police, if that's where you're headed. The last thing I need is them tracing my number and dragging me back there."

"What's your warning, Lily?"

"There's a crazy man out there. He kidnaps girls and takes them to a cabin in the wilderness. Keeps them as his personal sex slaves. He did it to me, but I got away when . . . when I had the chance. I just know he kidnapped Courtney Pearson."

She sounded a bit belligerent, as if she felt Ruth wouldn't believe her.

"Did you see Courtney at the hunting shack?"

"No, but I just know it was him. He wants victims in his lair at all times. Once Courtney died, I'll bet he reeled in that high school girl, Addie Donovan."

Ruth shivered at the startling accuracy of Lily's theory. "May I share your warning with the police?"

"That's the point of me calling, isn't it?"

"I appreciate your courage in calling, Lily. Do you want to talk about ways I can help you?" When the young woman sucked in her breath, Ruth added, "Strictly over the phone. We can talk about different types of therapy, different ways to cope with trauma in your life. Ways to cope so that trauma doesn't hold us back from happiness."

Lily scoffed at that. "It's too late for me."

"It's never too late to try."

"I passed that road a long time ago. But I've got a kid, and she's the one I worry about. Well, not a kid anymore. She's in high school now, and she's a really good kid, but it'd destroy her if she found out that . . . that . . ."

"That she's a child of rape?" Ruth asked carefully.

The quick end to the call was all the answer Ruth needed. Lily had been pregnant when she'd escaped.

God bless her.

* * *

Although Ruth usually used Fridays to catch up on case notes and paperwork, today she dropped Penny with the grandparents for dinner and drove into town. It was the beginning of the holiday weekend, and she had agreed to meet Ethan at the Lazy L Café to discuss Penny's progress and the possibility of continuing lessons. With Kit as his sidekick, he had taken over the lessons for the week, much to the delight of Penny and Jessica, who had enjoyed their time with the two expert riders with very different personalities.

Although Ruth was meeting Ethan at the Lazy L Café, she drove past the restaurant and stayed on Main Street for five more blocks, pulling up in front of the dingy storefront that housed the *Prairie Winds*. She felt that Woodcock's inappropriate behavior the other day had to be addressed. A few phone calls had confirmed that this was no anomaly, and she had to call him on it.

She pushed her way in the door, and Jimmy Woodcock peered out from around his computer monitor as the old bells jingled.

"Ruth! You came back."

"Only to drop off the check for the ad," she said, marching into the office and holding up a printed page with a check clipped on to it. "Remember the ad? You were going to get me a flier or a form or something. But you got distracted."

"You pay full price?"

"You never gave me a discount," she reminded him coolly.

He waved that off like it was a bothersome fly. "Have

you heard the latest on Courtney Pearson? The forensic investigators don't think the killer took her eyes out. Get this: they think they were plucked out by buzzards."

"I'm not here to get your latest scoop. I wanted to pay for my ad and tell you that I know about your porn problem. Your screen saver. Your collection of magazines. You spending hours on end alone in this office with nothing to show for it."

Woodcock squinted, a half smile on his face. "You're crazy."

"I talked to Audrey Cartwright, your former secretary. Remember Audrey? The gal who was with the paper from the beginning when your father founded it? She told me she had to get out. She couldn't tolerate your behavior."

"She's an old bag."

"And your wife isn't too happy about it, either."

"Desiree? You called my wife?"

"I ran into her at Molly's when I was getting coffee." The truth was that Cordelia had tipped her off that Desiree came in every morning with the kids, but Jimmy didn't have to know that. "For the sake of the children, we had a discreet conversation, but she confided that you've promised to address your problem, many times, to no avail."

Woodcock's face hardened into a sour scowl, and he tugged at his beard. "Have you heard of privacy, *Ruthie?*" He said her childhood name as if it were a taunt. "I would think any worthwhile therapist would know a thing or two about giving people their space."

"I know socially unacceptable behavior when I see it, *Jimmy,* and I will not be a part of your dysfunction. Do yourself and your family a favor and find a twelve-step recovery program in Jackson. At the very least, get yourself a therapist to take you through some Cognitive Behavioral Therapy."

"I don't have a problem."

"Denial, Jimmy. Best-case scenario, you'll alienate your family and friends and community people like me. Worst case? A large percentage of rapists report looking at porn. Do you want to go there, Jimmy?" She stood her ground, hands on her hips as her eyes met his cold stare. "Or maybe you've already been there?"

His expression darkened. "I think you'd better leave."

"I'm going."

By the time she joined Ethan at a table in the window of the café, the tremble that had riddled her body had quieted to a shiver. The waning sunlight did nothing to penetrate the deep chill she felt at facing off with Jimmy Woodcock, but she was glad she'd done it.

Someone had to stand up to him.

As a mental health professional, a mother, and just a basic citizen, Ruth wasn't going to tolerate offensive behavior that objectified and devalued women.

"Hey, there." Ethan smiled up at her as she slid into the booth across from him, and the vestiges of the boy she'd crushed on years ago softened her brusque mood.

She had planned to stick to water, but the frosty mug in front of him sold her on beer. She pushed her sunglasses back on her head as the waitress headed off to get her drink. "What a day." It felt good to have a peer to talk with. "I just read Jimmy Woodcock the riot act."

He squinted. "The newspaper editor?"

"Editor and porn addict," she said.

"What?" He winced. "Sorry. It's not that I don't believe you. It's just the way you blurted it out, as if it's a club or a job title."

"I should probably be more sympathetic and supportive, but I am fed up with the men in this town. Present company excluded. The Prairie Creek I grew up in seemed to be a quaint town. Yes, there were a few quirky personalities. Some eccentrics and local color. But now that I see this place with adult eyes, I've encountered a handful of men who are significant threats."

"Here in Prairie Creek? We live in the safest town this side of the Wind River Mountains."

"It's pretty much the only town this side of the mountains, so that's not saying much. I'm not naïve enough to believe that anyplace is truly safe, but when I brought my daughter here, I wasn't expecting to find death and kidnapping. Courtney Pearson's body recovered after being held captive for fifteen years? And Addie's disappearance . . . these things are a mother's worst nightmare."

As she spoke, her eyes lit on two cowboys walking down the street, both wearing black Stetsons and sunglasses. Recognizing one of them as Rafe Dillinger, she slid her sunglasses over her eyes and held the menu up to cover the bottom of her face. "Speak of the devil. There's Rafe Dillinger, looking like he's on his way to The Dog."

"Probably because he is. Friday night out." Ethan glanced toward the window.

After the two men passed, Ruth stared after the second cowboy, who was the same height and build as Rafe. "Who's that with him?"

"Looks like Scott Massey. He's a trick rider. He was in the rodeo with me, but he works on the Kincaid ranch now, or he did. You'll probably see him performing at the rodeo exhibition on the Fourth."

"Are you going to be in the parade?" she asked, thinking of the times she'd seen him riding down Main Street atop a majestic horse.

"Not this year. I'll be behind the scenes, horse wrangling for the Dillingers. Someone's got to take care of the animals."

"That was a bad scene on Monday." Ruth thought back on it, Rafe falling down drunk and still taunting her. "Does Rafe blame me?"

"He's acting like it never happened. Davis has had him out riding fences, especially mornings when the girls are around. He hasn't been a problem since then, but he owes you an apology."

Ruth raked her bronze hair back. "I chewed Davis out for assigning a man like Rafe to teach eight-year-old girls."

Ethan nodded. "He felt bad about that, but he's between a rock and a hard place. One of the female riding instructors went off to teach at a summer camp, and the backup teacher is Addie Donovan."

"Oh. That's awful. He didn't tell me that."

"He didn't want to spook you, but he never should have assigned Rafe to the girls. Actually, I would have been uncomfortable taking the girls on without Kit along. You have to be careful when you work with children. It's best to be cautious, for everyone's sake."

"I agree on that. It's one thing to take some chances on your own, but when kids are involved, you've got to keep them safe." She looked up and thanked the waitress, who placed a mug of beer in front of her. "I worry about Penny. But I came here with a mission, and I think I'm making some progress. Do you realize that the closest mental health professional is in Jackson?"

"That's pretty far, though it's not surprising for a town this size."

"But Prairie Creek has grown, and it's growing still. People in this town who need therapy are going to go without because they can't make the trip. I'm here to change all that."

"You're moving at a pretty good clip. You've got your office set up next to Emma's dress shop, and your hotline is up and running. I heard about it at Molly's."

"I'm glad the word's getting out."

"Any calls yet?" When she nodded, he smiled, his blue eyes glimmering with light from the late-afternoon sun. "I wish you luck. And once school starts, I'll put the word out there. I have a pretty strong network of guys—mostly athletes—who come to me when they have issues. I'd like the girls to know there's someone they can turn to."

"Any way you can get my name out there, I'd appreciate it," she said, "and no woman should worry about paying for counseling. Chrissy Nesbitt, the mayor's wife, has convinced a charity to subsidize my services for clients in need."

"That's great, especially if this town is as crazy as you say." Only the glimmer in his eyes hinted that he was poking fun at her.

Sipping the cold beer, she took a moment to enjoy the glow she felt in his presence. Throughout the week, she had tried to stay low key, but she had found herself looking forward to the brief moments she spent with him when she went to the ranch to drop off or retrieve Penny. Maybe it was because they had both left Wyoming and returned, or maybe it was just meant to be. She'd spent years holding back, suspicious and wary of men, and now, back at the source of her trauma, she'd found a man who filled the air around her with magic and warmth.

There was still wonder in the world.

"What are you thinking about with that lazy smile?" he asked.

"I'm thinking that you're probably the only reasonable person left in this town. Besides me, of course."

He ran his fingers over the condensation on his mug. "Does that psychobabble mean you like me?"

She laughed, feeling a flush of embarrassment. It was so "high school," but then that was where it had started for her. "Well, yes."

"Good, because I like you too. I'm hoping you and Penny will stick around awhile."

Basking in the light of his eyes, she took another

sip of beer and promised him that they weren't going anywhere—even if Prairie Creek was riddled by threats.

"Who are these menacing figures you've encountered? If that's not confidential."

"One is a client, so I can't talk about that. Then we have one of my parents' neighbors—" She looked around to make sure none of the other early-dinner patrons were listening. "Calvin Haney. Do you know him?"

"Is he a member of our church?"

"He is. My mother says he's an upstanding citizen, but I like to think of him as Creepy Cal." She told him about the hose incident with the girls and Cal's subsequent suggestive remarks. "Then there's Jimmy Woodcock—you know about that. There's the client and, of course, Rafe Dillinger. You know that story."

"You've had more than your share of local color, but I have to say you're pretty perceptive about people. Why do you think they've targeted you?"

"I . . ." She couldn't tell him about the rape, although that was the source of her overriding caution. "I don't know. Just a hunch," she said with a shrug.

"What can I do to make your welcome back to Prairie Creek smoother?"

"You've already done a lot," she said, opening her menu. "I'd like to buy you dinner as thanks for jumping in on the riding lessons."

"That's a nice gesture, but no." He watched her intently. "I'm old school on some things. The guy pays for the first date."

So it was a date. Something young and hopeful

trilled inside her, and she looked down at the menu to mask her unadulterated joy. "Okay, thanks." She smiled up at him. "In that case, I'll have steak."

From the Prairie Dog Saloon, he stared out through the warped, nicotine-stained glass at Ruthie McFerrron, the little girl with the big, round tits. There she sat, smack in the window of the café, a sitting duck. Maybe he should go back to her because after a suck-ass week of following Shiloh Silva from hill to dale, he was ready for something new. Damn Shiloh. She wasn't the wild risk-taker she used to be. Now Beau Tate stuck to her like white on rice. She never went anywhere without him or the younger girl.

He was getting sick of sweating in the hot sun, his throat parched and gritty as he waited for the right moment to snatch up Shiloh. Damned tired. But maybe the waiting game was over.

Ruthie here was a woman alone. She lived with her daughter in a quiet area at the edge of town. Not even a dog to make things challenging. And her body was ripe and ready, with hips widened by childbearing, and those big, round plums with rosy nipples that would brush against him when he pinned her down.

Lifting the long-necked bottle to his lips, he let the cool liquid stream past his teeth as he willed his dick to behave for now. Finishing the beer with a grunt, he waved down the waitress and ordered another.

Just killing time.

* * *

That night, Ruth still basked in sweet recollections of her dinner with Ethan as she stood in the doorway of Penny's room and watched her daughter sleeping. Penny's small body was turned away, hugging her fluffy white dog, but the steady rise and fall of her shoulder was like a soothing mantra to Ruth.

Keep breathing.

Stay safe.

Stay alive.

Ruth's contact with her new clients, women like Lily and Addie's mother, had reinforced her purpose in coming back to Prairie Creek. And yet, at the same time, the close brush with crisis was a reminder that catastrophe struck every life at one time or another.

It wasn't a matter of if, but when.

Ruth's first priority had always been keeping her daughter safe. Now, with the knowledge that there was a kidnapper and a killer out there, Ruth had become hypervigilant. She would be Penny's shadow and protector until this sociopath was found.

A breeze passed through the upstairs, stirring Ruth's nightgown around her bare legs. The cool wind felt good after the evening thunderstorm that had broken the three-day heat wave. She blew her daughter a silent kiss and trod down the stairs barefoot to close and lock the windows for the night. As she pulled down the dining room window, something moved outside, stirring the branches of the tall yew that bordered the neighbor's fence.

She froze, listening as she stared into the darkness. An animal? When she was a kid, her mother had nurtured a hedge of flowering arborvitae that was visited by a family of raccoons at night. Shining the beam of a flashlight on their gleaming eyes, she had felt intrigued and frightened at the same time. Nonetheless, she would check the hedge in the morning to make sure that nothing was nesting near her house.

She was closing the living room windows when she heard a buzzing sound from the kitchen. Her cell phone was ringing on the kitchen table, and it was a call from the hotline.

With a deep breath, she tried to muster a calm, professional tone as she answered. "This is the Sexual Assault Support Line," she said. "My name is Ruth. How can I help you?"

No one answered.

She kept the phone pressed to her ear as she closed the kitchen window and walked back toward the front of the house.

"Hello?" she said, stepping out to the screened-in porch. The cool air brought goose bumps to her skin, and the cement floor felt gritty underfoot as she padded to the front door, double-checking the lock. Maybe that was silly, as a home invader could simply slice through one of the screens, but checking the locks and windows was one of her nightly rituals.

She moved quickly, frowning at the thick cedar trees across the street. Their branches seemed to be moving, too. Was it the wind?

There was still no answer on the line, but she sensed a presence.

She scurried back into the house, throwing the bolt on the main door with a sigh of relief. "I can hear that you're there," she said. "And I can't help you unless you talk to me."

Silence prevailed as she went to the front window of the house, pulled the window down and turned the lock. Staring out at the cedars, she saw the flimsy branches flicker and got the distinct impression that someone was there. When she finished with this call, she might want to call the police and report a trespasser, as the park was supposed to close at dark.

Then came a whispering whoosh—a heavy breath. Not the sound of a desperate woman, it had the heavy timbre of a male groan.

"Who is this?" she asked crisply.

Another raspy breath, more like a satisfied sigh. Some asshole enjoying her fear.

Then came a deep, low chuckle as, before her eyes, the cedars stirred and a dark figure appeared between the bushes.

Her breath caught in her throat as fear surged through her, ice water in her veins.

"I'm watching you, darlin'," he ground out in a sickeningly smooth voice as he stepped into the street. "You've grown into quite a woman since I had you last. I bet you've learned how to satisfy a man. Why don't you come on out and let me give you a good pounding?"

Her knees trembled as he stepped closer.

"You know I'm gonna get you."

Chapter 18

Panic surged through her as he began to cross the street.

No, no, no! How did he find her?

Feeling naked and vulnerable in the window, Ruth wrenched off the ties of the lace curtains, fumbled to cover the glass, and then sprinted up the stairs to her daughter's room.

Thank God, Penny was undisturbed, still asleep. She closed and locked the window, then ducked into the hall and struggled to dial 911 with shaking hands.

"Prairie Creek Dispatch," said a female voice. "What's the emergency?"

"Someone's outside. Someone . . ." Ruth tried to control the shrill panic in her voice. "He was threatening me."

"Your location?"

Ruth gave her name and address.

"Is he armed?"

"I—I don't know. I didn't see a gun."

"Is he trying to break in?"

"No . . . I don't think so, but he could."

"Stay on the line with me, ma'am, okay? I'm sending a car over."

"I will."

As she waited for Naomi to dispatch a deputy, Ruth pulled on a robe and closed the rest of the upstairs windows. In less than ten minutes, a Jeep from the Sheriff's Department pulled up quietly on the street outside. No lights or sirens, thank God. So grateful she wanted to cry, Ruth thanked the dispatcher and hung up. Then she unlocked the front door and stepped onto the screened-in porch.

The fit officer who jogged up the porch steps turned out to be the sheriff himself. With dark hair and a medium build, Sam Featherstone seemed young to be a sheriff, though his calm manner made up for lack of experience. "You called about an intruder?"

"He was in the trees over there, by the park." Ruth pointed to the park across the street and explained that the stranger had called her and made threatening remarks as he moved toward the house.

"So it's someone who knows you? He had your phone number?"

She explained that the man had called the hotline. "It had to be someone who knows I manage those calls."

"Can you describe him?" Featherstone asked.

"It was too dark. I only saw a profile emerging from the cedars."

He rubbed his chin thoughtfully, looking up and down the street. "We'll take a look around at the park and check the yard."

She thanked the sheriff, hugging herself against the cool night. Watching from the doorway as he clicked on a high-powered flashlight and began to check the bushes and shrubs, she realized the threat was long gone. The man would have been crazy to stick around once the sheriff's Jeep pulled up.

Hugging a mug of coffee, Ruth sat with her feet propped up on the sill of her bedroom window and stared at the glorious gold and orange of the sunrise. She had slid the big red chair around to face the window, not wanting to take her eyes off the tall, dark cedars.

On watch. On alert.

She had changed into terry-cloth shorts and an oversized Santa Barbara sweatshirt, just in case she saw something that sent her running out to the street. Which didn't make sense at all, as she would not leave her daughter alone in the house to run out and make herself a target. But sleep deprivation was wearing away at her logic.

Now, looking ahead at the Fourth of July weekend, she realized she needed a plan, a way to safely get her daughter through the next few hours and days without . . .

Without Penny knowing that a predator was watching her mom.

Without being vulnerable to attack.

If only she could whisk her daughter out of town for the weekend, back to California so that Penny could visit her dad or Disneyland. But a last-minute flight would cost a small fortune and a great deal of disappointment. Ruth and her mother had sold Penny on the events of the holiday weekend, beginning with the Lions Club pancake breakfast around two hours from now. People came from a hundred miles away to see the Fourth of July parade. Prairie Creek did it right.

Ruth yawned, raking her hair back with one hand. She hadn't slept at all last night, too afraid to close her eyes, but she couldn't stand guard at this window forever.

After the breakfast, the parade would overtake Main Street—a western-style parade with plenty of horses, cowboys and cowgirls, and American flags. Probably an old stagecoach and a surrey with the fringe on top, just like in the song. There'd be classic cars and local politicians. Maybe some guy dressed as Uncle Sam on stilts and another one dressed as Abe Lincoln. Half the kids in town would be riding at the tail end of the parade on bikes decorated with red, white, and blue ribbons and streamers.

Ruth would be sure to keep Penny at her side every single moment.

After dark, some people would head up to the ridge road to watch fireworks over the valley. Penny loved fireworks, but Ruth didn't think she could bear the feeling of vulnerability, surrounded by strangers in the dark.

On Sunday, everyone would head over to the fairgrounds for a barbecue, country music, and a rodeo exhibition—a taste of the events to come the following weekend when the rodeo came to town. Maybe she could talk Penny out of that part?

Either way, she couldn't go on like this.

She had to come clean with her parents, the cops, even with her kid. And she would have to tell Ethan everything . . . or as much as he wanted to know. Right now, any involvement with her was a liability, and she wanted to make sure he knew the risk before things went any further. Maybe he would want to back off.

She let out a groan as her head lolled back against the chair cushion. There were definitely going to be fireworks this Fourth.

It was time to talk to Kat. Time to get it out there. Everything that had happened. Her pulse raising, she called the non-emergency number Sheriff Featherstone had given her.

"I'm trying to reach Detective Starr. Kat Starr?"

"She's not in yet, but we're expecting her shortly. It's all hands on deck on a day like this. You want me to put you through to her voice mail to leave a message?"

Ruth hesitated. "No. No, thanks. I'll catch her another time."

She rose from the chair, stretching as she stared out at the bushes across the street. In the light of day, the landscape of the small park and the street of two-story homes seemed safe and tidy. Grabbing her robe, she headed into the bathroom for a quick shower.

On the short drive to her parents' house, Ruth brought up the topic. It was sort of the coward's approach, dropping the bomb during casual conversation in the car, but she hoped the relaxed atmosphere would get the message across without alarming Penny.

"You know that Mommy used to live here when she was in high school?" she began. "Back when I was a teenager, something bad happened. A man hurt me."

"What did he do?"

"Let's just say he was a bad guy, like Hans in *Frozen*." A turncoat villain.

"Mean and sneaky," Penny said.

"Exactly. He got away, and in my case the police never found him, so he wasn't punished."

"Oh. Are you mad at him, Mom?"

"I am, but mostly I want the police to find him." Ruth glanced at her daughter in the rearview mirror. Absolutely unfazed. "I just wanted to let you know in case you hear the police or my parents talk about it. Because they're still trying to catch the bad guy."

"Okay." This made sense in an eight-year-old world. Penny was cool. "I hope they catch him, Mom."

"I do too."

The outdoor pancake breakfast went well, probably because Ruth was too exhausted to talk much, which allowed her parents a chance to shine and show off their granddaughter to anyone who stopped by their table. Buoyed by coffee and pancakes, Ruth was beginning to feel strong enough to make it through the day when she spotted Kat Starr working with the security detail at the edge of the park.

She turned to Bev, who was talking to a mother of one of the other girls playing on the swings. "Stay with Penny for a minute, okay?" she asked.

"Of course."

Although her heart was thrumming in her chest, it

brought her some relief to think that this whole mess was spiraling to an ending. Soon the secrecy would be over.

Kat's petite frame seemed somehow substantial in her deputy's uniform. Her dark hair was tied back in a twist, adding to her intensity. She acknowledged Ruth and stepped away from the other deputy. "Ruth."

"I'm sorry I haven't returned your calls. I couldn't. I wasn't ready."

Kat accepted that. "The chief told me about your intruder last night."

"It was him," Ruth said under her breath. "The man who raped me. It was him." Kat frowned and seemed about to argue the fact, so Ruth rushed on. "I know that sounds paranoid, but he's after me." A sudden stab of emotion thickened her throat, infuriating Ruth. After all these years, she should be able to talk about her attacker without getting all choked up. "That was him last night."

"Could you identify him? Are you sure? It's been—"

"I know, fifteen years. Look, I can't talk right now, and . . . I don't mean to sound desperate, but maybe I am. The news about Courtney and Addie was bad enough, but now, to think that I'm a target . . . I'm going to put the truth out there, Kat. I've got to. I just need the weekend to tell my folks and . . ." Ruth was going to say "your brother," but she said instead, "Just another day or two, and then we'll talk. I don't know who it is, but I have a few ideas. I've been pro-filing and compiling a list of suspects."

"Ruth, that's our job. You don't need to do that."

"It's already done. I did it for my own protection—

for myself and my kid. I'm not just profiling my rapist. I'm thinking of the man who attacked Courtney and Addie too."

Kat glanced over at the children on the swings. "I'm glad to hear you agree there might be a connection. That's why I want you to go on the record about your assault. But don't jump to conclusions, Ruth. You're not working the investigation. There are facts of the case that you're not taking into account . . ."

"I'm dealing with it in my way, okay? I'll call you when I've got things settled at home, and then I'll come in and make a statement."

"Okay."

Kat sounded relieved, and maybe she was. Ruth flashed back to the girl Kat had once been, a respectful but stubborn kid who'd somehow had the good nature to let Ruthie tag along. Something about that goodness brought tears to Ruth's eyes now. If it weren't for the rape, they might have become good friends. If it weren't for the rape, well . . .

"When are you coming in?"

Ruth thought about trekking to the department and relating the story of her attack to Sheriff Sam Featherstone. A trickle of sweat ran down her spine. She'd counseled others to come forward, but it was never easy. "Soon," she said, bolstering up her flagging courage. "Soon."

She dropped her parents off after the breakfast, parked, and followed them inside.

It was now or never.

She settled Penny in the den, telling her that mom

needed some adult time with grandma. "Can I watch Nickelodeon?" Penny asked.

It was a special treat, as they did not have cable at home. "Sure."

With Penny tucked away, Ruth returned to the kitchen, where her mother stood at the sink.

"I'm making a pot of decaf," Bev said. "It's a long ways from here to the fireworks tonight. I may need a nap."

"A man was outside my house last night, threatening me."

"What?" Bev shut off the water and turned away from the sink.

"I don't know his identity, but I think it's the same man who attacked me one summer years ago, back when I was in high school."

"What are you talking about? You were never attacked."

"I was, Mom. I was raped, but I didn't tell anyone. I was embarrassed and afraid that you and Dad would be mad at me. That you would think it was my fault."

Her mother's hand flew to her chest. Hearing a noise, Ruth turned to the doorway and found her father standing there, his face void of emotion.

"Ruthie," he warned. "What are you talking about? Now, don't go exaggerating, like you do."

"It was rape, Dad," Ruth said evenly. "The night I snuck out. I'm not going to let you dismiss it and marginalize the trauma."

"Oh, Lord help us!" Bev cried, tears in her eyes.

"The night you snuck out," he repeated reprovingly. "Why are you telling us this today? With all your mother does for you, cooking for you and taking care of Penny, you seem to go out of your way to create problems."

Ruth struggled to keep the fury from her voice. "I just wanted to give you fair warning because I'm going to the police, and you know how gossip flies around this town."

"If it happened when you were in high school, why open this can of worms now?"

"Because someone came to my house and threatened me last night, and I think it was the man who attacked me. I need to tell the police the history so they can stop him before he hurts me again. Or Penny. Or anyone else."

"Now, wait. Let's not exaggerate," he said. "Who was this fellow?"

"I don't know. I hope the Sheriff's Department can find him."

"Can they deal with it in a discreet way?" Bev asked. "They don't have to put your name in the papers or interview you on television, do they?"

Ruth paused in frustration. She had expected her mother to be more supportive, but instead she was concerned with keeping a clean reputation. "They won't release my name, but people are going to figure it out. There are few secrets in a town like this."

She turned to her husband. "It's so unfair. People are going to be talking about us, Rob, saying we didn't raise our daughter right."

"Because I was raped?" Ruth asked in disbelief.

"Please." Her father sat down heavily at the table. "Stop saying that word."

"I know this is upsetting for all of us, but can we

please talk about damage control?" Bev wiped her hands on the dishtowel, tears in her eyes. "Your father and I shouldn't have to suffer embarrassment from something that happened ages ago. I say you just drop it, Ruth. Please, honey, let it go."

"And do nothing about a rapist who's still out there, watching my house? Possibly a danger to me and other women?"

"The sheriff can pursue this intruder from last night," her father said. "We need to stay out of it."

Bev was nodding. "Dad's right. Leave it to the sheriff to find this man. Probably just a burglar or some drunk going home to the wrong house."

"No need to bring up unpleasantness from the past," Rob agreed. "If you're struggling with it, offer it up to the Lord and get yourself some counseling, but don't inflict your personal problems on our community."

"That's right; that's the right thing to do." Bev let out a sigh of relief. "You're so good at managing these things, Rob."

As her parents went on some more about how a person needed to keep their problems to themselves, Ruth felt as if she were watching a scene in a farce. Their focus was on saving face, without a trace of concern for the terror and trauma Ruth had endured.

They don't care about me. They're making this all about them.

It hurt to realize the level of her parents' selfishness, but then again she wasn't surprised. They had never truly been her advocates. They hadn't noticed when the bottom dropped out of her world fifteen years ago, and they weren't looking out for her now.

I'm on my own.

The realization was liberating in some ways. No longer would she be tethered to getting her parents' approval for her life choices.

"Well, that just wiped me out." Bev pressed her fingertips to her temples. "The stress has gone straight to my head. I'm going to take a nap." She shuffled out of the kitchen, leaving the coffee unmade.

"I hope you've learned something here," Rob said. "You can't spring bad news on your mother like that. She's a strong woman, but she's worked hard to maintain a pristine reputation in this town. We both need people to think the best of us."

Ruth replaced the plastic lid on the coffee can and left the pot of water. Her father could make his own if he wanted coffee. "It must be a terrible thing, to care so much about what other people think," she said calmly. "I've learned to let that go, since you have no control over it."

She turned to her father, unafraid of the stern set of his jaw. "I've also learned that people of character judge you based on your actions, not your looks or social reputation."

He drew in a sharp breath. "It must be nice to be so free and breezy. Did you get that from California?"

"No, Dad. I got it from extensive therapy. You and Mom might want to try it sometime." She went to the door and paused. "I'm going to the police. Sorry to inconvenience you, but it's the right thing to do."

With one last look at the sour, uncompromising man he had become, she went off to retrieve her daughter.

* * *

Main Street was lined with folks dressed in red, white, and blue, some waving flags as the high school marching band strutted past playing "Yankee Doodle Dandy." In some spots, the crowd was three deep, and people were jammed up around rolling carts with vendors selling hot dogs, lemonade, ice cream, and popcorn. They had taken a spot at the heart of Main Street, where a wooden walkway lined the shopfronts— a throwback to the old western frontier towns. The swarms of people and activity seemed to thrill Penny, though Ruth couldn't help but suspiciously eye every man who crossed their path or bumped into them.

Is it you?

Are you the one?

It would be too easy to slip into paranoia, so she forced herself to remain objective. Nothing was going to happen to Penny or her in the light of day in front of the entire town. Safety in numbers.

But she sensed that he was here, watching, calculating.

Is it you? she wondered as Rafe Dillinger, decked out in full cowboy gear and a black Stetson, rode down the street waving at the crowd. His sunglasses covered his eyes, but she got the distinct impression he was staring at her, hating her.

Bone-achingly tired, Ruth took a deep breath and pulled Penny's clasped hand to her breast.

After the cowboys and cowgirls came a few trick riders from the rodeo, and the crowd gasped and applauded as Scott Massey seemed to slide off his horse headfirst, then turned his body and flipped back into the saddle. The trick-rider had a huge smile for the crowd, but his gaze seemed to catch Ruth, holding her in his sights as if he knew her.

He fit her memory of her attacker too. As she watched, he leaned down to a woman who was standing at the front of the crowd and clasped her hand. She tilted her head upward, and he managed to slide sideways and kiss her on the lips while still in the saddle, which elicited claps and hoots from the crowd.

Someone yelled, "That how you always kiss your wife, Massey?"

"Always," he called back, grinning.

"Mom, your hand is all sweaty," Penny said, extracting her own hand and wiping it on her shorts. "Do we have to hold hands?"

Forever and ever, Ruth thought. "Just stay close," she said as an ice cream vendor wheeled a cart close behind them. They had to press into the family in front of them to make room.

"Mom, can I please get a Popsicle? It's so hot, and they have cherry."

The red-hot sun dead overhead was unrelenting, and the close crowd made the street seem airless and oppressed. "That sounds great." She paid for two Popsicles and handed one to Penny. Hoping that the cool treat might chase some of the numbing exhaustion from her mind, Ruth worked on the Popsicle as she watched a handful of classic cars roll past. The sweet frozen treat eased the dryness in her throat, but it was gone too quickly.

"Mom . . . a little help, please?"

Ruth looked down and saw that Penny's Popsicle had dripped all over her hands. "Let me get a napkin." But the ice cream cart was long gone. Ruth glanced back toward the nearest store, Menlo's Market, just a few yards away. "Come with me."

"Noooo . . . I'm all sticky."

"I don't want to argue with you."

"Mom." Penny glared at her.

"Then stay right there."

Quickly, she ducked into the nearly empty store. She felt an immediate surge of relief at the cool air as she headed straight to the checkout counter to explain her problem. The older woman with a crooked front tooth, Pearl, handed her two paper towels, and she scurried back out.

Ruth burst out the door onto the wooden walkway and started toward her daughter . . .

But Penny was not talking with the little toddlers who had been watching the parade in front of them or holding her sticky hands up in the air. She was not straggling behind the rest of the crowd or waiting by the door of the store. Ruth looked right and left, but her daughter was nowhere in sight.

She was gone.

Chapter 19

"Penny?" Ruth called, trying to still her racing heart, to quiet the deafening roar of fear. Why had she left her alone? What had she been thinking? Oh God! Oh God! All the stories of children who had been snatched away from their parents and never returned swirled in Ruth's mind as she searched for her girl up and down the boardwalk in front of the market. Ruth had only been gone a minute, maybe two.

Oh no, oh no, oh no. Where was her girl?

"Have you seen my daughter?" Ruth asked the couple in front of her.

The woman turned around, baby on one hip, and shook her head. "The little girl with the red hair?"

"Yes!"

The mom shrugged. "She was just here."

"She went off with some man," said the husband, a well-muscled young man with a shiny, shaved head. "I think he was her uncle or something. He was giving her a hard time about dripping the Popsicle all over herself."

Ruth's heart stilled, but then a rush of relief. *Her grandfather!* "Was he tall with graying hair? Reverend McFerron?"

"I don't know who that is, but he wasn't gray. Younger than that." He pointed down toward the Stallion Barbershop. "They went that way, across the street so's she could wash up in the drinking fountain beside the horse trough."

The fountain—of course.

Ruth turned in that direction, but she couldn't see anything beyond the side street because of the food carts parked there and the people lined up around them. Her throat was dry, and perspiration dripped down her back as she hurried into the fray, bumping into people and cutting through lines. At one point she tripped on the edge of a stroller, banging her toe. She caught herself and hobbled on as a stern woman with a star-spangled T-shirt scolded her to take it easy.

There was no time to explain that her daughter was missing.

At last, she made it through the crowded side street and wove through the crowd on the wooden walkway. She had a rough idea where the fountain and trough were located, but she couldn't make them out in the throng of people, some lined up to watch the parade, others moving down the street in a stream behind them.

"Penny?" She pushed her way toward the fountain, telling people she was looking for her daughter. They moved aside, responding to her distress, but when she spotted the fountain, Penny wasn't there.

Fear welled in her throat as she turned away and

appealed to the crowd. "I'm looking for my daughter, Penny. She's eight, with bright red hair. Have you seen her?"

"I'm sure she's around here somewhere," an elderly man said, trying to reassure her.

No, she's not! Ruth wanted to snap at him, but she held her tongue and fished her cell phone from her pocket. Time to call the sheriff.

She was unlocking her phone when she thought she heard a thin voice calling "Mom!" Scanning the crowd, she spotted her: a tiny square of red T-shirt, pale face, and a hand waving her over.

Penny was next to a broad-shouldered man in jeans and a long-sleeved shirt. He was turned the other way, his head covered by a dark baseball cap. And he was pulling her away by the hand.

No. No, no, *no!*

Ruth lunged ahead, pushing through the crowd to get to her daughter. "Penny! I'm here!" Up ahead Penny turned back to her. The man shot a quick look back and then moved on.

A crazy pulse beating in her throat, Ruth scrambled past Betty Ann's Bakery and finally moved around a trio of large, lumbering women to reach her daughter.

"Penny!" She fell to her knees in front of the little girl, whose dark eyes shone wide as saucers. "Oh my Lord. Oh . . . oh. You gave me such a scare."

Ruth hugged her daughter close, loving the feel of her tiny body in her arms. Then she pulled her to the empty vestibule of an office entrance and checked her over, gently stroking her arms and head. "What happened? I told you to wait for me."

"I know, but he showed me where the fountain was."

"Did the man hurt you?" Ruth asked.

"No. He was kind of mean, though. He gave me the stink eye, like Grandma says, and he told me I needed to wash up, that I was a piggy. He had a bag of flags he was selling, and he kept trying to get me to buy one, but I didn't have any money." Penny's brown eyes looked worriedly at Ruth. "I told him I was waiting for you, Mom, but he took me to the fountain . . . it was just across the street, so I . . . I . . ." Her bottom lip began to wobble as her face puckered in a sob.

"Okay, honey. You're okay." Ruth pressed her girl against her, running her palm over the coppery sheen of hair as she thanked God Penny was safe. "But you know not to do that again."

"I just wanted to go to the fountain." Penny sniffed.

"It's okay, pumpkin. You're fine now." From now on, Penny would not be out of her sight. Later Ruth would have a talk to warn her daughter about trusting anyone in this town. But for now, she wanted Penny to know she was safe.

"Do you want to watch the rest of the parade, or go home?" she offered, trying to restore some normalcy.

"Can we stay? I want to see how Jessica decorated her bike."

"Okay. But I'm not letting you out of my sight, little bean."

"Okay," Penny repeated, clasping her hand tight.

*   *   *

After the parade, Penny had some friends over to splash through the hose in the backyard. Watching them through the kitchen window, Ruth mixed red and blue sprinkles into vanilla cake batter to make cupcakes for Penny's Sunday school class. The plan was to have the girls frost the cupcakes, a task that would keep them busy once they tired of playing in the hose and sprinkler. As she poured the batter into paper-cup-lined muffin tins, she sorted through everything she knew about her attacker that might help identify the man Penny had encountered at the parade.

The flag man.

Something about him seemed a little off. Unlike her attacker, who had seemed more squared away, brazen, and strong-willed. A stubborn cowboy type.

She scraped the last of the batter from the bowl with a spatula, thinking that Kat had been right. Ruth was out of her league in terms of really investigating these people. Maybe she could help with the profiling, and she was going to make sure Kat took a good look at the list of suspects she'd compiled, but operating in the vacuum of her life, Ruth didn't have access to the background information and details Kat had at her fingertips.

A knock sounded from the front of the house, and she put the mixing bowl down and licked her finger as she went to see who it was. Ethan stood on her doorstep, hands resting loosely on his belt just above the hips, looking as relaxed and handsome as any cowboy she'd ever seen.

"Hey, there." She opened the door, inviting him in. "You got my text."

"I did." He stepped into the screened porch. "How's Penny doing?"

"She's a little scared, mostly because I was so freaked out, though I tried not to show it."

"I got that. But to know that someone's watching your house, and maybe following your kid around too? That's scary stuff."

"And that's just part of it."

"I sensed there was more." He looked into the house. "You got a minute to talk?"

"Come on into the kitchen. I was just about to put cupcakes into the oven."

He sat at the table, and as she popped the trays into the oven and washed the bowl, she told him about the intruder from last night and the "flag man" from today. She filled in the many details that she couldn't include in a text message. His questions showed that he took the threat seriously, though he was baffled at what the motive might be. "It begs the question, why you? Do you have any idea who might be targeting you?" he asked.

Ruth took a breath. "The truth?"

"Always."

"I think this is related to something that happened fifteen years ago. The thing is, when I left Prairie Creek, I wasn't just going off to college. I was escaping this town." She turned away from the chatter of the girls in the backyard to gauge his reaction. He nodded, his steady gaze telling her to go on.

"When I was sixteen, still in high school, I was attacked." As she stared out the window at the girls, she told Ethan the secret she'd held all these years. The whole story, from the innocent escapades of three teenaged girls to the rape, the secrecy, and the shell of a person she'd become until she finally got counseling. "I did seek help when I got to Santa Barbara and found the rape crisis center. There were people there who wanted to help me, people who taught me that I wasn't to blame and that I could heal and move on with my life."

Ethan absorbed that with a slow nod of his head. "That explains your dedication to your practice here and the hotline."

Ruth exhaled, realizing belatedly that she'd been holding her breath. "I can't let the same thing happen if and when another girl gets raped here. It's up to me to set up some sort of treatment program that will outlast me."

"And now that you're back, and someone is threatening you, you think it might be the attacker from fifteen years ago, still targeting you?"

Ruth lifted her palms. "When I first returned, I was looking for my attacker everywhere, even subconsciously checking men I encountered to see if they had the same features. And then, when Addie went missing and the deputies found Courtney Pearson's body in the same week, I started to wonder if it could all be related. Could it be the same man, coming upon girls who can't defend themselves out in the wilderness, sweeping them away to be his captive? If that's true, he might have done the same to me if Kat and Shiloh hadn't returned to save me."

He shook his head. "That's a big *if*. But if it's true, we need to tell Kat."

"Kat's made the same connections on her own. She's been pressuring me to go on the record with what happened fifteen years ago. I'm ready, but my parents are freaking out. I guess the fur still goes flying when folks find out that the family of a minister is human."

"There's definitely a double standard there. So, you've talked to Kat?"

"I ran into her this morning. Truth is, I've been avoiding her. But today I told her I'm ready."

"Good."

Ruth's hands were sweating, and her heart began a slow, hard beat. Was she ready to go on record? She needed to be. "I'll get together with her tomorrow or Monday, maybe while you've got the girls for their lesson." Looking at the week ahead, Ruth wondered if her mother would continue to watch Penny after their disagreement. Bev could be very forgiving, but she hated losing face in the community. Maybe it was time to talk with Jessica's mom about watching the girls for part of the week. Fiona would be a great backup.

"You should tell Kat about the flag man too," Ethan said, explaining that he'd run into his sister at Menlo's Market, where she'd been taking a report about a theft. Someone had stolen a box of flags that Don Menlo had put on an endcap for the holiday. "It's petty thievery, but that's not to diminish your instincts that this guy is a threat. I believe in the power of fear. If you're afraid of someone, usually there's a good reason."

"My instincts have run amok. I see my attacker everywhere now."

"You can't blame yourself for that," Ethan said. "You've returned to the scene of the trauma, and now you've got a daughter to protect. The stakes are high here." He rose from the table and stretched. "You know, it wouldn't hurt to have a little muscle nearby." He summoned her closer and flexed one arm. "See that?"

The close proximity stirred something deep inside. She wouldn't mind having an intimate look at the rest of his body. "Nice guns," she said with a smile.

"At your disposal anytime." When they both laughed, he added, "Seriously. Let me be your bodyguard. I've got to run over to my father's place for a cookout, but after that, I'm free for fireworks or whatever."

She placed a hand on his upper arm, testing the steely ridges there. "That sounds like a plan."

A moment passed where Ruth's hand still lay on his arm. Ethan gazed down at her, and the sudden, silent intensity shot a thrill through her. He took her in his arms and swept her close. Ruth closed her eyes as his hands moved down her back, leaving a trail of sweet sensation, pinpoints of light and desire as he cupped her bottom and held her against him. He wanted her; she could feel that in the hard ridge of his lean body, and she wanted him too.

He leaned down to kiss her, and she welcomed the touch of his lips on hers, the spark of desire there, the sweet opening that hinted of more. Desire, like warm, lazy honey, oozed through her veins, making her knees weak. But as her legs softened, he held her to him and kept her from falling.

Keep me from falling.

She wanted to stay this way forever, safe within his strong arms. She wanted to make love all day and all night. But there were little girls to corral, and the oven timer was beeping, drawing her away. Damn, but it was hard to pull back.

When they finally pulled apart, there were promises simmering in his eyes.

Later could not come soon enough.

Time was marked only by the sun, now a fat, roiling dandelion in the window overhead. From her calculations, Addie believed today was the Fourth of July, and she hoped the festivities would be reason enough to keep him in town and away from her, his rough, thick hands off her body, his salty man smell out of range. Besides, she needed time to get her work done—a tedious task, with pathetic progress, but right now it was the only hope she could cling to. Each day, after she was sure he had left the shed, she squatted next to the tin bucket and worked a section of the chain link over the rim of the bucket. If she did this every day, as often as she could, she believed that one day the chain loop would wear down enough that she could break free and make her escape. The scraping had barely made a dent so far, but the bucket was the hardest edge she could find in this old, moldering shack.

Back and forth, back and forth. She gritted her teeth as the metal scraped against metal. Occasionally she would stop and check her progress, allowing herself a frown. But she had given up on cursing and crying, realizing that it only sucked her energy away and tugged her down into an even lower pit of misery.

Today, when she went to check how far she had worn the cuff chain away, she noticed the marks she was making on the bucket. The bucket's rim was now a shinier shade of silver, with hairline scrapes feathering this way and that—evidence of her escape efforts.

Would he notice?

Probably.

She lowered herself to the cot and leaned back against the beam of what was supposed to be a wall. What excuse could she give? That she'd been chewing on the edge of the water bucket because she was hungry? She actually didn't have much appetite. The takeout burgers and peanut butter sandwiches he brought her had little appeal because they came from him. She kept hydrated with creek water, but it gave her satisfaction when he would return and find that she'd barely picked at the food.

Maybe she should tell him that she'd been trying to file down her nails? That would be a laugh. She had asked him to bring some shampoo, toothpaste, and a manicure kit. She had planned to use the latter for the sharp edges she'd find inside, though she had made a pitch about getting sexy for him. He was always telling her what a failure she was as a whore. Like that was going to motivate her. Right. If you don't like it, asshole, let me go.

But Monster Man had simply brought her a toothbrush and toothpaste and told her he wasn't running a resort. The bastard. She started scraping again, fiendishly, desperately.

When she stopped, the chain link appeared bruised, but not compromised at all. Leaning back with a sigh, she wiped the fine sheen of sweat from her forehead and gingerly touched the tender area of her wrists under the handcuffs. The nasty acetate made her wrists sweat and left a raw, crusty ring around her wrists. She reached her fingertips into the water bucket and came back with droplets to flick over the wound. Hardly a first aid kit, but better than nothing.

She blew on her wrist to dry it, and then tugged the cuffs back toward her fingertips. The ring began to slide along the butt of her palm.

What?

She stared at it with eyes wide open, tugging again. The cuffs were definitely closer to sliding off than they had ever been before.

She gaped in wonder. Were her bones collapsing? Or maybe it was because she was barely eating and losing weight.

Whatever was causing it, she had a chance of sliding out of these in the future.

A chance.

Leaning toward the bucket, she cupped a handful of water, splashed it over her neck, and leaned back against the wall. The water helped to cool her as it trickled down over her breasts and shoulders.

She closed her eyes and dreamed of stepping into the icy waters of the creek with Dean beside her, holding her hand.

Someday, the dream would be real.

Someday . . .

Chapter 20

"Did she settle in?" Ethan asked as Ruth came down the stairs from tucking Penny in.

"She crashed soon after her head hit the pillow, but that's no surprise. It's been a long day."

True to his word, he had swung by after dinner and given the three of them a ride in his truck to the ridge. Penny had been happy to meet up with her friends there, and Ruth had been thrilled to have entertainment of her own as she and Ethan sat and watched from a blanket. Overhead, fireworks sizzled and exploded in the sky. Back on solid ground, Ruth experienced a few thrilling tremors of her own as Ethan reached across the blanket and covered her hand with his. And when the temperature began to drop quickly on the open hill, he was quick to get his denim jacket from the truck and slide it over her shoulders.

Don't fall too fast, Ruth kept warning herself as the night went on. *You don't know him all that well.*

Which wasn't entirely true, as she had known him

for more than fifteen years. And just as she knew
there was something seriously off-balance about the
man who'd come to her home last night, she knew
that Ethan Starr was a good-hearted man with two
boots on solid ground.

After the fireworks, when he pulled up in front of
their house, she didn't hesitate to invite him in. Penny
changed into her pajamas and came downstairs with a
collection of books, from which Ethan performed
Green Eggs and Ham, leaving them all in stitches.
Penny's father, Sterling, could be a performer too,
though he didn't allow himself to go to the silly
places that eight-year-olds enjoyed.

"You're good with kids," she said. "I'm surprised
you don't have any of your own."

He shrugged. "I'm not dead yet."

She smiled down at him, loving the light in his
eyes. Nope, definitely not dead. "Thanks for doing
the story tonight. It's been a long day, and I didn't
sleep last night."

"That's no good."

"After I saw him in the street, I didn't feel safe. I
was afraid to close my eyes."

"Where did he come from? Can you show me?"

"The park across the street." She unlocked the
door to the porch. "You can see it from out here."

The screened-in porch was cooler than the house,
the night air punctuated by the hoot of an owl and
the rumble of the neighbors' air conditioners. "He
emerged from those tall trees, the cedars that border
the park."

"Right across the street? This guy's brazen. No
wonder you were scared."

The darkness seemed to have black pockets of un-identifiable hazards. He could be hiding anywhere, under the Hendersons' canoe or behind a bush in the park. She turned away with a shiver. "It was a relief when the sheriff came out, but I can't expect to have cops guarding my house every night. What if he comes back?"

He looked over at the porch swing, then at the outdoor sofa with its blue-and-green-striped cushions. "I guess I know where I'm sleeping tonight."

"Ethan, really, that's nice of you, but—"

"It's what friends do for friends in these parts. You said it yourself: you were too afraid to close your eyes. And he could come back. And if he does, I'm your first line of defense. Guy like that isn't going to mess with me. Predators prey on fear. A woman alone, a kid in the house."

The thought of having him here in her home filled her with relief and excitement, and she honestly didn't know which emotion was stronger. "I'd owe you, big-time."

He smiled and raked his hair back. "I'd settle for one of those cupcakes you baked today. Or actually, a real date. I've got this invite to the Dillinger wedding."

"Colton and Sabrina?"

"Are you already going?"

"No, I don't know them that well. But I've heard about it. Talk around town."

"Colton's a friend. I might actually enjoy the festivities with you there. Want to be my plus-one?"

A dreamlike image of dancing in Ethan's arms came to mind, sweet and ethereal. "I'd love to. My first big event back in town." She yawned. "Let me get you a blanket. I don't know how comfortable this couch is. Do you want a sleeping bag?"

"A sheet and a pillow would do it."

"Or maybe the couch inside?"

"This is better. I like the fresh air, and I don't want Penny to hear me snoring when she comes down for her morning cereal."

"Penny . . . I didn't think about that. It can be traumatizing for a kid when a parent begins dating."

He gave a skeptical look, crinkles forming at the edges of his eyes. "I think she'll hold up just fine, Dr. Ruth."

She brought him sheets and a blanket, then went upstairs to get ready for bed. She was slipping on her nightgown when she realized he needed a pillow. She grabbed two from her bed and took them downstairs.

"Ethan?" She called from the open screen door. "Are you awake?"

"Sure thing."

Pillows clutched to her chest, she stepped onto the screened-in porch and felt her eyes grow wide at the sight of him, bare-chested, on her couch. His thick biceps and broad chest tapered down to a narrow waist. She longed to run her hand along the line of hair that began below his navel and ran down into his jeans. Damn, but he looked good. Better than her teenaged imaginings.

"How's the couch?" she asked.

"Pretty comfortable." He patted a spot beside him. "Give it a try."

As if she hadn't sat on that thing a dozen times,

she settled in beside him, drawn to him. "I brought you pillows."

"Thanks." He took them and tossed them on the sofa behind her, his eyes sweeping over her in appreciation. "That's a nice nightgown."

She looked down, suddenly aware of the transparency of the cool summer cotton revealing the pink, round nipples of her breasts, the flare of her collarbones, the dark triangle at the juncture of her legs. "That's a summer nightgown for you," she said. "Might as well be naked."

"Might as well." He leaned in with the clear intention of a kiss, and realizing that she wanted more, so much more, she closed her eyes and opened herself to him, body and soul. Their kissing was accompanied by exploring hands, tentative at first, and then more confident, more teasing. She thrilled to the hard planes and edges of the muscle and bone beneath his skin, while his fingertips left a trail of fire that swept through her skin and licked at long-buried desire.

This is how it's meant to be, she thought as he moved over her, the last vestiges of clothing long abandoned. *This is how it feels to make love, to be loved.*

"Are you sure?" he whispered, holding himself tight above her. "I mean, the neighbors . . ."

"Are asleep with their air conditioners humming," she said. Her conscious mind told her it was a bit brazen, but the half-wall of the porch and the surrounding shrubs provided enough privacy in the night.

"Are you really ready for this? We could wait."

"Yes, yes. No waiting," she gasped. She had been waiting for this all her life.

He lowered himself to her and began to move,

slowly at first, treating her with a combination of tenderness and driving need that nearly brought her to
tears. Out in the cool night air of the porch, with fireworks from one of the neighbor's yards crackling in
the dark sky, Ruth felt the storm clouds race over the
horizon of her shame, a clear sky at last. Only clear
skies.

He stood behind the lilac bush by the fence, only a
few feet away from the rutting sounds on the porch.
The whore.

He sheathed his knife and pressed it to the crotch
of his pants. He was rock hard, eager to get in on the
action, hungry for another taste of her. He should
never have let her get away. Her bare, naked fear had
intensified his thrill that night. He'd had her, and he
would have kept her if it weren't for her friends coming after him.

And then she'd left town. Gone, just like that.

But she'd come back, all high and mighty. All edu-
cated. A *therapist*. Like she was better than everyone
else. But he knew the truth. Strip off the fancy clothes,
and you had a simpering whore like any other. She was
supposed to be his that night, his way to get the crazi-
ness out of his system so he could fly straight and leave
those other bitches alone. She slipped through his
fingers then, but he'd gotten smarter, better at the
game. This time, he was taking home a trophy.

She would know that soon enough. He had left
her a gift in the mailbox—a snapshot of their time
together.

A promise that he would keep coming around until he could have her again—this time for good.

Sleep was a panacea for so many things.

After a night of rest in the safe comfort of Ethan's protection, Ruth awoke to the smell of freshly brewed coffee from downstairs.

He'd made coffee.

Never in her marriage to Sterling, child of privilege, had he ever lifted a finger in the kitchen. It was such a simple gesture, but it filled her with hope for the future and a sizzling excitement about their relationship. She threw on a robe and met him downstairs in the kitchen.

"G'morning." He was putting his boots on.

She was sorry to see him go. "Leaving already?"

"I've got to get going. Shower and church. Will I see you there?"

"I take Penny to Sunday school at the Unitarian Church."

"Sounds like a father-daughter issue, but I get it. Been there with my own father, and I didn't have those hellfire and brimstone sermons to deal with."

"I've been trying to avoid church with my father since I returned. And now that I've told him I am going public with the rape, I want to keep my distance more than ever."

"He wasn't supportive about that?"

"Hardly." She took a sip of coffee. "I'll explain that later."

"Maybe for dinner? I could pick up something to

grill here," he said. "Or if you have plans, I can come over later to man my post on the porch."

She was about to tell him he didn't have to stay, that a good night's sleep had restored her confidence, but in terms of her personal security, nothing had really changed. Right now, she needed him. "Dinner would be great," she said.

He headed out the door, pausing on the way to pull her close and kiss her good-bye. He left her a little breathless and wanting more.

She was dropping off the cupcakes in the Sunday school office when her phone buzzed—the hotline.

Panic squeezed her tight as she thought of him. Was he here at church, watching her? She looked behind her and saw Daisy, the church secretary, talking with a mom. Down the hall, a handful of ushers were chatting, but she was too far away to make out their faces.

She pushed her way out the door to the pebble walkway lined by thirsty pansies and braced herself for his voice.

"This is the Sexual Assault Support Line," she said flatly.

"Um . . . is this Ruth?" A female voice.

Ruth allowed herself to breathe again. "Yes. Please, tell me what happened to you."

"Uh . . . this is Lily."

"Yes, I remember your voice." Ruth moved rapidly, putting some distance between herself and the church complex so that congregants did not hear her conversation. "You usually call at night."

"Is it a bad time?"

"No, no. Don't hang up."

"I . . . I just left church and, I don't know. . . . Everywhere I turn, I see signs that I should tell the police what I know. That girl Addie going missing, and the dead girl's body. And this morning in church, the minister kept saying, 'The truth shall set you free.' It was like he was talking to me. He kept looking at me. This is killing me."

"I know Addie Donovan's disappearance has been weighing on you, Lily." *Just as it's been killing me.* "I think it would help you to talk to the sheriff."

"I can't do that. I can't risk my girl being . . . no. I told you, you can pass on the stuff I remember if you think it will help the cops nail him."

"I'm happy to do that, but the investigators will want to meet with you."

"No."

"What if we met somewhere of your own choosing? There's a female detective with the sheriff's office who's very easy to talk with."

"I can't . . . I don't know what to do. He's all I think about now." She was starting to panic.

"When you're ready, Lily," Ruth soothed. "You can do it. There's a vicious brute out there, and he needs to be stopped. We can do this together." Ruth knew that Lily would not understand how difficult it was for Ruth to also come forward, but maybe she would sense the urgency and commitment in Ruth's voice.

"I'll think about it," Lily said. "But I can't come to Prairie Creek."

"Detective Starr and I will meet you halfway."

"I'll think about it. That's the best I can say now."

And without another word, Lily ended the call, leaving Ruth stranded alone two blocks beyond the church parking lot in a residential neighborhood so quiet she could hear bees buzzing in the hedges.

As Ruth walked back toward the church building, she looked warily toward the parking lot and then toward the church lobby—both empty, now that the service had begun inside.

Was he out there, watching? Planning. Waiting to pounce again?

Her heartbeat raced faster than the click of her heels as she returned to the relative safety of the church building. She couldn't go on like this much longer. She was grateful for Ethan's presence at night, but she was out of her league in the investigation of a potential kidnapper and rapist. After all the avoiding, now she couldn't wait to talk with Kat.

After church, the afternoon loomed long on a scorcher of a day without a breeze or a cloud in sight. "It'll be too hot to sit through the rodeo," Ruth told her daughter. The fairgrounds had very little sun cover—just a few tents and hardly a tree in sight. "Why don't you invite the girls over to splash around in the backyard?"

"We did that yesterday," Penny said, though she clearly didn't mind giving up the rodeo. "Can we go to Bonny Lake?"

Although Penny had been to the small waterfront swim park with other friends and their moms, Ruth had avoided the place, only because it was a vague reminder of another, more desolate lake of summers gone by. But if she was going to insist that Lily face her fears, then Ruth would need to move in that direction too.

"Let's pack some snacks and drinks," Ruth said. "And don't forget sunscreen."

An hour later, Ruth was backing a car full of girls out of the driveway when she saw something sticking out of the mailbox. Huh. There was no mail delivery on the Fourth of July or on Sunday. She put the car in PARK and opened her door.

"Mom? Come on!" Penny called to her.

"Just one second." She grabbed the large, gold envelope, closed the box, and returned to the van to stash it in her tote bag. "Okay, girls, we are rolling."

The swim park was more crowded than usual, but Ruth helped Penny and her friends stake out a spot in the shade of the tall pines where they could spread out the blanket and set up. Although two teenaged lifeguards watched over the swimmers from tall chairs, Ruth was glad to have her camp chair set up close enough to the shoreline that she could watch the girls in the water.

At half past the hour, the lifeguards pulled all the kids out of the water for a ten-minute safety break, and Ruth counted the four girls huddled together on the dock before turning to her bag for her cell phone. That was when she remembered the gold envelope.

She removed it quickly, noticing it was unstamped, without an address. Probably from the landlord. Curious, she opened it and pulled out a single sheet of paper—a photo.

Three naked girls.

Fear seeped through her as she recognized the sixteen-year-old version of herself standing on the dock, shoulders hunched in embarrassment. Next to her, a more confident Kat was reaching up to swipe dark, wet hair from her face. At the edge of the dock stood Shiloh, a proud, golden lioness with arms extended overhead, as if enjoying the sheen of lake water cascading down her body in rivulets.

One fuzzy black-and-white photo, and the bottom dropped out of her world.

He was here, watching her, wanting something.

With trembling hands, she grabbed her phone.

Sunglasses offered the best camouflage; no one could see that he was staring. At a picnic table nearby, he tuned out the perennial chatter of her voice and scanned the teenage girls lethargically sunbathing, their flat bellies shiny with lotion, a tiny triangle of cloth covering the area begging to be plundered. Something about seeing girls near water turned him rock solid every time.

It had to be ninety in the shade as he watched. Part of him wished one of the older ones would take a little jog into the wooded trail at the edge of the park so that he could take her here in the bushes. But . . . no. He didn't need any more young ones. He had one at home. A young, pretty one. Hot body, but lacking in experience.

But that Ruth . . . she was older and experienced enough to know her way around a man's body. She would know when to go soft and when to ride hard. Nothing like a woman with experience.

The sight of all these kids at the water reminded

him of that long-ago night when he came upon the three girls skinny-dipping. He flashed to the memory—the three of them naked together.

He'd thought they were a gift from God, but no. The Lord giveth, and the Lord taketh away. Just a short taste of Ruth, and then they had gotten away.

But not forever. And he owed them all for what they'd done to him. He rubbed the back of his right hand with the fingers of his left, then touched his forehead. They'd attacked him, the damn whores. He was pretty sure it was Patrick Starr's daughter who'd gotten him with the screwdriver. *Bitch!* He'd make her pay all right, when the time came.

But now, staring at Ruth, he wanted to just dive inside her. Fiery red hair, ripe breasts, shapely legs that would wrap around him nice and tight. Ruth would be a good fit. And this time, he would not let her go.

She found it difficult to focus on Kat's voice as she watched Penny and her friends take turns diving from the dock. Something about clearing her morning schedule.

"He sent Shiloh a photo too," Kat said. "She just let me know. Sounds like the same one."

"He sent her one too?" Hearing her voice rise, Ruth stopped herself, then whispered, "What the hell does he want from us?"

The silence on the phone indicated that there was no good answer to that question.

"I can have the night patrol come by your house," Kat suggested. "Or maybe you want to pack up your daughter and stay with your parents for a while."

"Not my parents. Ethan is going to help me."

"Ethan, my brother?"

"He's going to stay at my place until this blows over."

"Okay." Kat sounded a bit nonplussed, but then said, "Glad you're not alone. With the way things are developing, it's good you're coming in tomorrow, Ruth."

Wide girth, furry skin, thick hands.

Ruth vividly remembered the taste, look, and feel of that evil.

Closing her mind to the dark memories, Ruth thanked God for Ethan—for the love and protection he was offering so soon in their relationship. The stoic part of her told her that it was too much too soon, that she was a professional woman capable of taking care of herself. But in reality, those arguments were riddled with cracks and holes, like the metaphorical wall she had constructed to keep people out when she was raped. The wall had been built upon fear; it was time to bring it tumbling down.

Time to recognize her own humanity, her need for love and protection.

Shivering despite the heat, Ruth counted the girls on the dock for the umpteenth time. Everyone was safe, and she planned to keep it that way.

Part Four

Kat

Chapter 21

Katrina brushed her teeth with vigor and spat tooth-paste into the sink. She looked at her reflection in the mirror: serious brown eyes, messy dark hair pulled back into a loose ponytail, gleaming white teeth, and—

She turned quickly to the toilet as bile rose in her throat, leaned down, and promptly threw up blood. She gasped in horror at the sight, breathing so fast and hard she thought she might pass out. Then she realized the color came from Betty Ann's red velvet cupcakes, which had called to her yesterday after-noon after she left work; she'd brought home a half dozen more, eating them for last night's dinner and today's breakfast. Not the healthiest meals on record, but then she hadn't been making the best food and drink choices for a while. She pretty much fueled up on whatever was handiest. It was a bad routine that she swore she was going to fix, but she hadn't man-aged that yet.

Relieved, she flushed the toilet, then rinsed her

mouth under the faucet and began the tooth-brushing process again.

Pregnant.

The word slipped into her consciousness unbidden, and she immediately dismissed it. Nope. Not pregnant.

But you could be, her nagging conscience reminded.

Feeling another wave of nausea, she braced her arms on the sink, spat a couple of times, heart pumping, stomach rollicking. Sweat broke out on her forehead, and the feeling took a couple of minutes to pass. She drew a deep breath and hung her head. Maybe she was just sick, fighting a bug. That had to be it. In any case, Ruth was making her statement today, and she wasn't going to miss it.

Yep, the flu. A summer bug, she decided. Naomi had been out sick for a few days a couple of weeks ago. Kat hadn't been paying attention, but the dispatcher had definitely caught something.

Still, now that she thought about it, she'd been feeling weird for a couple of weeks, off and on. She'd put it down to the intensity of the job, the need to find Addie Donovan, the guilt that followed her around from not confessing about Ruth's rape. She'd nearly upchucked at the sight of Courtney Pearson's corpse, but then she'd known Courtney. Not friends, but classmates. A part of Kat had admired Courtney's wildness, the way she thumbed her nose at convention. The same traits that had drawn Kat toward Shiloh. The same traits that had led Kat toward some bad choices of her own.

Odds are you don't get pregnant from a one-night stand.

She stared at her reflection again, her mouth tight-ening. She catalogued her wan cheeks and sunken eyes. *Since when have the odds been in your favor?*

"Don't be a pessimist," she muttered. She'd certainly felt enough of that over the years. Her father's obses-sion with the missing girls—*and your own, Kat. I mean, let's be honest here*—and the sadness that had fol-lowed her around since her mother's death . . . and now Addie's disappearance, and discovering Court-ney . . . it had certainly left her feeling that life was hard.

Well, to hell with it. She was determined to have a better outlook.

She splashed cold water on her face and pinched her cheeks. Then she pulled out the under-eye cream and added more liner and mascara than normal. It was going to be extremely difficult for Ruth to bring up the events of that night, but it would be no picnic for Kat, either. Everyone she worked with—Sheriff Featherstone, Detective Ricki Dillinger, and all her other coworkers—would know about Kat's continued silence, and though they might not say anything to her directly, judgments would be made. It was a small price to pay for finally getting the information out there, and it was nothing compared to Ruth's trauma. Nonetheless, it was something Kat had to face—and she already felt like death warmed over.

Walking into the bedroom, she glanced at the clock. Seven-thirty in the morning and hot as blazes. After pulling on her jeans, Kat slipped on a short-sleeved, tan blouse. She only wore a uniform for spe-cial duty—like the parade. Most of the time, like the other deputies, she chose street clothes.

But what if you're pregnant?

She put a hand to her stomach and tried to imagine that future. Her mind was a blank.

The flu, she reminded herself sternly.

Climbing into her Jeep, she drove to the station, pulling into the back lot a few minutes before eight. Naomi Simmons was already at the reception desk when Kat walked in.

"When you were out for a couple days a few weeks ago, was it the flu?" Kat asked the dispatcher. "I was trying to remember."

"Nah, it was a sinus infection. Complications from my allergies, which were horrible a few weeks ago, and not a whole lot better now."

"Oh . . . right."

"If it isn't the trees, it's the grass, and if it isn't the grass, it's the flowers. Don't even talk about it because now I feel like I want to sneeze." And with that, she did.

Kat started to move off. Not the flu, huh.

"Fresh cupcakes from Betty Ann's in the break room," Naomi called after her.

Kat's stomach lurched, and she was forced to inhale a careful breath. "Thanks."

"They're just the best, aren't they?"

"The best."

She headed into the central squad room, a space shared by most of the officers. Easing herself into her desk chair, Kat forcefully shoved thoughts of her possible condition aside. She didn't have time to think about it today.

Footsteps sounded behind her, and she looked around to see Detective Ricki Dillinger heading her way, a red velvet cupcake on a plate. "Talked to your dad, and he said these are some of your favorites." She set the plate on Kat's desk.

"Thanks. You talked to Dad?" Kat kept her gaze averted from the cupcake, her stomach leaping madly, as if it wanted to catapult from her body. She put one firm hand over it.

"You sent him a copy of one of the pictures you took of Courtney Pearson."

Kat went cold inside. Yes, she had given her father a copy of the photo she'd taken with her cell phone, and it was against all department rules. "I—I wanted his opinion. When we were all chasing that other killer a few years back, I went to him for advice, even though he wasn't on the force anymore. You were leading the charge on that one, but Dad's got great insights and—"

Ricki held up a palm. "Stop right there. I know why you did it, and there's no denying that Patrick's a professional. But he's no longer with the department."

"I'm sorry." *Hell, Kat, are you going to get fired today?*

"You just need to give me a heads up before you go off page."

"Sure, sure." Kat's heart was racing with adrenalin. It wasn't like her to be a lone ranger, as a rule.

"Sam and I talked it over, and I said I'd talk to you about it. We're clear, right."

"Clear. Absolutely."

"Okay, good." She grimaced, then smiled a bit sheepishly. "I wouldn't have known, but Patrick called me, not the other way around. He looked over the photo and had some thoughts. He agrees that the gasoline may have been because the killer planned to burn the body."

Kat nodded, glad they'd moved on. Was it wrong to feel a teeny bit betrayed that her father had called Ricki first? Probably. She was lucky she'd gotten a reprimand and that's all. Working to keep her feelings from showing on her face, she nearly missed what Ricki was saying.

"—right about that barbed wire. It's Dillinger, all right. Old style, though. We don't use it around the Rocking D anymore."

"The barbed wire around Courtney's wrists?" Kat asked, playing catch-up.

She nodded. "Your father zeroed in on it. Told me to do the same, so I did, and I ran a close-up of it. I'm taking that picture to my father this afternoon. If anybody knows anything about Dillinger barbed wire, it'll be Ira. I was wondering if you wanted to go with me."

"Yes," Kat said immediately.

"Good."

As Ricki started to move off, Kat said, "Um . . . Ruth Baker's coming in this morning."

Ricki turned back to her. "She have an idea about who was lurking outside her house the other night?"

"No . . . this is something else, though it could be related. She's . . ." Kat swallowed hard. Her uncertain stomach hadn't settled down. She started breathing rapidly, aware that she could throw up at any time.

"You okay?" Ricki asked, frowning at whatever she could see on Kat's face.

"Man, I could use a club soda." At The Dog she'd

told Shiloh that she was drinking club soda because she was on duty, which was the truth, but she hadn't been feeling right even then.

"You sick?"

"More like hungover," she lied. She wasn't ready to tell Ricki or anyone else about her suspicions. What she really needed was a pregnancy test. Then she would know the good, the bad, and the ugly. *Please don't let me be pregnant*, she silently prayed. "Ruth just has some things she wants to go over with us."

"Like Skip Chandler?" Ricki asked.

"Skip?" Kat repeated.

"Apparently he stole some miniature flags from Menlo's during the parade and handed them out to the kids. Ruth talked to Sam and said Skip used one to lure her daughter away."

"I know. I talked to the store manager about it." Skip Chandler was one of the top three names on her father's suspect list.

"Oh, that was you. Okay." She nodded. "Sam talked to Skip, and he says he just told the girl where the fountain was, and she followed after him to wash off her hands. I'm not saying Skip wouldn't lie, but it doesn't sound like coercion. There's probably more to the story. The man's a thief and lewd and unreliable, and at least once a year he gets in a fight at Big Bart's or The Dog and lands in jail. But he's never been known to engage with children. It's not part of his MO, but we're still keeping an eye on him."

"He's always been a little off," Kat said.

"Stealing the flags from Menlo's . . . that's exactly the kind of dumb thing Skip does. He's compulsive. Never thinks of the consequences, or just doesn't care. Probably a little of both." Ricki stopped, but seemed to want to say more.

"What else has he done?"

"It's not that. You know Sam went to Ruth Baker's house the other night because she said she was being stalked."

"Yes."

"She's had us watching her house since because of someone she says she saw in the bushes, which is ending today."

"You don't believe her?"

"She saw something," Ricki acknowledged. "Whether it was real, or imagined, I don't know. And this Skip Chandler thing with her daughter on the heels of it . . . I just want to know if there's a credible threat to her, or if she's been influenced by the discovery of Courtney Pearson's corpse and Addie Donovan's disappearance. What do you think?"

The picture Shiloh had slipped to Kat inside an envelope when she'd stopped at the station played across the screen of Kat's mind. "Open it when you're alone," Shiloh had warned. "It was left in my mailbox. Don't call me; I'll call you." Shiloh had been accompanied by her half sister, Morgan, at the time, so Kat had followed instructions, waiting until she was home before gingerly pulling out the photo. A black-and-white picture of the three of them, naked. From that night at the pond.

The image had had a profound effect on Kat. All those memories had bubbled to the surface anew. She was still waiting for Shiloh's call, figuring if she hadn't heard from her by the end of the week, she'd be doing some calling of her own, whether Shiloh liked it or not.

But then Ruth had told her she'd received a picture too.

"I believe it's a credible threat. She's a therapist, and she's not overly hysterical," Kat said. "She has her reasons, and that's why she's coming in."

"I'm curious what she has to say." When Kat didn't comment, she said, "All right then. Call me when she's here. Oh, and we're getting the ME's full report on Courtney Pearson later today. Maybe we'll get some more answers." As Ricki started to move off again, she added, "I think I saw some club soda in the break room fridge."

Kat looked up in surprise. "Do I look that bad?"

"You look tired" was the diplomatic answer thrown over her shoulder.

Half an hour later, Kat had grabbed her cell phone to call Ruth when it rang in her hand, and she nearly dropped it. She looked at the screen. *Ruth.* "Well, finally," she muttered, then answered, somewhat impatiently, "Where are you?"

"I can't do it, Kat. I've thought about it and thought about it. All night and this morning. I'll give my statement to you, but I can't come into the station. I'm sorry. I can't face them all yet. I should be stronger. I *am* stronger, most of the time. I talked to my parents and your brother, but I can't just waltz into the station and talk about the rape. I've pictured myself walking up those front steps in my mind, and I always stop before I open the station door."

"Okay. I get it. Now, let's—"

But Ruth barreled on, "I'll talk to you. I've been thinking about it all night. The stalker and that picture . . . someone's after me, and if they try for my daughter—"

"That's why you need to come in," Kat interrupted.

"I'll come to you," she said. "Only you."

"Fine. Okay," Kat said hurriedly, thinking hard. "Where do you want to meet? My house?"

"Maybe a restaurant? Betty Ann's?"

"Someplace else." Kat was clear on that. Betty Ann's was too close to her father's office. *And those red cupcakes . . .* "How about Molly's Diner?"

"I know everybody there."

"The Dog?" Kat suggested. It wasn't exactly Ruth's kind of place.

"Well, I wouldn't know anyone there," Ruth admitted. "And I suppose if someone there recognized me and told the Reverend . . . so be it."

"Amen," Kat said.

Ruth choked out a laugh. "But I don't think I could talk about what happened in The Dog."

"Let's just meet there and see how it goes. Say an hour?"

"I've got to make arrangements for Penny, and I'm going to think this over."

"Don't take too long."

"I'll see you there," she said, though the uncertainty in her voice made Kat wonder.

With another glance at the clock, Kat swept up her purse. She eyed the red velvet cupcake on her desk. Her stomach managed to handle the sight, but she wasn't taking any chances. Leaving it where it was, she walked down the hall to the break room, opened the refrigerator, grabbed one of three club sodas and began sipping it carefully as she headed out to her Jeep.

Her father wasn't at his office when she knocked, and Kat made a sound of impatience as she pulled out her cell phone. Next door, Betty Ann's was doing a thriving business, but the tinkling of the bell over the door grated on her. It damn well brought back her nausea, which pissed her off. Climbing back in the Jeep, she reversed quickly out of her parking spot. *Beep!* A horn blasted, and she slammed on the brakes and looked back. Blair Kincaid's truck was right behind her, and he was sitting in the driver's seat, staring at her through the windshield. He lifted his hands from the steering wheel and held his palms skyward in a "What gives?" gesture.

She gritted her teeth, shook her head, and drove off. She could feel the color creeping up her neck. Of course it had to be him. If she was pregnant it was his fault. Jesus. How had she gotten herself into this mess?

Alcohol. Lack of protection. One-night stand.

She drove to the edge of Prairie Creek to a fairly new chain drugstore. She'd been there once before and hadn't recognized any of the employees, so she was hoping she would remain anonymous. She just didn't need one of the town busybodies showing up, but most people she knew frequented Bomburn's Pharmacy in downtown Prairie Creek.

Walking inside, she glanced at the girl behind the counter. A young woman who looked to be in her early twenties. She seemed faintly familiar, but Kat couldn't place her. It was no one she knew well.

Feeling conspicuous, she walked down the aisle, waiting until a middle-aged woman who'd been examining the contents of some baby cream finally wandered away. Glancing around like a thief, she picked up the pregnancy kit, grabbing a two-pack just in case she needed further corroboration. Then she walked to the counter with a certain amount of trepidation. If she'd had the time, she would have driven to the next town, but she didn't, and the need to know was killing her.

The girl had on a name tag. RHIANNA BYRD.

Oh. Lord. God. Help. The youngest Byrd daughter.

"Hi," the girl greeted her with a smile as Kat placed the kit on the counter. She rang it up and asked, "Will that be all?"

"Yes, thanks." Kat scrounged in her purse for cash. No way was she putting her credit card out there. She hoped to God Rhianna didn't recognize her.

The girl took the money and handed her back her change. As Kat pushed back through the door, Rhianna's voice called after her sweetly, "Have a nice day, Ms. Starr."

Shit.

Fifteen minutes later, Kat was in the bathroom of her own home, staring at the two pink lines that had appeared on both tests. She tossed both sticks in the trash, washed her hands, and stared at herself in the mirror.

You can't wash it away.

Her cell rang from where she'd left it on the bathroom counter. She looked at the number, saw it was her father. Less than an hour ago, she'd wanted to talk to him about Courtney Pearson and the barbed wire. Now she just wanted to crawl back in bed.

She debated about letting the call go to voice mail, but she growled under her breath in frustration, then answered, "Hi, Dad," as she grabbed up her purse again and headed out. It was almost time to meet Ruth.

"I heard you stopped by to see me this morning," he said. "I was over at the grave site, visiting your mom."

Ah. Made sense. Patrick went through cyclical periods of going to Adam's Cemetery and communing with Kat's mother. It had been a while since the last time, but that was before Courtney's body was found and Addie Donovan went missing. It was one of the ways her father dealt with emotional trauma, while Kat had her own methods, one of which was engaging in reckless behavior, apparently.

"Who told you I stopped by?" Kat asked as she climbed back into her Jeep.

"Blair Kincaid. He was going to Betty Ann's. Picks up breakfast almost every morning there." A pause. "Guess you almost rammed his truck."

Kat's fingers flexed around the steering wheel. "I was backing out, and he came up behind me." Did she sound defensive? Probably. "Didn't even know he was there 'til he blasted me with his horn."

"Well, no harm done. I thought Hunter made a mistake bringing him back to the Kincaid ranch and then putting him in charge. I mean, Blair's always been good with livestock, has been since he was a boy, but he and trouble were pretty good pals back in the day too, and there was that time—"

"I don't want to talk about Blair Kincaid," Kat stated flatly.

"—that Blair and Carl Perkins were in that fight at the Buffalo Lounge. Blair wasn't old enough to be drinking there, but he was, and he took offense because Carl thought he'd stolen his girl."

"Dad, that was Rafe Dillinger, and the girl was Darla Kingsley."

"I'm talking about the one who had the baby."

"I know which one you're talking about. It was Darla. And it was all rumor anyway." Kat was impatient. "She might never have been pregnant in the first place."

"I thought Blair confessed to being the baby daddy."

"No. Blair and Carl were fighting about some bet at the rodeo that summer. It had nothing to do with Darla. Courtney was the one who planted that rumor because Rafe was her boyfriend."

"Okay." He sounded slightly taken aback at her sharp tone.

"I just came by to talk about the barbed wire. Ricki and I are going over to the Dillingers this afternoon and talking to Ira."

"He should know about the wire," he said in a contained voice. She knew she'd hurt his feelings at her abruptness, but she couldn't help herself.

Kat thought about Courtney. All that high school drama was so trivial now. Exhaling heavily, she said, "The photo I gave you of Courtney . . . I shouldn't have given it to you without checking with Sam or Ricki first.

Ricki let me know this morning that it wasn't protocol, and I'm just lucky no one's taking it any further."

"Everyone knows how involved I've been with those missing girls," he protested.

"You couldn't have called me first? Given me a chance to explain it?"

"I didn't think about it. I just wanted to tell them what I found. Ricki's a Dillinger. Part of the family."

"Well, it got me a talking to. Which I probably deserved."

"I'm sorry, honey."

He was so shocked and contrite that she lifted up her hands. "Forget it. Ricki's okay now. And it's a great lead."

"You sure?"

"Yeah. What have you got?"

"I pulled out my magnifying glass and really examined it. Back in the day, these ranches all had their own special wire. The way the barbs are twisted on it. This one had a double twist, and a reversal. Gives it an upward tail. Knew I'd seen it before, and it was either Dillinger or Kincaid."

Kat mentally reviewed the picture she'd taken of the barbed wire, but her brain was focused on the torn flesh around Courtney's wrists.

"It's all pretty much a thing of the past now. Thought about asking Blair about it, when he was here, but I'm leaning toward Dillinger. That's what I told Ricki." He paused. "I should've called you first."

"I should've gone to Sam and Ricki first. It's all right." Kat forced the image of Courtney's wrists from her mind.

"This wire wasn't for sale just anywhere. It was made special for the ranchers for their livestock. You couldn't buy it at a store."

"You're not saying you think Courtney was held prisoner by a Dillinger or a Kincaid, are you?"

"Not necessarily, but Rafe Dillinger's one of the top three on my list," he reminded her.

"It could be anybody who had anything to do with either family, or maybe this guy just found this wire somewhere. It could be completely unrelated."

"There's likely some of it still around the Dillinger property," he mused. "Coulda been thrown out over the years, I suppose, but I don't see Ira cleaning out all the outbuildings on the ranch. That's where it would be, unless this kidnapper took it all. But I bet there's scraps there."

She was pulling into a spot across from the Prairie Dog when he asked again, "You sure Blair didn't get the Kingsley girl pregnant? I hate to think my memory's not what it used to be."

"Pretty sure."

"Well, neither Rafe Dillinger nor Blair woulda made much of a father, so let's hope that's all it was."

Kat fought back a strangled sound.

"What?" her father asked.

"Nothing."

Chapter 22

The Prairie Dog hadn't improved since Kat had been there with Shiloh, not that she'd expected it to, but she looked at it with new eyes now that Ruth was joining her: same worn stuffed prairie dog, Zipper, sitting on a shelf behind the bar; same rough-hewn floor, beaten down by cowboy boots and wooden chairs; same bleary-eyed clientele in Stetsons and baseball caps; same everything. It wasn't going to work, Kat could already see, but she chose a table in a far corner that offered privacy and gave her a view of the door. She pulled out a notebook and a recorder, though she wasn't sure how Ruth would react to that.

Five minutes later, Ruth showed up in black pants and a white blouse with a loose tie at the throat, her expression sober, her red hair tamed by a tortoise-shell clip at the back of her neck. She looked professional and approachable at the same time.

She crossed the room to Kat self-consciously, and they both said as one, "We need to go somewhere else."

Ruth saw the recorder and the notebook as Kat tucked them back in her purse. "Oh," she said. She swallowed, then she drew back her shoulders and said, "I can do this. I was thinking on the ride over that maybe we could go back to the park where you and I talked the last time . . ."

Right after the attack. "I'll meet you there," Kat said, gathering up her purse.

Kat led the way in her Jeep, and Ruth followed behind in a small SUV. It was a short trip, but Kat's mind was jumping all over the place. She had too many things to think about, not the least being she was pregnant.

Pregnant . . . knocked up . . . with child . . . motherhood bound . . .

Blair's brother, Hunter, and his new wife, Delilah Dillinger, had just had a baby boy they'd named Joshua. The night he was born, Kat had run into Blair at Big Bart's Buffalo Lounge, a sprawling restaurant and bar that was a larger version of The Dog, with better food and more tables, but the same overall clientele.

Blair was in jeans and a denim work shirt, the cuffs rolled up along his forearms, leaning back in his chair, his booted feet propped on the seat of an adjoining one. His hair was dark, tousled, and longish, the remnants of a hat ring adding a raffish air. A dove-gray Stetson sat on the table next to a nearly finished mug of beer.

"Another Kincaid in the world. Baby Joshua has arrived," he called out to Kat, who'd gone to Big Bart's for their Cobb salad. Being single and living alone in a small apartment close to the station, Kat rarely cooked for herself, and the food at Bart's was surprisingly good, a cut or two above the usual bar fare.

Blair moved his feet and pushed out a chair in invitation as she walked up to the bar to pay for her order. She ignored him, so he slid to his feet and headed her way, beer in hand.

"How's Ethan?" he asked, leaning a hip against the bar.

"The same."

"Both he and Colton Dillinger, bronc riders, and now domesticity." He spread his arms wide and shook his head slowly from side to side, as if their lives were over.

Kat tried not to look at him. He was just put together too well. Something about that untamed hair, and the way his jeans rode low on his hips, the silver buckle at his flat waist, the strength in his biceps. And that face. Silvery blue eyes and a hard jawline, a slightly mocking smile, firm lips. He was just too good-looking for his own good, and hers. Around him she always felt a womanly response right to her core, a thrill, a heightened awareness, which always pissed her off.

"Want to have a beer and celebrate with me?" he asked, almost boyishly eager.

"Oh, I can't," she said. No way. He was far too tempting. The Blair Kincaids of the world weren't the kind of men to start something with that you wanted to last. They weren't made that way. Period. And Kat wasn't looking for a maybe on/maybe off romance.

"C'mon," he whispered, grinning like the devil he

was. "What's it gonna hurt? I'm an uncle. To a half *Dillinger*. That's gotta be a reason to drink."

The barkeep handed her the brown paper sack that held her salad. She looked at it, and then at Blair. She saw the stubble on his chin and got lost a moment thinking about how it would feel to rub her fingers over those whiskers.

"I don't really drink beer," she said.

"Wine? Whiskey?"

"Vodka, once in a while."

"Rustle up the lady a vodka martini, Grey Goose, three olives," he told the man. He swept an arm toward his table, but when Kat hesitated, he said, "Uh oh. You prefer a lemon twist, don't you?"

"No, it's fine." In reality, she'd never had a straight vodka drink. She generally stuck with lemon drops, or cosmos, or vodka tonics, something with a mixer.

But her drink came up, and Blair carried it to his table. She sat down across from him, setting the brown bag that contained her salad and her purse on the table next to his Stetson. He leaned back and surveyed her with a soft smile. "Katrina Starr," he said.

"Yes."

"Little Kat."

He'd known her brother, Ethan, better than he'd known her, as they were closer in age. Blair had left Prairie Creek somewhere during his high school years, a time when he'd had "trouble as his best pal," to quote her father. But he'd returned a couple years back at the behest of his brother, Hunter, who'd wanted help running the ranch after their father, the Major, died. Kat asked him some questions about his family, skirting the sensitive issues, but mostly making conversation, as she worked her way through the martini.

As soon as she got to the bottom of the glass, Blair ordered her another, even though her head was already swimming. She protested, but the protest fell on deaf ears, and Blair ordered a Maker's Mark for himself, both drinks arriving in minutes.

And she got plastered. It happened so fast. One moment, she was telling a story—something she thought thigh-slappingly hilarious at the time but couldn't recall the following day—the next, she was in his pickup with him, practically ripping off his clothes out in Big Bart's lot.

"Slow down, Little Kat, we've got all night," he breathed in her ear, which sent up a warning bell from the depths of her drunkeness, a warning she ignored as she let him drive her to the Kincaid ranch.

He wasn't half as drunk as she was, she realized much later. He knew what he was doing, and did it anyway. She, on the other hand, was beyond hope, and just trying to hang on to some vestige of respectability. "I'm a cop, goddamnit," she told him proudly as they walked through the house and upstairs to a huge bedroom that opened with double doors. "I don't drink, and I don't smoke, and I drive within the speed limit, mostly."

"You don't drink?"

"Usually. I don't drink, usually. But this is a special occason . . . occasion . . . after all, you're an uncle!"

"I am. That's for sure." He nodded. "I did give up smoking. Bad habit. But I do drink, and I always drive at least ten miles over the speed limit."

326 Lisa Jackson, Nancy Bush, and Rosalind Noonan

"We're made for each other," she said happily. "God, this is a big room."

He looked around as if seeing it for the first time. "Hunter moved out and gave it to me." He sat down on the end of the bed. "You should drink more," he told her. "You're a lot less uptight."

Kat was immediately incensed. "I'm not uptight."

"Okay, but you're a lot less uptight now, so . . ." He shrugged.

"Why is this room so big?" she asked, feeling dizzy as she looked toward the vaulted ceiling.

"It's the master suite, and I guess I'm the master?"

"No . . ." She laughed.

"I'm not?"

"No . . . wait, are you?"

"Maybe."

And after that he reached a hand out to her, and she willingly fell into his arms. They kissed like they were drowning for each other, then he pulled her onto his lap and she straddled him, and they began rocking together, and her fingers caressed his beard, and she felt how hard he was beneath her crotch, and she squirmed down on him until they were both gasping and then stripping off their clothes.

She'd had very little experience with sex, except for some trial and errors with a couple of guys from college who'd been more or less test cases rather than serious romances. She'd just never found a guy she wanted that much.

But this was something else. She *wanted* him. Wanted him driving deep inside her. She wanted to scream and flail and beat her fists on his back. She wanted to arch her back and bite his ear and make love like this was the one and only night in her life.

Well.

She did all that and more. She unbuckled his belt and pulled down his jeans and took him into her mouth as if she'd done it all her life. She heard him groan and pull away, and then she was down on her back, pressed into the satin coverlet, and Blair was atop her, pushing into her, and she was grabbing his butt and helping, begging, wanting everything so fast and hard.

"Jesus, Kat," he murmured.

"Don't stop."

"God, no . . ."

God, no, she thought now, grinding her back teeth together, as she pulled into the parking lot at the east side of the park. The rest of that night was a blur, the morning after embarrassing; she'd tried not to wake him as she gathered up her clothes. A hammering headache hadn't helped. Nor had the fact that he'd woken up and watched her fumble around as she hopped on one foot to get into her jeans—forget the underwear, she never found it—and struggled with clasping her bra, something she could usually do in her sleep but couldn't seem to manage, and then she swore under her breath when she saw that two of the buttons had been ripped off her blouse.

He'd gotten to his feet and yanked his own jeans on, also commando style, and said in a drawl she'd found sexy the night before but was like fingernails on a chalkboard the morning after: "You need a ride home."

"Yes . . ."

His gaze flicked to the mussed covers. Neither of

them had made it beneath the sheets. "It's still early, we could . . . ?"

She felt like hell. No. No. No. But her mouth again said, "Yes."

And that time, he'd been tender, and she'd floated, somewhere between pleasure and pain, because the horrible hangover that attacked her hadn't quite come into play yet, and the feel of Blair's body inside her made so much of it disappear beneath a wave of desire that swept through her womanhood and made her cry out with joy.

She'd gone to work with two little men clanging hammers against a gong inside her head. She'd thrown up twice in the station bathroom, then gone home and crawled into bed feeling like she might die. She'd awakened at two o'clock in the morning, nibbled on cheese and crackers, then forced herself to crawl out of bed to go to work the next day, too. She felt better by that evening—and like a complete idiot. She was scared at how many bad choices she'd made. It was so unlike her.

Blair called her sometime that second night. "How're you doin'?" he asked.

"Okay," she lied.

"I'm going out of town, but I'll be back next Wednesday."

"Okay."

"You want to get together again?"

Yes. Of course she did. But this time her brain took over and made her mouth answer the way she should. "I don't know. What do you think?"

"Well, sure. I'd like to."

It was so casual. Too casual. She had a distinct chill

run through her when she realized that it was all in a day's work for Blair Kincaid. No big deal. Happened all the time. And her mind tripped to Paula Gregory, who not that long before had been crying over Blair at Molly's Diner, blubbering into her cheap Chardonnay. "It's just sex to him," she said on a hiccup. "He doesn't care about me, but I don't care. I want him, and if I can only have some of him, that's what I'll take." And then the tears had really started flowing, and her girl-friends at the table jumped up to offer handkerchiefs and tissues and mascara and eyeliner for makeup re-pair.

Kat had felt sorry for her and suddenly saw herself in the same position, crying over Blair Kincaid, who she knew was bad news, romantically speaking.

"I don't think it's such a good idea," she said, and then she hit the END button on her cell phone.

And that, as they say, had been that.

Did she feel a little sorry? Of course. Was she going to change things? No.

And the baby?

Couldn't think about that now, she decided, as she pushed open her door, climbed out of the Jeep, and waited for Ruth to park.

They walked to a picnic table not far off the path they'd wandered down together fifteen years before. Kat set the recorder and her notepad on the weath-ered planks of the fir table and settled onto the bench. Ruth sat down opposite her, her eyes on the recorder.

Kat pressed the ON button, aware of the whisper-ing birch leaves above their heads, caused by an errant breeze that had cropped up, and the caw of a rattled crow that clearly didn't like their interference in its domain. The machine could pick up ambient noises, but it would record their voices loud and clear. Kat stated the date and time, who and where they were, then asked Ruth for permission to record their conversation.

"Yes," Ruth said in a barely discernible voice. Then, stronger, "Yes."

"Go ahead," Kat told her.

It took a few starts and stops, but Ruth managed to relate the events of the rape fifteen years earlier by an assailant she couldn't identify. After laying out the particulars—that Shiloh and Kat were with her while they were skinny-dipping in the pond—she gained momentum and went on to explain that they'd all scattered, but that Ruth was captured by the man, and that Shiloh and Kat had returned to rescue her. She finished with, "If they hadn't come back for me, I believe I would have been kidnapped. That's what I think happened to Addie Donovan. That's what I know happened to Courtney Pearson, and maybe Rachel Byrd, and Erin Higgins. I'm sorry I didn't come forward sooner. So sorry."

Her voice weakened, and Kat stopped the tape. They both were silent for a moment, then Ruth said, "I've tried to block it out, but it doesn't work that way. So I've been concentrating on the details of what I remember about him. Wide girth, furry skin, thick hands. That's my mantra. That's what goes through my head when I think of him."

"I'll take the tape to Sheriff Featherstone and Ricki.

They'll probably want to talk to you themselves," Kat warned.

"I feel better now that it's out there. I'll be okay. Sorry I panicked. I had this mental image of me in a room with silent police officers, all of them staring at me, and it just didn't work."

"Arms folded across our chests. Cold judgment in our eyes."

Ruth choked out a laugh. "I know that's not how it would be, but . . ."

"You don't know how it'll be until it happens. It's okay."

"Thank you, Kat," Ruth said, heartfelt. "I have a hotline, and I get calls from women who won't come in, won't finger their attackers, even if they know who they are. I know how they feel. The fear is crippling." Ruth gazed, clear-eyed, at Kat. "But hiding the truth only delays justice. Speaking up is the only way to get these guys."

"Maybe we'll find him now," Kat said. "The one at the pond."

"He's still here in Prairie Creek, and he hasn't changed. I think he took Addie. You think so too."

Kat nodded.

"He would have kidnapped me, if you and Shiloh hadn't stopped him. I'm actually one of the lucky ones." She reached into her purse and pulled out a notebook and an envelope similar to the one Shiloh had handed her earlier. "This is my list of suspects. There's also one who's a client, but I didn't put him on there for professional reasons. And this is the photo he left in my mailbox."

Kat accepted the items. "He hasn't left one for me."

"Yet," Ruth said seriously. "Be careful, Kat. I'm spending almost every minute with other people. Ethan's with me every night." A faint blush stole into her cheeks. "Tell Shiloh to watch out too."

"She's staying at the Tate ranch with Beau Tate. They're taking care of Morgan, and they've got a dog."

"Ethan says you try to have dinner once a week or so, but that you haven't been able to get together lately. Maybe we can all find some time in the near future?"

"Sure."

"I'll call you," Ruth said, looking a little uncertain about Kat's monosyllabic reply. The truth was, currently Kat couldn't imagine ever eating again.

Three hours later, Kat and Ricki were in Ricki's Jeep rattling down the long driveway that led to the Rocking D, Ira Dillinger's ranch. Kat had tried to think of something to eat for lunch, but the image of the blood-red remains of her breakfast in the toilet was something she couldn't get out of her head. She held on to the panic bar as they bumped along, hoping she didn't upchuck on the upholstery. Finally, they hit the blacktop, and the ride smoothed out for the last quarter mile.

Ricki had asked her if Ruth had come in, and Kat had said no, without explaining that they'd met in the park. Kat was waiting until after this meeting with Ira Dillinger about the barbed wire to bring up Ruth's recorded statement and the rape. She planned to present the facts of the crime to both Ricki and Sheriff Sam Featherstone at the same time, and the sheriff had been out of the office all morning.

"Still waiting on that full report on Courtney Pearson, but preliminaries are grim," Ricki said now, her eyes straight ahead, her expression set. "Indications suggest she was subjected to rough sex, probably for years."

Kat swallowed.

"Someone doused her in gasoline, inside and out. Maybe they meant to burn the body, or maybe they thought it would disguise DNA. It's not clear. Her cause of death was from exsanguination."

"She bled out?"

"That cut on her wrist was from the barbed wire. Not the wire that was binding her wrists. A separate piece, apparently, that wasn't with the body."

"He cut her wrist to kill her?" Kat said slowly, disbelieving.

"Or maybe she'd had enough and did it to herself."

"Oh. God."

Kat hung her head and felt saliva gather in her mouth. She swallowed quickly, several times.

"You want me to stop the truck?" Ricki asked.

"No."

"Hangovers can really be a bitch," she said sympathetically as they pulled up in front of the wide front porch of the two-story rambling mansion of wood and stone.

* * *

Ira Dillinger sat behind the huge desk in his den, his gray-white brows capping a pair of sharp eyes. He looked rawhide tough and weather-beaten, and he gave Kat a hard looking over as she entered his office behind Ricki. Kat nodded to him, then focused on the multi-generational photograph of the Dillinger family prominently displayed behind him. It had been taken years earlier, when Ricki was much younger. She was standing in front of a gray barn with a brilliant blue Wyoming sky behind them. Beside her were her brothers, Colton and Tyler, and her sisters, Delilah and Nell. Kat knew them all by sight, though none of them very well, other than Ricki.

"What is it you want me to see?" Ira asked his daughter.

Ricki pulled out the snapshot of the close-up on Courtney Pearson's wrists. "Patrick Starr thought this was Dillinger wire," she said, pointing to the barbed wire. "I figured you'd know for sure."

He dragged a pair of wire-rimmed glasses out of his pocket and perched them on his nose. When he made no immediate comment, Ricki explained, "It was wrapped around the wrists of Courtney Pearson, who had been missing for fifteen years."

Ira shook his head. "Well, it's Dillinger, all right. Haven't used it in years. Don't like them finding it and using it for God knows what purposes."

"We believe someone used it as a means of binding."

"I can see that." He shoved the picture aside. "I don't like what I'm thinking about it."

"I know," Ricki agreed.

Before she could go further, he pointed a finger at

her. "This is no job for a woman. I've said it before; I'll say it again."

"Dad." Ricki was long-suffering.

Ira shot Kat a look. "Your father's the one who realized it was Dillinger wire. You're Patrick Starr's daughter."

"Yes." She pegged Ira as late sixties, early seventies, maybe older, but he was in great shape, so it was hard to say.

"How's he like you being a cop?"

"Dad," Ricki said again, exasperated. "Where would someone get their hands on our wire? Is there any left on the property? In some corner of the barn or one of the outbuildings?"

"Well, I don't know. Ask Colton. He's all over the property."

"When did you stop using this particular design?" Kat asked.

He gave her another hard look but answered readily enough. "We never really went back to it after the old homestead burned down twenty years ago. All the old barbed wire's been replaced."

"Ricki, is that you?" a female voice called from somewhere outside the office. Both Kat and Ricki turned, and soon a pretty, blond woman wearing a Baby Bjorn appeared, a sleeping, dark-haired infant leaning against her breast. Delilah Dillinger Kincaid. And with her was another woman, tall and beautiful, carrying a garment bag over one arm.

"Sabrina, is that your dress?" Ricki asked.

Delilah answered first. "It's a bridesmaid dress she wants me to try. I don't think I can fit it." She puffed out her cheeks and gestured to her stomach.

"You don't have an ounce of baby fat left on you," Sabrina told her.

Ricki leaned in to touch the baby's head, and Kat looked at the velvety hair on his head and felt her heart beat painfully hard.

Ira growled, "Bring him over here."

"Hi, Katrina," Sabrina greeted her with a smile. "Good to see you. How's your dad?"

"Good." She cleared her throat.

The front door opened and shut again, and soon a tall man with a long stride came into view. Dark hair, slashing grin. Colton Dillinger. Sabrina's husband-to-be. "What is this, a family meeting?"

"We're just stopping by to see Ira," Delilah said, gently extracting the baby from his carrier and handing him to Ira. "And to try on a dress that won't fit."

"It'll fit," Sabrina assured. "Are you coming to the wedding?" she asked Katrina.

Kat blinked at her. "Um . . ."

"You got an invitation, right?" Sabrina looked alarmed, like she'd forgotten to send it.

"Yes, thank you," she said. Patrick had received one for the whole Starr family, though Kat had determined she wasn't going; it was just one more event to avoid because she didn't want to run into Blair Kincaid. "Unfortunately, I have a conflict, but I'll make sure Dad sends back the reply—"

"I'm so sorry," Sabrina said, too polite to ask what Kat's conflict was, which was a relief since Kat's mind was currently a blank. She couldn't think of anything she would be doing six weeks from now.

Except maybe starting to show . . .

"Can I talk to you a moment?" Ricki asked Colton.

"Sure," he said.

"If something changes, just let me know," Sabrina told Kat. "We're keeping it casual, so the guest list is fluid."

"Thanks." Kat swallowed.

"We'll be upstairs," Sabrina called after Colton, who was already heading out of the office with Ricki.

Kat followed them all into the front entryway. She glanced back to see Delilah putting baby Joshua into Ira's stiff arms. "Relax," Delilah laughed at her father. "He's a sound sleeper. He won't even notice."

Kat dragged her attention away from the baby as Ricki showed Colton the picture of Courtney's barbed-wire-wrapped wrists and explained what he was looking at. His expression grew sober, and he made a sound of unhappiness. "What the hell?"

"Dad says it's Dillinger barbed wire, so somebody got it from here. You think there's any left on the property?"

"Possibly." He rubbed his chin.

"Mind if Kat and I take a look around?" Ricki asked.

"I can do it later for you, if you can wait. I gotta go into town right now, but—"

"Don't worry about it," Ricki cut in. "We've got this."

Ira yelled from the office. "Let Colton do it!"

Ricki shook her head in exasperation, and Colton nodded in understanding. Ricki motioned for Kat to follow her, then stalked through the house and kitchen, out the back door. "Any way he can get me to not do my job," she muttered as she stomped into the hot sunshine. "He was about to give you a lecture on policework, but we were saved by the wedding."

There were a number of buildings around the property, used for machinery and storage, and there were several barns as well. They went into the first one, and Ricki ordered Kat to start in the back and go room by room, stall by stall. The musty smells of dust, horse, and grain didn't help Kat's uncertain stomach, and her mind's eye was still filled with the sight of Blair's nephew, the sweep of the baby's lashes, the lips sucking in sleep, the sweet, smooth skin and fat cheeks. She clenched her jaw and continued the search by sheer willpower, but she couldn't stop the thoughts and images that stayed with her: Courtney's body and the barbed wire; a shadowy man dragging Addie Donovan away from her horse; the hard planes and sinewy strength of Blair Kincaid's body; the two pink lines; the sheriff's office where she would soon explain all the years of silence over Ruth's rape . . .

They worked through two of the buildings, then entered an older one with a weathervane atop a cupola. Ricki took the front, while Kat walked to the back, her nose registering new smells, oil and gasoline. She'd discovered a hay baler, a rototiller, and a couple of ATVs. There were various pieces of junk parked against the back wall, which she looked over and around, and at the far end of the room was a low door that Kat had to shove her shoulder against. It opened with a groan, and she entered another room with more junk: a pile of metal machinery pieces; blocks of wood, one split by a rusted axe; and along the back wall, tiny remnants of rusted barbed wire.

Heart rate accelerating, Kat moved closer and

picked up a piece, turning it over in her hands. She recognized the pattern. "Found something!" she yelled jubilantly.

"I'm coming!" Ricki called back.

She appeared a few moments later, her rapid footsteps thunking on the wooden planks. She leaned down beside Kat, and they examined the pieces. "That's it, but not a lot of it." She then stood and looked around. "I suppose anybody could have gathered up strands at any time." She picked up the largest pieces.

"They'd have to have access to your father's ranch," Kat said. A distant part of herself was glad the bits of wire had been found where it was expected, on Dillinger land, not Kincaid. Not that it proved anything, but still . . .

"Who would know to steal it? Someone who worked here? Had access? Did they just come across it and decide to take it?" Ricki glowered at the thought. "There've been a lot of hands through here over the years. Need to narrow it down some."

Kat said, "Dad has a list of suspects he compiled about the missing girls from fifteen years ago. His top three left about the same time the girls stopped disappearing, but all three of them are now back in Prairie Creek."

Ricki squinted at her. "Rafe Dillinger fits that category. He on the list?"

Kat nodded.

"Rafe drinks too much, and he's a mean drunk, but I don't know. Doesn't seem like him. Ira tried to straighten him out when he was in high school, and it didn't take." She dusted her hands on her jeans. "Who are the other two?"

"Cal Haney and Skip Chandler."

"Chandler's name just keeps coming up. I'm not sure either one of them has ever worked at the Rocking D, but they could have been around."

"There are more names on his list. I know them by heart. It's been Dad's obsession. I can write 'em down for you."

"All right. Sam should be back by now. Let's go talk to him."

Ricki gave a curt good-bye to Ira as she and Kat traversed the lodge, in through the back and out the front. Delilah and Sabrina were still upstairs, and Kat heard the baby fussing and Delilah's soft cooing as she shut the front door behind them and climbed into Ricki's Jeep.

On the way back to the station, Kat's brain was cluttered with thoughts of the wedding, Blair, and the baby, and she forced them aside with an effort. She was deeply involved in this investigation, and her personal life needed to be put on hold. "Ruth has a list of suspects too," she said. "Mostly the same names as my dad's, but a few extras."

Ricki wheeled into the back lot. "We'll put them together, toss around ideas, and see what shakes out. Sam went to interview Debra and Jeremy Donovan again, and Addie's boyfriend, Dean Croft. Volunteers are still walking the fields, but there's been no sign of Addie. She might have been transported by vehicle, and her abductor could have gone back on the road and be miles from Prairie Creek by now."

Kat didn't feel like he was that far away. But then she had the information Ricki didn't know about yet. "I want you and the sheriff to hear a tape I recorded this morning from Ruth. It's about a crime that took place fifteen years ago. A man attacked Ruth and raped her."

Ricki's head swung around. "That's what she was coming in about?"

"I was there too, and so was Shiloh. He snapped a Polaroid of us skinny-dipping, and we all ran. But he caught Ruth."

"*What?*"

"I know. We fought him off her, but he chased us. He wore a mask. We never saw his face. We were kids, and we swore to Ruth that we wouldn't tell," Kat said grimly. "We kept that promise, but Ruth has finally come forward. Listen to the tape. It's all there."

"Okay."

"Ruth thinks her rapist is still around, and that there's a strong possibility he's related to Addie's disappearance and Courtney's kidnapping. I don't think she's wrong."

Ricki gave Kat a long look but apparently decided to let the matter lie for the moment. Kat didn't elaborate. Soon enough the whole world would know anyway. As soon as the PLAY button was pushed on the recorder.

Chapter 23

Sheriff Sam Featherstone punched the OFF button of the recorder and then sat back in his chair. Ricki and Kat were in chairs across from him. He had already slid the black-and-white photo of the three girls from its gold envelope, which had made Kat clench her teeth in embarrassment, then slipped it back inside once he'd taken the measure of it. He'd also looked at the one Shiloh had given Kat, its matching envelope now beneath Ruth's. The pieces of barbed wire Ricki had picked up from the Dillinger outbuilding were sitting on his desk next to the recorder.

Sam said, "We'll fingerprint the envelopes, but it sounds like they've been well handled, and it's unlikely our doer would be careless enough to leave prints."

It wasn't really a question, but Kat nodded. Sam then reiterated what she had told him when she and Ricki had first walked into his office, his eyes on Kat. "You and Ruth both think her attacker from fifteen years ago is involved in Addie Donovan's current disappearance and Courtney Pearson's death."

"Shiloh and Ruth got those pictures recently, so he knows where they are and dropped those envelopes in their mailboxes. Courtney was reported missing about a month before the attack on Ruth. Erin Higgins and Rachel Byrd disappeared earlier. Everyone concluded they were runaways."

"Your theory is they all were kidnapped," Sam said.

"Yes. Now. Shiloh wasn't kidnapped, she just left town, so it seemed like maybe those other girls left on their own too . . . but Erin and Rachel had no history of running away. Courtney was wilder, but even she hadn't left home, according to her mother. Ruth was attacked about that same time, and now we discover Courtney's body just after Addie Donovan disappears . . . Yes, I think there's someone out there kidnapping women and holding them hostage."

"As their own personal sex slaves," Ricki said softly.

Sam's face was grim as he picked up a strand of barbed wire. "Courtney could have been held somewhere on forest land behind where she was found. There are lean-tos and sheds all over hundreds of miles of acreage. Not supposed to be built, but they are, and hunters use them."

Ricki said, "We're already checking into the backgrounds of anyone who worked for or was somehow connected to the Rocking D."

"Your father always believed those girls weren't runaways," Sam said to Kat.

"He compiled a list of suspects, and Ruth made her own list." Kat pulled Ruth's small notebook out of her purse and handed it across the desk to Sam.

He glanced at the list of names in the notebook.

"Ruth thinks one of these is her stalker, and the man who attacked her fifteen years ago?"

"She believes it's a strong possibility. My dad is the one who really knows this case."

He handed the notebook back to Kat. "Go ahead and talk to Patrick."

Kat was relieved to get the okay from the sheriff himself. They discussed the case a bit more, then Ricki and Kat returned to Kat's desk, and they went over Ruth's list, comparing it to the names Kat knew on Patrick's.

"Dad doesn't have Jimmy Woodcock on his list," Kat said.

"Find out why Ruth added him," Ricki said.

"Ruth hinted that one of her clients should be on the list, but she wouldn't name names."

"Well, we'll start with these and see how far we get."

Ricki was called away by the arrival of the ME's report on Courtney Pearson. Alone, Kat picked up her desk phone to call Ruth, who answered right away. When Kat posed the question about Woodcock, Ruth explained about his obsession with porn and how it was often seen with sexual predators.

"You mentioned a client that you thought should be on your list," Kat nudged.

"You know I can't reveal his name. I'll think about how I want to handle him."

"Well, don't do anything rash."

"Don't worry."

Kat's attention was grabbed again by the red velvet cupcake, still sitting on her desk. She'd hardly noticed it since getting back from the Dillingers, but now her stomach trembled. Damn, this was getting old. "I wanted to ask you, how'd it go when you told your parents?"

Ruth made a disparaging sound. "I didn't expect them to understand, and I was certainly right. But at least it's out there. Other girls need to be warned. We have to stop him, catch him, put him away for good."

"We will," Kat told her with certainty.

After she hung up, her phone rang almost immediately. It was Ricki. "They're pretty sure Courtney's death was a suicide, but the barbed-wire manacles were there a long while. Handcuffs. Looks like she was held against her will. Probably the reason she killed herself."

Her eyes drew back to the cupcake. It sat there . . . sweet . . . red . . .

"Lividity shows the body was moved, otherwise all the blood would have pooled in one area, and it didn't. She may have killed herself, but someone transported her to where she was found. Could have trucked her from anywhere across that forest land."

Blood red . . .

"So, maybe he's here and maybe he's not. We're looking, but there are thousands of acres behind where Courtney was found. A lot of property butts up to Forest Service land, a lot of makeshift roads. If she was kept hidden somewhere in those acres, it's going to take a while to find where, maybe a long while."

Ricki signed off, sounding somewhat down. Kat felt the same way. She swallowed hard, feeling her throat tighten. She swept up the cupcake, walked quickly toward the break room, and veered toward the bathroom. Without hesitation, she tossed the confection in the trash.

Then she ran for the toilet and vomited again and again.

Shit.

* * *

"Who do you think this guy is that's going to see Ruth professionally?" Patrick asked Kat two hours later. She'd called him on her cell as she was heading back to her apartment and told him about Ruth's list, so they were comparing names. Most were the same, but Ruth had added Bryce Higgins to her list, Erin Higgins's brother, who'd been big and burly since puberty, and had been loud and angry, damn near obnoxious, when his sister went missing, then later on had acted as if the deed had never happened, as if all his earlier actions were just posturing. Her father had decided to move Scott Massey up on his list because he was an avid hunter whose property was remote and nestled up to Forest Service land on a trajectory to where Courtney Pearson's body was found.

"I don't know who he is, and she wouldn't say." Kat reached one hand into her glove box as she drove and came up with a pack of gum. She pulled out a stick, unwrapped it, and folded it into her mouth, proud of her one-handed dexterity. "She's professionally bound."

"Her office is right across the street from Goldie's Used Furniture," he said reluctantly. "I could stop in and see her. Ask her a few things."

Kat could have laughed out loud. Goldie Horndahl was one of Prairie Creek's snoopiest, most gossipy women. Anything you ever wanted to know about anybody, and a lot that you didn't, came flying out of Goldie's mouth every time you ran into her. She'd also been sweet on Patrick Starr for as long as Kat could remember. "You'll just encourage her, and she'll never tell you anything that matters."

"Bet she knows every one of Ruth's clients."

"I'm not taking that bet."

"I could take her out to dinner, see what she says."

"You'll never get rid of her," Kat warned.

Her father humphed. "On the list there are the guys who left Prairie Creek and came back, and there are the ones who were here the whole time. I'm starting to lean toward the guys who've been here the whole time. Courtney was held somewhere around here all those years."

"We don't know that," Kat said. "He could have brought her back. She's been missing a long time."

"Why would he bring her back? Doesn't make sense. He was getting rid of the body."

"I'm inclined to agree with you. I just don't want to jump to conclusions and make a bad decision."

"You couldn't make a bad decision if your life depended on it," Patrick said with a chuckle.

Oh, boy. She hadn't told him about Ruth's rape and the events that led up to it yet. She'd only mentioned that Ruth had compiled a list of names based on her own recent encounters with Cal Haney, Rafe Dillinger, and Skip Chandler and her experience as a therapist.

Wait until he finds out about the baby . . .

"Kat?"

She realized she'd missed whatever he'd just said. "Yes?"

"I asked who you wanted to interview first."

"I'm not sure." In truth, she had much still to do at work. Some texts on Addie's phone to her boyfriend,

Dean, had sounded like they were planning to secretly meet, although they were mostly from Addie and could be hopeful yearnings rather than a serious plan. Nevertheless, Ricki wanted to talk to Dean Croft again, and Kat did too.

Her father said, "I'll take Rafe Dillinger."

Kat just managed to keep from rolling her eyes. "You still don't believe me that Rafe was the one who got Darla Kingsley pregnant," she accused.

"Doesn't hurt to follow up."

"Ricki's already talking to him. He's a Dillinger."

"I'll take Massey then. I know where he lives, and I'll check on him."

"Maybe I should go with you."

"No. Dad." She fought her annoyance. Everything seemed to irritate her these days. "This is what I do for a living. I'll make sure Ricki and Sam know who I'm interviewing and when. And Massey's married. I don't see our kidnapper having a wife in the picture. You're the one who needs to be careful during interviews. You're not a cop anymore."

He grunted. "It'll work in my favor. Less official."

She knew he didn't really believe that. He missed being on the force, but she wasn't going to argue further. "Ricki and Sam have got their eyes on Skip Chandler, among others." She'd told him about Skip's interaction with Ruth's daughter, Penny. "I'm not planning on doing anything tonight. I'm just heading home." All she wanted was a hot bath and something to eat, though she wasn't sure exactly what that was going to be.

"Guess I'll give Goldie a call."

Hearing the reluctance threaded through his voice,

Kat said, "You don't have to. The department's all over this. You and I both have enough suspects to hold us for a while."

"No time like the present."

She shook her head. Her father was nothing if not tenacious. It's what had made him such a great detective. Her mind touched on the picture of the three of them skinny-dipping that Ruth's rapist, and possibly Courtney's killer, had sent to Shiloh and Ruth, and she said, "I think Addie's been kidnapped by the same man who kidnapped Courtney."

"We both do." They'd already been over that.

"This guy left Courtney's body close by because he wanted us to find her. Maybe it was convenient. Maybe that's why he chose the spot he did. He had to get rid of her. But he also likes to taunt. And he may be the same guy who stalked Ruth a few nights ago at her home."

"He's gone active again." This too was something they'd gone over. "That's why I don't want you seeing Massey alone."

"I'll make sure Joleen's there. But I'll stop by your office, and we'll talk before I go out there. Right now I'm going home." She pulled out her wad of gum and stuck it inside its leftover wrapper. It had helped slightly, but she was still feeling uncomfortable in the midsection.

It turned out that Kat missed a half day of work the next day, and a full day the next. She blamed it on the flu, but in truth, she was pretty sure it was her pregnancy keeping her in bed. On the third day, she dragged herself to work and was at her desk, catching up, when Shiloh breezed in and plopped down in the chair opposite her.

"I want to help," she said determinedly, her blond hair a braided rope down her back, her face sun-kissed, her blue eyes hard. "Stop freezing me out."

"I'm not freezing you out. I haven't been at work."

"Did you see today's paper?" She tossed a copy of the *Prairie Winds* onto Kat's desk, and it sailed into her lap.

"What is it?" Kat asked, picking it up and scanning the front page. Jimmy Woodcock's headline writing was as sensational as ever: THERAPIST VICTIM OF RAPE HERSELF. "Oh no."

"Apparently word leaked from your department here, and Woodcock ran with it, although there's not much there, just that it happened a long time ago and she was finally coming forward."

Kat quickly read the article. It was more innuendo than fact, but it did mention Ruth's name. "Woodcock put in that Ruth thinks there's a link between her rape and the missing girls from past and present."

"Kinda throws it all out there," Shiloh said.

"This is what we all wanted, but it's still hard to see it in the paper. Good thing Ruth already told her parents." *And my brother.*

Shiloh grimaced. "Hope she handles it okay."

"Yeah," Kat said soberly.

"Woodcock also says Courtney Pearson's death was a suicide and the investigation is ongoing. Beau and I talked it over, and we want to be a part of it."

"Thanks, but we're good."

"This is what I mean. You're freezing me out."

"I can't talk about the investigation. You know that, and I already got my hand slapped once."

"Why? What do you mean?"

"Nothing." Kat shut that down right away. She didn't need Ricki, or anyone else on the force, overhearing her talking to Shiloh about the case. She'd already had enough trouble with her father. "There's nothing for you to involve yourself with."

"Don't say you can't use more help," Shiloh said. "Those K-9 teams I see all over the Croft property are coming up empty. Helicopters haven't found anything on forest land?" When Kat didn't respond, she said, "And no clues from where we found Courtney's body and where Addie disappeared." She leaned in and added in a low voice, "You know we know Ruthie's rapist."

Kat frowned. "What do you mean?"

"He seemed familiar to us. He sure did to me, and he did to you too."

"We never saw his face."

"All I'm saying is, he's not a complete stranger. And I want to check out some of the guys around here, see if they ring any bells."

"We're already doing that. Don't get in the way," Kat warned.

"This is what I've been saying! You're freezing me out." Shiloh got to her feet. "I'm going to do some checking on my own."

"Shiloh, *no.*"

"I've got Beau with me. I won't get in the way of your investigation." She started down the hall.

Kat ground her teeth together and said in a stage

whisper to Shiloh's back, "I just don't want anyone to get hurt. Leave it to the authorities."

Shiloh lifted a hand in acknowledgment but didn't turn around. Kat stared after her, irked, then got up to follow after her friend. Shiloh was just too bull-headed for her own good sometimes.

Brrrinnngg. Her desk phone rang before she had taken two steps. She hesitated briefly, then turned back and snatched up the receiver. "Yes?" she answered tightly.

Naomi said, "Phone call for you. Mr. Blair Kincaid."

Blair.

"I can't take it right now, Naomi. I'm in the middle of something."

"He's pretty insistent. Says it's something about a kid named Noel Brinkman getting into trouble on Kincaid property?"

Kat made a strangled sound. The Byrds' grandson again? "Okay, put him through."

A few seconds later Blair's familiar drawl raised goose bumps on her arms with, "Hey, Kat. How're you doing? This kid here says you're the one to talk to."

"Noel Brinkman's on your property?"

"That's the one."

"What's he done?" She just stopped herself from adding *now*.

"Well, we're not far from Hal Crutchens's place, and apparently Noel and some of his friends opened up the gate and let Crutchens's old nag out. The beast ended up on our property, and, well . . ."

Kat silently swore inside her head. "What? Is the horse okay?"

"Right as rain. 'Cept for the 'F-word' and 'you' spray-painted on his haunch."

Dammit. "And Noel's with you now?"

"Mike, my foreman, caught him and a couple other of the little delinquents before they ran away. I was about to start taking names, when Noel offers up his own name and says to call you, like you're his lawyer."

"Have you contacted his parents?"

"John and Rinda. I was about to—" There was a commotion on the other end of the line, and then Blair said, sounding faintly amused, "Your client wants to talk to you, counselor."

"Detective Starr?" a young, thin voice warbled, sounding near tears. "Don't call my parents. Please, please, *please* don't call my parents. It was Reed and Ben's idea. It's water-based paint. It won't hurt him none."

"Noel, it's not up to me. You're a minor. Your parents are your guardians."

"I said you'd help us! I said we wouldn't go to jail!" He dropped the phone, and Kat heard a scuffle and then someone barked out, "Stop right there!" then silence.

"Noel?" Kat asked, alarmed. "Noel?"

The phone was picked up again, and Blair said, "It's all right. Flight from custody averted. Mike stopped them from running. They are all now shaking in their boots on the back porch, waiting for the long arm of the law to come crashing down on them."

"I'll be there in twenty minutes . . ."

"I'll call their parents," Blair said. "See you soon."

* * *

354 Lisa Jackson, Nancy Bush, and Rosalind Noonan

The Kincaid ranch sprawled over hundreds of acres of farmland and was close to the size of the Dillinger ranch, maybe even as big or bigger. Kat hadn't been back to it since that night with Blair, and she approached with a feeling of extreme weariness. She wanted to find Addie Donovan. She wanted to find Ruth's rapist and Courtney Pearson's kidnapper. She wanted to know what had happened to Rachel Byrd and Erin Higgins. She wanted to scream and rip out her hair and lie down on the ground and sob.

She'd put in a call to Ruth on the way, sick at heart that Jimmy Woodcock had sensationalized her story as only he could. When Ruth picked up, Kat immediately began apologizing for the leak in the department, swearing she would get to the bottom of it, but Ruth told her not to worry.

"I spoke to Woodcock myself," she revealed, to Kat's surprise. "I called your cell, but you didn't pick up, so then I phoned the department. You weren't in, so I ended up talking to Ricki. She was so sympathetic and determined to get the guy that it was easy to talk to her. It was good, and then I asked myself what I was waiting for. She knows, Sam knows, my parents know. So I called Jimmy and gave him the bare bones story."

"You left Shiloh and me out of it."

"He didn't need every detail. He just needed to report that I was raped. He was bound to add his own spin, but it could've been a lot worse. Honestly, Kat, it's really helped to have Ethan here, encouraging me. Woodcock's a lowlife, and it's too bad he owns the paper, but . . . so what. We need to catch this guy." Kat could almost hear her brother's words coming from Ruth. "This is going to sound weird," she'd gone on, "but I think Jimmy was deeply shocked by my story. Shocked that it happened to me. You know, good girl, Ruthie, and all that. He could have been covering up, I suppose, but I just don't think he's that good of an actor . . . so I'm thinking of moving him down on my suspect list."

They'd talked a bit more, but then the entrance to the Kincaid ranch had come into view, and Kat had wound down the call.

"Maybe my story will help get this guy. Someone might remember something, or maybe it'll give them courage to come forward. Something," Ruth had added hopefully just before they hung up.

"I'm glad you're with Ethan," Kat blurted back, meaning it.

Now, she drove through the gates and down the long drive that circled in front of the sprawling two-story ranch house with its flanking wings. There were new boards on the porch, and the shutters looked freshly painted. She took in three deep breaths and exhaled them and was staring at her hands, still clenched around the steering wheel, when her cell phone rang. She dug through her purse, completely aware that she was glad of the distraction. It was her father, and that gave her pause, but in the end she answered, "Hi, Dad."

"Where are you? Are you at work?"

"Yeah . . ."

"You don't sound too sure. You're not on your way to Massey's, are you?"

"No, I'm at the Kincaid ranch." She gave her father a brief update, fully aware she was going against department protocol since this wasn't part of the Pearson investigation, but she wanted Patrick to know what and whom she was facing.

He understood immediately, warning grimly, "Be careful with the Byrds."

"I can't seem to get away from them," she said on a sigh.

"What does that mean?"

"Nothing. Look, I gotta go deal with this, so I'll talk to you later."

"I wanted you to know that I had dinner with Goldie."

"Great. Can we talk about this later?"

"Sure enough. Ruth's client is probably Hank Eames. That's the only guy Goldie's seen going into her office who fills the bill."

Kat had a mental image of Eames, and a cold feeling settled between her shoulder blades as she recalled Shiloh's words: *You know we know Ruthie's rapist. He seemed familiar to us. He sure did to me, and he did to you too.*

Could Hank Eames be the guy?

What was Ruth's mantra? Wide girth . . . something . . . thick something . . .

Kat had mostly seen him in profile, but his face had been obscured. His body, though . . .

"Katrina?"

The ranch house front door opened, and Blair strolled onto the porch. Through the windshield, her gaze moved upward from his cowboy boots, to his jeans with the dull-silver belt buckle, to his insouciant smile, the amusement in his eyes below the tip of his hat. A rush of emotion ran through her—an-

noyance, breathlessness, a rush of inexplicable desire. Man, she didn't want to want him. It was down-
right perplexing that she did.

"I'll call you, Dad." She clicked off and stepped
out of her Jeep into a blasting July sun. Her scalp
prickled with the heat. Mentally tamping down on
her uneasy stomach, she strode his way.

"Thought I was going to see that back bumper in
my grill the other day," he drawled, nodding toward
her Jeep.

"You snuck up on me," she said shortly.

"Did I?"

He was staring at her in a way that made her feel
he was asking a different question than the one she
heard, but she ignored him. "Where's Noel?"

"Out back. Come on through." He opened the
screen door and pushed in the oak front door with a
booted foot. Kat heard an approaching vehicle and
looked around.

"The Brinkmans," Blair said. "And the Byrds."

They both waited as Rinda and John Brinkman,
the Byrds' oldest daughter and son-in-law, and silver-
haired Paul Byrd and his wife, sad-eyed Ann, moved
toward them. John's face was a study in contained
fury, while Rinda's face was flushed with color—embarrassment, it turned out. Paul glared at Kat as if
the whole thing was her fault, while Ann regarded
her anxiously, apparently feeling the same way.

"Come on in," Blair invited, holding the door for
all of them. Kat waited to bring up the rear with Blair,
who whispered in her ear, "You do something to piss
off Grandma and Grandpa?"

"I'm Patrick Starr's daughter."

"Ahh . . ."

They all trundled through the house to the back porch, where Mike, the foreman, a brawny, fifty-something man with a wide chest and muscular arms, was leaning against a back rail and whittling on a small piece of wood. Three tween boys were seated in a row on a wooden bench, all sitting with straight backs and sober expressions. Their eyes swung as one to the Brinkmans, and when Noel saw his father, he shrank back and looked at the floor.

Paul Byrd looked around, glaring, then his angry eyes landed back on Kat. His gaze skated down her slim frame, centering on her mid-section, and Kat felt herself go cold. *He knows. Rhianna told him.*

"What happened?" John Brinkman asked Noel, but it was Mike who brought him up-to-date on the horse prank. Noel's father looked stricken, and Noel's chin sank down further. His friends tried to look at anything but the group of adults on the porch.

"What were you thinking?" John demanded.

"I dunno," Noel mumbled.

Paul Byrd said evenly, "I'd prefer to keep this matter out of the hands of the Sheriff's Department."

"That will be up to Mr. Crutchens," Kat answered.

"Has he been told yet?" Byrd was laser-focused on Kat. She wasn't certain the others were aware of their silent little war, but she sure was.

"Not yet," Blair put in. "But it's kinda hard to hide the, uh, sentiment on the horse's hide."

"He's just such an a-hole," Noel muttered.

"Noel!" Rinda cried.

"Well, he is."

Byrd looked like he was going to yank his grand-

son to his feet and shake him. Kat stepped forward
instinctively, and so did Blair. Everyone else looked
stunned.

Byrd rounded on Kat. "If Hal Crutchens wants to
file a report, he can file a report. We don't need you
keeping score!"

"What's going on?" Blair interjected tautly before
Kat could respond.

"I'll be talking to the sheriff," Byrd assured him.
"He's a good cop. Diligent."

Kat felt her face flame, but she told herself not to
rise to the bait.

Blair, however, wasn't known for holding back.
"You got something to say, you better just say it."

"You her boyfriend?" Byrd challenged.

"Dad," Rinda said, discomfited.

Blair's brows raised. "What're we doing here?" he
asked.

"The sanctity of marriage shouldn't be laughed at,
especially when there's a new life on the way." He
swung his gaze meaningfully toward Kat, and everyone else looked at her too.

There was a buzzing in her head, and the sunlit
field behind the Kincaid ranch house began to swim
in front of her eyes.

Shit.

Chapter 24

She didn't completely pass out. After several seconds, her vision righted itself, and with the attention off him, Noel seized the opportunity to plead his case, whining that old man Crutchens deserved everything coming to him because he was a mean, nasty, old *bastard*.

Ann Byrd stepped between her husband and his grandchild, and Rinda and John Brinkman looked at their son like he was a creature from another planet. They decided to walk Crutchens's horse back to him with the help of the truants who were desperate to wash off the water-based paint before he saw his horse. They wanted to go alone, but their parents ignored them, and the whole family trooped toward the Crutchens property.

Mike had diplomatically disappeared to one of the outbuildings, and Kat pulled out her phone, glanced at the screen, and said with false lightness, "I'd better go. Duty calls. It's in Hal Crutchens's hands now, and hopefully he won't be too hard on them."

"Are you pregnant?"

Of all the scenarios she'd thought of, and there had been a few that had run through her mind, about how, when, or even if she would tell Blair he was about to be a father, this was one of the worst.

"I'm . . ." She stopped. There were no words she could think to say. She wanted to deny it all. She wanted to lie. She couldn't do it, so she just stopped.

Blair was regarding her through incredulous blue eyes. "Is it mine?"

"No."

"It's not mine?"

"It's . . . I'm . . . I haven't figured this out yet, and I'm . . . taking some time to, uh . . ."

"But you are pregnant?"

"I haven't seen a doctor. Nothing's for sure."

"Whose is it?"

"I don't know."

"You don't know?" he bit out. She didn't like the way he was gazing at her so intently.

"No, I don't know. It could be any one of the guys I've been seeing," she snapped.

"What guys?"

"The . . . the ones I've been dating."

"Name one."

"It's a secret. They don't know about each other, and it's gotten worse, the stakes are higher now with the . . . this . . ."

"Name one," he insisted. He took a step toward her, and it was all Kat could do not to step back.

"You threatening me, Kincaid?" she demanded.

"You're pregnant, and it's my baby, and you weren't going to tell me."

"You're making assumptions!"

"Tell me I'm wrong."

"You're . . ."

"Kat," he whispered when she couldn't go on.

"I don't know what I'm doing, Blair! You don't know anything about me, and that's the way it's going to stay!"

"What's with you, Kat? Two months ago . . . practically three . . . we end up making love, and then you won't talk to me, and now you don't tell me that you're *pregnant?*"

"I just learned, okay? I got a pregnancy test from that pharmacy at the edge of town, and the Byrds' daughter works there, and she saw me. Don't tell me that you have any rights because you don't! I don't want to hear that from you."

"Well, you're going to." His lips were pressed blade thin.

"To hell with you."

"To hell with you," he shot right back.

They glared at each other.

Kat was a mess inside. She couldn't believe she was having this verbal skirmish, all of it out in the open. "I haven't seen a doctor yet. Or told my dad. Or people at work."

"Well, you'd better do it soon," he growled. "'Cause the word's out."

"I'm not sure I'm keeping it!" The words rang out between them. They were false. She'd already determined she wouldn't be able to go that route. But she was alarmed. He was alarming her! Where did he get off being so proprietary?

"Kat," he said in disbelief.

"I gotta go."

She turned away from him, yanking open the back door, hurrying through the house, blinded by her own tumultuous thoughts. He was right on her heels, and when she ran onto the porch and slammed the front door into the outside wall, he grabbed her arm. The door banged back into him, but he wasn't fazed.

"Kat. Wait."

She tried to shake him off. "Stop it. I don't want the Byrds to come back and see us fighting. Just let me go."

"Come on, I'm sorry. You shocked me. I don't want to fight. I just need to talk. You and I. Talk."

There were tears rising to her eyes from the depths of her soul. *Oh. God. No.* She couldn't break down. She didn't even feel like breaking down. It was her out-of-whack hormones. "I can't right now. I'm working. I've got . . . things to do."

"What kinds of things?"

"Addie Donovan's missing, and Courtney Pearson's dead. *Would you let me go?*"

He dropped her arm. "Is it mine?"

She shook her head, glad that he wasn't one hundred percent sure.

But his words followed her to her Jeep. *Yes, it's yours. There's been no one else.*

She tore away from his ranch, seeing his image retreat in her rearview mirror as he watched her leave. What was it that made her act like an adolescent around him?

"You should've told him," she muttered through her teeth.

She glanced down at her cell. It would be a simple matter to put that right.

But she didn't pick up her phone.

Blair Kincaid watched the plume of dust that followed Kat's Jeep down the long drive that led to the ranch. He was a mass of conflicting emotions, which really pissed him off. The credo of his life had been to be a rolling stone, and when he'd accepted his older brother's invitation to work the ranch with him, Blair had turned a corner he hadn't been sure he wanted to turn. But he'd dug in, side by side with Hunter, and together they'd brought the ranch back to its glory days . . . well, maybe not quite that far, but it had been in real disrepair until the Kincaid brothers had gotten to work, and now it was a whole lot better.

Blair had given up smoking . . . and drinking to excess . . . and women with great bodies and no interest in him beyond a one-night stand. Not that he'd been anybody's idea of a catch for most of his adult life, although the way some of the single gals around Prairie Creek were looking at him now said they'd noticed the change.

Or maybe they just knew he was in charge of the Kincaid ranch, and he rattled around the house all by himself now that Hunter, Delilah, and baby Joshua had moved to a house in town. Hunter still worked the ranch, but he still had one foot with the Prairie Creek Fire Department, a job he kept trying to quit and one that kept dragging him back with offers of promotions. He'd actually turned the fire chief's job down twice, but Blair expected they'd be asking him again.

He stretched and closed his eyes, tamping down a feeling of frustration entirely new to him. Katrina . . . Little Kat . . . She'd gotten into his blood. He'd known it before the whole baby discovery.

A baby . . . his baby . . . He knew it damn well was his. Had to be. No matter what she said.

God.

He opened his eyes, staring at the dissipated dust that still hung in the air in the wake of her leaving. Was that how it was? One day you were just gobsmacked by a woman, one who didn't act like she even liked you?

The Byrds and Brinkmans returned and called his name from the back porch. He went back to meet them and help shepherd them through his house and to their vehicles. They seemed to have worked things out with Hal Crutchens. Blair suspected money had changed hands because that's what would be required to get Crutchens to not take the matter to the authorities. Old man Byrd's face was red with suppressed anger, and the Brinkmans looked worn out and anxious to just leave and put it all behind them.

Blair was glad to be rid of the lot of them, although the incident had brought Kat back to the ranch, the only way it would happen since she didn't want to have anything to do with him.

Mike had returned to the back porch, nearly finished with his whittling of a tiny dog, which looked like some kind of Lab. "Nice people," he remarked with faint sarcasm.

Blair snorted.

"Katrina Starr's a bit of all right," Mike admitted.

Blair slid him a look, wondering how much he'd overheard. He'd wandered off the porch when the Byrd/Brinkman entourage had headed toward Hal's place, but he could have wandered right back and maybe overheard when he and Kat were arguing on the front porch. Blair hadn't shut any doors and windows, and sound traveled . . .

"She the same gal you had over here that night awhile back?" He held up the wooden dog and blew across its back, removing dust.

"What makes you think that?"

He eyed the little dog and gave a grunt of satisfaction. Then he set the figurine near the porch post nearest Blair. "For the baby," he said, then strolled back toward the barns, whistling tunelessly.

Two days, Blair determined. He would give her two days, and if she hadn't contacted him, he was going to go find her and have it out with her.

"Helicopters scoured a lot of the forest land behind the Donovans and the Tates and beyond," Ricki said to Kat the next morning, "and haven't turned anything up. We need more manpower for trekking, and we just don't have it."

"You think he's keeping Addie somewhere around here. Maybe where he kept Courtney. Where he would've kept Ruth, if she hadn't gotten away."

"Isn't that your theory?"

Kat nodded. Yes, it was her theory. Her mind was just so full of her own problems that it sometimes helped to reiterate their thoughts on the case precisely. So far, Rhianna Byrd hadn't shouted Kat's pregnancy to the rooftops, but then, she'd never admitted to it, either. She could've been picking up that kit for someone else. That wasn't out of the realm of possibility. And Blair hadn't taken things further, but then it had only been one day . . .

"It's been a lot of years since Ruth's rape," Ricki said. "Could be a different guy, I suppose. I don't want to assume too much. But if it's a different guy, then maybe he did take Addie away. Pretty dangerous to keep doing what you're doing with all this attention."

"Unless you think you're smarter than everyone else."

"There's that," Ricki agreed.

Kat not only believed it was the same guy, she also believed it was someone on her father's list. And Ricki believed it too. She was just making sure they didn't jump to one conclusion.

"I don't think it's Rafe," she said. "Not because he's a Dillinger. Like I said, I just don't think he's made that way. I know. Totally unscientific and arbitrary. Just a gut feeling."

"I don't think it's Rafe, either."

"I've talked to him and talked to him, and all I've done is piss him off, which I don't care about, but it just doesn't read right."

Kat wondered if her father had interviewed him, like he'd said he was going to. "I'm going to talk to Cal Haney. Ruth had a run-in with him, and he scared her."

"What kind of run-in?"

"Haney lives with his wife near Ruth's parents' place, and Ruth felt he was a little too familiar with her daughter and Jessica Calderon. Turns out Haney is Jessica's newish uncle. He married her mother's sister. Haney was spraying the girls with a hose, and they were screaming. Ruth ran to where they were, panicked, and apparently Haney acted like she was a crazy woman."

"Hmm."

"I know it seems like Ruth overreacts, but Cal Haney is too familiar, as a rule. I don't know him well, just of him."

"He is a little smirky," Ricki agreed. "You going out there today?"

"That's the plan."

"Maybe you should take someone with you."

"You just said we don't have enough manpower. I'll be fine," Kat said. "Reverend McFerron and his wife are right there, and Haney's wife too, probably. I've got my cell. I can always call for backup, if need be."

"If he's the guy, he's dangerous," Ricki reminded.

"Oh, I know."

Her mind returned to those moments in the clearing, when the bastard had looked up from raping Ruth and Shiloh had thrown the rock at him. She shivered. If this guy wasn't Ruth's rapist, he was just as bad or worse.

Kat was getting ready to head home when she got a phone call from Hank Eames that was so blistering it felt like it took the top layer of skin off her ear. ". . . Sneaky little bitch! I'll get her credentials yanked!" he practically screamed. "I didn't have anything to do with that girl's disappearance, and the one that's

dead too. Pearson. And I wouldn't touch Ruth Mc-
Ferron if you paid me a million dollars a year! Not
then, not now, not ever! You tell your dad to stay
away from me!"

"Ruth didn't say anything about you, Mr. Eames,"
Kat assured him. "We're interviewing lots of people."

"I didn't hurt nobody. I told her that. It was all
consensual!"

"Mr. Eames—"

"You Starrs think you're better than the rest of us.
You . . ." He couldn't seem to find his voice for a moment, then flashed, "You tell your little friend to stay
out of my way. She's a lying bitch who probably
spread her legs for that guy and now wants to cry
rape!"

Kat replaced her receiver carefully, feeling how
fast her pulse was racing. Patrick had told her he'd
met with Eames, and that the man hadn't been happy
about the questions he'd posed. But Jeez Louise.

Her father had also told her that he'd had some
questions for Rafe Dillinger, and the man had gotten
in his face. "First Ricki, now you. I been checking
things out. Found out when that girl disappeared. I
was putting in a shift at Big Bart's at that time. Everybody says she was doing the Croft kid. You should be
looking at him, not me."

Patrick had added that Rafe was fairly colorful
about what he could do to himself, then added somewhat ruefully, "Checked his alibi, and it holds up.
You know who vouched for him? Darla Kingsley . . .
can't think of her married name. By all accounts,
she doesn't like him much anymore. Rafe never was
much of a father, not that she apparently cares any-

more. Anyway, she works at Big Bart's part-time, and Rafe was there the day Addie disappeared for all the hours that matter."

An alibi for Rafe Dillinger. Maybe it could be broken, but Kat also knew that Darla had no love for Rafe, so she was inclined to believe it.

At least Dad knows Blair wasn't the one who got Darla pregnant.

Small comfort, in the scheme of things.

Kat picked up the phone to call Ruth. Might as well warn her about what Eames was saying before she was blindsided. She didn't get through, though, so she left a message on voice mail for Ruth to call her, and then as she headed out of the station, her cell phone rang and she fished it from her purse and saw it was Ruth. "Good thing you didn't call me back at the station, as I'm just heading out," Kat said as a hello.

"Call you back? Was I supposed to? No, I'm calling for a different reason." There was suppressed excitement in Ruth's voice.

"What?"

"You know I have a number of call-ins on my hotline who keep checking back with me. One of them, 'Lily,' is ready to talk to the police. Kat, she's alluded to the fact that her rapist is from around Prairie Creek, and I've tried to get her to go to the authorities for a while, but she couldn't make herself. But she saw my story, and now she's ready to talk!"

"That's great, Ruth."

"I told her you were with me when I was attacked, and she only wants to talk to you," she rushed on. "But she lives out of town, and she won't come back to Prairie Creek. Can you get away for a day, drive maybe to Jackson to meet her?"

Jackson was quite a ways. Kat had already missed a day and a half of work, and though this could be construed as related to their investigation, she didn't want to have to ask for time off. "Any chance she could come closer? Say Saturday? Maybe Wheeler City?" The town was about an hour away. "I'm off that day."

"I'll ask her," Ruth said. "And see what her schedule is."

"Good."

"You were trying to call me, you said?"

"My dad interviewed Hank Eames as a potential suspect, and Hank, uh, thought you'd given him up." Kat then related what Hank Eames had said about Ruth. She absorbed the message in silence, then thanked Kat for telling her.

"I wouldn't give him up. You know that."

"I know it. And my dad knows it, but Hank doesn't."

"He wasn't on my list because I couldn't talk about him. Was he on Patrick's?"

Time to come clean. "Um . . . more like my father has been seeing a little of Goldie Horndahl, whose furniture store is right across the street from your office. If you know Goldie, she's not known for holding back."

"I know Goldie," Ruth said dryly.

"Dad might've initiated that friendship to see who was going in and out of your building."

"Might've?" Ruth asked, though there was a trace of humor in her voice that encouraged Kat.

"Oh, he'll pay the price for it, believe me. Goldie's not the kind of woman you have a couple of dates with and then let go."

"I'll tell your brother," Ruth said, a smile forming in her voice. "Ethan and I can handle Hank. I'm relieved it's out there, to tell the truth, and I'm just so happy Lily's finally coming forward."

They ended the call on good terms, and Kat headed to her Jeep feeling better than she had all day. She parked in front of her apartment—an older home that had been converted to a four-plex, with two units on the ground floor and two on the upper floor. Kat was on the ground floor in the back, and she walked down a narrow walkway to the rear entrance and let herself inside.

She immediately made herself a peanut butter sandwich. She seemed to have developed a craving for peanut butter over the past few days, and she was trying to balance it with a few salads, with limited success. She was mulling over calling her gynecologist. She needed an initial appointment, but like Goldie spying Hank Eames entering Ruth's building, someone would surely see her if she stopped in at Dr. Cady's office. She could claim it was for an annual appointment, but with the Byrds already alerted and Blair aware she was pregnant . . .

"Oh, hell," she muttered, placing the call. She got Dr. Cady's receptionist, asked if she could have an appointment ASAP, and was informed that Dr. Cady was on vacation and would be back the week after next. Kat scheduled the first time available and hung up in relief. One more hurdle to put off a while longer.

But how long will Blair wait?

She gritted her teeth and shook her head. No use borrowing trouble. He wasn't completely sure the baby was his, so maybe he would leave things alone for a while. She knew better than to believe he'd let it go completely.

All I need is a little time to figure things out. After Addie's found, I can think about myself. And Addie has to be found soon. She can't suffer the same fate as Courtney Pearson.

Her thoughts spurred her to action. She'd called the Masseys while still at work and spoken to Joleen, who'd said her husband wasn't around, but that she would give him the message. So far he hadn't returned her call.

But there was still Cal Haney. She'd told Ricki she was going to interview him, and Cal lived closer in than the Masseys.

No time like the present . . .

She headed back to her Jeep and drove through the early-evening shadows toward Cal Haney's place. Ricki and Sam were dealing with Skip Chandler, who, much like Hank Eames, had been affronted and furious that anyone would dare impugn his character when Ricki had convinced him to come to the station.

Kat's cell rang just as she reached Cal Haney's place. Seeing it was Ruth, she took the call and learned that their meeting was a go for Saturday.

"She's really nervous," Ruth added. "This is hard for her, and I can definitely relate."

"Glad she's going through with it. When was she kidnapped?" Kat asked, eyeing the leaf-choked leaves of the Haneys' gutters.

"A while ago. She had a daughter who's a tween now, I think. She hasn't been totally upfront. She's scared."

Kat didn't tell her friend where she was. It was police business, and she didn't want to involve Ruth and earn herself another reprimand. And in that arena, Shiloh and Beau weren't helping her cause. They'd taken it upon themselves to interview Bryce Higgins, the missing Erin Higgins's brother, who'd been so vocal and energized when his sister had first gone missing, then had stopped speaking out, like someone had turned his spigot off, almost as if he knew his sister was never coming back. He'd been affronted as well, and Shiloh had been frustrated in her attempts to get any information from him.

"Kind of an asshole," had been her report to Kat, who'd once again told her nicely to stand down.

Haney was a wildcatter who, by all accounts, spent more time at The Dog and Big Bart's bending an elbow than he ever did making a living. Kat drove up to his place and could feel adrenalin rush through her veins. It would have been a lot better meeting with him at the station, but though he'd been invited several times, he'd showed no inclination to do the deed. So now she was here.

She stepped out of the car and looked around. There was a garden of sorts to her left. She didn't believe Cal had anything to do with growing vegetables; it just wasn't in the man's DNA. She concluded the ragged rows must be his new wife's doing.

And then she saw the ten-by-four mound of dirt near the garden. It looked as if the ground had been bulldozed and then tamped down. It looked, in fact, like a grave.

Her heart started pounding in her ears. *Addie Donovan?* No. Surely, if he'd killed her, he wouldn't bury her body in his own backyard!

The front screen door screeched open and slammed shut, and Cal Haney, all six foot two of him, stood on the concrete porch and glared down at her.

"What're you lookin' at?" he demanded.

"Is this your wife's garden?" she asked.

"Well, it sure ain't mine."

She swallowed. "Then you didn't dig up that part of the yard and fill it in with dirt?" She pointed.

His gaze landed on the suspicious mound, and he blinked several times. A dark flush crept up his neck and cheeks, and he said in an ugly tone, "I don't know what you think you know, but you get that right outta your head. I was building me a patio, but the dickhead landlord told me no. So that dirt's just sitting there. You wanta dig into it, be my guest. There's nothing there but more dirt."

She believed him. He was too sure of himself, and she didn't think he was bold enough and stupid enough to risk burying a body in his own backyard. But it didn't mean he was innocent.

"I know why you're here. That scaredy cat, Ruthie, told on me for spraying her kid with the hose. She was with my niece. I was just playin' with 'em."

"We're asking people to help us find Addison Donovan, who's been missing for—"

"You think I did it. That's why you're here."

"Mr. Haney, we're just trying to find her, make sure she's all right."

"Don't lie to me! You think I took her? Go ahead and arrest me. Take me to your Fearless Leader." He held out his wrists and glared at her. "Do it, or get the hell off my property!"

Chapter 25

It was terrifically hot inside her four walls, but Addie had almost grown used to the oppressive, airless cell. She'd worked and worked and worked to break the chain of her handcuffs, but it was no use. He hadn't noticed the scrape marks she'd left on the bucket, but she hadn't made any more progress, either. She'd have more luck sliding a wrist out of the pink-acetate-covered cuffs themselves, but since her initial thrill that she could almost get her hand free, she'd failed in that over and over again, bruising and further chafing her wrists, making them swell. The cuffs were still a smidge too tight.

And he was coming back tonight. She just knew it. He said he would try to stay away, but he just couldn't. She understood that now. He didn't have to say it. He would take her and relieve himself, and then do it again, three times most often, and she would escape the moment by going to that heavenly place in her head where she and Dean were together, lying on a blanket together and looking at the stars, telling each other how much they loved each other.

However, the last time he'd actually slapped her and yelled at her to wake up. "C'mon, honey. Don't lie there like a sack of manure. Put your lips around me, *here*." And he'd shoved his sex in her face, and she'd tried not to gag, but it had been no use.

He'd left more tense and angry than when he'd shown up.

He'll kill you if you don't get out.

Addie gazed helplessly down at her swollen wrists. If she could just twist one loose. Get it past the widest part of her hand . . .

She heard the faint sound of his truck's engine, and her heart clutched with fear. It was a ways down the dirt track through dense trees to this cabin. She remembered that much when he'd first driven her here. Would she be able to lead someone back here if she managed to escape? She didn't know. She sensed how isolated the cabin was, the mountains rising behind it. Sometimes she caught sight of a sliver of the moon or twinkling stars through the high window near the rafters. If she did manage to free herself, she didn't trust that she would really be able to get away.

She braced herself, as she heard the truck approaching. If only there was something to bash him with, but apart from the barbed wire stretched ominously through a ring on the wall, just out of her reach, the place was carefully empty. Her captor had put everything away.

"Call me Lover," he'd told her, when he stroked her hair after the first time.

She couldn't. She just couldn't, so she'd remained silent.

"Say it," he'd insisted, and his hand had squeezed her breast a little too hard, a warning.

"Lover," she managed to whisper in a tremulous voice.

"That's my name. Say it again."

"Lover."

"Louder."

"LOVER."

And for that he'd kissed her hard and bitten her lip, mounting her again, coaxing her to *fucking move*.

Now, she glanced down at her wrists again, stubbornly held in their unforgiving, fuzzy, pink vises.

If she couldn't free herself, she hoped to hell she had the courage to end it all.

Late Saturday morning, Kat pulled into the parking lot of the Wheeler Hotel, a wattle and daub relic from a previous century that had been recently painted and sported a café at street level with ivory lace curtains and antique tables and chairs clustered throughout a main room.

On the drive over, she and Ruth hadn't talked much. Kat's mind had been dissecting the various suspects' reactions concerning Addie Donovan's disappearance, wondering if all the anger-fueled bluster and the attacks on Ruth's, Patrick's, and her own integrity were simply a means to hide their complicity. To a man, they had been verbally vicious . . . but then

they'd basically been asked if they were serial kidnap-
pers and rapists. Innocent men would be offended.

"Your daughter with your mom?" Kat asked now,
as they both got out of the Jeep.

"Yeah. It's strained between Mom and me now,
and my father's not really talking to me, but I just
have to wait for them to work through it. My mother
still wants to be with Penny, but she has trouble looking me in the eye."

"I'm sorry," Kat said, meaning it.

Ruth acknowledged that with a nod. "I knew this
would happen. I'd hoped it wouldn't, but I knew it
would. But it doesn't matter. I had to tell my story,
and it's led Lily to us, so that makes it all worthwhile."

They reached the café's front steps. "I don't see
anyone inside who could be Lily," Kat observed, peering through the windows as she opened the door.

A server in a gingham skirt and white blouse came
up to them with a smile. "Sit anywhere you like," she
invited.

There were several older couples and a family of
four with a young boy of about two, who held onto a
ball for all he was worth, until he hurled it across the
room. The mother yelped and chased after the ball
as the father scolded the boy and the older sister
drank from a straw in a glass of juice, her eyes sliding
back and forth between her parents. The little boy ignored his father and tried to follow after his mother,
but his father held him back. He started moaning
loudly, working up to a scream, when Mom hurriedly
returned with the ball. As Kat and Ruth selected a
table toward the rear of the room in an alcove that

could afford them some privacy, the boy wrested himself free of Dad's grip and started howling like a banshee.

"The check?" harried Dad asked the waitress through a strained smile.

Ruth made a sound of commiseration low in her throat. "I remember Penny running around the room of a restaurant one time and Sterling trying to catch her. She was laughing, and it was funny, and I tried not to laugh, because Sterling did not find it funny at all."

"This is your ex?"

"Yep. A sense of humor he did not possess."

Kat's gaze lingered on the little boy. Two years old. In a couple of years, she would have a child the same age.

She could see Blair's tense face. *Is it mine?*

The family collected themselves and made for the till, Dad picking up the now-sniveling boy, who'd turned into a limp rag. Their waitress rang them up in record time, and as they pushed through the door, a woman entered behind them. She was tall, and her hair was scraped into a ponytail. She wore no makeup, or very little, and her gaze skated over the room, landing on Kat and Ruth. The three of them stared at each other a long moment.

There's something familiar about her, Kat thought, her mind jumping to the truth just as Ruth sucked in a startled breath and whispered, "Oh my God. It's *Erin Higgins!*"

It had been more than two days.

Blair turned in the saddle and slid off Willie's back,

then handed the horse over to Mike, who'd ridden with him out to the cabins at the far reaches of their acreage, his mother's idea for making money when the ranch had been failing. Both Hunter and Blair had considered the idea pure folly, but the fact was the cabins were there, and they either needed to be repaired or taken down. There was a side access road that could be expanded, but neither Blair nor Hunter had been certain which way to jump.

He swept off his gray Stetson and slapped it against his leg, feeling the July sun beat down on his head.

"I'll take the horses," Mike said, grabbing Willie's reins from Blair.

Blair watched the horses' haunches sway back and forth as Mike led Willie and his own mount into the barn. Blair had been a little short with the foreman, not for anything Mike had done or said—he'd stayed pretty much silent after his initial comments about Kat and the pregnancy—but because the issue was between Blair and Kat, a burning secret neither wanted to touch.

Resettling his hat on his head, Blair squinted up at the sun. He'd let too much time go by, half hoping Katrina would contact him, but it looked like it was going to have to be the other way around. With a sigh, he stalked from the barn toward the ranch house's back porch.

He could call her, but it would be better to just show up.

Erin Higgins looked remarkably the same, Kat realized as the woman headed toward their table. Older, yes, but the eyes that looked out at her and Ruth were hauntingly the same as the ones from the picture that had been distributed on the flyers her family had posted around town. There was no smile now, however. This thirty-plus-year-old woman was as sober as a judge.

She seated herself across from Ruth and to Kat's right, facing the door. Her tension was palpable. Both Kat and Ruth couldn't help staring at her, and she flicked her gaze from one to the other, then toward the door, then back, settling on Ruth. "You're Ruth."

"That's right. And you're Erin Higgins," Ruth responded.

None of them had known each other when they were in high school, but Kat and Ruth had seen Erin's picture over and over again, as they had Courtney Pearson's and Rachel Byrd's. How Erin recognized Ruth she didn't say, possibly because of Ruth's fiery hair.

"I'm Lily now. Lily-white." She grimaced. "I needed to be somebody . . . pure . . . after he . . ." She stopped herself and just said firmly, "After."

"I'm Detective Starr," Kat introduced herself, shaking Erin's hand. "Do you know who he is? Could you identify him in a lineup?"

"Maybe. I don't know. He was mostly in disguise. Part of the fun, he said." The corners of her mouth turned down, and her eyes kept up their restless search of the room.

Ruth said, "You're safe here with us. Take your time."

"I haven't been this close to . . . where he took me . . . in a long time."

"How did he take you?" Kat asked.

"I snuck out. With my brother. And he left me in the woods, thought it was a great joke. But he was there, just waiting to pounce."

"Where's your daughter now?" Kat asked.

"At a friend's."

"How old is she?" Ruth inquired.

"Almost fourteen." She looked panicked for a moment and pulled out her cell phone, checking the time. "I can't stay long."

"We won't keep you," Kat assured her. "It's just that we think the man who kidnapped you could be at it again."

"I know he is," she whispered. "He won't stop. Ever."

"And he may be the same man who attacked Ruth."

Kat looked at her friend, who said, "We need to find him. We need to know where he kept you."

"I don't know where that is."

Kat picked up the thread. "Ruth said you escaped from him. How?"

"I wandered around for what seemed like forever. There was a dirt road, but I knew that's where he came from. Where he would look for me first, so I went into the woods. I wandered around and finally stumbled across another hunter's shack. I was afraid to stay there long. Afraid he'd find me." She shivered and hunched her shoulders in memory. "So I left and finally came across some guys camping. They looked . . . scary, so I hid in the bushes until one of them finally got in his truck. Then I climbed in the back and tried to hide, but I didn't have to. He was drunk. Really drunk. Thought I might die on that ride out of there, but I didn't care. I was free."

"Your abductor kept you near Prairie Creek," Kat said.

"Yeah . . . when I got away, this is where the drunk guy came first."

"Wheeler City?"

"I about stood you up when I heard this is where you wanted to meet," she informed them. "This is too close. But then he drove farther, and I stayed in the truck until morning. By that time, I wasn't that far from Jackson. From there I called Bryce, and he helped me."

"Where did your abductor keep you? What kind of place?" Kat asked.

She swallowed. "It was like the hunter's shack."

"Do you think you could find where you got into the truck?"

"I . . . don't know. It was dark. I was scared . . ."

"Could you try?"

"Kat . . ." Ruth murmured, giving her a look. She knew she was pushing, but she was desperate for information.

"Can you describe the shack?" Kat tried.

"We each had a cot."

"Two of you?" Kat was surprised. "You and . . . Courtney?"

"No. Me and Rachel. He musta got Courtney after I ran away."

"Can I get you all something to drink?" the waitress suddenly interrupted with a big smile, dropping off menus.

Kat looked around impatiently, but Erin said, "Chardonnay."

"I'll have the same," Ruth said after a moment.

They looked at Kat. "Just water, please," she muttered.

"All righty," the waitress said, stuffing her menu pad into the pocket of her white apron. "You all should try the sourdough biscuits and the fruit compote. We make it fresh daily."

As soon as she departed, Erin moaned, "Oh God, you're on duty. Of course you are. It's all too real."

"Actually, this is my day off," Kat assured her. Erin was on the edge of her seat, as if she was about to bolt. "You were at the shack with Rachel Byrd?"

"Yes."

"For how long? What happened to Rachel?"

"Take your time," Ruth intervened.

"Rachel's still missing," Kat said. "Along with another missing girl, Addie Donovan."

"I know."

Ruth said to Erin, "I haven't revealed anything to Detective Starr. This is your story. Take as long as you need to tell it." Another meaningful look Kat's way.

Kat forced herself to stop peppering Erin with questions. "Yes, take your time," she agreed, though she could hear a clock ticking in her head. Long moments passed, and Kat couldn't stand it any longer. "Is Rachel still with him?"

"I don't know. Maybe . . . maybe not. She was . . . they were fighting. That's how I got away. It was her turn to play, and she refused, and I got my ties off."

"Play?" Kat didn't like the sound of that. "Your ties? Barbed wire?"

She looked blank. "It was rope. I worked on them, but he kept retying them, always so tight, my hands behind my back. He never gave me enough time to get them completely off. But I worked 'em loose, and then he came for Rachel. I knew I'd be next. He was never . . . satisfied. But Rachel hit him with something, and he went down. I got myself free, and she was almost there too, but he grabbed her. My ropes were off, and I just *ran.*" She suddenly covered her mouth with her palm, and tears ran down her cheeks. "I left her there."

"You had to get away," Ruth assured her.

"I wanted to go back for her. I really did. I just couldn't. I told Bryce when he came to get me, but by then I knew I was pregnant."

Bryce Higgins . . . *Kind of an a-hole*, according to Shiloh. He'd certainly raised holy hell after Erin disappeared but then had stopped. Never once had he told them about Erin, and Kat felt anger boil up inside her.

"Bryce told me he tried to find her," Erin said, as if following Kat's thoughts. "But he never could."

Really? Kat fought back her anger. Bryce was on their list, but Erin surely would have figured out the man was her own brother. Still, he could've owned up to the truth and stopped this sicko years ago. "You said your kidnapper was partially disguised," Kat said. "In what way?"

"He wore a baseball cap. Mask. Long-sleeved shirt. When it was time to play, he blindfolded me and warned me if I took the blindfold off he would kill me. But he screwed up a time or two. I saw him once, a little bit, when he was . . . with Rachel."

"Is there any chance it was someone you knew?" Kat asked.

"No. But I'd know his voice if I heard it now."

"Wide girth. Furry skin. Thick hands," Ruth said.

Erin looked at her and began to tremble violently. "That's him," she said unsteadily. "He told me he had a sex problem and needed us to help him stay true. Without us, he would go after other women. Looks like he has."

The waitress came with their drinks, but almost as if they'd planned it, no one took a sip. They all sat with their own thoughts, Kat's being: *And Courtney committed suicide after years of abuse . . .* What did that mean for Rachel? Was she alive? His captive?

As if reading her mind, Erin finally said in a voice so low they could scarcely hear it, "I think he might've killed Rachel. He had a gun, and he hit her with it, I think. I was outside the shack." She covered her eyes with her hands. "It's all my fault."

"It's your abductor's fault," Ruth told her firmly.

"What's his name? Your abductor," Kat asked. "Did he tell you?"

Erin reached for her wine, holding it in an unsteady hand, "He made us call him Lover." She put her lips to the glass and gulped half of it down until tears stood in her eyes.

"Have you decided what to order?" The cheery waitress suddenly reappeared. She'd swept up behind Kat and was once again holding up her menu pad.

"We might need another minute," Ruth suggested.

The cheery smile evaporated, and she turned sharply on her heel. When they were alone again, Kat said, "I know you don't want to, but if you could come into the station and meet with a sketch artist so we could get a basic idea of what he looks like—"

"No."

"—it would be easier to narrow in on him. Just your impression of him."

"No."

Ruth said soothingly, "Erin, we don't want to push you, or make you feel uncomfortable."

"Well, you are. I told you I'm not going back there. Ever." She knocked back the rest of her Chardonnay.

"I understand," Ruth began.

"No, you don't. You can't. I'm—I'm sorry for what happened to you, Ruth. I really am. Maybe it was him, or maybe it was somebody else, but you can't know how I feel."

"I didn't mean I knew—"

"Stop. Please." She pressed her hands over her ears and shook her head. "I'm sorry. I'm really sorry. I just can't do this."

"All right." Ruth lifted her hands.

Erin said, "I've gotta go." And with that, she jumped to her feet, jangling silverware atop the table and nearly toppling Ruth's untouched wine. Ruth grabbed for her glass just in time as Kat scrambled to her feet as well.

But Erin had moved off already, blasting through the tables, causing exclamations of surprise as she bumped diners and snagged the edge of a tablecloth.

Kat followed after her, ignoring Ruth's, "Kat! Wait! She'll call. Let her go."

Kat ran after Erin onto the porch, but Erin yanked open the door to an older model Chevy sedan and threw herself inside. She started it up, and the engine coughed violently.

"Erin!" Kat called.

Without looking, Erin reversed in a U that faced her nose-out to the road. Kat memorized the license plate, as it appeared Erin was bolting. She was turning back to the door, feeling slightly defeated, when the blast of a truck's horn shattered the air with a loud WWWOMMMMM. She looked back, and everything seemed to go into slow motion as Erin's car leapt onto the road, directly in front of a Ford F1.

CRASH!

Shrieking metal. Erin's car spun crazily. A scream of "OH NO" ripped from Kat's own lips.

Then silence and steam rising from the radiator, and Kat was running to the scene, running to Erin, running . . .

Chapter 26

The next three hours passed in a blur. Patrons boiled out of the restaurant at the sound of the crash. Ruth was one of the first to reach Kat, who'd dialed 911 and learned that an ambulance was dispatched. The truck driver staggered down from his cab, more shaken than hurt. Kat wrenched open the driver's door and checked Erin's pulse. Found it steady, but she was unconscious. With Ruth's help, she held people back until the EMTs arrived and Erin was pulled from the wreckage and placed on a gurney. The doors on the ambulance slammed, and they learned they were headed to the closest hospital, Prairie Creek.

"She didn't want to go back," Ruth whispered to Kat, stricken.

"She doesn't have a choice," Kat said.

"I know, but I feel responsible."

"Yeah."

Kat then called Sheriff Featherstone's cell and told him what had happened. When he learned it was Erin Higgins, he said he would send extra officers to the hospital to protect her and that he would alert Bryce Higgins.

"Bryce knows his sister's alive," Kat said. "He's been in communication with her from the moment she escaped her kidnapper."

"All right, I'm on my way. Ricki's with me," Sam said.

"I'll meet you there," Kat said. Ricki and Sam had been dating for a while, and there was something about the way he'd said her name that resonated with Kat. What would it be like to have a partner you wanted to share your life with? Even though she was having his baby, she certainly couldn't feel that way about Blair . . . could she?

The local police arrived on the heels of the EMTs and began interviewing everyone on the street, including Kat and Ruth, and it took another call to Sam to get free of the questions and be allowed to leave. Kat drove Ruth directly to the Prairie Creek Hospital, whereupon they were met by Sam, Ricki, and Ethan, whom Ruth had called on the way over. Ethan folded Ruth into his arms, and Kat found her throat tightening at the sight.

"I should have never asked her to meet us," Ruth said for about the fifteenth time, sick with guilt.

"This isn't your fault," Ethan assured her, the same words Kat had uttered as they'd driven to the hospital.

And it's not mine, either, she reminded herself. *Though it sure as hell feels like it.* "We gotta get this prick," Kat said to her brother. "For Erin, for Courtney, for Rachel . . . and for Addie. It's the same guy. I know it."

"And for Ruth," Ethan said.

"Oh yes." Kat was grim.

Erin was taken to emergency surgery for abdominal injuries, but the hospital staff assured the sheriff that, barring complications, she would pull through. Then Sam and Ricki questioned Ruth and Kat in a private waiting room, while Ethan stood by. Kat brought them up to date on their meeting with Erin, and Ruth explained about how Erin, "Lily," had called in on her hotline.

It was late by the time Erin was out of surgery. Ruth had called her mother, and her daughter, Penny, was staying the night with Ruth's parents. She, Kat, and Ethan had gone to the cafeteria before it closed, and Kat had managed to keep down a cheese sandwich and a cup of vegetable soup. Her stomach seemed to be holding its own for the moment.

As they finished their meal, Ruth said, "I've always thought the rape was the worst moment of my life, but it could have been far worse. He could have taken me away too. Locked me up for years. Abused me countless times."

"But he didn't," Ethan said.

"That's right," Kat reminded fiercely. She was filled with so much anger toward this monster. She wanted to get him. Make him pay.

"Because you and Shiloh were there to help save me. You saved me, and I'm one of the lucky ones. But what about the others. Erin and Courtney . . . Rachel and Addie? And now Erin's fighting for her life. She never wanted to come forward. I urged her to. I pushed her."

"Erin wanted to help too," Kat reminded. "She

made that decision. That's why she met us today. You know that."

"I know. It just doesn't feel that way," Ruth said on a sigh, and Ethan put his arm around her and drew her close.

Kat knew they would be heading home together, and it reminded her anew of her own screwed-up situation with Blair.

Don't compare yourself to them. You've made a mess of things, but you'll get it sorted out. You will.

With an officer planted outside ICU, who would then follow Erin to her hospital room once she was moved, Kat was satisfied that she would be safe. She stifled a yawn, and Ricki and Sam, and Ruth and Ethan, coupled up and left the hospital. Kat waited until they were gone and then followed after them, phoning her father, who was on another date with Goldie and seemed to be enjoying himself. Who woulda thunk?

But when she gave him the update, he said, "We need to get together and go over the case. I'm still trying to meet Bryce. I know you said Shiloh and Beau already talked to him, but now that we know he knew about Erin, I want it to be one of us who interviews him. He kept that secret a long time."

"You want to meet tomorrow?" Kat asked.

"Tomorrow's Sunday."

Her father wasn't one to attend church, but she sensed he was thinking about spending time with Goldie. And Kat felt all in. This pregnancy was taking its toll. "Let's talk tomorrow afternoon," she said.

"Good enough."

She walked along the pathway that led back to her

apartment. The night was hot, and she felt sweaty and weary. But as she mounted the two steps to her door, she felt a chill between her shoulder blades, as if hard eyes were staring at her. She whipped around, but there was nothing there. Not even a breath of wind pushing the branches of the trees at the edge of the small yard. Quickly, she let herself inside and closed and locked the door, drawing the chain. She stood for a moment in the silence, then because her stomach was starting to get fluttery again, grabbed some soda crackers from her cupboard and munched them down, then stripped off her clothes, dragged on her pajamas, and fell into bed, exhausted.

Erin Higgins was alive and at the Prairie Creek Hospital!

His heart pounded hard and fast, painful. Erin Higgins. That bitch. That sneaking whore. It was because of her that he'd lost Rachel. He'd had to hit her hard, over and over again, with the butt of his rifle once he'd gotten her off him that night. And then he'd jumped in his truck and driven down the dirt lane, enraged at Erin. She couldn't run away. *She couldn't!* She could identify him. Rachel had ripped his mask off, and Erin might have been gone by then, but she'd seen enough of him to know. He had to catch her, fuck her, kill her . . .

But she hadn't been on the lane. She'd gone into the woods, and he'd searched but never found her. By morning, he'd had to go back and bury Rachel. If for some reason Erin made it through the forest, he had to cover up.

But she didn't make it through. Weeks went by, and there was no sign of her. He'd started to feel less panicked. She'd probably died out there. And then he'd found Courtney . . .

Katrina Starr and Ruth McFerron . . . they'd found her. And Shiloh was asking too many questions too. Those three!

His hands fisted in fury, and he had to fight to relax them. He was at The Dog, having a beer, and everyone was abuzz at the news. Hank Eames had taken a fall and was at the hospital and overheard, though they'd been trying to keep it quiet. "They think whoever took 'er's going to come after her," Eames said loudly. "That Ruthie thinks we're all guilty!"

He'd learned as much as he could, his pulse racing, and then had headed out. He'd driven by Ruth's place, but the bitch had been with Ethan Starr, so he went instead to Katrina's, watching from the pines along the back fence, staring at her hard, until she suddenly turned back and stared right back in his direction.

You can't see me, whore. But I see you.

He'd watched her lights go out, one by one, then had cruised by her door.

Feel me, bitch?

His boner was damn near painful in his jeans. Addie . . . he thought, wishing she would give him something. *Anything.*

But it didn't matter. He would take her, but his mind would be on Shiloh, and Ruth, and Katrina Starr . . .

* * *

Kat slept hard, though she had to get up to relieve herself several times—another aspect to pregnancy she'd have to get used to, as she'd always been proud of her steel bladder. Still, it felt like she'd barely been asleep when there was a loud pounding on her door. Rolling onto her back, she groaned, staring up at the ceiling. Seizing a pillow, she pulled it over her head, covering her ears. It was way too early to rise.

Bang! Bang! Bang!

Growling under her breath, she tossed off the pillow and stalked in her pajamas to her door, peering out cautiously. She made a strangled sound in her throat, then threw it wide.

Blair Kincaid stood on her small porch, in jeans, boots, and his Stetson.

And in one hand was the same kind of gold envelope that had been given to Shiloh and Ruth . . .

Blair took in Kat's tousled hair, the satiny green pajama top and matching knee-length pants, the dark circles under her eyes, and the cautious, almost resentful, way she looked at him. It was six-thirty AM and he knew it was early, but he'd tried reaching her the night before to no avail.

Her eyes were focused on the envelope. "Where'd you get that?" she asked sharply.

He looked down at it. "It was sitting on top of your mailbox with just your name on it. I saw it as I went by."

One hand reached for the lapels of her pajama top and held them tight. He smiled at the gesture, noticing her slim legs and small feet. Her toenails were a soft pink.

But her gaze was still glued to the envelope. She reached a hand for it, holding it so gingerly, he asked, "What is it?"

Instead of answering, she responded with, "Why are you here?"

"Well, you've been avoiding me, and we need to get past that. You're pregnant. I'm the father. We gotta make some plans and—"

"*Shhh.*" She grabbed his arm with her free hand and yanked him inside. Her lapels parted, and the mounds of her breasts peeked over her pajama top. "Hold your voice down. This was on the top of my mailbox?"

"Yep. I take it you haven't told your father yet."

"It wasn't there last night. Did you see anyone?" she asked as she shut and latched the door, drawing a chain across it.

He shook his head, mystified. "What the hell is it?"

"Nothing."

"Come on, Kat."

She shook her head.

"Well, open it up," he said. He wanted to put the issue of whatever was in the envelope to rest and get back on topic.

"I'd rather not."

He lifted his hands in disgust. "Then let's talk about the baby. *Our* baby."

"I'm too busy to get into this now."

"I know what you think of me," he went on, ignoring her. "And okay, I probably deserve it. I've been— unreliable—and making this baby probably adds to that. But it's time we addressed this issue. What are your plans? I mean, really Kat, what are they?"

"I don't have any plans. I'm working on a case."

"Give me a straight answer. This is my baby too. Are you keeping it?"

"Of course I'm keeping it!"

"That's not what you said."

She pulled herself up short. "I know. I didn't mean it. I just . . . I don't owe you an explanation." She stalked toward the tiny kitchen and set the envelope on the table, then stared for a moment at the coffeemaker, before pulling out a bag of coffee grounds and a filter and filling up the carafe with water. "I'm going to make coffee," she said unnecessarily, "and then I'm getting ready for work."

"I heard about Erin Higgins."

She whipped around in surprise. "How?"

"It was all over The Dog last night. Bryce had a lot to say."

"Oh God. Bryce . . ." She shook her head as if clearing cobwebs.

"He seemed kind of pissed off. But it's good that she turned up after all this time."

"He knew she was alive."

"He did?"

She nodded, then peered up at him quizzically. "How much do you know about Erin?"

"Just that she's been missing, and she had an accident yesterday, and that's when it was discovered who she was."

"She came forward to Ruth and me in Wheeler City yesterday. I was there when she drove in front of the truck."

"Jesus . . ."

"Luckily, it seems like she's going to be okay." She

turned her attention back to the coffeemaker. "She was kidnapped and held against her will. Like Courtney Pearson."

"That's for certain?"

"That they were both kidnapped, yes."

He slowly shook his head. "And this is the case you're on? You shouldn't even be working."

"Oh, don't go there. You sound like my father."

"Then at least let me help you," he said to the back of her head.

"No."

"Why not? Because I was a screwup? Those days are over. Hunter didn't think it would work out with me at the ranch, and I've been making damn certain to prove him wrong. I want to help you. I want to see you. What the hell do I have to do to get you to turn around and *look at me*?"

Kat was staring at the brown liquid dripping into the glass carafe with a concentration worthy of a surgeon. Slowly, she slid her dark gaze his way. Her body was as stiff as a board, and her expression was forcibly neutral. "I don't care that you were a screwup."

Blair's brows lifted. It was, in its way, the most encouraging thing she'd said to him.

"But I don't need a keeper, or someone telling me what to do."

"That's not what I'm about."

"This baby is mine . . . and yours . . . ," she admitted reluctantly. "But I've got to figure this out my own way. I've got to tell people, and . . . think about the future . . . and make plans."

"So do I. Maybe make some plans together?" His gaze drifted down her lovely back and hips, and it was all he could do to keep from stepping forward and wrapping his arms around her. Instead, he stayed put and said, "I've done a lot of things ass-backward, so let's make it one more. How about a date? Get to know each other. Stuff like that."

"It's too late for that."

She slowly turned around, her fingers clasped around the edge of the counter. Blair looked at her, and she looked right back at him. Seconds ticked by. The huff and gurgle of the coffeemaker punctuated the silence. He reached forward and pulled an errant curl of her dark hair toward him, pressing it between his thumb and finger, his gaze focused on the trapped silky strands. Then he lifted his eyes to hers. "I want to kiss you."

She stared at him. Was he imagining it, or had something flared in her eyes, a fire to match his own? She inhaled shakily and said, "Okay."

He dropped the strand of fine hair and moved his palm to the slope of her jaw. Her skin was satin. He ran his thumb pad over her lips, which she pressed together in a moment of restraint.

"Actually, I should—"

"No," he cut her off. "Don't think so much." He kissed her lightly, and his hand slid downward over the green satin to cup her breast. He could feel the nipple through the smooth fabric.

She pulled back from the kiss. "No . . ."

"No?"

She laughed faintly. "This is how I got into trouble."

"How we got into trouble," he amended.

"How we got into trouble," she agreed.

He looked down at her. He hadn't imagined it. Her eyes shimmered with desire.

He leaned in for another kiss, and she lifted her mouth to meet his. And it wasn't long before they were grappling for each other, struggling out of their clothes, dropping to the floor, her legs wrapped around his hips. She was as eager as he was, and with desire pounding in his head, Blair made love to her like it was his last moment on earth.

Brring . . .

The cell phone brought Kat out of her sex-induced stupor like an electric shock. They'd moved to the bedroom and made love a second time, and now Blair was stretched out beside her, his finger drawing desultory circles on her abdomen, his head propped on his other hand, his eyes heavy-lidded, watching her, that insouciant smile pasted to his lips.

She shot off the bed and ran to the kitchen, buck naked. Her cell was in her purse on the counter. The gold envelope lay on the table. She dragged her eyes away from it and pulled her phone out.

It was her father.

She didn't take the call. Just carried her phone back to the bedroom, where Blair lay stretched atop her covers, also naked. She sat down on the edge of the bed, and the phone finally stopped ringing.

"You didn't answer." He gathered her into his arms, and she told herself to resist, but she went down to him like wax.

"I can't talk to him naked."

"Who?"

"My father."

He drew a line of kisses from her mouth to her neck and down her abdomen. "Hi, Baby," he whispered against her skin.

She stared at the ceiling, aware that her traitorous stomach was having no problem with Blair's lovemaking. "I'll have to call him back."

"Do it tomorrow."

And when he moved lower yet, she grabbed the bedclothes, closed her eyes, and groaned with desire.

"We have to eat," Blair said an hour later while they were in the shower together. Between bouts of lovemaking, he'd asked her all sorts of questions about her pregnancy. Half-embarrassed, half-impatient, she realized she had very few answers for him. She knew what she knew, but she hadn't furthered her knowledge. "I have an appointment with Dr. Cady in about a week," she said somewhat defensively.

But now that he was interested in food and in truth, so was she. The uncomfortable fluttering had started again, and she knew that if she didn't eat something soon it would get worse.

"We could go to Betty Ann's and get some—"

"No. No baked goods." Kat shuddered.

"Really? Huh. Okay. How about Molly's Diner then?" He was soaping her back, and she was letting him, with no qualms, while water ran over her head, aware that they were acting like a couple who'd been dating for ages.

But his words panicked her. "We can't go out in public."

His hands stopped. "Still don't want anyone to know?"

"Not because of you. Because of everything. If I'm seen with you, and then Paul Byrd or his daughter or your foreman says something . . ."

"You could beat them to the punch, y'know."

"I have to figure out how to tell people, and I can't just start hanging around with you without a whole lot of questions." She pulled away from him, rinsed off, and opened the door to the shower, letting the water run out.

"Hey!"

He quickly cut the taps as she shut the door behind her. "I'm going to get dressed," she said. Then she practically ran back to her bedroom and yanked out a pair of jeans and a dark blue shirt that buttoned up the front. By the time Blair appeared a few minutes later, a towel slung around his lean hips, his hair still dripping water, she was dressed and had dragged a comb through her own wet locks.

"So, we can't be seen together." His eyes were glacial blue.

"Not until I tell my father about the baby, and I don't want to do that until this case is over."

"You want to sneak around in the meantime?" he drawled. "I can do that."

She fought back a frustrated chuckle. "No. You have to go now. We'll . . . see each other soon."

"You said you need to make plans."

"Yes. Alone. At least for now." But she was laughing, and he tried to pull her into his arms again. She sidestepped and said, "Stop it. You're making me crazy. This is crazy."

She left him and headed into the kitchen. Her eyes immediately went to the gold envelope. She knew what was in it, and she knew what it meant: a threat, a warning, a reminder that he was out there, watching and waiting. Did he know that she and Ruth had connected with Erin?

Her cell phone rang again, and she started guiltily. Sure enough, it was her father. She thought about putting him off some more, but that would only create more questions later.

"Hey, Dad," she answered.

"There you are. I tried to call earlier, but you didn't answer."

"I turned my phone off and forgot to turn it back on."

"You want to get together this afternoon? I've already got a call into Higgins, but he's not answering. I might head to the hospital."

"This afternoon?" She glanced at the clock. It was eleven AM.

"Have you seen today's paper? Jimmy Woodcock sure learned quick about Erin Higgins showing up again."

"It's already in the paper?" She felt a stab of fear, and that reminded her of how she'd felt the night before, and that made her wonder if she'd sensed the intruder. Maybe he'd left the envelope for her then.

"I've got it right here." Her father read her the article, which explained who Erin Higgins was and theorized that Rachel Byrd had been abducted about the same time, and considered Courtney Pearson and Addie Donovan as victims of the same abductor.

Ruth's name was added to the mix too. It was all there, Kat thought a bit dispiritedly. Everything Erin Higgins was afraid of having come from her.

She hoped to hell she was safe.

Blair appeared, fully dressed. His dark hair was still damp, and her mind momentarily tripped to their moments together in bed, and she lost the last part of her father's recitation. But she got the gist of it.

"It finishes up with naming you and Ruth as the ones who made the initial connection with her," Patrick said.

Kat grunted in acknowledgment, and her eyes strayed to the envelope. "I should be the one to talk to Bryce," Kat thought aloud. *Kind of an asshole,* Shiloh had said.

She glanced at Blair, then had to look away as he seemed to fill the room.

"Nah, I'm already on that one."

In truth, she had no wish to tangle with Bryce. He was ornery and belligerent by nature, and she suspected he wouldn't appreciate Erin's secret coming to light unless it was his idea, which she supremely doubted it was. "Then I'll go see Scott Massey, see if I can get him to come into the station. Let's meet tomorrow and see what we've got. Maybe Erin will be awake by then," she added hopefully.

"Can she identify the guy?"

"I think so, though he was disguised most of the time. But she definitely knows his voice." She was conscious of Blair overhearing her. "Look, I gotta go. I'll call you tomorrow."

"Be careful when you go to see Massey. Maybe you should—"

"Always," she cut in, then clicked off before he could say anything more.

"Food?" Blair reminded.

"I've wasted most of today already. You have to go." She headed to the door and waited for him.

"I'll bring you back something from Molly's Diner. No baked goods. How about bacon and eggs?"

"God, no." She shuddered.

"Pancakes? Waffles? French toast? Or are those baked goods? How about granola?"

For whatever reason, her mind hooked on that. "Granola. Wow, that sounds good."

"Great. I'll be back in a flash." He glanced at the envelope. "And then you can tell me what that's all about."

Chapter 27

Kat ate every last bite of the granola with yogurt and an array of blueberries, blackberries, and raspberries. Blair had a stack of pancakes with eggs and bacon, and they both drank the forgotten coffee Kat had prepared earlier.

They sat across from each other at the table, and when they finished, Blair said in a tone that brooked no argument, "What's in the envelope?"

Kat had opened it after he'd left—the same photo given to Shiloh and Ruth—but the sight of the three of them, naked in the black-and-white photo, even though it was exactly what she'd expected, still made her breath catch in her throat. She'd stared at it for long moments, and her mind had traveled back to that night: the heat, the smells, the sounds, the rutting monster with his ski mask atop Ruth. It had opened a thought in her mind: the bastard had brought a camera with him. It hadn't been a cell phone. She was pretty sure of that. Hadn't she actually seen the camera the moment after the flash? Wasn't it substantial? He must have dropped it before he captured Ruth.

And people just didn't carry that size of camera around as a rule, unless they were tourists, or if it was the person's job. He couldn't have planned to find them at the pond because their plans had been last minute.

Bad luck and bad timing, but what had he been doing out there with that camera?

Kat waved an arm toward her bedroom. "It's to do with a case. I put it away."

"So it has something to do with your work?"

"That's right."

"Somebody left you an envelope with just your name on it, no address, and it has to do with your work. And you looked at it in horror."

"I didn't look at it in horror."

"You did," he assured her. "What was in it?"

"It's none of your business."

"Is it connected to the Erin Higgins case? And Courtney Pearson and Addie Donovan?" He eyed her closely.

She didn't immediately answer, and they sat in silence for several long minutes while Kat considered. Should she tell him about the night Ruth was raped? That she and Shiloh were there? That they'd grabbed Ruth and run from her attacker? It was for Ruth to tell, but Ruth had gone public already, maybe not about all the details of that night, but close enough. "It's a picture," she finally admitted. "Of Ruth, Shiloh, and me. Skinny-dipping. The guy who took it attacked Ruth right afterward."

"You were there . . . and Shiloh?"

She nodded.

"Show me the picture."

"No, Blair . . ."

"Please."

For reasons she didn't quite understand, she fetched the envelope, watching as he withdrew the photo, seeing his lips tighten into a thin line as he looked down at the black-and-white print. After a moment, he slid the picture back inside its envelope.

He clarified, "He left you and Ruth and Shiloh copies of this picture. All of you. The guy who raped Ruth."

"That's right. Ruth thinks she's lucky because she got away. We think he's the guy who abducted all the others too."

"And this is the case you're working on now," he reiterated carefully.

"Yes." Kat was firm. A bit reluctantly, she related everything about the case that was already public knowledge, only leaving out the part that the barbed wire around Courtney's wrists had come from the Rocking D, which was still under wraps. When she was finished, she added, "We've been talking to a number of different men around Praire Creek who are . . . persons of interest."

"Suspects," Blair stated flatly. "You and the department."

"And my father. He never believed the girls were runaways, and other than Shiloh, it looks like he's right. And this guy has Addie and maybe Rachel, still, and he made sure Ruth, Shiloh, and I each got a copy of the photo." She gestured to the envelope. "He's sending a message."

"I get it. And that's why you need to let someone else handle this," Blair said seriously. "You need protection. All of you."

"I'm a detective, Blair. And Sheriff Featherstone knows the whole story. He knows our list of suspects. Searchers have been looking for Addie since she disappeared. And with Erin's testimony, we'll get him."

"But you're *pregnant*."

"I know that. You don't think I know that?" She glared at him. "Doesn't mean I still don't have a job to do."

"This is a little different than saving a horse from four-letter words."

Kat flushed. She thought about Patrick, who was torn between being proud of her and fearing for her safety. And she recalled how Ira Dillinger had complained about Ricki working in law enforcement. "I'd like to believe I have enough skill at my job that people trust me to do it," she said dryly.

"It's not about that."

"Isn't it? You just said you wouldn't get in my way."

"I know, but—"

"Don't do this, Blair."

"What? Care? Worry?"

She could tell he was working himself up, and she was almost glad when her cell rang again and she could sweep it up. Her father once more. "Hey, there," she said tersely.

"I know you won't appreciate it, but I've been thinking. Why don't you wait to interview Massey later, maybe after Erin wakes up?"

"Erin told Ruth and me all she knew, and it wasn't

enough. I'm not stopping my job for you or anybody else," she added fiercely.

"Okay, okay. What's got into you?" he asked, clearly set back on his heels at her tone.

"I can take care of myself, that's all."

"I know that, honey. But you know as well as anyone what this bastard's capable of. I'm just asking you to stand down and let me do the heavy lifting on this one, Katrina."

She thought she might scream. She could feel it boiling up inside her. And the worst of it was, she *was* scared. The picture had scared her deeply. If that's what the bastard's message was meant to do, it had worked. And she wasn't going to let him win.

"I'm going to interview Massey, maybe today," she said. "And if I have to, I'll go back to Haney, and Rafe Dillinger, and Woodcock and Chandler and Bryce Higgins . . . *whoever!*" She could have added, *I took care of Mom when you and Ethan couldn't even look at her, and I'm perfectly capable of running my own life,* but she knew that would be opening wounds long forgotten by her father and her brother. Instead, her eyes on Blair, she said heatedly, "You just need to stay out of the way and let me do my job."

"Kat . . . ," Patrick protested.

"You said you were going to talk to Bryce. I've got Massey."

"Tell me when you're on your way to his place."

"Okay, this is me telling you. I'm on my way now. I don't care that it's Sunday. He might be actually home for once."

"You're going now?" Blair asked.

"Is someone there?" her father questioned.

"It's the television, Dad. I'll call you when I'm back home." She clicked off before he could say anything more. "I said that to shut my dad up. I don't know when I'm going. I don't even know *if* I'm going. Maybe I should wait for Erin to wake up . . . but Erin's already told us all she knows. I wasn't wrong about that. She wants us to find this bastard more than anybody. That's why she crept out of her hiding place to meet with us. But then we spooked her by asking her to come down to the station in Prairie Creek and meet with a sketch artist. It got way too real for her, so she bolted for her car . . . and drove into traffic without looking." Kat took several deep breaths. "And yeah, it feels like our fault. Mine and Ruth's. And I want Erin to be okay. I want them all to be okay! That's what I want. So don't get in my way." Tears were burning behind her eyes, and she blinked madly to keep them at bay.

"I want to help," Blair said.

"Blair, seriously. I already got in trouble at work for talking to my dad before it was sanctioned. I'm not going to get in trouble again."

"I'll go with you when you interview these guys. Jesus, Kat, one of them could be the guy you're looking for! I don't have to go in. I'll just stay in the truck and wait for you. But I'll be there. You should have a partner with you."

"I'm going in my Jeep. By myself." She drew a breath. Truthfully, the idea of having backup with her wasn't a bad one, but she sensed it was a slippery slope with Blair. *He could take over your life, and not in a good way.*

"You think I can just stand by and let you wander

around asking probing questions of a bunch of guys, any one of which could have kept Courtney Pearson a sex slave for twenty years?"

"Fifteen."

"Fifteen. You think I can just stand by and let you piss off the same guy who raped your friend? The same guy who sent you a picture from that night of you all *naked*?"

"The word 'let' isn't in this discussion."

"I can't do it, Kat. You're carrying my baby. I've got to be involved. I need to help."

"And if I weren't carrying your baby?" she asked testily.

"I'd still be crazed with worry. I'd still want to be with you. Come on. Seriously. Don't go off alone and try to prove something."

"It's my job," she said, stung by the "prove something" comment. But she wasn't completely foolhardy, either. "And it's not that dangerous. Scott Massey has a wife, Joleen. I don't think they're kidnapping girls and turning them into sex slaves together."

"Maybe he hides it from her."

"Maybe. Maybe not."

"Are you going to meet with him today?"

She drew a breath. What the hell. "Might as well. Dad and I are meeting tomorrow to go over everything."

"Okay, then, I'll follow you in my truck. Massey has a long drive to his place. I'll stay at the end of it. No one'll know I'm there, but I'll be nearby."

Some of her annoyance dissipated as she listened to his plan. In truth, she appreciated his concern, and maybe it was because of her pregnancy, but she felt oddly weepy and, even stranger, thrilled that he seemed to be staking some kind of claim on her.

Don't get carried away, Kat. He's not declaring undying love. He's still Blair Kincaid.

"Hey, Little Kat," Blair said softly, upon seeing she was blinking back tears. He drew her into his arms, and she let him, laying her head on his shoulder. She wanted someone to lean on. She'd been the strong one for a long, long time.

Soon she and Blair wound up back in bed together, making love with a tenderness neither had been willing to wait for earlier. And then her cell phone rang once more, and Blair groaned, "This is your day off?"

"Shhh." She saw it was her dad, and she answered, "Yes?"

"Have you left yet? You said you were leaving."

"Dad."

"This guy's a sexual predator, and girls like you are his prey. I think it might be best if you let a man do the interviewing on this case from now on."

"I'm just going to invite him down to the station for an interview. That's all. Okay?"

"Okay." He was grudging.

"So how're things going with Goldie?" she asked as a means to change the subject.

"It's all business."

"Sure it is."

Blair's head was back under the covers. She could feel his tongue on her belly button, and it was moving lower. Sucking in a quiet breath, she gritted her teeth, then said, "Okay, let's make this the last call, okay?"

"I want to hear from you after the interview."

"Fine!" she gasped.

"You okay?"

"Fine!" she said again. "I'll call you after . . ." She snapped off the cell phone, and it slipped from her hand to clatter onto the night stand. "My God, Blair . . . stop!"

But he didn't, and she was soon floating in liquid sensations that had her fingers clutching the bed-clothes and her body writhing.

She left for Massey's ranch in the late afternoon, hoping to catch Scott at home. Blair followed in his truck, bound and determined to be Kat's protector. She kept looking at him in her rearview mirror, though he kept his vehicle way back from hers.

She was practically in a fever all the way to Massey's property, which was tucked up against Forest Service land, nestled up against rolling hills that led into the mountains. She watched the fence posts whip by in a blur and patchy white clouds flutter overhead, her mind on Blair. She saw the stuttered white lines that split the two-lane road run into one long ribbon, her mind on Blair . . .

Blair's lovemaking had turned her into a puddle. His hands . . . and mouth . . . and well, the feel of him thrusting inside her, body straining, the hot passion in his eyes . . . the taste of his probing tongue . . .

Just thinking about it brought a flush to her cheeks, and she flexed her hands on the wheel. One tire suddenly slipped off the pavement onto the hardpan on the side of the road, and she yanked the

Jeep back on course. *Shit.* With an effort, she forced aside the vision of their lovemaking, dragging her thoughts back to her driving. She didn't want to miss the turnoff to the gravel road that led to the Massey house. As the thought crossed her mind, she damn near drove right by it and had to stand on her brakes, looking in her rearview for approaching vehicles, then reversing to make the turn.

Blair's truck was just easing up at the end of the Massey drive as she turned into it. He pulled over to the side of the road, nodding toward her, his Stetson tipping forward. She lifted a hand in acknowledgment, then drove farther along, watching in the mirror as Blair's truck became a dark speck behind her, then disappeared behind a rise. On either side of the dusty drive lay pasture land currently covered with a blanket of bright, bobbing wildflowers in blues and pinks, yellows and reds, and shades of purple from lilac to magenta to grape. Someone had strewn seeds, she thought, as it was such a riot of color as far as the eye could see down the long drive. Joleen, Scott's wife, probably.

It was half a mile to the house, which was a small, tired-looking ranch-style with a barn and several outbuildings in much better repair behind it. Kat knocked on the door and heard light footsteps heading her way. The door opened, and Joleen Massey peered out. Kat had seen her a number of times but had never made her acquaintance.

"Mrs. Massey? I'm Katrina Starr from the Sheriff's Department."

Joleen stared at her blankly, a little unfocused. Her expression grew worried. "Yes?"

"I've talked to you a few times, but I've never connected with your husband. I was wondering if he's home now."

"Oh." She was peering somewhere near Kat's left ear, and Kat recalled vaguely that Joleen had some vision problems. "I'm sorry. Scott's out hunting for that poor missing girl."

"He's searching for Addie Donovan?"

"Yes. He knows these woods inside out." She half-turned toward the back of the house and swept a hand behind her to indicate the forest rising behind their property.

"He's an excellent hunter."

"I saw him at the parade," Kat said, her gaze searching the interior of the house. "He's a trick rider, isn't he?" She noticed a series of black-and-white photos of Scott on a galloping horse, making some intricate moves, along the wall above a flight of stairs that led down to a lower level.

"Well, yes, but mostly he helps out at some of the spreads around Prairie Creek, and he loves to hunt." She smiled. "There's nothing like venison."

It wasn't deer hunting season yet, but that didn't stop some of the men around Prairie Creek who felt it was their God-given right to go after game any time.

As if she'd spoken aloud, Joleen added, "He's always been a good provider. I'm having some trouble with my sight these days, but I can still help trim a deer."

Kat could almost smell the scent of animal blood, but wondered if that was just her jittery stomach reacting to the mere idea.

Joleen tilted her head. "Are you Patrick Starr's daughter? The policeman?"

"Yes, he used to be with the Sheriff's Department," she allowed, "but he's retired now."

"Scott always said he was one of the good ones."

Kat smiled. With Paul Byrd being so down on her father, it was nice to hear someone else praise him. "Would you have your husband call me?" She gave Joleen the number and expected her to write it down, but she said she had an excellent memory and didn't need to.

"The one good thing about losing a sense. The others make up for it," she said.

At that her nose wrinkled. "Although the smell can be pretty rank."

So the odor was real. Massey must have killed something recently.

"I'm lucky because he usually does most of the skinning at his hunting shack."

"Is that one of the outbuildings?"

"It's further away. Into the woods."

A hunting shack in the woods.

The hair on Katrina's arms lifted. She envisioned Scott Massey tramping through the undergrowth, stalking prey. She gazed thoughtfully to the hills behind the Massey house. Hunting . . . in the off-season . . .

"Do you know which direction he went to search for Addie? Is he with other rescuers who are looking?"

She shook her head. "I'm not sure. But he should be back soon. He always makes sure I'm settled before it gets too dark."

Kat lifted her chin toward the photographs on the back wall, forgetting Joleen probably couldn't see. "Those are great pictures of Scott along the back wall. Who took them?"

"Oh, I did. Before my eyes started going bad."

"You were a photographer?"

"Of sorts. Scott's really the one who knows cameras. He's taken pictures for lots of people around town, some of the best families. You know the Dillingers?"

"I actually work with Ricki Dillinger."

"Ira's daughter? Well, Scott took some pictures for Ira of the Dillinger family a number of years back," she said proudly.

Kat remembered the photograph in Ira's office with him and all of his children. She would have to ask Ricki about it.

"Would you like to come in for an iced tea?" Joleen invited. "Scott should be back any minute."

"You know, I think I'll have to pass this time, but thank you."

"Oh, there he is now," she said, cocking her head.

Kat faintly heard an approaching engine. Joleen's superior hearing had picked it up sooner than she had. Panic spread just beneath her skin. Why hadn't Blair alerted her that Scott had passed by him?

Her purse was slung over her right shoulder. She stuck her hand inside and pulled out her cell. No message. Had something happened to Blair?

"I may have to take a rain check," she started to say.

"Nonsense. He'll want to talk to you too. Wouldn't it be marvelous if he found that poor girl?"

Kat had turned around and looked back the way

she'd come. Nothing but the wildflowers and blue sky that was just starting to darken. Then she realized the truck was coming from a different direction. The woods. Forest Service land.

The hunting shack.

She was still holding her cell phone, and she glanced down at it, looking for Blair's number. Favorites. No, she hadn't put Blair there yet. But he was in Recents. She pushed the button for his number as the truck roared right up to her, so close that she jumped back in alarm. Joleen peered out from the doorway sightlessly. Scott leapt out of his truck and slung a rifle to his shoulder in one smooth motion.

"Drop it," he said, leveling the rifle directly at her.

"Scott?" Joleen asked, sounding afraid.

In a soft voice, he said, "Joleen, honey. Go back in and get both Ms. Starr and me a cold lemonade. Can you do that?"

"Did you park right by the porch?" she asked.

"Sure did. Gotta haul some equipment out of the back."

Kat could see the bed of his truck was empty.

"Go on, then," he said, a smile in his voice. "We're both dying of thirst."

Chapter 28

Joleen blinked worriedly in Scott's general direction, then said, "Um . . . okay. Ms. Starr? You want that lemonade, then?"

Massey's finger tightened almost imperceptibly on the trigger. Kat felt a line of sweat trickle down her back. She had a gun inside her purse, but there was no way to reach for it with the rifle's muzzle pointed at her.

"Drop it," Scott mouthed this time, staring at her.

The phone slipped from her fingers and landed in the dust with a tiny *thunk*.

"Ms. Starr?" Joleen asked.

"Lemonade would be fine," Kat told her in a surprisingly strong voice.

"Go on then, honey." Scott shooed his wife.

Joleen disappeared, and immediately Scott strode toward Kat, whose brain was sizzling with one word: *run*. But that barrel stared at her, a round, black eye, and she stayed stock-still. The man was a hunter and desperate. She didn't doubt he would shoot her cold and claim an accident, and she couldn't risk it. Not now. Her thoughts were tumbling, one after another in the space of a nanosecond. *I'm pregnant. I have a chance for a future with Blair. I love him. I cannot die now. I have to live. For the baby, for Blair . . .*

When he reached her, he dropped the rifle and grabbed her neck with both hands. Her knee shot up, but he twisted away, expecting the move. She grabbed at him, reaching for his face. She'd gouge his eyes out if she could. But he shook her like a rag-doll, and pinpoints of light formed behind her eyes. His hands tightened cruelly. *Air.* She needed *air.* Her fingers scrabbled and dug at his, wrapped hard around her throat. She gasped and fought as he stomped hard on her cell phone over and over again, effectively killing it.

"You were the one with the screwdriver," he whispered in her ear, his breath hot and fetid.

The trees . . . the wildflowers . . . the colors darkened and faded, and she was gone.

Blair snatched up his cell phone. *Katrina!* He clicked on.

"Hey, there. You okay?"

No answer. A thumping sound and . . . strangled breathing?

Then nothing.

A pocket dial?

Hell no.

He put the truck in gear and turned down the Massey drive. He tried calling Kat back, but the phone went straight to voice mail. He didn't want to piss her off and crash her party, but he didn't like any part of this.

If he was barreling in where he wasn't wanted, so be it. It wouldn't be the first time.

Kat woke to a raw throat and a sense of movement. She was in a vehicle, bouncing hard. She opened her eyes to a scene of passing trees and then a small clearing with a small building on one edge, its roof obscured by a canopy of fir boughs. Her hands were caught behind her back, so tight she was losing feeling. Massey . . . the rifle . . . *you were the one with the screwdriver* . . .

". . . no, honey, I'll be back soon," he was saying. "Ms. Starr remembered she had a previous engagement. See ya before the sun goes down."

He dropped something into the side pocket of his door. His cell phone, she figured. She started to turn her head but stopped herself, sliding her eyes instead.

But he was watching for her. "I don't want to hurt you," he said. "Even though you hurt me." He turned his hand so she could see the mark she'd left with the screwdriver fifteen years earlier, a small scar. He clucked his tongue. "You and your friends showing off what God gave you that night . . . I knew what I had to do."

"You raped Ruth," Kat tried, her voice a rasp.

"Made a woman of her," he corrected. "She wanted it. You all want it. You just like to pretend you don't."

"That's what you told Courtney? And Rachel? And Erin, before she got away from you . . . ?"

His face darkened. "You and Ruthie met with her," he growled. "And look what happened. She's going to die too."

"She's going to live. And she's going to finger you."

He jerked the truck to a stop beside the shack. She realized the boughs would make it difficult to see. Where were they? She had the sense she hadn't been out that long, so maybe they weren't on Forest Service land at all. No wonder no one had found them. "This is somewhere on your property," she said.

"You're smart," he said. "Too smart."

She reached around for the handle, trying to shove open the door. She managed, but he was laughing as he came around from the driver's side and yanked her out the rest of the way, tossing her onto the ground. Her head reeled. He'd damn near killed her, she thought dizzily, cutting off her air. He grabbed whatever held her hands—a rope?—and dragged her toward the shack. She kicked and fought, but he cuffed the side of her head, and she saw stars.

He left her to insert a key in the padlock on the door. She tried to crawl away, but he picked her up like she was a rag doll and hauled her over his shoulder. Someone gasped, and Kat focused to see a naked and dirty Addie Donovan sitting up on a cot, handcuffed to a long chain that extended from a metal ring on the wall behind the cot.

Oh God.

He grabbed Kat and cut her loose from her bonds. Baling twine, she saw. Then he picked her up once more as if she weighed nothing and carried her to the wall where the head of the cot stood. A thick metal ring was nailed halfway down its length, near the ceiling, and it was strung through with barbed wire. Rocking D wire, she realized. Head aching, she kicked at him and connected with flesh. His grunt of surprise brought her a brief flash of satisfaction, then he was standing her against the wall, grabbing her flailing fists, wrapping them in the barbed wire until her arms were stretched over her head. Her legs were free, and she kicked again, but this time he easily sidestepped her. The barbs bit into the flesh at her wrists, and she had to stand on tiptoe to keep them from hurting her.

"You asked for this, bitch. Remember that. You always get what you ask for, right, Addie?"

"Addie," Kat said, turning to look at the frightened girl who cowered against the wall. Her eyes were large and bruised.

"Right?" he demanded of her, leaving Kat for a moment to stomp closer to her.

"Right, Lover," she whispered.

"Don't talk to her," Massey warned, glaring at the girl who looked away from Kat and crossed her arms over her bare breasts in embarrassment.

He grabbed one of Kat's legs, and she tried kicking him with the other, but then she was yanked down on the barbs at her wrist. She yelped in pain before she bit off the sound, hanging from the wire. He lashed her leg to the wooden one at the head of Addie's cot. She wriggled as best she could, but he caught her other leg and lashed it to a hook on the far side. She felt panic rise inside her. She hung before him, the pain at her wrists excruciating.

Then he stood back, looked at her, and smiled. "You've got the place of honor," he said. "Right, Addie?"

"Right, Lover," she whispered, her eyes downcast. Kat wanted to weep for her. She was so broken.

"Addie here doesn't know how to please a man. She's got a lot to learn. But you know what to do, don't you, Katrina? All of you out there, swimming and splashing. You know what to do."

Kat shrank against the wall as Massey came toward her. He slowly undid the buttons on her shirt and then moaned in delight at the sight of Kat's breasts pushing up from her bra. His hand cupped one breast, and she automatically twisted violently away from him.

"Come on now," he whispered. "That's not how we play."

Addie started to whimper, and he snapped his head toward her. "Look at me," he demanded. When she didn't comply, he shouted, "LOOK AT ME!"

She slid him a terrified look. He stared at her for a moment, then turned back to Kat. "You see? She doesn't know the first thing about fucking. Courtney, now, she learned. She learned real good."

Kat said through her teeth, "Courtney killed herself because of you. You had to take her body away from here, toward the Donovans. That's how you found Addie. You poured gasoline on Courtney to hide your DNA, but it didn't work. They have a sample of your semen."

His eyes flared with alarm, and Kat met his eyes with a confidence she didn't feel. The lab hadn't found anything, as far as she knew, but Massey didn't have to know that. He yanked her bra down, expos-

ing her breasts. Kat steeled herself, looking for anything to help her escape. Anything! Her head was
slowly clearing, down to a dull ache now as adrenaline raced through her veins. She had to save her
baby. She had to save herself.

"Erin's going to identify you," Kat pressed.

"Erin didn't see me."

"Oh, yes, she did. She saw you. And she knows
your voice. And your semen will seal the deal."

"You *bitch!*" he roared.

Addie cried out as he pinched one of Kat's already
sensitive nipples, hard. Kat closed her eyes and counted
to ten. When Massey had first kidnapped Erin and
Rachel, he'd attempted to hide his identity. He hadn't
wanted his victims to see him. Chillingly, now he didn't
care about that any longer. There would be no escape.

"Rachel's dead too, isn't she? She fought you, and
that's when Erin got away. She got free of you, didn't
she?" Kat said triumphantly.

"Well, you never will!" he shouted, then, "You need
to shut your fucking mouth!"

"You buried Rachel here somewhere," Kat guessed.
"But not Courtney. Why?"

He didn't answer, and as Kat struggled to find how
to free herself, Addie's voice came tremulously from
the corner. "Rachel haunts him."

He whipped back toward her. "Shut up!"

"He keeps saying he loves us all," Addie said. "He
didn't mean to kill her, and it hurts him to have
Rachel nearby."

"Another mistake," Kat said. "They're adding up,
Massey. You won't get away."

Massey went over to Addie and backhanded her,

hard. Then he strode back to Kat and unzipped his fly. Kat jerked her left leg, the one with the rope tied to Addie's cot, and tried to free it. The rope stayed taut, but the cot moved. Kat threw Addie a look, and the girl scrambled to her feet. Massey was jerking at his pants, pulling them down as Kat wrenched her leg again, hard. Addie scrambled forward, allowed enough movement by her own chain to get a hand on the rope attached to the cot and yank at the knot.

Scott Massey let out a roar of fury when he saw what she was doing. He stumbled toward Addie and grabbed her hard. She shrieked with fear, cowering backward, but the deed was done. Kat hauled her leg free and swung it at Massey's head. He turned back to her just as she caught his chin. He howled and stumbled backward toward Addie.

"Addie!" Kat screamed at her.

The nearly paralyzed girl looked at Kat, then at Scott Massey, who was struggling to his feet, his jeans around his ankles, then back at Kat. She lifted her arms and slid her handcuffs over his head, pulling back hard, the chain between them cutting into the flesh of his throat.

He jerked to his feet like a marionette, Addie hanging with him on his back. Supported by her freed leg, Kat swallowed and called on her courage, then kicked forward once more, catching him dead in the crotch before her weight dropped her down on the barbed wire again. She cried out in pain as Massey collapsed on the floor, writhing and swearing. Addie was still on him, and she threw her weight against the chain, strangling him. He garbled, his eyes bulging, his fingers clawing madly at the heavy links cutting into his

throat. He stumbled forward, digging at the chain.
With a roar, he yanked himself free, and Addie tumbled back onto the cot. Wild-eyed, he vaulted upward
and lunged for Addie. Kat shot her leg out, tripped
him, then fell against the barbed wire with an aching
moan.

"You bitches!" he screamed, his face red, his eyes
bulging.

BANG! CRASH!

The door suddenly splintered inward and slammed
against the wall. Kat looked up and saw Blair in the
aperture. In his hand was Kat's gun.

"Stop, or I'll shoot," Blair said.

In a blind rage Massey hurled himself at Blair, who
slammed the gun into Massey's nose. Blood gushed
as he hit him twice more alongside his head. Massey
collapsed, and Blair stared down at him, the gun leveled at his head. "I lied the first time. I won't a second. Go ahead and rush me and die. Do us all a
favor."

Massey looked at Blair through blood running into
his eyes and then broke down and cried.

"I'm fine. Just fine," Kat said for about the hundredth time as Blair looked blackly at the cuts on her
wrist from the barbed wire. "Luckily, I recently had a
tetanus shot."

"I wish he'd let me kill him."

They watched as Massey was led toward the back
of an ambulance. He had superficial wounds from
fighting with Blair, but everyone was following protocol. Sheriff Featherstone was there with the Dono-

vans, who'd brought Dean Croft, and the lot of them were hugging Addie, who was also due for a trip to the hospital to be checked out, but no one wanted to be the first to let go.

"I'm still taking you to see the doctor," Blair told Kat as one of the EMTs temporarily bandaged her wrists. "That damn barbed wire's nasty."

"In a bit. I want to go back to Massey's house. I need to see what's in the basement." Ricki had radioed that Kat should take a look.

"Seriously?" He gestured toward the rustic shack. "You haven't had enough of this?"

"It's on the way." When Kat gestured toward his truck with one bandaged hand, he gave in, moving ahead to open the door for her.

Ricki had already been inside the Massey house and had told a frightened and disbelieving Joleen that her husband was being arrested for kidnapping and holding Addie Donovan against her will. Other charges would be filed later. Completely shattered, Joleen had immediately phoned her sister in Cheyenne, begging her to come straighten things out. The sister couldn't understand the extent of Scott's crimes yet, but she was already on her way to come to Joleen's aid, and that was all that mattered.

Now Kat and Blair walked inside the house, aware of Joleen softly weeping in one of the back rooms. It hurt Kat, and she felt tears spring to her own eyes.

Massey had wounded his wife as well as all of his other victims.

They headed down the stairs, past the black-and-white photos of Scott trick-riding, and entered a long, low-ceilinged room broken only by posts that held up the floor above. It was unremarkable except for one corner where she could see the remains of what looked like a dark room. She instantly had a mental image of Massey developing the picture of the three of them skinny-dipping.

She shivered, and Blair put his arm around her, whispering in her ear, "You okay?"

"Yes. He's caught. So, yes, I'm okay." Her eye fell on a familiar photograph, tacked on the wall and curling at the corners. It was a smaller duplicate of the one of the Dillinger family. But then she looked more closely and drew a breath. It wasn't a perfect match. In the background was a roll of barbed wire. Rocking D wire, she would bet, if she could get a close look at it. Maybe it was even the reason he decided to use the barbed wire in the first place, moving it out of the shot for the one he made for the Dillingers, coming back for it later.

"Sick bastard," she muttered.

"What?" Blair asked.

She shook her head. There would be time enough to tell him everything later.

Epilogue

The Pioneer Church was filled to capacity as Sabrina Delaney and Colton Dillinger stood at the altar together, hands clasped, their gazes constantly meeting as they smiled at each other throughout the ceremony. Colton's son, Rourke, was best man, and his brother, Tyler, was his other groomsman. Sabrina had chosen Ricki to be her maid of honor and Delilah Dillinger Kincaid as her other attendant. Delilah kept glancing back to her husband, Hunter, who sat in one of the front pews holding baby Joshua, who missed the whole event as he blissfully slept through it all. He was directly in Kat's line of sight, and she could see the little sucking motions his lips made and the shape of his fingers as they curled around Hunter's larger ones. Colton's sister, Nell, was seated beside Hunter, along with Ricki's daughter, Brooke. Tyler's wife, Jen, was nowhere to be seen as they'd recently separated, and Jen hadn't made the trip from Colorado.

The church still had that new pine smell from

when it had been rebuilt after a fire several years earlier. Kat inhaled deeply and felt Blair's arm steal
around her shoulders. His other hand rested posses-
sively on her abdomen, its slightly rounded form
growing more so every day. Soon her pregnancy would
no longer be a secret.

Now she slid a look into his blue eyes. How had
she ever thought they were icy? The warmth in them
was impossible to miss. Catching her glance, he tickled her middle, and she clamped a hand over his ma-
rauding fingers and warned him with a mock angry
look to behave.

It had been six weeks since Addie had been rescued. In that time, she'd started healing, though it
was going to be a long haul. Her family's support
was everything, and Dean Croft, even though he was
only eighteen, seemed to be hanging in there with
her, a surprisingly strong and mature presence to
help her recover from the dark time of her capture.

Erin Higgins had woken up that same night and
been told about Addie's rescue. She'd been given
several six-packs of pictures, and she'd unerringly
picked him out as her abductor. Apparently he hadn't
been all that adept in his disguises even with the first
girls he'd kidnapped.

Paul and Ann Byrd had moved Rachel's remains
from the makeshift grave behind Massey's shack to
an honored place in the Pioneer Church Cemetery.
Kat and her father had attended the small ceremony
at the new grave site, and Paul had even managed to
shake Patrick's hand after it was over. He'd nodded
to Kat, too, then tossed a glance at her burgeoning
waistline, but he hadn't said anything. Still, it had

made Kat realize she was putting off the inevitable
for no good reason. From the night of Addie's rescue, she and Blair had been an item, and it was no
longer a secret. Blair had even invited her to move into
the master bedroom of the Kincaid ranch, though she
hadn't given him an answer yet.

She had, however, visited that room a few times
since, the first time discovering her missing panties
draped over a corner of the bed.

"Funny man," she'd told him, to which he'd
laughed, then given her a small silver box with a
white ribbon around it.

She'd almost been afraid to open it, afraid to hope
for something that might be still too much to ask for.
She'd been slightly disappointed and confused to
find a hand-carved miniature of a dog shaped out of
wood, until Blair said, "For the baby. Mike made it."

"You may kiss the bride," Reverend McFerron said
with a flourish, and Colton dipped Sabrina over his
arm and laid one on her while the church exploded
with cheers and clapping.

The guests then all returned to their respective vehicles and drove in a line to the reception at the
Dillinger ranch. Half the town had been invited, and
they spilled through the doors to the backyard, which
was lined with picnic tables covered with red and
white checked tablecloths. The noise level grew bois-
terously loud as toasts were made to the bride and
groom, who accepted it all in good grace, grinning
happily.

"Here you go," Blair said, handing Kat a glass of
lemonade.

Seeing he had one as well, Kat said, "You teetotaling along with me?"

"You gotta be kidding." With a sideways smile, he pulled out a flask from inside his suede jacket and poured vodka into his glass. "I heard there was only wine and beer, so I brought my own."

"I think you heard wrong. That bartender's pouring whiskey for Ira Dillinger."

"Okay. You got me. I just like carrying the flask. I can pretend that you and I are sharing its contents."

"I think it's time I let the world know about the new Kincaid."

"Finally." He grinned. "Who are we telling first?"

At that moment, she saw her father enter with Goldie Horndahl clinging to his arm. "I don't know, but we'd better do it quick because as soon as Goldie catches the news, she'll be trumpeting it to the masses."

Kat realized Patrick was looking a little woebegone, and she chuckled to herself. He'd planned to use Goldie's nose for news for his own purposes, but she'd reeled him in with the cunning of an old fisherman. Kat wasn't sure what her father really felt about the gossipy Goldie, but he wasn't really complaining too hard.

"What?" Blair asked.

"My dad."

His gaze followed hers, and amusement threaded his voice. "Got more than he bargained for."

"Maybe."

Just then Kat caught sight of Shiloh waving from across the room, and soon her friend was corralling

Beau and Morgan over to join Blair and her. Shiloh was wearing a silvery blue dress, and her hair was caught in rhinestone clips. She still looked like a cowgirl somehow, but she seemed less aggressive, more relaxed, these days. Happiness had done wonders for her, Kat decided.

"Have you seen Ruth?" Shiloh asked. "I saw her at the wedding, but she's not here."

"She and Ethan and Penny were stopping for ice cream first, and then Penny's going home with the Reverend and Ruth's mom." Ruth had confided to Kat that she and her parents were carefully tiptoeing into the new field of their relationship. The Reverend and Bev McFerron were still struggling with their daughter's rape; they had no coping skills, apparently, when it came to their own child. But with all of Prairie Creek and the surrounding areas alerted to the extent of Massey's crimes, and a general outpouring of sympathy and understanding for the victims, they were attempting to find a way to acknowledge and accept the truth of what had happened to Ruth.

"Mostly they just want to run and hide," Ruth had said. "But they can't, and at least they're talking about it some. My father wants to be judgmental, but everyone's been so supportive that he can't make those kinds of statements without losing face, something neither of my parents handle well. So, they're trying. It isn't all that I could ask for, but it's as much as they can give."

"Sounds like you're getting over how they treated you when you told them about the rape," Kat had told her.

"More like I've shoved it aside. We'll see if they

can sustain. I think my father's embarrassed about some of the comments he made, about me and about Colton's son, Rourke, being conceived out of wedlock. Who cares? It's old history. The important thing is Colton found Sabrina and they're happy. My dad can't help but see that."

"There's Ruth now," Shiloh said, and Kat turned to spy Ruth's red hair, and then her brother's dark head as he turned toward her and whispered something in her ear. Ruth lifted a hand to Kat and smiled. She too was clearly healing. Catching Massey had taken away the bogeyman for all of them. The mystery of the missing girls was solved, and Addie Donovan was safe with her family again.

"So, you're sticking around?" Kat asked Shiloh. As far as Kat could tell, her friend hadn't made any serious plans to get back to her old life.

Shiloh shot a glance at Beau, and then one at Morgan. Both of them were regarding her expectantly. "Yeah, I guess," she said, pretending to think it over.

Morgan said, "You've gotta stay. You promised me my own horse."

"Did I?"

"You did! You did!"

"Yeah, you did," Beau reminded, getting into the game. "You made a lot of promises."

"I don't remember any of them."

For that, Beau grabbed her and tickled her, and she started laughing. Morgan joined in, and the three of them hugged each other tightly.

As they moved off, Blair remarked, "Shiloh Silva, who'da thunk."

"Blair Kincaid, who'da thunk," a female voice said

behind them. Kat turned to see Delilah with baby Joshua. She was smiling at her husband's brother and said, "You know, Hunter wasn't really sure you'd domesticate all that well when he asked you to help rebuild the Kincaid ranch. And now look at you." She waved a hand to include Kat. "Dating a detective with the Sheriff's Department."

To Delilah's surprise, Blair lifted Joshua from her arms. "You don't know the half of it. I might just have to get me one of these."

Delilah gazed at him with mock horror. "You must be a pod person. Blair and babies . . . ?"

Kat grinned, but she felt her face flush. Blair and Delilah joked some more, then Blair settled Joshua back in his mother's arms. As Delilah moved off, Blair said, "Okay, who's first? I can't keep this secret much longer."

"Okay."

"And we're going to make that baby a Kincaid."

Kat looked at him, startled, unsure if she knew what he meant.

"Katrina Starr, will you marry me?" he asked.

"Don't you dare get down on one knee!" she hissed, when he started to kneel.

"What's going on here?" Patrick asked from somewhere to Kat's right.

She jumped about a foot. "Blair's just horsing around," she assured him quickly, shooting Blair a dark look.

"Sounded like a proposal to me," Goldie said, still hanging on Patrick's arm, her expression avid. She was like a bloodhound on the scent, whenever there was news to be had.

"It was," Blair told her. "I'm just waiting for an answer."

Kat shook her head and smiled. "You *are* a pod person."

They were interrupted by the descent of most of Blair's family on them: Hunter and his two sisters, Emma and Alex, came by in a group. Only Mariah, Blair's older sister, hadn't made the trip. The rest of the Kincaids started talking all at once. Just the fact that Blair and Katrina were an item was news enough, but Patrick held up an authoritative hand. Immediately, they all fell silent. Patrick Starr might not be lead detective for the Prairie Creek Sheriff's Department any longer, but he still commanded a lot of respect. "I believe there's a proposal on the table," Patrick said.

"What proposal?" Hunter asked.

"I've asked Kat to marry me," Blair said blithely.

"WHAT?"

"You're kidding?"

"Good God . . ."

They all spoke at once and caught the attention of Shiloh and Ruth, who were talking with each other. They drifted over to the Kincaid group just as Hunter, taking a cue from Patrick, held up his own hand. He looked at his brother, eyes smiling, then he turned expectantly to Kat.

Kat looked at them all, and then beyond to the amber fields beneath a warm September sun, and then to the mountains. Like Ruth and Shiloh, she had reached a new peace. All the bad and sad feelings over the loss of her mother were gone. All the fear and hurt and anger over Ruth's rape had slowly dissipated. They'd found the missing girls, and Addie Donovan was safe again.

She looked over at Shiloh, whose brows had lifted, as if she knew what was coming, and then to Ruth, whose smile was growing wider. Like them, Kat had found her happiness.

What was she waiting for?

"Yes, I'll marry you, Blair Kincaid." She placed his hand over her abdomen once more. "After all, we need to give our baby the Kincaid name . . ."